in the
UNLIKELY
EVENT

L.J. SHEN

*Sometimes you meet people who are out of this world,
so you make them a part of yours.*

A one-night stand born from vengeance in a foreign land.

An explosive chemistry neither of us could deny.

We signed a contract on the back of a Boar's Head Pub napkin that said if we ever met again, we would drop everything and be together.

Eight years and thousands of miles later, he's here.

In New York.

And he's America's music obsession.

The intangible Irish poet who brings record executives to their knees.

The blizzard in my perfect, unshaken snow globe.

Last time we spoke, he was a beggar with no intention of becoming a king.

But a king he became, and now I'm his servant.

I'm not the same broken princess Malachy Doherty put back together with his callused hands.

I have a career I love.

A boyfriend I adore.

An apartment, a roommate, a *life*.

I changed. He changed, too.

But Mal kept the napkin.

Question is, will I keep my word?

Dedicated to Kristina Lindsey, one of the kindest souls on this planet, who left us prematurely while I was writing this book. Every snowflake that falls, every time a light bulb flickers, we're thinking of you.

"I cannot let you burn me up, nor can I resist you.
No mere human can stand in a fire and not be consumed."
—A.S. Byatt

in The

UNLIKELY
EVENT

Present day

Rory

MY LIFE IS CONTAINED IN A ROUND, BEAUTIFUL SNOW GLOBE. The kind no one has bothered to pick up from the dusty shelf in years. Unshaken. Quiet and still. From the outside, my manicured Swiss village looks perfect. And it is. Kind of. At twenty-six, it appears I have my life together.

Perfect job.

Perfect apartment.

Perfect roommate.

Perfect boyfriend.

Perfect *lies.*

Well, they're not lies, per se. All my accomplishments are real. I worked hard for them. Problem is, I promised eight years ago to give them all away in the blink of an eye if I bumped into *him* again. But back then, I wasn't the same person I am today.

I was lost. Grieving. Broken. Confused.

Not that it matters, because that was then, and this is now, and it's not *him* I'm staring at. Nope. There's no way.

It's *not*.

…Then why can't I tear my eyes from the mysterious stranger who glides through the doors of The Beerchman Hotel's ballroom, turning every head along the way?

Ruddy cheeks tarnished by the unforgiving winter, an aristocratic square jaw, Roman nose, and lips made for the darkest sins and most sordid pleasures—all framed by tousled, coal black hair curling at the ears like ivy, rumpled in a thousand different directions. His slanted, brooding eyes, broad shoulders, and narrow hips make him more than handsome. He's perfect. *Too* perfect.

As with all cruel, fairy-tale princes, I long to spot something that would indicate his immortality, a lack of humanity. Something that would prove his perfection truly is impossible.

Pointy ears. Long fangs. A little tail.

C'mon, God, give me something to work with here. Anything.

He is tall, but not enough to demand any special attention. No, Malachy Doherty doesn't need imperial height, fancy clothes, or millions in the bank to justify the awe he triggers in people. His existence alone is enough to make women fall to their knees. I saw it then. I see it now.

All eyes at the ball are on this enigmatic man, mine included.

Stop it, Rory. It's not him.

If only I could see his eyes. Then I'd be able to put this to rest, to know for sure. No one else has those eyes. A rare shade of violet, like crushed crystal candy.

"*Lack of melanin mixed with light reflecting off red blood vessels,*" Mal explained the night he took my innocence, heart, and panties all in the same breath.

I watch as the man strides past security and into the VIP area without missing a step, ignoring the curious glances and lip-biting female admirers. Even celebrities throw themselves at him, chasing his lazy stride, trying to strike up a conversation as the large, bald bouncer unhooks the red velvet rope separating the mortals from the deities.

The man who cannot be Mal ambles toward the bar, his eyes ze-roed in on something. Or rather *someone*: record label tycoon Jeff Ryner, who has up-and-coming R&B darling Alice Christensen, known onstage as Alicious, sprawled in his lap. Jeff's forty-something face is hued pink by excessive drinking and cocaine.

As the man approaches, Ryner stands, letting Alicious slip from his lap, her ass hitting the floor with a thump. Stepping over her body, he rushes to Mystery Man, falls to his knees theatrically, and plucks a large stack of cash from his breast pocket to wave in the stranger's face. The man who *is not* Mal lets loose a cold smirk, plucks the money from Ryner's sausage-like fingers, and slips it into his coat pocket, say-ing something that makes Ryner stand up in a rush.

Well, that puts a lid on things.

Mal would die before making a deal with a bigwig like my boss. Set himself on fire before attending a glamorous gala. Drink cyanide straight from the bottle before associating himself with the likes of Jeff Ryner.

Mal is not cold, or arrogant, or high-browed. He cuts his own hair and high-fives strangers and thinks brown sauce is the cure for all of the world's problems. Mal hates lavish events, entertainment journals, mainstream record labels, and elegant food. He loves his mammy, having the craic, getting shit-faced, and songwriting while lying un-der the flawless night sky in his backyard. He *refused* a check for six-teen-grand a pop sweetheart tried to give him to buy one of his songs, simply because he had a good laugh watching her confused manager and agent try to decipher the word *no*.

But that was eight years ago, a little voice inside me points out. *For a period of twenty-four hours.*

What do I know about today's Malachy Doherty?

What did I ever know about him at all?

"There she is."

Callum's arms wrap around my waist. I jump in surprise, his posh, English accent startling me for a second.

"The belle of the ball." His lips, still cold from the outside, brush my ear from behind.

"You made it." I turn around, wrapping my arms around his neck and giving him a peck on the lips, like punching a time card. He's still wearing his pale gray suit from the office.

"Don't I always?" He scrunches his nose.

He does. Callum is the most precise, trustworthy man I've ever dated. The exact opposite of spacey, unreliable Mal. When I look again, I see that my boyfriend has remembered to wear my favorite tie. Dark green with strings of gold. When we spotted it in the store, about two weeks into our relationship, I told him it reminded me of Ireland, and he immediately bought it.

I yank the Nikon D18 he bought me for my birthday from my purse and snap a picture of him, capturing his rich-boy, pouty smile as he searches my face for approval.

I've been freelancing as a photographer for Blue Hill Records ever since I got my arts degree four years ago. It pays next to nothing, but next to nothing is still better than actual *nothing*, which is what I got paid when I interned here for the first three years. I work a part-time job as a bartender to pay my astronomical Manhattan rent.

It's not that I have to live the poor Manhattan girl cliché. I have an inheritance from my late father, but I refuse to touch it. Using it never even crossed my mind. I'd burn the money if I could, but that would give my mom a heart attack, and I don't want that on my conscience.

I never wanted the money. I only ever wanted my dad in my life.

"You look gorgeous, love." Callum captures my chin with the back of his thumb, tilting my head up.

Do I, though? I'm the opposite of what a man like Callum would usually go for. I have pale, borderline-sickly skin, big green eyes always framed by an industrial amount of eyeliner, a nose hoop, and an undying love for everything punk rock, which is probably getting a little old at my ripe age of soon-to-be twenty-seven.

Right now, my red-gold roots are showing at the top of my long, silver-ombre hair. *Like strawberries in the snow,* Callum says when my roots are showing. I'm wearing a messy ponytail, and I have on a striped red and white dress, which I paired with Toms and a studded choker. Put simply, I could pass as a Victorian ghost who got lost at Spencer's.

Sometimes I suspect that's what drew Callum to me in the first place. That eccentric, vibrant shell that could elevate his status more than any plastic trophy wife could.

"Look how open-minded and hip Callum is, with his hipster, artistic, holds-on-to-an-actual-job girlfriend. Her breasts are unenhanced, and she is not on a first-name basis with the saleswomen at Neiman Marcus."

"I look like something from the cast of *Beetlejuice*." I laugh, kissing his neck. His low rumble vibrates against my body.

Callum removes a lock of my hair that has escaped my hair tie with the back of his palm and presses his lips to the flesh he just exposed at the base of my neck.

"I like *Beetlejuice*."

He's never watched it. He told me so on our first date, but correcting him seems redundant, and like I'm trying to find non-existent issues in our relationship.

"You know who else I like?" He dips his head down for another kiss. "*You*, in that Tiffany's necklace I bought you."

Eh, yeah. The one he gave me, along with a sensible dress, because I'm cool, but not always cool enough to look the way I do next to *his* friends.

"Careful. I'm turning twenty-seven in a couple months. You might give me ideas," I tease. The words feel empty on my tongue, but I know how much pleasure he takes in hearing this.

"My father told me not to threaten a whore with a dick. Do you know what that means, Aurora Belle Jenkins?"

That's my tall, stockbroker, Wolf of Wall Street boyfriend. With his Eton and Oxford education. With his impeccable manners and dirty mouth.

The man whose only fault is being exactly what my mother wished for me.

Rich. Powerful. Well-bred.

Stable. Sweet. Boring.

What Mom doesn't know is I like Callum *despite* all of those things, not because of them. It took me six months to relent to his persuasion, because I knew she'd like him, and the things my mother likes are usually artificial and shallow.

He'd been chasing me around for months. Finally, he showed up at the bar located beneath his apartment—coincidently the one I work at—and slammed his palm against the counter.

"Tell me what it'd take to make you mine," he slurred that night.

"Stop looking put together and on the sanity spectrum," I deadpanned. "You remind me of everything my mother wants. And my mother wants all the wrong things."

"Is that why you keep saying no?" He frowned, confused. "I come here every night, begging for a chance, and you turn me down because your mother could like me, God forbid?"

I shrugged, reaching for another steaming-hot glass, wiping off the condensation.

"I'm a clusterfuck, love. I failed my first year at Oxford. Miserably. And not for lack of trying."

I arched an eyebrow, giving him a *really?* smile. I needed more to work with.

Callum blew out air, shaking his arms like he was getting ready for a marathon.

"All right, let's see. I have a birthmark the size of my fist on my arse. I still eat Lucky Charms for breakfast. Every. Single. Day. My personal trainer says I have the arms of Rhys Ifans, also known as Hugh Grant's roommate in *Notting Hill*. I...I...I can't swim!" He threw his arms up in the air, triumphed, as everyone around us lifted their heads from their drinks and smiled.

I chuckled, shaking my head. Maybe he was imperfect, but he

was far from the kind of mess I was usually attracted to. Debbie, AKA Mom, had always complained that I only went for the last of the litter. The broken, misunderstood, messed-up ones who couldn't offer me more than a heartache and STDs.

It wasn't untrue. I didn't look at men very much, but when I did, they always came with more issues than *Vogue*.

Callum had leaned forward then, his entire torso plastered on the counter, and framed his mouth with his hands, pretending to whisper in my ear.

"Can I tell you a secret?"

"I've a feeling you will, anyway."

"I think you were put on this earth to destroy me."

I laughed, taking a step back. The conversation with Mal from all those years ago floated to the front of my mind, reminding me I'd heard those words before. Things Mal and I said to each other always lurked in the recesses of my thoughts.

Mal had told me I could kill him.

He didn't know that in a way, he'd killed me, too.

Every day I lived without him slugged by like a snail, leaving a trail of slimy goo in its wake.

"Okay, fella. Time I call you a cab." I tapped the back of Callum's hand.

That was before I knew he owned the penthouse upstairs.

"I'm serious," he pouted again.

He knew he was attractive. Knew his angles, the charm in his accent, how to work a girl into giving him her number. Unfortunately, I was immune.

Putting another clean glass aside, I threw the cloth over my shoulder.

"Can I tell you another secret?" He dragged his thumb across his lips.

That's when I noticed his lips were ridiculously kissable, even without the pout.

"Do you always ask for permission before you say things?" I cocked my head.

He laughed. "Usually, believe it or not, I'm the one people ask permission from. Anyway, I'm not even drunk. This beer? It's the only pint you've served me tonight, and it's full. I don't come here to get pissed, Aurora. I come here because of you."

I paused, my eyes glued to his pint. He was telling the truth. I knew because I served him every night. It occurred to me that he was the exact opposite of Mal—the fancy clothes, the properness, the sobriety. Maybe he was what I needed to rid my mind of lingering thoughts of the Irish poet.

Which meant Callum was also the exact opposite of my father.

Which meant that for the sake of my sanity, I should at least give him a chance.

He was my redo. My second chance. My redemption.

"So? Would you give me one date?" he begged. "I promise to prove to be wonderfully unstable, with a dash of incompetence, and provide you with plenty of unpredictability."

"Fine." I rolled my eyes with a giddy smile.

"Ha!" He slapped the bar in triumph. "It was the unstable bit that did it, wasn't it?" He settled himself back down, pushing his beer away like he finally could, like it revolted him. "Always gets the ladies," he said.

I take a deep breath, meeting Callum's eyes in the ballroom. "I'm sure you're about to tell me all about the whores and the dicks," I say, his erection throbbing between my legs through his cigar pants and my dress.

For the record: Callum lied that night at the bar. Not one bone in his entire body is messy, risky, or uncalculated. As for the birthmark? His skin is as unmarred as a blank new sheet of paper.

Callum Brooks is attractive in a Nantucket-summer-house, two-point-five-children, Polo-shirts-and-golf-tournaments kind of way, with his pulled-up white socks, sandy blond hair, impressive height, and runner's body. Summer, my best friend, likes to joke that he looks like David Duke's dream candidate.

He looks into my eyes. "I'm a serial monogamist, thirty-two, and have been dating you for almost a year. Commitment doesn't scare me, Rory. If I have it my way, you'll move in with me tomorrow morning."

I unbutton his blazer and loosen his tie, just to do something with my hands. I like Callum, too, but a year is still early in our relationship.

It took you twenty-four hours to promise Mal your forever, says the voice in my head.

I was also new to dick and non-self-induced orgasms. I proceed to make excuses for my eighteen-year-old self.

Callum ushers me to our table. We sit down next to a bunch of suits from accounting and marketing, who munch on their first-course ceviche and talk about hedge funds and newly popular beach towns that are driving people out of the Hamptons. Callum slides into the conversation effortlessly, sticking to his club soda—as he does, still without a drop of alcohol. I focus on my colleagues, trying to put the man in the VIP area behind me.

As I said before, it's not Mal. And, okay, fine. Let's humor the craziest part of my brain and say that it *is* him—so what? He didn't see me. And I'm not going to approach him, either. He's probably in town for a few days. Mal's extremely devoted to his family, his farm, his country. I knew that when I met him. That man wouldn't move to America. Not even for a girl.

Especially not for a girl.

Definitely not *this* girl.

As for money? He doesn't care for it. Never did.

I nibble on a breadstick, down two glasses of wine, and find myself engrossed in a heated conversation, which has taken a turn from beach houses to the best public restrooms in Manhattan (Crate and Barrel on the corner of Houston and Broadway is in the lead), when Whitney, Ryner's bitch-from-hell assistant, sashays over to our table, her hips swinging like a pendulum. Her short, platinum bob is cut with a precision that implies her hairdresser uses a ruler. She is wearing some sort of BDSM gown made of leather stripes that cover her nipples and midriff, and not much more. She cocks her head, pouting her scarlet lips.

Everyone stops talking, because Whitney knows how to keep a secret like I know how to stay away from carbs. Exhibit: breadsticks and wine.

"Aurora," she purrs, parking a manicured hand on her waist.

Everyone calls me Rory, but Whitney calls me Aurora. I made the mistake of expressing my dislike for my name once during a pop star's photo shoot she attended with Ryner. Since then, I've been Aurora to her. If I told her I was allergic to money, she'd immediately wire the company's entire budget into my bank account.

There's an idea.

"Whit." I pop the last piece of breadstick into my mouth, not bothering to meet her eyes.

"Mr. Ryner would like to have a word with you on the balcony." She glances at me under pinched eyebrows. I swear Whitney takes orgasmic pleasure in clearing her throat and adding suggestively, "*Alone*."

Squeezing my shoulder blades together and tilting my chin up, I head toward the VIP area's terrace, knocking back my third glass of wine for liquid courage. Ryner is always two hundred pounds of sexual harassment, but especially when he is high and drunk. Which he definitely is right now. I tuck the napkin with the hotel logo into the pocket of my dress. Glancing back, I see Whitney sliding into my seat and casing her red-nailed claws on Callum's shoulder, shooting him a sugary smile. Whitney would love nothing more than to prove she's better than me. And she certainly is, if the criteria is best *Desperate Housewives* imposter from a plastic suburban neighborhood.

The last thing I catch is her whispering something intimate to Callum. He frowns and shakes his head, *no*. Whatever she told him, he seems upset by the suggestion.

Walking through the double doors, I find the balcony completely empty. It's colder than my mother's heart in here. I rub my arms, cursing myself for leaving my coat inside, and gait to the railing, admiring the view.

Not only is it freezing, but I'm always cold. Ever since I was born, ever since I can *remember*, I wear sweaters and fluffy jackets everywhere. It's like there's an invisible layer of ice coating my skin at all times.

I look up, blinking back at the stars, admiring their beauty even in this weather.

Approaching footsteps clack on the floor behind me. Something heavy falls on my shoulders. A rich wool coat, still warm from body heat. It smells masculine and expensive: clean earth, pine, smoke, and the type of cologne that's too pricey for mass retail. A shadow looms by my side. He puts a glass of whiskey on the wide marble bannister, his elbow next to mine, almost touching, but not quite.

I twist my head, expecting to see Ryner, and come face to face with...*Mal.*

My Mal. It is him after all.

Malachy Doherty, with the lilac eyes. With the hypnotic smile. With the contract I signed on the napkin.

With the piece of my heart he never gave back.

Only he is not smiling anymore. It doesn't look like he's happy to see me.

He said if we ever met again, he'd marry me, no matter what. But that was almost a decade ago—under the influence of alcohol and lust and youth. Of *possibility.*

Mal opens his mouth. "Hello, *darlin'.*"

At his rough Irish accent, my knees buckle, and I find myself grasping the bannister.

The first flakes of snow fall around us. On my nose. Eyelashes. Shoulders. A storm is brewing inside my snow globe.

Eight years ago

Rory

I PROP MY BACK AGAINST MY FATHER'S HEADSTONE AND PLUCK A few blades of grass, throwing them in the air and watching as they float down onto my dirty Toms. The church bells chime, the sun slinking under green mountains.

"You could've waited, you know. Laid off the alcohol for a month or two so I could meet you," I mumble, yanking out my earbuds. "One" by U2 still plays distortedly until I kill the music app on my phone and throw it beside me. "Sorry. That was rude. I'm cranky when I'm tired, which…you probably would have known, had you decided to actually *meet* me. Jesus, Dad, you suck."

But even as I say those words, I don't believe them. He didn't suck. He was probably the best.

I bang my head against his tombstone and close my eyes.

I'm freezing in the middle of summer, as per usual, and exhausted from the long flight from Newark to Dublin. And from arguing with the hostel's receptionist for forty-five minutes because my reservation got lost in cyberspace and they ran out of rooms. After I unloaded my small suitcase at a hotel off Temple Bar Square, I took a shower, ate half a bag of stale mini-bar chips, and freaked out over the bill I was going to pay for my unforeseen accommodations, which no doubt is going to kill my dream of purchasing a new camera before I leave for college.

Then my mom called, informing me that I was dead to her for traveling to Ireland, in her highly diplomatic way.

"What is the meaning of all this?" she demanded. "First of all, he's dead. Second, you were better off without him. Trust me on that one, sweetie."

"So *you* say, Mom. You never gave me a chance to find out myself."

"He was a lazy drunk and a terrible flirt."

"He was also talented and funny and sent me gifts every Christmas and birthday. Things that were much more interesting than your Sephora gift cards and eyebrow-enhancing creams," I mumbled.

"I'm sorry I wanted you to get yourself some nice things. You could've used it to buy better makeup to cover your birthmark. It's easy to be the cool parent when you don't do the actual parenting," she huffed. "Are you looking for your half-sister? Bet she lives in a fancy-schmancy house. All that money ought to have gone somewhere."

What she meant by *somewhere* was *probably not to you.*

I want to look for my half-sister, but I don't know where to start. To be honest, I haven't really planned this trip. I just wanted to see the place where my dad was buried. Expecting…what? Some magical connection with the cold stone beneath me? Probably. Not that I would ever admit that aloud.

"Anything else, Mom?"

"Don't you give me this attitude, young lady. Not when I did my best to raise you and all he did was drink your inheritance."

I grunted.

Money, money, money. It's always about the money.

"I can't believe they buried him near a church," she mused. "Hopefully the grass won't grow black, like his heart."

She hung up after a string of complaints about her too-prominent new highlights and milking a promise from me that I'd buy her a carton of duty-free Parliament cigarettes on my return trip.

Now here I am, in a cemetery in central Dublin, staring at a gray squirrel who is eyeing the bag of chips peeking from my backpack. I envy its coat of fur. I'd legitimately consider walking around with a sheet of fur all over my body to protect myself from the constant chill.

"They're not even that good. Who puts vinegar on chips? It's barbaric." I yank the bag out of my backpack, pull a chip out, and throw it its way. The squirrel jumps back in fear, but then gingerly makes its way to the snack. It sniffs the chip, grabs it with its tiny paws, and makes a run up a nearby tree.

"Where I come from, you get jailed for assisting a murderer," a voice cracks behind me.

I look around with a jerk. A priest is standing a few paces behind my father's grave—black robe, big cross, all-ye-sinners-are-doomed expression, the entire shebang. I jump to my feet, grabbing my bag and phone, and swivel to face him.

Okay, so he doesn't look super dangerous, but being all alone in a foreign land makes me hyperaware of my vulnerability.

"Now, now."

The man takes slow steps down the rolling green hill on which my father is buried, his hands knotted behind his back. He looks like he lived through both World Wars, the Renaissance…and Hannibal's invasion of Italy.

"No need to be scared. I reckon you're highly uninformed regarding the gray squirrels and their hidden agenda."

He stops behind my father's tombstone, gazing at the prominent birthmark on my temple. I hate when people do that—stare so openly. Especially because it looks like a scar. A crescent-shaped thing, it is somehow even paler than my normal shade of dead. Mom always encourages me to do something about it. Cover it with makeup. Remove it with a laser treatment.

14

Something flickers in his eyes when he sees my birthmark. He has fluffy white hair and a face stained with age. His eyes are so small under heaps of wrinkly skin, I can't even make out their color.

"The gray squirrels endanger the red squirrels, driving them out of their own territory. The reds were here first. But the grays are better at problem solving. Street smart. The grays also carry a disease that only affects the red squirrels." He removes his reading glasses, cleaning them with the hem of his robe.

I swallow, shifting my weight from foot to foot. He slides his glasses back on.

"'Course, the grays also eat the reds' food and are better at reproducing. Red squirrels don't reproduce under pressure."

I stare at him, not sure if he is an avid environmentalist, an awkward conversationalist, or simply batshit crazy. Why is he talking to me about squirrels?

More importantly—*why* am I listening?

"I, um, thanks for the info." I play with the hoop in my nose.

Leave, Rory. Start walking in the opposite direction before he gives you a lecture about ants.

"Just an interesting anecdote about squirrels. And maybe about how unwelcome guests sometimes take over territory simply because they're better than the locals." He smiles, tilting his head. "And you are?"

Confused and excessively emotional. "Rory." I clear my throat. "Rory Jenkins."

"You're not from here, Rory."

"America." I kick a little stone at my feet, somehow feeling like a punished kid, though I've no good reason to. "I'm from New Jersey."

"That's why you fed it." He nods. "Should I take a guess why you're here, or are you in a sharing mood?"

I'm too embarrassed to tell him I came here to find closure before I go to college, practically flushing all the money I've saved the past two years working at Applebee's down the crap-stained toilet.

"Neither." I fling my backpack over my shoulder. It's time to go back to the hotel. Nothing is going to come out of this stupid trip. "Thanks for the fun facts about squirrels, though."

It was totally worth the trip across the ocean.

I'd taken my first steps toward the cemetery's gate when I hear his voice behind me.

"You're Glen O'Connell's daughter."

I stop, feeling my shoulders tense. My whole body turns to stone. Slowly, I swivel on my heel, muscles frozen.

"How do you know?"

"You're the third offspring to visit his grave. I'd heard the last one was supposed to be American. We've been waiting for you."

"We?"

"Well, I."

"Where are the other two?" I look around, as if they're hiding behind tombstones.

"One lives just a short drive from here. Known her since she was a wee baby. Still attends this church with her mammy every Sunday. Glen was in her life as much as he could be, considering his…er, limitations."

Translation: Alcoholism. Strangely, I still envy her.

"And the other one?"

"Lived up north. County Antrim."

"Why the past tense?"

"He passed away a few weeks ago. Leukemia, would you believe? Such a young lad. He met his da a couple times, but never got to know him quite well."

My heart sinks like an anchor, clawing at the bottom of my stomach. I had a brother who died, and now I'll never get to meet him or know him at all. I have a potential *family* here. This guy…I could have hugged him, comforted him in his last days.

I know next to nothing about my father. Only that he died at age fifty of a heart attack that wasn't unwarranted, considering his affection for fast cars, fast women, smoking, drinking, and artery-clogging food.

He was born in Tolka, the son of a butcher and a teacher, and shot to fame writing "Belle's Bells," a Christmas song that exploded all over the charts in Ireland, the UK, and the US, giving Mariah Carey and George Michael a run for their money. The Christmas song was his first and last brush with labor, or anything similar to a career, but it was enough to secure him a house in Dublin and an annual budget for food and booze.

He was a womanizer. The kind to bed everything that moved. He met Mom at a bar in Paris while she was backpacking with friends and he was trying to find his muse again. They had a one-night stand, and he gave her his address so she could write to him if she ever happened to be in Ireland looking for a good time. When she *did* write to him, informing him I was in the oven, he invited her to come live with him, but Mom never did. Instead, he sent child support money every month. Sent me gifts, letters…but everything was always carefully monitored by my mother. I hated that she controlled our relationship.

So I rebelled. From a young age.

I'd tried to get in touch with him on my own over the years.

I wrote him letters my mom wasn't aware of—sent him pictures, emails, poems I'd ripped from books at the library. I begged Mom for crumbs of information about my mysterious sperm donor. I never heard from him, and I thought I knew why. He knew how much of a bossy bitch Mom was, and he was afraid if she found out we were talking behind her back, she'd cut off his communication with me completely.

Dad agreed to only talk to me through Mom, and never on the phone, out of respect for her. He once wrote to me that he was ashamed of his voice, of what had become of him. He'd said he slurred now even when he wasn't drunk, and his voice shook all the time.

I didn't care what he sounded like. I just needed his voice in my ears.

I wanted a dad.

Not even a particularly good one.

Seriously, *any* sort of dad would do.

My father died two months before I graduated high school. I was walking into the kitchen to get a glass of water when Mom got the phone call. I plastered my back to the hallway wall so she couldn't see me.

She wasn't sad. Or angry. Or broken. She just grabbed the vintage, corded phone, lit a cigarette, and sat down at the dining table, flipping her hair behind her shoulder.

"So he finally kicked the bucket, huh?" She coughed. "Only sad thing about it is I'll have to tell Rory. She doesn't deserve this heartache."

I didn't know who she was talking to, but I wanted to throw up. He was my father, and he was a part of me—presumably a part of me she wasn't too crazy about.

If Glen had waited just a little longer, I could have met him face to face. Now, I'm meeting him grave to face, hearing about his legacy of out-of-wedlock offspring from a priest.

Class act, Dad.

"Father...?" I eye the giant cross on his chest.

"Doherty," he provides.

"Father Doherty, did he ever say anything about me?"

In that space of time, between my question and his answer, I feel the entire weight of the world pressing against my shoulders, ready to bury me.

"Yes. Of course. He spoke of you all the time. You were the apple of his eye. He bragged about your photography. Whenever he got out of the house, he made a point of shoving pictures of you in people's faces and saying, 'This, right here, is my daughter.'"

Whenever he got out of the house.

His situation was so awful. Mom never once tried to help him. Why?

"How come he never wanted to see me?"

I don't know why I decide to unload all these questions on this stranger. He couldn't have known my dad too well. It's not like Glen used to attend church regularly...at least I don't think.

"He sent you money every month and loved you from afar, knowing you were better off not knowing him." Father Doherty evades the painful question. "Some people are weak, but not necessarily bad. He'd been battling depression and alcoholism, and wasn't in a state to take care of a child."

Maybe Dad did save me from himself. *The important thing is that he talked about me, right? That he took care of me in his own, roundabout way? Yeah, I can work with that.* But I can't shake the nagging feeling that Mom had a hand in the fact that we never met.

A trickle of warmth sneaks into my chest. "Can I meet my sister? Do you know where she lives?"

I'm grasping at straws at this point. I can hear the desperation in my voice, and it makes me actively dislike myself. *Get it together. He didn't even leave you a letter before he died.*

"Ah, poor thing's in a state. I'm afraid she doesn't want to be reached. However…" He strokes his chin, mulling an idea. "I know someone who could help you. Follow me."

I shadow Father Doherty into the church, all the way to the dim back office, where he sits at a heavy oak desk and scribbles an address on a piece of paper. He talks as he writes.

"My grandson busks on Drury Street. He knew your da well enough. Glen taught him how to play the guitar. I'm sure Mal is full of stories about Glen. Why don't you talk to him over a few pints, eh? But not too many, unless you want the stories to take unexpected, bizarre turns." He chuckles, sliding the address across the desk along with a fifty-euro note.

"Thanks, but I can't take your money." I grab the address and shove it into my corduroy jeans' pocket, leaving the note untouched.

"Why?"

"Because you owe me nothing." I hitch one shoulder up. "And you've already done enough."

He looks up, the tenderness in his eyes leaving me with stupid thoughts—thoughts like I wish he'd adopt me. I wish he'd be *my* granddad. There's nothing quite like feeling you don't belong. Floating rootless on this planet, without anyone to fight for you. Well, there's Mom, but she has a weird way of showing her love.

"*Show me unfailing kindness like the Lord's kindness as long as I live, so that I may not be killed.* Samuel 20:14. We all owe each other a little kindness, Rory. A little kindness goes a long way."

His teeth are as yellow as the shards of light cutting through the tall church windows. I swallow, not making a move for the money.

"Now, go before my grandson's finished. Malachy rarely stays in one spot. There's always a lady friend or two lurking, and they always drag him into hell-knows-where doing God-knows-what."

I have a pretty good idea as to the *what* part. Anyway, his playboy grandson's sex life is not something I want to talk about in a church. Or, you know, *ever.*

"How will I know who he is? There must be more than one singer on Drury Street."

"Oh, you'll know." He folds the money between his fingers and hands it to me.

I hesitate, but take it. "And if I don't?" I furrow my brows.

"Just yell his name. He'll stop everything at once. Malachy never could resist a pretty girl or a stiff drink."

I already dislike this Malachy guy, but if he can give me closure, I can ignore the fact that he sounds exactly like my father: a flirt, a drunk, and a man who avoids responsibility like it's the plague.

"Can I take a few pictures of his grave before I go?"

He nods, looking at me with sheer pity, the type that crawls under your skin and takes residence. The type that defines you.

"You will prevail, Aurora."

Aurora. I never told him my name. Only Rory.

"Aurora?" I lift an eyebrow.

His smile vanishes, and he clears his throat. "Your father told me, remember?"

Yes. Of course. So why does he look so...*guilty*?

Two things hit me in that moment as I regard Father Doherty:

1. The man's eyes are mesmerizing—a weird shade of violet dipped in blue that instantly warms you up.
2. I will meet him again, someday.

Next time I do? He'll change my life. Forever.

I shoulder past the thick wall of female bodies that crescents the street artist. Drury Street is an explosion of colors, scents, and sights. Red, exposed-brick buildings covered with vibrant graffiti. An Asian market peeking from a corner, a parking garage, a bus stop, and little hipster shops. It looks like a picture, and I can't help but stop everything and make it one, capturing the beauty of the street with my old camera.

A bus, passing in a blur, slicing through the colors like the stroke of a brush.

Click.

Two suited men walking past **FUCK CAPITALISM** written on a wall.

Click.

A lone beer bottle lying on the pavement, tucked between junk food wrappers like a sad drunk.

Click, click, click.

When I finally come face to face with the street artist standing on the side of the pavement, his guitar case open and full of rolled-up notes and change, I understand why his grandfather told me I'd recognize him with the self-assurance of an avid believer.

I've never seen someone like him before.

He is beautiful, true, but that's not what stands out to me. He is *radiant.*

It's like his presence has a presence. He sucks the air out of everything in his vicinity, making it impossible not to look at him. Malachy is tailor-made for a huge, colossal heartbreak. Everything about him—his tattered jeans, filthy boots, white shirt, and leather jacket that was broken in decades ago—screams trouble. He looks like a seventies heartthrob. An icon. A Terry Richardson muse. Bruce Springsteen pre-fame.

His voice is like honey and warm spices. It lulls me into a place in my mind I've never been before, even though it's far from beautiful. It is gruff, throaty, and smoky. When someone bumps my shoulder to get closer to him, I snap out of my reverie and realize what I'm listening to.

"One" by U2.

The coincidence is strange. I try to tell myself it's nothing. This is Ireland. U2 is a national treasure.

His eyes are squeezed shut as he sings. It's like no one exists other than him and his guitar. Something warm rushes through my skin, like a heat wave, and I shudder in delight.

Warmth.

I always thought there was something melancholy about street performers—the way people walk past them, ignoring their music, their art, their passion. But this guy, he's the one doing the ignoring. The tables have turned. He's got the crowd eating from the palm of his hand. Every woman here is under a thick, sweet spell. He's got that Harry Styles quality that makes girls want to bed him and older women want to adopt him. The men are a cross between impatient, annoyed, and jealous. You can see it in the way they tap their feet, check their watches, nudge their wives and girlfriends to move it.

The song ends, and Malachy Doherty cracks his eyes open and stares directly at me, like he knew I'd be here. Like he watched *me* watching *him* through closed eyes. Disoriented—and for some reason wanting to do something, *anything*—I throw a bill into his guitar case and look away, realizing to my horror that I threw the fifty euros his grandpa gave me. Everyone around me murmurs and whistles. They think it was intentional. I can feel my face flaming red. I bet he thinks I want to sleep with him.

Do I? Probably. *But should he know that?* Hell no.

Too late to take the money back now without looking like a crazy person, though. And between crazy and an easy lay, I think I'll go with the latter.

Flushed, I back away. Malachy leans forward, grabs my wrist, and tugs at it. Electric heat courses through my veins, like a snakebite. I gasp.

I'm staring down at my shoes, but he crouches and peeks into my face, a brash, lopsided grin playing on his lips.

"Any requests, Baroness Rothschild of good fortune?" he drawls.

Can I get my money back? I need to buy you drinks with it so you can tell me about my father, I try to convey to him with what I'm sure is a sweet-but-seriously-psycho look.

"None that I can think of." I slant my gaze sideways, playing nonchalant but secretly wanting to die.

Bright side: I'm no longer thinking about my dead father. Silver lining and so forth.

"The Copacabana!" someone suggests.

"Cavan Girl!" another shouts.

"Dick in a Box!"

Malachy looks around and laughs, and the minute his eyes leave my face, the warmth is snatched away. Still, his rolling laughter is like hot wax seeping into my stomach.

He straightens up. "Who's the rale Bulgarian who suggested that?"

Some guy in a green beret and orange tweed jacket raises his hand and waves his fingers.

"Not Bulgarian, English." He grins smugly.

"Jesus, much worse," Malachy deadpans, and everyone around us erupts in more laughter.

I use the opportunity to gentle my pulse back to normal, smiling along. *Ha-ha indeed.*

Malachy swaggers back to his spot and secures his guitar strap over his shoulder. He has the slender, yet muscular body of someone who works in the field, not in the gym. He points the guitar pick at me, and everyone's heads turn to see who he's pointing at.

"I'm not keen on girls who don't know what they want." He quirks a dark, thick eyebrow. "But I've a feeling you're here to change that."

He starts playing, and maybe it's because I'm feeling small and vulnerable and broken, but I allow myself to cave to the sound of him, close my eyes and let go. I can tell this one is an original, because I don't know the lyrics. It's too good not to be a hit. He sings it completely differently from the way he did "One." Like every single word cuts through his flesh. A welt, a scar, a burning thing.

Weakness, hate, desire,
How I'd love to light your soul on fire,
In a room full of pretty lost girls and bad broken boys,
You will find me, dip me in ice, and drown all the white noise,
I want to see the world through your eyes and fall in love,
But most of all, I am frightened you don't really exist,
Because then my fairytale has no beauty,
Just a sad, lonely beast.

This guy can move me without touching me, and touch me without laying a finger on me. His grandfather was right. He's trouble.

Everyone is so quiet, I begin to doubt this moment is real. I stop swaying and open my eyes. To my astonishment, I find the entire street staring at him. Even waitresses stand on the thresholds of restaurants and at café doors, admiring his voice.

And Malachy? He is staring at *me.*

I snag my camera and take a picture of him as he sings.

When he finishes the song, he takes a little bow and waits for the claps and shouts to die down. He wiggles his brows at me with a grin that tells me he's going to sleep with me, which is stupid, because I'm eighteen, and not the sleeping-around type.

I've only slept with one person in my life: Taylor Kirshner, senior year, because we'd dated for a while and both of us didn't want to leave for college saddled with our awkward virginity.

But I believe Malachy. We will.

I believe him because he is *that* guy. Someone like my dad must've been. A completely unhinged, typhoon-souled, damaged Romeo who would break your bed, heart, and resolve if you let him.

Not maliciously, no. And not because he wants to. He simply cannot help himself. He would wreck everything in his way. This misunderstood, beautiful, brilliant boy who is burdened with gifts he never asked for, but unwrapped nonetheless. His talent, charm, and beauty are a weapon, and right now they're aimed at me.

I watch as he scoops the money from his guitar case, stuffing it into his pocket. The circle of people around him thins and dies away. Two college-aged girls approach him, tucking their hair behind their ears. He flirts with them shamelessly, shooting me a look every now and again, making sure I'm still standing here.

I'm only here because of my father, I want to clarify. I'll tell him that as soon as he's done.

Since Malachy feels comfortable keeping me waiting, I don't feel guilty taking out my camera again and snapping a picture of him just as he hoists the guitar case over his shoulder, awarding one of the girls with a kiss to the knuckles.

"Flattered, but see, I promised this generous, albeit clingy lass, I'd let her buy me a pint."

I lower my camera and arch an eyebrow at him. He beams at me as both girls scatter along to a bus stop, giggling breathlessly and swatting one another.

"I think *you* can afford to buy the generous, albeit clingy lass, a drink, everything considered." I tuck my camera back into my backpack, throwing the hood of my jacket over my head.

"Only if she sends me a copy of that picture." He juts his chin to my backpack, flashing me a lazy grin.

"Whatever for?"

He thumbs the strap of his guitar case as he saunters over. Stops when we can breathe each other in. "So I'll have her address."

"Who's being clingy now?" I fold my arms over my chest.

"Me." He grins, the world likely tinted a dramatic shade of mauve through his mesmerizing eyes. "Definitely me. You American?"

I nod. He scans me.

Purple eyes, like his grandfather's. But different somehow. Clearer, with depths that suck you in if you're not careful.

I turn around and start walking, knowing he'll follow me. He does.

"What's the story?" He shoves his hands into his front pockets.

"Can we sit somewhere?" I ignore his question, looking around us.

I could use a drink and something to eat. I'm guessing any normal guy would have a hundred and three questions about what I want from him, but Mal seems nowhere near the normalcy spectrum. He motions with his head in the opposite direction, and we turn around. Now I'm the one doing the following.

Turning the tables. This street performer is good at that.

"You have a name?" he asks.

I catch his footsteps. Barely.

"Aurora."

"Aurora! Princess Aurora of…?"

"New Jersey." I roll my eyes. What a flirt.

"New Jersey. Of course. Known for its processed meat, goldfinch, and Jon Bon Jovi, although I won't hold the latter against you."

"That's incredibly considerate."

"What can I say? I'm a charitable soul, too. Mind you, everything I know about New Jersey I learned from a little show called *Jersey Shore*. Mam is a goner for the one who's got enough gel on his hair to fill up a pool."

"Pauly D." I nod, smiling.

Suddenly, I feel hot. I need to get out of my army jacket. Maybe even my hoodie. De-onionize. Peel off my layers of clothing.

"That's the one." He snaps his fingers. "Although, I'm sure you and your family are nothing like him and his orange mates."

I chew the side of my thumbnail. "Actually, my mom is pretty much the queen of those people. She's twenty-five percent fake tan, twenty-five percent hairspray, and forty percent skimpy clothes and hair dye. She is, like, super flammable."

"Where's the other ten percent?" He chuckles, shooting me a look I can't decode.

"She's not very good at math," I deadpan.

Malachy throws his head back and laughs so boisterously, I feel it vibrating in my stomach. Back home, a boy like him would elevate his looks to his own benefit somehow—become an actor, model, a social media persona, or some other made-up job. My mom would have a heart attack on impact if she ever saw Malachy laugh. He laughs with his entire face, practically *inviting* wrinkles. Every inch of his flesh is squeezed tight.

"I'm Mal," he says.

Since we're mid-walk and he can't shake my hand, he bumps his shoulder against mine, tugging my hoodie down to reveal more of my face.

"What about you? Are you going to smash any Irish stereotypes?" I ask.

Mal takes a sharp turn onto a corner street. I follow.

"Afraid not. I'm Catholic, a mammy's boy, and a mostly functioning alcoholic. My grandfather...actually, he's not technically my granddad. Father Doherty's a Catholic priest, but Mam's da died young and Father Doherty, his brother, kind of took care of her like she was his own. Anyway, he taught me how to make stew, which, to this day, is the only food I know how to prepare. I live on a farm with a staggering amount of sheep, all of them arseholes. I prefer stout to lager, missionary position over doggy, think George Best was a god, and reckon brown sauce can cure anything short of cancer, including but not limited to hangovers, a badly cooked meal, and possibly hepatitis C."

"We're…incredibly stereotypical representations of the places we come from." I roll my nose hoop, moving it around inside its hole. I do that when I'm nervous. Keeps my hands busy.

"Stereotypes exist because they have a seed of truth." He stops, turns around, and raps the roof of an old Ford the color of bad teeth. "Now, come. We have places to go, things to see, and I'm afraid you must do the driving."

"*Huh?*"

"Have you not seen any decent romance movies, Princess Aurora from New Jersey? All the best meet-cutes in cinematic history involve the woman driving the man somewhere. *When Harry Met Sally, Singin' in the Rain, Thelma and Louise…*"

"The last one wasn't a meet-cute. And Geena Davis is not a man." I can't help but laugh. How dare he thaw me before I'm ready to defrost?

"To-may-to, to-mah-to." He throws a set of keys into my hands, and I catch them on instinct. "Your carriage awaits, Madame Semantics."

This guy is sleek, charming. The worst type of heartbreaker—not compassionate enough to let you know he's an asshole by actually behaving like one. I bet he leaves a string of half-beating, bleeding, broken hearts in his wake wherever he goes—like Hansel and Gretel left breadcrumbs to find their way home by following the trail. Only I know where this path is leading: destruction.

"Wait. Before we go anywhere, I have something I want to ask you." I raise a hand. Best to set the expectations right now.

"All right." He throws the passenger door open, sliding inside. I'm still standing on the pavement when he shuts the door, rolls his window down, and rests his arm on its frame, sliding his aviator sunglasses on.

"You coming?"

"Aren't you going to ask what that is before you let me in?" I frown.

He raises his aviators and flashes me a smile that can hold up the entire universe with its magnitude.

"What's the point? I'll give it to you, anyway. Be it money, a snog, a shag, a kidney, a liver. God, I hope it's not my liver you're after. Unfortunately, mine has seen some mileage. Come on now, Aurora."

"Rory."

"Rory," he amends, dragging his straight teeth over his bottom lip. "Much more fitting. You don't look like a princess at all."

I arch an eyebrow. I don't know why his statement annoys me. He's right. I look nothing like the princess my mother wanted me to be. My best friend, Summer, says I look like a suicidal pixie.

"You look like the more beautiful stepsister in a Disney movie. The underdog who gets the prince at the end. The one who wasn't born with the title, but earned it," he explains.

I can feel myself turning red, thinking that ironic, as I just found out I *do* have a half-sister.

"Oh, she is blushing." He raises a fist in the air through the window. "All is not lost. I still have a chance."

"Actually, you don't." I douse his enthusiasm in cold water. It makes him laugh harder, because he already knows. The bastard knows he is winning me over.

"I won't have a one-night stand with you," I say.

"Of course, you won't," he agrees easily. Freely. Not believing a word.

"I mean it," I warn. "Over my dead body."

Laughing harder, he taps the passenger door.

"Chop-chop now, Princess."

Mal directs me out of Dublin in his own peculiar way ("Take a left. No, your other left. Never mind, the original left"), and though I'm terrified driving on the other side of the road, and despite the fact I *don't* have an international driver's license, I still find myself behind the wheel.

Maybe it's the setting that unchains me from any type of reasonable logic. Maybe it's Mal himself. All I know is I'm eighteen, newly orphaned by a dad I didn't know, and I feel like I'm suspended in the air, like a marionette. Between sky and earth. Nothing to lose, nothing to gain.

We roll into a small village, tucked between green hills a stone's throw from Dublin, with a white wooden sign announcing our arrival in Tolka, Co Wicklow. There's a river to our right, an old stone-arch bridge over it, and old houses with bright red doors edging the town's entrance. It's more like a main street with a few houses scattered around it, like spots of hair on an otherwise bald head. We drive down Main Street, passing a bright blue house, a church, a row of inns, pubs, and a little cinema Mal tells me offers actual individual seats, and the people operating it still use traditional reels.

The road winds, snaking up and down, and my heart feels strangely full when I park the car, as instructed by Mal, a few buildings down from a pub called The Boar's Head.

When we exit the car, I stop and take my camera out. The pub is painted stark white, with green windows decorated by flowerpots with marigolds and cornflowers spilling out of them. The Irish flag hangs on a pole by the door.

It looks like something out of folklore, a tale my late father would have told me in another life.

"What's keeping you, Rory?" Mal turns around mid-stride into the pub and catches me crouching down on one knee, squinting and aiming the camera at him.

"Make love to the camera, gorgeous," I say in a creepy, old-man voice, expecting him to tell me to quit it.

Instead, Mal breaks into a huge grin, covers an imaginary blowing-in-the-air dress, and sends a kiss to the camera, a la Marilyn Monroe. Only his dripping masculinity makes it look one hundred percent hilarious and zero percent feminine.

Click. Click. Click.

I stand up and walk over to him. He offers me his arm. I take it, too tired to resist.

"Is this where you live?" I motion around us. "In this village?"

"Just under that hill." He runs his fingers through my hair to pull it out of my face, and my spine tingles in unexpected delight. He smiles, because he notices. "With all the arsehole sheep I told you about earlier. You'll meet them in a bit."

"I have a flight to catch tomorrow." I clear my traitorous throat, which keeps clogging with all sorts of emotion.

"So?"

"I can't stay long."

He stares at me with a mixture of confusion and mirth. I think this is possibly the first time he's been rejected. Then he does the unbelievable and reaches to run his thumb over my birthmark, staring at it, mesmerized.

"How'd it happen?" he asks, his voice so soft, it sounds like it's fading.

I feel so warm I can practically sense the sun beating down on my skin, even though it's cold and gray out.

"It didn't. I was born with it."

"You were, huh?" His thumb drags from my temple to my lips. Was he expecting some crazy story about a car crash or a freak accident?

I pull away.

"Anyway, I can't stay. I have a hotel booked in Dublin."

"I'll drive you back to check out." He snaps out of his weird trance. "You'll be staying with me tonight."

"I'm not going to sleep with you. Over my dead body, remember?"

He cups my cheeks in his hands. They're rough and confident, an artist's hands, and my heart thunders with newly found pity for my mom. Now I get why she slept with my dad. Not all Casanovas are slimy. Mal isn't.

"Don't let your feelings get in the way of facts."

"Meaning?" I frown.

"Just because you don't like the fact that you're going to sleep with me doesn't mean it's not going to happen." He brushes his thumb over my lips. "And just because we've only met doesn't mean we're strangers. Do we feel like strangers?" he asks, jerking me to his body.

No. No, we don't. He feels like he's never left my side. Like I carried a tiny part of him with me from the moment I was born, and now that he's here, we can fit the part I kept with the rest of him, like finishing a puzzle.

I gulp, but say nothing.

"Exactly. Now, you're cocking up our perfect meet-cute. Geena Davis is rolling in her grave."

"Geena Davis is not dead, Mal!"

"Come, Madame Semantics. Let me feed you."

Three corned beefs and a shepherd's pie later, Mal points at me with his half-finished Guinness pint—his fourth. I'm still nursing my first vodka Diet Coke.

"You wanted to ask me something." He squeezes one eye shut, like he's zeroing in on me with a gun, licking the white foam of the Guinness from his upper lip.

Here goes…

"I came to Drury Street on your granddad's advice. He knew I was Glen O'Connell's daughter. He said you'd be able to tell me more about him." I study his face carefully.

He takes my hand, flips it, and trails the lines on the inside with his finger. The little hairs on the back of my neck stand on end.

"I used to go to Granddad's church every Sunday when I was a kid. Glen lived behind it. He'd let me listen to his records. He taught me a few notes and helped me string a sentence together when I started writing songs. Taught me how to bleed onto a page. So, yes, we knew each other quite well. Well enough for him to tell me he'd kill me if I ever touched his daughter."

Huh?

"The other one." He shakes his head, laughing when he sees the look on my face. "Not you. God, Glen would have died on the spot had he met you in person. He would've appointed an army to protect your virtue."

"From you?"

"And the rest of Europe." He smirks.

Is that his weird, Mal way of telling me I'm pretty?

"Why didn't Granddad send you to Kathleen, Glen's daughter? She lives right down this street." Mal frowns, finishing off his pint.

Kathleen.

My sister's name is Kathleen.

The penny drops, and he realizes I didn't know her name.

"You knew you had a sister, yeah?"

I nod slowly. "My mom refused to tell me her name. She said it shouldn't matter, because no one here particularly wants to know me. How come this entire village attends a church in Dublin if you all live here? Kinda weird." I circle the straw inside my drink.

Mal sits back. "Not the whole village. Just us. Mam works weekend shifts at Lidl, so Kathleen's mam took us both to Sunday mass to support my granddad's Dublin gig, essentially babysitting me. I usually went home with Granddad, but sometimes I stayed with Kathleen when she hung out with Glen afterwards."

"What kind of father was he to her?"

"A good one," he says, then frowns and amends, "but not good enough for you."

"And how old is Kathleen?" I ignore his attempt to make me feel better.

"My age." Mal still studies my hand like it's the most interesting thing in the world. "Twenty-two," he adds.

"You must know her well."

"We grew up together." He clanks his empty glass on the sticky wooden table. "Why he would direct you to me and not to her, I wonder."

"He said she was in a state and didn't want to see anyone."

"Bollocks. Kathleen's more social than a penguin."

What an odd thing to say. I try not to smile at his choice of words. Everything about him is so…different.

"What's she like?" I feel like an FBI agent, but it's hard to keep myself in check when I want to learn everything there is to know about Dad. About my sister. Plus, if my lips keep moving, I don't have to stop to examine the stain of jealousy in my voice. Kathleen had years of growing up with Dad. And being next to Mal.

"Sweet. Nice. Saintly. You'll see. Let's go see her. She must have a load of photos of him."

"I don't know if that's a good idea."

"Well, I do. You're not getting out of here empty-handed. Let's go."

He takes my hand and yanks me to my feet. He slaps a few bills onto the table, and I don't even attempt to pay for my portion of the meal, because with the hotel, I'm already deep in the red on this trip.

My hand clasped in his, Mal blazes through Main Street like a bullet. It starts to rain, and I duck my head, trying to dodge the downpour.

He laughs, his voice muffled by the storm. "I can't believe it's raining in the summer. It's like you brought winter with you, Rory."

It is weird, but it keeps us close and touching, so I don't care.

"Why not take the car?" I yell.

"Her house's right in front of my car, actually. Besides, she'll have mercy on us if she sees us wet and miserable."

"I thought you said she was saintly."

"Even the godly have their limits, especially considering I've been ignoring her for three consecutive months." He snorts.

"Mal!" I shriek, but he only laughs harder.

We arrive at a white-bricked, black-shuttered Victorian house. Mal raps the door and runs his fingers along his dripping hair. It sticks out in a thousand different directions, making him look annoyingly delicious. A few seconds pass before the door swings open and a girl who looks like a rounder, less-edgy version of me appears. Her hair is ruby red, a few shades lighter than my original light orange, but she has the same big, green eyes and bony nose and downturned, pouty lips. She has freckles, like me, and the same beauty mark by her upper lip.

But as far as appearance goes, this is where our similarities end. She's wearing a sensible white cardigan with a long, blue A-line dress underneath. Her leggings are pristine white, like bones. I shift in my Toms and hoodie and jam my fists into my pockets to stop myself from playing with my nose hoop.

"Mal!" she cries when she sees him, throwing her arms over his neck and burying her face in his shoulder. "What are you doing here? God, you're soaking wet!"

"Kath, I want you to meet my friend, Aurora, from New Jersey." He flashes her a big, goofy smile and motions to me as if I'm some kind of a prize in a game show.

We're still on her doorstep, the rain pounding our faces. But even that doesn't stop Kathleen from taking a sharp inhale, her eyes bulging when she notices me for the first time. Mal is too busy kicking the rain off his boots and shaking his head like a dog to recognize the delicate situation he's just created.

"You said you always wanted to meet her, and she told me she doesn't even have any pictures of Glen. Well, bumped into her in Dublin and reckoned it was high time for a reunion. Thank me later." He winks, knocking his shoulder against hers, his fists stuffed in his jacket pockets.

So my mom was right about one thing. Men do have the emotional intelligence of underdeveloped bricks.

I blink at her, refusing to dwell on the fact that Father Doherty insisted she didn't want to see anyone, yet Mal says she's been dying to meet me. Only one of those things is true, and I have my hunch.

Kathleen assesses me—not that I can blame her, it *is* a bombshell—and I immediately feel guilty for going against Father Doherty's word. She shakes her head, snaps out of it, smiles, and flings her arms around me in a hug, throwing herself into the rain. I stagger back and return a squeeze.

"Oh, God. Oh, God. Oh, God." She crushes my bones with her hug.

I melt into her and burst into laughter and tears at the same time. It's a total case of emotional diarrhea, but it's not every day you meet your half-sister for the first time.

"You're both drenched! Come! Shall I make some tea?" She disconnects from me, tugs my hand, and ushers us inside, padding to the bathroom and coming back with two warm towels. We wrap ourselves gratefully.

"Tea!" Mal exclaims, like it's the best idea he's ever heard in his life. "The magic word. Rory, did you know Kath makes a mean cup of tea? Best in the county. No joke."

Kath swats Mal on the chest and giggles like a schoolgirl on our way to the kitchen. We follow a narrow hallway with coats and scarves piled on hangers. Everything is small and neat and cozy. The house has a '70s feeling to it, with green wallpaper, brown furnishings, and yellow lights. It is soaked with familiarity. Fully inhabited—not just a space with furniture like Mom's house in New Jersey.

"Country, not county," Mal amends.

Kathleen swats Mal's shoulder and keeps her hand on him, possessively. Sighing like it's a job, he captures her wrist, turning her around and pinning her against the hallway wall in one swift movement. I halt, watching the situation unfold. He holds her like a farmer holds cattle, rough and without passion, but she is breathing hard. Her eyes, heavy-lidded and dripping lust, daring him to make another move. She lets out a little moan, flinching at her own lack of control and turning bright red. He looks down at her like she's a chewed toy. The familiar, old type that is too nostalgic to throw away, but no one wants to play with anymore.

"How's school, Kiki?" he asks with a pang of regret in his voice, like he hates to do that—string her along.

Then why does he?

He knows exactly what he's doing to her, and that bothers me, because I can see just how much he oozes control. She is locked in the moment, but he's an observer, the gatekeeper keeping her in a foolish dream, the key far from her reach.

"Grand." Her voice shakes. "I...I tried to call you a few times. Dropped by on Sundays after mass. Your mam said you've been busy."

"I have."

"Not too busy for Aurora, apparently." She turns scarlet again. There's nothing mean about her tone. Just desperate.

My loyalties are torn between the boy she loves, who is trying to help me, and the sister who's falling apart because of him.

"She prefers the name Rory." Mal removes a lock of hair from Kathleen's face, tucking it behind her ear.

I want to punch him in the balls on her behalf, then kick him in the knee on mine.

"Sorry, Rory." She flashes me a nervous smile, snapping her eyes back to him, like he could disappear at any moment. "I missed you."

She *missed* him.

She *loves* him.

I can't do this to her. I can't kiss him or sleep with him or do any of the things I want to do with Mal. Because I'm leaving, and she is staying. Because she seems lovely, and even if she isn't lovely, she's still my sister.

I tiptoe my way to the kitchen without making it apparent that their seemingly friendly conversation is making something in my chest collapse, brick by brick.

"*Stay*," Mal snaps behind my back. He doesn't sound so nice anymore.

I halt, but don't turn. Kathleen's obviously got it hard for him, and I want to show her I'm not a threat.

"You guys are…" I start.

"Nothing," Mal clarifies. "We're just friends, right, Kathleen?"

She clears her throat, smoothing her dress. My heart is dust in the wind. Poor her.

"Of course."

What an asshole. Before I know what's happening, Mal is at my side, plastering his hand at the small of my back. He ushers me into the kitchen, leaving Kathleen behind. I turn my head to her as I go, and she flashes me a tired smile, waving us to move along.

"I'll just go wash my face," she mumbles. "Turn the heater off, maybe. I'm feeling a bit flustered."

I take a seat at the dining table and study the family pictures hanging on the walls with hungry eyes. But there's no one who looks like he could be Glen. Just Kathleen and her mom, Kathleen and the family dogs, Kathleen kissing young Mal's cheek while he looks horrified and disgusted to the core, as boys do at that age. Even toddler Mal gives me butterflies. What the hell is wrong with me?

Everything, apparently. He's just like your dad.

My half-sister serves us tea and shortbread as she tries to make conversation. She explains to me that she studies veterinary medicine and jokes about Mal hiring her when he eventually takes over his family farm.

"Actually, it was Mal who told me I should become a vet. Remember, Mal? The day I tried to save that pigeon? I think it was the Christmas we turned eleven."

Mal stares at me. "Yeah. Sure."

He doesn't remember. Kathleen's eager smile doesn't collapse.

"He's just being modest. You just wait till I graduate, Mal. You have plenty of sheep and cows. You can do so much with them, if you only put your mind to it. Renting out the land to other farmers is a bad investment. I could help."

"I'm a musician." He pours half a carton of milk into his tea, staring intently at his cup. "I've no interest in farming."

"You still help the Boyles here and there, though."

He shrugs. "When they need help, yeah. I also take shits. Doesn't necessarily mean I want to be a plumber."

I almost spray the tea in my mouth all over the table. *Almost.*

"How are you a musician, Mal? You don't want to be a singer, and you don't sell your songs to anyone, even when they make you an offer." Her eyelashes flutter, her cheeks staining pink.

There's more back-and-forth on that front, then Mal stops Kathleen's stream of questions and arguments and says, "We were wondering if you could share some memories of Glen with Rory. Since she never really met him. Surely you don't mind?"

"Oh, of course. I didn't want to point out the elephant in the room." She smiles, angling toward me in her seat. "Of course, Rory, anything. What would you like to know?"

"Hmm." I tap my knee under the table. "What was he like?"

Did he ever talk about me?

Did he miss me?

Did he care?

"He was the best, Rory. We had a great relationship. He had a wicked sense of humor and a massive musical talent. In fact, the only guy I know who's more talented than him is Mal. Da used to call me McNugget, because I was small and a bit pudgy when I was a kid. Remember that, Mal? I was so offended for the longest time."

She reaches and squeezes Mal's shoulder. He is still looking at me. Kathleen's words sound detached, but I chalk it up to her being upset over Mal showing up here with me.

"Did he have a lot of freckles, like us?" I ask, the question sounding dumber than it was in my head.

Thing is, I've never seen my dad. Ever. My mom told me he

had dark hair and light eyes and three chins. Forever a poet, this woman.

"No." Kathleen chuckles. "His face was pale and smooth. I got mine from Ma."

I guess I got mine from my mom, too.

"Do you have a picture of him?" I fidget with my fingers under the table.

"I don't believe I do." She scrunches her nose. "Have you not seen him?"

I shake my head, swallowing the ball of tears settling in my throat. Maybe it was a mistake to come here and see the real family he left behind.

"Surely you have a picture or two of Glen, Kiki." Mal frowns at Kathleen.

She bites her lip. "I'm sorry. Mam did a massive cleanup a few weeks ago and moved everything to the attic. She's got the key for it, I suppose, but she's out. I wish I could have known you were coming, Rory. I'd have asked her to leave it here."

"Did he ever mention me?" I ask into my cup of tea, not wanting to see the pity in her face when she answers.

Even staring down, I can see Kathleen in my periphery putting down her cup of tea and sighing heavily. Almost theatrically. I don't know why I do this to myself. Each question puts another nail into my self-esteem's coffin.

"Oh, Rory, I really am so sorry."

I lift the cup and bring it to my lips. The scorching liquid burns a path from my tongue down my throat, but I'm practically chugging it, longing to feel anything—even pain—to distract myself from what's going on inside my head. Mal eventually lowers my hand with the cup.

"I'm sure he did here and there. He'd have loved you!" Kathleen tries desperately. "Da loved everyone, didn't he, Mal? Even that stook, Jared, who sold knockoff Burberry on the street corner every Sunday."

Mal gives her a weird look I can't decipher, then stares at me in a way that makes me feel naked of clothes, skin, and bones. Like he's looking into my soul, dissecting it with a knife and a fork.

He snaps out of it, stretching in his seat. "Excuse me, ladies. Nature's calling, and it has a three-gallon piss for me to depart in the jacks."

He stands up and saunters to the bathroom. I realize he knows this house by heart—been here probably dozens of times. He and Kath share history, chemistry. I should feel happy that Kathleen might end up with a guy like Mal, if she ever manages to tame him. Funny and charming and handsome.

But for some reason, I don't.

As soon as Mal is out of earshot, I shake my head and smile. "He's a wild card, huh?"

Kathleen's sweet smile drops. She plucks a tube of lip gloss from her handbag on the table and squeezes a generous amount onto her pinched lips.

"What he is and what he's not shouldn't matter to you. He's mine." Her warm voice is now a cold, pointy blade running along my neck.

"Excuse me?" I slant my head back.

She smacks her lips, lifts her teacup—pinky in the air—and takes a slow sip. "The problem with Malachy is he has a weakness for strays. No matter how dirty, no matter how rabid." She narrows her eyes at me. "No matter how *dangerous*."

I study the way her face twists in revulsion, my mouth parting in shock.

Fake.

It was all fake.

My sister is not nice or timid or disoriented. She is the devil.

She hates me. She's always hated me. That's why Father Doherty wanted me to stay away. That's why he directed me to his sweet grandson. Kath just puts on a mask for Mal.

"You know, Da said he'd made a terrible mistake when he came from Paris and it became known he'd impregnated the American slag. But personally, I've always wanted to meet my wee half-sister. Until he died and it became clear you'd go after his money. I didn't want to believe it. I truly didn't. I even wanted to write to you."

"Yet you didn't." I grit my teeth, holding her gaze now. "How convenient of you to say you wanted to reach out, but never did."

I feel cold again. I want Mal to come back, to soak the room with his warmth.

She flashes a mocking smile.

"Fancy seeing you here a second after he drops dead."

My nostrils flare, and my heart kicks up. Whatever she's insinuating is complete BS and far removed from the truth.

"I'm not here for his money," I hiss, narrowing my eyes and hoping to God I look as menacing as I feel. "I'm here to see his grave, where he lived and grew up. To take some pictures, so I can look back at them and tell myself I came here and connected to my roots. There's half of me I don't even know. I'm carrying a stranger's genes in my body, for crying out loud."

"Why not sooner, then?" She rolls her eyes on a sarcastic smile.

"I wasn't of legal age to make that decision!"

"Is that why your mam sent a letter to my grandparents asking to see the will? So you can connect not only with your heritage, but also a nice Gucci bag?"

It's a surprise my jaw doesn't hit the floor. I want to kill Mom. Or at least I think I should. I don't know what I'm entitled to or not. I don't *care*. I'm not gonna use his stupid money. This is not what this trip is about.

"Listen, I—" I start, but she cuts me off.

She leans forward, clutching my hand in hers across the table. Kathleen squeezes painfully, crushing my bones, her plastic smile making an unexpected comeback. Now I know that when she hugged me at the door, she really did mean to hurt me. She looks like the kind of girl who'd drown her old dog to get her parents to buy her a puppy.

"No, you listen to me. You're not going to see a penny from Da's money. He left everything to me, and for good reason. I'm his *legitimate* child. You and the other poor sod who kicked the bucket, on the other hand, are nothing but mere unfortunate accidents. Also, you can shag Mal all you want for however long you're here, but it is *me* who will marry him. So just remember that when you're writhing underneath him and letting him use you. He'll fuck you, because he can, but it's me who will warm his bed forever. And that's you in a nutshell, Aurora. A cheap version of me. In Da's life. In Mal's."

Her grip tightens even more around my hand. I pull away, but she is strong, and I'm too stunned to move. Her lips twitch and widen. "And please don't embarrass yourself by trying to pull your mother's trick and get knocked up. Surely you know he won't follow you to America, and if you expect to dump your spawn at my door, you're in for a terrible disappointment."

I stare at her, wondering how I could be genetically linked to this cardigan-wearing, fire-spitting green-eyed monster.

"You've got it all wrong." I try to yank my hand away again, but she tugs harder, digging her manicured, neutrally colored nails in.

Usually, I'm a take-no-crap kind of person, but right now, the shock of being in a foreign land and hearing this from my only living relative besides Mom freezes me to the spot. Turns out, I'm not a fight, nor a flight type of person. I'm a let's-sit-here-like-a-log-and-see-how-it-pans-out chick.

"Stay away from Mal. He is mine. The money's mine. Everything you see here, everyone you meet, belongs to me. *Leave.*"

"You think I'm after the money? Your *crush*?" I spit the last word.

Moments ago, I'd have died before laying a finger on Mal. But right now? I would likely hump him on her dining table, preferably as she eats her dinner in front of us.

"I think you're a gold-digging whore like your mother. She ruined my father and everything I knew and loved. You're the reason I lost him for a while."

A while? What does she mean by that? Pointless to ask, as she seems less than cooperative with me.

"You're a bitch," I retort.

Not the most eloquent of comebacks, but one that comes from the heart.

She smiles. "Well, I'm the bitch who owns everything you want, so I'll happily take the title. Now, now, don't look so riled up. Mal loves me more than life itself. If you tell him I said any of those things, he'll kick you to the streets."

Mal reappears at the kitchen door with perfect timing, plopping back on his chair. He notices Kathleen's hand on mine. She pats the back of my hand in a motherly way and straightens her spine.

"Bonding. I like it." He looks between us, yawning. "What'd I miss?"

"Nothing important," she purrs, blinking in my direction with a sugary, meaningful smirk. "I just brought Rory up to speed."

3

Eight years ago

Rory

"KNOW WHAT'S IRONIC?" MAL ASKS WHEN WE EXIT Kathleen's house.

I'm still shaken and nauseous from our visit. When I told Mal I'd had enough of our friendly chat, Kathleen altruistically volunteered to drive me back to Dublin. She really is a saint. *Not.* Mal, who has been blessed with the diplomacy skills of a soiled diaper, informed her that we were planning to spend the rest of the night together.

It was the first—and I hope the last—time in my life that I took pleasure in someone else's misery. She could burn in hell at this point and I wouldn't even hand her sunscreen.

The sky is a blue and orange velvet blanket. The scent of fresh earth rises from the concrete and trees, enhanced by the rain.

My head is still reeling from the hateful words Kathleen threw in my face like grenades.

Gold-digger.

Stray.

Whore.

"Earth to Rory." Mal grabs a lamppost and spins around it like in the movies, jumping into a puddle and splashing me. "What's eating you? Can't be me, or you'd have a smile on your face."

"You're not funny," I snap, still walking.

He catches my wrist and spins me to face him. We're in front of his car. I don't feel like driving. Or talking. Or breathing. I just want to go home, to America, with my tail between my legs, licking my wounds. I don't have a family in Jersey other than Mom, and I sure as hell don't have one here. At least I have Summer.

"What's wrong? Did Kathleen say something to upset you?" Mal frowns, placing a hand on my shoulder.

A little voice inside my head tells me to keep my mouth shut about Kathleen's Don Corleone speech—not because I want the best for her, but because I want the best for Mal, and he doesn't deserve to know his childhood friend is a bitch. I have a twenty-four-hour shelf life in Ireland. I'm merely a smear of ink in the elaborate painting called his life. Why disrupt their relationship—if he'd even believe me? Besides, I saw how he looked at her. There's no attraction there. Amusement, yes, but he'll never be with her.

In a moment of sheer madness, I do something I've never done before. I slant my eyes toward her house, making sure she's at her window, watching us.

She is.

Kathleen is messing with the top button of her cardigan. *Button, unbutton. Button, unbutton.* Her lips pressed together, her hawk-like eyes watching my every move.

Slowly, I raise onto my toes.

"Everything is mine. Nothing is yours."

We'll see about that, sister dearest.

I press my lips to Mal's. Tentatively. Shyly. Uncertainly. I've never kissed a boy before. It was always the other way around. But I'm not here to enjoy the kiss. I'm here to prove a point.

His mouth, warm and soft, latches on mine delicately. He wasn't expecting to be kissed. But he is molding into the shape of my body so we're pushed against each other everywhere. Seconds pass. I watch Kathleen watching us kiss, my eyes wide open while Mal's are closed. I drink from the well of Kathleen's misery for long seconds before I sink down to the pavement, disconnecting from him. I peek behind his shoulder again. She is red, her lips so thin, they're non-existent.

"No," I hear Mal grunt.

I look up at his face, and something about it sucks the air out of my lungs like a vacuum. A black cloud passed over his features while I gave him that kiss. No part of him is playful or cute anymore. He looks like a demon, out for blood—thick eyebrows pulled together, eyes crackling with thunder, mouth twisted and sharp, like an icy storm.

"No?" I whisper.

"No. This is not a fecking kiss, and this is certainly not *our* first kiss."

Before I know what's happening, he pulls me at the waist and slams my back against his car. I arch and moan when his hands find my cheeks, my neck, my hair; they're *everywhere*. He's an octopus, wrapping himself around me, no longer molding, but conquering, and it's crazy, but the rain stops abruptly, the sun peeking through the clouds.

The rays pierce my cold skin, and Mal does the rest of the job, pouring heat that swirls and dances in my stomach.

When our lips connect again, they don't meet, they crash. He shoves his tongue into my mouth, growling. Our tongues twist together, roaming, exploring, fighting. He's an animal, acting on a carnal instinct, devouring me like a beast. We kiss and we kiss and we kiss and *boy*, does he know how to kiss. He smells amazing, he *tastes* divine, and when his head drops to suck on my neck, my eyes widen as I remember Kathleen is still there.

She watches us through the window, tears rolling down her

47

cheeks as her palm presses against the glass, ghost-white from the pressure she puts on it. I can feel the pressure of her touch like my skin is the glass.

Mal and I are no longer kissing. We are full-blown making out in the middle of the street, his lips closing around my tongue and sucking it into his mouth.

"Christ," he mutters, moving his mouth to the sensitive flesh of my shoulder, dragging it up my chin and back to my lips again, still oblivious to our audience. "You burn under my fingertips, Rory. How do I give you up?"

Burn, I think. Strange choice of words, seeing how I'm always cold. But I feel it, too. The pull. The ache. It is not necessarily sweet or nice or called for. I'm aflame at the stake, a redheaded witch, watching his fire consume me.

I rip my mouth from his and mumble, "We can't do this here."

He kisses my mouth again. Then my nose. Then my forehead. He can't stop. No part of him is in control.

"Let's check you out of that money-sucking hotel and head back home. I want to spend every waking moment in you until you leave."

"*What?*"

"*With* you. Get your mind out of the gutter, lass."

"You put it there!" I laugh.

"You say carjacking, I say borrowing. Why are we still here discussing it?"

Dazed, I slip into the passenger seat of his car, fastening my seatbelt. Mal gets behind the wheel, revving the engine. He drank quite a bit of Guinness a few hours ago, yet he looks oddly sober. I look up one last time, catching Kathleen's gaze. Her eyes are puffy and wet. It's not in my nature to be a bitch, but it's not in my nature not to fight back, either.

Mal doesn't look back and doesn't appear to notice Kathleen as he rolls down the road, taking a U-turn back to Dublin. Our hands touch, and there's a moment I can't explain. It feels like more than just our flesh links us. I tell myself it's nothing, that I'm the only one feeling it, but then I slip my hand back between my thighs and we both shudder in unison, like someone unplugged us from an electric outlet.

To burn under your fingertips, I think, *is to come alive.*

During the drive, I realize what Father Doherty was talking about. I'm a gray squirrel, an unwanted pest who steals from the locals. The cunning, street-smart, diseased, rat-like thing. But villains are just misunderstood heroes. I learned that the day I realized my mother's archnemesis—Glen—was the protagonist I wanted to meet the most.

I sit back and let Mal reach over, grab my hand, and lace his fingers through mine over the gearshift.

Life is too short not to kiss the one you want.

Midway into Dublin, I remember something. "Mal?"

"Princess?" he answers naturally, like we're well-versed in conversations with each other.

"You said something was ironic, but never got to tell me what it was."

"Did I?" He feigns innocence.

"Tell me."

"Even if it's no longer true?"

"Especially so."

"Well, my name, Malachy, means angel, but Kath used to tell me I was the devil when we were teenagers, that I'd be the very thing to kill her one day. She was eighty-percent joking, I'm sure. I was always up to one shenanigan or the other. Climbing trees, lighting homemade torches, attempting to ride the cattle…"

There's a twitch in his mouth that tells me he's trying to school his face, that he's tasting a calamity that's yet to happen.

"But twenty percent of it, I felt she truly believed. Which is why I've always kept my distance from her. A subconscious part of me has always been worried I'll hurt her."

I squeeze his bicep. "It *is* ironic that the angel is someone's devil."

"The second part of my name—Doherty—means unlucky. Yet, Mam claims the luck of the Irish is with me."

"So why is this part not ironic anymore?" I ask.

"Because I don't feel so unlucky right now." He moves his eyes from the road, his gaze finding mine.

My throat closes on a declaration. *I like you, Malachy Doherty. More than I should. Definitely more than my half-sister allows me to.*

I turn toward the window, clearing my throat. "Do you like her? Is that why you're afraid of hurting her?"

"Sure. I like her fine."

"You're playing with her feelings."

"She enjoys it."

"She enjoys having her heart broken?" I blink, incredulous.

I'm concerned about what it says about him that he's using Kathleen as blood sport. No matter what I feel about my half-sister, she doesn't deserve it.

He stares back at the road, rolling his bottom lip with his teeth. "Between being ignored and being toyed with, Kathleen would prefer the latter, which is why she's at my door twice a week. Look, I tried telling her it isn't going to happen. She cried. She broke things. She even slept outside my door one winter night. This is what she wants. A sliver of hope to hold on to. I think Kath is a grand lass, but I don't fear her capabilities over me. Isn't that the essence of love? Find someone worth killing for? Someone with the power to ruin you?"

Silence stretches between us. I always thought of love as something sweet, fun—not melancholic, dark, and all-consuming. Then again, I've never imagined I'd fall in love.

"You, on the other hand..." He taps the steering wheel. "You can slay me any day of the week."

"So, you can kill Kathleen, and I can kill you?" I ask, watching the landscape zip by. "That's a morbid way to look at things."

The fields sprawl like bed sheets under the darkening sky. Tomorrow I'll see them in full daylight, and then I'll never see them again. I have nothing to look for here. Ireland turned out to be a sweet, unfulfilled promise.

"Life's morbid. Spoiler alert—we all die at the end." Malachy shrugs.

"Well, I'm a pacifist, so don't worry about me. I'll never kill you." I turn back to face him.

He smiles a sad smile I haven't seen on him before, takes my hand, and kisses my knuckles, his eyes still on the road. The energy I felt earlier when our hands touched returns, and I can't put a name to it, but it's electric. Tangible. It even has a taste.

"You already have."

Mal carries my suitcase to his car, then proceeds to spend the next hour arguing with the hotel's receptionist, trying to get them to let me go without paying for the night I've booked. The receptionist looks to be in her mid-fifties, baggy-eyed, with no patience to spare. They each ping-pong the merits of their argument. I take Mal's hand and tug, pleading for him to drop it. I'll pay. I don't care about the money. (Actually, I do, but I care more about not wasting the few hours I still have in Ireland watching them argue over my bill.)

Mal shakes me off and continues bickering with the woman. He tells her to climb inside my skin and walk in it, referencing—I shit you not—*To Kill a Mockingbird*. I want to simultaneously hide under a rock and kiss him silly.

"This girl right here came all the way from New Jersey to mourn the father she never met." He points at me. "Her hostel reservations got cocked up, and she checked in here only to have somewhere to put her suitcase."

"Sir, I understand, but we have policies in place…" she argues.

Mal lets out an exasperated sigh and takes his wallet out of his back pocket. He throws a stack of bills onto the counter.

"You win. I hope this makes you very happy and pays for your boss' Ibiza villa and three illegitimate children with his secretary."

The woman looks down at the notes scattered between them. "Actually, sir, it's three hundred euros per night."

"Holy F…*forks*." He sucks in a breath, throwing more notes at her, plus a few gum wrappers, a handful of coins, and what looks like a fortune from a cookie. He turns around and grabs my hand.

We gallop out to the chilly street. My heart is pounding in my chest.

"You didn't have to do that. I'll pay you back."

"Like hell you will, darlin'."

He turns to me, and to my amazement, he is all smiles. In fact, he looks like nothing happened. Totally over it.

"Aren't you mad?" I blink.

"What about?"

"Uh…spending all the money you've earned this week for a room we won't be using, for one thing."

He waves me off, laughing now. "That was a minute ago. It's time to move on. Don't let the little things in life bother you, yeah?"

Crazy as it sounds, I get what he means. Life *is* too short to get caught up in the small things.

We get into his car and drive back to the village. When we pass Kathleen's house on the way to his farm, I can't help but sneak a peek at her window. She's not there.

We get to his Tudor-style cottage, which is white with black logs running across it, a dark roof, and a heavy oak door that's thoroughly chipped. It looks small, but in a charming, quaint way, at least in the dark. We fight bushes and overgrown grass that lash at our ankles as we make our way to the door.

"Mam's in Kilkenny visiting my big brother, Desmond, so it's just you and me," he says.

"That's cool that you have an older brother." I watch the back of his head as he pushes the old door with his shoulder, applying force. It whines open, and we pour into his living room. Wide-plank floors, wrought-iron lighting, and salvaged wood everywhere tell me I'm no longer in America. Save for the tattered orange-yellow couch and flat TV, this place could pass as a Regency household.

"Six," he says, dumping his keys into a vase by the door before turning around and pulling me into his arms.

I melt in his hands. "You have six brothers?" I burrow into his heat, torn between astonished and jealous.

He shrugs. "Six siblings. Five brothers and one sister. Catholic family, you see. Dez is the oldest. I've also got five nieces and four nephews. Don't get me started about the pets."

I clear my throat. "And your dad?"

"Kicked the bucket young. Heart attack at forty. I was a wee boy when he died. Joke's on him because I don't remember him enough to miss him."

"I'm sorry," I say anyway.

He takes my hand and leads me to the narrow, old kitchen with a yellow, decaying breakfast nook. He pushes another door open, and we spill into his backyard, which I can see is huge, even in the dark. There are a few divided paddocks where they must keep the cattle.

I can't imagine Mal as a farmer. Clearly, he can't imagine himself one, either, because he prefers to perform on the street for a living. He leads me to a patch of grass and tells me to stall the ball. He disappears into his house and comes back with blankets, a bottle of whiskey, and an orange pack of something called Hobnobs. We lie on the grass next to each other, staring at the stars as they fade into the clouds.

"Do you believe in God?" I munch on a chocolate-covered cookie. It's so much easier to ask weird questions when darkness engulfs you. I can see a glorious Mal-smile cracking in my periphery.

"When it suits me."

"When does it suit you?"

"When I need to have a word with Him or when Ireland needs a prayer during the World Cup games. My turn to ask a question."

I already roll my eyes, psychic that I am.

"Why don't you like your scar?"

Birthmark, I itch to correct. "How do you know I don't like it?"

"You didn't want to talk about it," he says.

I sigh. "There's nothing to like about it. It's ugly. It stands out."

"It's the most beautiful thing about you. It makes you more than a generically beautiful face," he says.

I shake my head. I don't want to think about it. "My turn. Do you sometimes feel like we're all just burning alone?"

"All the time," he croaks. "Less so when I'm with you, though. My turn—have you ever climaxed with a guy?"

I choke on crumbs from my cookie, twisting my head to him with a frown. He still stares at the stars, completely serene.

"What the hell, Mal?"

"I'm sorry, is that more intimate than asking if I believe in God? 'Sides, you're never going to see me again, remember? Who will I tell? My arsehole sheep?"

He's right. Our little world has an expiration date.

"No. I mean, I'm not a virgin. I just…anyway, no. I think I'm too inside my head when I'm intimate with a dude. My turn," I say quickly.

I hate that he's smiling. I hate that his smile makes every inch of my flesh tingle. But most of all, I hate that he illuminates all my senses, like a drug, and soon, I'll have to quit him.

"Do you really hate money?" I ask.

"Loathe it," he confirms. "I'll never make large sums of it. Knowingly, anyway."

"So, Kathleen was right? You can sell your songs and don't?"

He tilts his head toward me, cupping my cheek. Fire licks at the inside of my belly. "Not needing money makes you rich in another way, Rory. A better way. The less you depend on it, the less it limits you. My turn—do you think you'll marry a rich, boiled-balled man when you're older?"

"Boiled-balled?" I laugh.

He takes a swig from the whiskey, but still stares at me, dead serious. "Yeah. Rich men like taking flying classes. It boils their balls, and then they blame their wives for not being able to conceive when actually their sperm count is in the shitter. I've read about it at the dentist's while I was waiting to get my teeth cleaned."

"Thanks for the anecdote." I try to stifle a giggle. "No, I've no plans to marry a rich guy. Why?"

"Because I don't want you to, and you have that something that drives men crazy."

"What's that?" I eyeball him.

He shrugs, taking my hand in his and kissing my open palm. "You're cool."

"Have you ever been in love?" I lick my lips.

"Ask me that question tomorrow before you go. My turn. Ever had an orgasm from a kiss?"

"Excuse me?" My eyebrows shoot up to my forehead.

His face cracks with a mischievous grin that lights up the entire backyard. It shines right into me, keeping me warm. "You heard me."

"No," I hiss, narrowing my eyes at him. Is he for real? I just told him I hadn't orgasmed with a *guy.*

Mal leans down and thumbs my cheek, the rest of his fingers curling around the back of my neck. He feathers his lips against mine. I let him, my eyes still open, guarded and waiting. He darts his tongue out and licks the tip of my nose unexpectedly.

I snort out a laugh, letting my guard down. "That's not gonna do anythi—"

Mal slams his mouth against mine, and before I know what's happening, he's on top of me, pinning my wrists above my head in the damp, cold grass. I groan into his mouth as I feel his body cover mine completely in all the places that matter, because he is hard and hot everywhere, the opposite of my cold, soft self. It's like we aren't even made out of the same material.

His tongue finds mine, and somehow—*somehow*—they dance together sensually and in perfect unison, like we've practiced it before. He is an *excellent* kisser, pulling me into a swirl of passion that makes me blind with need. I feel my panties becoming damp and sticking to my body. This kiss, this kiss is everywhere, down to my curled toes, and just when I'm starting to believe in his orgasm-from-a-kiss silent promise, he lets go of my wrists and pulls back, wiping his mouth with the back of his hand.

"You didn't make me come," I rasp through swollen, numb lips. It's more of an accusation than a taunt. Almost a whine.

"Are we going to sleep together tonight, Rory?" he asks seriously, looking away.

"It…it's not your turn to ask a question," I stutter.

He is the most direct person I've ever met, and I don't know what to make of it.

"I'll owe you one. Now answer."

This time, he turns to look at me, and our eyes meet in the dark. The grass is crisp and dewy, even under the blanket. It's chilly, but for once, that's not the reason goosebumps blossom all over my skin. My breath catches in my throat. *Jesus.*

"I want to," I confess.

The muscles of his neck move when he swallows.

"But we shouldn't, should we?" I whisper. "Not when we already like each other so much."

"I don't know," he rasps. "I don't want to spend the rest of my life wondering what you feel like."

His hand drags down to my neck, wrapping around it, and he leans forward, kissing me so softly, I shudder from the delicacy of his touch. His tongue slides into my mouth, and he rolls on top of me, his hands caressing every inch of my body—my arms, my shoulders, my waist, my stomach…my breasts. He bunches my jacket and hoodie up and flicks a puckered nipple through my shirt. I'm wearing a sports bra, but the chill and the moment make everything in my body impossibly tense and erect and needy.

We groan at the same time, so he flicks it again. Then he moves back up to kiss me, and we smile into each other's mouths. I don't know how it happens, but all my upper layers—jacket, hoodie, top— find themselves thrown beside us. He unclasps my bra with one hand, while shoving the other into my corduroys.

"Anyone ever touched you there?" he asks, brushing his middle finger along my slit. I jolt in pleasure, clenching everywhere.

"Yeah." My mouth waters.

"And like this?" He dips his finger into me, and we can hear how wet I am. I turn maroon between his arms.

"Hmm-mm. My ex-boyfriend, Taylor."

"Did Taylor do this, too?" He drags his wet finger to my clit, massaging it in slow circles.

I throw my head back, closing my eyes. It's not that Taylor didn't know where to touch me. I've just always felt too removed from the moment to fully enjoy it. Like I was putting on a sexy act. This? I feel this. Everywhere. I'm delirious, hot and wet underneath him. Mal takes my left nipple into his mouth and sucks. Stars explode behind my eyelids like fireworks. Everything tightens with delight. I like that he thinks about me first. I like that he is still fully clothed. I like that he knows exactly what he's doing—even if that means he's practiced on other girls. On many girls, no doubt.

"God," I moan.

"Partial about him, remember?" Mal jokes, kissing his way up from my breasts to my shoulders and neck, biting and teasing me as I begin to buck my hips forward and ride his hand that's shoved inside my pants. He rubs my clit back and forth faster, and I prepare to explode. He dips two fingers into me and lets out a groan. Then, when my climax hits me from my toes to the top of my head, he reaches into my bag with one hand, takes the camera out, and snaps a picture of my face as I come.

He captures me in such a vulnerable moment, I want to scream at him, but when he dumps the camera on the quilt next to us and looks down, I let it go. He doesn't look smug or happy or offhanded about it. He looks...*tortured.*

"Rory."

"Hmm?"

"I made you come."

I blink, looking down at my wrinkled corduroys pushed halfway down my thighs.

"And you're going to make me come now," he says. "Hopefully *after* I put my dick inside you. Feck, I can't stop staring at you. You're beautiful."

He unbuckles his belt, lowers his pants, flips his wallet open, and begins sheathing himself with a condom. I kick my corduroys down, refusing to dwell on the fact that he has condoms ready at any given moment.

I don't get a good look at his penis, purposefully avoiding eye-to-dick contact. Penises freak me out. Especially uncircumcised ones. They look like sweater sleeves curled inwards after a wild ride in the washing machine.

When he's all wrapped up, he looks down at me, his arms braced on either side of my head.

I blush, covering my face. "Stop looking at me like that."

"Like what?"

"With a grin that says you pissed in the Jacuzzi everyone's chilling in and got away with it. You gave me an orgasm; you didn't discover the cure for cancer."

"Night's still young," he jokes, dropping a kiss at the crown of my head. "Ready?" he asks, angling himself between my legs.

God, yes. I nod.

He thrusts into me, our eyes lock, and when he starts to move inside me, almost shyly—and definitely not as smoothly and skillfully as I'd imagined—we find out Taylor didn't really do a stellar job taking my virginity after all.

I squirm. Mal gasps. He kisses me with so much passion, I can feel his kiss twisting my stomach in delicious, messy knots.

Without warning, he presses a hand to my left breast, frowning and looking skyward, still inside me.

"What...?" I trail off before realizing what he's doing.

I told him I'd sleep with him tonight over my dead body. I can't help but giggle underneath him.

"Still breathing," he confirms, diving down for another ravenous kiss. "And oh, how alive you are against my fingertips."

"It hurts," I moan into his open, welcoming mouth, clinging to his shoulders.

"Don't worry, Princess Aurora," he growls, hot and velvety and alive against my skin. "I'll make sure to rock your castle if it's the last thing I do."

2:00 am

I stir awake in Mal's bed. The room is so dark—no light from lampposts or passing cars or electronic devices—there's no difference between opening my eyes and closing them. I feel his hot, wet tongue between my thighs, lashing hungrily as it swirls deeper between my legs.

"What are you doing?" I moan.

"Tasting you." He dips his tongue into my folds, and I squirm with pleasure. "Christ on a cracker, Rory. You taste like heaven."

"Mal, what are you..."

But then his tongue brushes my clit, and his lips clamp down on it, sucking. I squeeze my thighs against his face and grab his hair, arching against the pillow and moaning as I press his head into me.

"You'll wake England, darlin'." He dips a finger into me, flicking my nub with his tongue at the same time.

"What do you care? You have a beef with them."

He laughs as he French kisses my clit, his fingers curling to find my G-spot as my toes coil deliciously.

I come again, his name on my lips.

3:00 am

"It's more about enthusiasm than technique," Mal explains, his penis staring back at me.

It's thicker and longer than Taylor's. Angry-looking and purplish. I finally found something about him that's less than perfect, even though it does feel good inside me.

"Just give it your best go. Honestly, I'll probably come after twenty seconds, anyway. You're a ride, Rory."

I wrap my lips around his shaft, then realize he was right when he pushes me back not fifteen seconds later, coming on my chest. We fall from the bed to the floor, limbs tangled, laughing hysterically.

"Rory!" he thunders. "I pre-ejaculated. Now I must kill you to keep my secret safe."

"Relax. I'm not going to tell on you." I roll on the floor, mid-yawn, hitting the door. I can still taste his salty flesh. My mouth feels full of him. "Besides, we'll have an ocean separating us, remember? Who will I tell? My pet fish?"

"You have fish?" He looks startled, like it hurts that he doesn't know everything about me.

"I'll get some to make you feel good about yourself."

"Just admit that I can kill you, too," he says from across the room now, both of us lying on the floor, staring at the ceiling.

"Why?"

"Because you're stealing my breath, so you're already halfway there with the killing part."

I shake my head, zipping my mouth with my fingers.

He grabs a guitar pick from the floor and throws it at me. "I'll let you hold on to your heart for a little longer. Just don't get attached."

I laugh, but then he stops and looks at me, and I swear there's regret etched on his face.

"Forgive me?" he asks.

"For what?" I scrunch my nose.

He looks away, swallowing. "Good question. For not giving you what you came here for, I suppose."

4:00 am

"Sometimes you make music. Sometimes the music makes you," Mal explains. We sit on his bed, sharing a pack of something he calls candy rolls, drinking milk from the carton. "And when it makes you, it changes you, and when it changes you, you never know how you're going to come out of it."

"Same with photography." I nod. "I feel like a director, showing you what I want you to see. I can make the field behind your house gorgeous or creepy, sad or happy. It's all in the angles, and filters, and composition."

"I don't want to sing. Attention doesn't get my dick hard."

"I know." I smile. "That's why I hide behind a camera, too. It doesn't…make me wet, I suppose, either." I blush.

"So you understand." He smiles, relieved. "I won't sell my songs. They're mine."

"Do what makes you happy. The world will understand. If it doesn't, it's the world's problem, not yours."

Silence.

"Marry me, Rory." He turns to me. "Let's just stay here and feck and make music and take pictures."

I laugh and pop another candy into my mouth. But he seems serious, waiting for an answer.

"Mal…" I say.

Jesus. He's still looking at me, waiting for an answer.

"I have school. I'm going to college in a few weeks."

"We have colleges here."

"I've already enrolled. Paid. I have a dorm room. My best friend, Summer, is coming with me."

"I have some savings," he insists. "I'm good at what I do. I can provide for us."

"You're insane."

"I never claimed not to be." He scowls, and by the edge in his voice, I can tell he's finding it hard to keep himself calm. Then he shakes his head, smiles, rolls on top of me, and covers my face with hot, wet kisses.

He taps the nightstand, trying to find another condom. There aren't any. We ran out. He lifts his face from mine, wordlessly asking for permission. I can feel the weight of this decision pressing against every bone in my body. Especially considering how I came into this world. This is where I become my mother. Where I let my need and lust override my logic.

I give him a little nod. "Pull out, please. It'd be hard to take care of a baby during finals."

"Feck you, Rory."

"Please do, Mal."

In the morning, I insist on treating him to breakfast before we head to the airport. He paid for my hotel and my meals since I got here. It's the least I can do.

We end up at The Boar's Head, which is apparently the only place locals eat. Tourists from all over the world come to Tolka for the small town, Irish experience, to work the land and tour the local brewery. I've learned this place is also known for its butter. The pub is jam-packed when we walk in, but a beautiful, blonde bartender finds us a table when she spots Mal.

"Missed you, rascal." She winks at him.

It's pretty easy to see they share a history.

Mal flicks the back of her ear. "Been a minute."

"Call me this weekend?"

"Depends on a certain bell," he says. *Bell* means a ring, a booty call, a one-night stand. But *Belle* is my name, too. Not that he knows that.

My whole body is sore from having sex with Mal five times last night, not to mention the extracurricular activities we did in addition. We don't discuss the one time without the condom, because he did pull out. I tell myself nothing bad will happen, but just to make sure, I'll buy a morning-after pill at the airport's Boots pharmacy.

After placing our order at the bar, I wince as I sit down. Mal grabs my hand and presses it against his lips.

"Let's try this again in broad daylight." He clears his throat. "Stay."

I tear open a pack of chips and throw one into my mouth, chewing to buy some time.

"As I said, I'm starting college in two weeks."

"Feck college."

"What about my mom?"

"Don't feck her. That's the kind of kinky I'm not quite into. But you hate her, Rory. Besides, we'll send her hairspray every month. And plane tickets every Christmas. Easter, too, if you insist." He reaches for his Guinness—yes, in the morning—taking a generous sip. "Stay, Rory. It's kismet. Tell me you didn't notice the rain stopped when we kissed yesterday."

I open my mouth to say it means nothing, but then the power goes out. It's daylight, but it still freaks me out when the hanging TVs go dead, the *Lord of the Dance* music stops, and the humming of industrial fridges ceases.

The silence stretches between us. Everyone seems to have gone quiet. I'm not sure, but I think some people are staring at us. They must've heard the last part of the conversation when the music died, and are waiting for my answer.

Do they know Mal proposed? I swallow, staring at my hands on the table.

"Rory?" he asks.

"I don't believe in kismet," I say quietly, keeping my eyes trained on the open bag of chips. "You're twenty-two, and I'm eighteen. We both know it won't last."

Am I working against my own fate?

The electricity comes back on. This serendipity crap is borderline paranormal. Annoyed, I take comfort in the fact that the football playing on the TVs and the music will drown our conversation, and the rest of the locals go back to their chitchat.

Mal says nothing. His face falls, like he just realized I'm right. I pinch the hoop in my nose and slide it back and forth.

"Hey, what about doing a long-distance thing? I'm planning on getting a job while I study, so I can probably visit you next summer. Maybe even Christmas, depending on the ticket prices."

As I say this, I try to convince myself it really can work. I'll only need to pay for the tickets. Mal has a car and a house.

But he shakes his head, sitting back and balancing his chair on its two back legs. "I'm an all-or-nothing type of lad, Rory. There's no way in hell I can manage long distance."

His answer angers me a little. So he wants me, but only on his conditions? That's shitty. If someone isn't willing to wait for you, they don't really deserve you.

I can't tell him to uproot himself and come to the States, to leave six siblings, his nephews and nieces, a mother, an elderly adoptive grand-father, and a mourning childhood friend who is pining for him and probably wants to wear my skin.

And after the offhand way he treated me when I brought up long distance, I won't even try.

"We could stay friends on Facebook or MySpace—" I start, but he cuts me off.

"And watch as you move on with other guys? Nah, thank you. I try to keep my self-hatred below suicidal level. And we both know watching each other fecking other people would be dazzlingly stupid."

I give him a hard stare, folding my arms. "Fine. Then we go cold turkey."

"I can't go cold turkey," he says.

God, he is difficult. "You leave no room for much else," I grit out.

"False," he retorts.

"What do you suggest?"

"A contract." He lets his chair slam on the floor as he leans forward. "You Yanks love legally binding shite, yeah?" He reaches for my bag next to me, flipping it open. He takes out my camera and a pen, sprinkles the utensils out of a folded napkin, and straightens it on the table.

"It's not the right time to be together, I agree. But if we meet again, under any circumstances, any time in the future, we're making this work, Rory. Feck spouses. Feck boyfriends and girlfriends. Feck the world. If kismet happens, we are letting it happen, no matter what, you hear?"

I stare at him like he just fell from the sky. What is he smoking and how do we make sure it never falls into the hands of our youth?

"The chances of us meeting again are less than zero."

"Bzzz. Wrong again. They are slightly more than zero. I would put it at zero point fifteen percent," he says cheerfully.

I don't know how he can be so nonchalant about it, but I guess I can't complain. He proposed to me, and I'm almost sure he was serious. I turned him down. Publicly, too.

"What if one of us seeks the other person out?" I ask.

"That's cheating." Mal shakes his head. "It needs to happen organically. We can't look for each other."

"But what if someone does?" I have a feeling this someone is going to be me.

"Then the contract is terminated, and you don't have to marry me."

"I have to marry you if we meet again?" My eyes flare, but I'm smiling.

He shrugs. "High stakes make good stories, Princess Aurora of New Jersey."

"So much for me having the power to kill you. You won't even give me your phone number," I mumble, sipping my Diet Coke.

"I'm not giving you my number *because* I don't want this to kill me," he grinds out, his eyes darkening.

I'm trying not to hate him right now, because I know everything he says is right and true. We can't be together, and keeping in touch would leave both of us craving more. Mal jots the terms of the contract on the napkin. Then he signs it and slides it toward me.

"Whenever you're ready."

I read it first.

We, Malachy Isaac Doherty, and Aurora what's-the-rest-of-your-name? hereby promise each other that, in the unlikely event we meet again, under any circumstances, under any rules and conditions, at random, we will make this work. No matter the casualties or consequences. We marry each other. We live happily ever after. With kids and dogs and arsehole sheep.

The rules:
No looking for each other on the internet.
No seeking each other out.
But if it happens—it's on.

Malachy
_____   _____
Malachy Isaac Doherty   Aurora McGorgeous O'Cool

In the unlikely event.

He knows it. I know it. Still, you can't make someone be with you. You can't force them to commit to something doomed. I have no plans of moving to Ireland after I graduate, and Mal's entire life is here.

I amend my name to Aurora Belle *Jenkins*, so he'll know it—I already want him to cheat—and sign. I consider only briefly the fact that I never told him my middle name, and he's referred to it. He takes a picture of the napkin and passes me my camera. "Your copy of the agreement, for safekeeping."

Mal tucks the napkin into his back pocket and takes a sip of his Guinness.

"I mean it." He shrugs. "I'm getting this notarized and apostilled."

"I know." I throw another chip into my mouth, trying to act nonchalant.

"Let's just hope I don't die from heartbreak first." He downs the rest of his Guinness.

I think about Kathleen's open arms and the herd of girls who follow him everywhere.

"Oh, I think you'll survive."

A NOTE FROM THE NAPKIN

Look, I don't have high hopes for this spur-of-the-moment contract. You think it's my first rodeo? I'm recycled, bitch. I've been around the block—long enough to know how this works. They will keep their promise for a few weeks. Maybe a month, if they're really into each other. Then I'll start to wrinkle, stink, and fall apart, or his mother will find me and throw me away, muttering profanity at her untidy son, who, of course, by that time will be balls deep in someone else and not actually present.

I'm just the victim of their knee-jerk decision. I should have died gracefully, in a recycling bin, tucked comfortably among other napkins, plastic bottles, and stray leftovers the workers here are too lazy to scrape off to the other bin.

Also, and not on a completely unrelated note, I have a ketchup stain the size of a pea on the word *casualties*, and it itches like hell.

This has mess written all over it.

When we reach Dublin Airport, I fling my backpack over one shoulder, grab my suitcase from Mal's trunk, and insist he doesn't come in with me. He double parks, rounding the car on a jog.

"I hate airport scenes in movies. They're morbidly tacky. We're better than that, Mal." I tuck my hair behind my ears, chuckling at my feet.

Truth is, I'm already crushed, and if we share any more intimate moments, I might spend the entire trip home crying, which would be beyond embarrassing.

He rubs his thumb over my lower lip, smiling. "Safe travels."

"Thanks." But I'm still standing here like an idiot. Waiting for… what, exactly?

I don't want to go. I don't want to leave you.

I remember something important. I unzip my suitcase, rummaging for my Polaroid camera. When I find it, I jump up and take a picture of us together. I hand it to him.

"It's not fair that I'll have all these pictures of us, and you'll have nothing."

"I won't have nothing," he amends, smiling. "I'll have the memory."

"And our contract." I squeeze his shoulder, but I can already feel our bodies growing apart. Like we're strangers again. "You'll have that, too."

He rolls his eyes. "Let's hope I don't wank on it to death the first week you're gone."

I laugh and glance at the napkin in question, relieved that it's an inanimate object, but it's a mirthless kind of laugh.

He takes my face in his hands and kisses me so deeply I lose balance. His heart is beating so fast and hard, it sounds like it could tear his chest open. *Maybe*, I think desperately, *it should*. I want to snatch it and take it with me—somewhere Kathleen won't be able to get to it.

We disconnect slowly, like we're glued together.

"Don't be with Kathleen." I look up at his face, whispering, "She doesn't kill you."

That Bukowski quote pops into my head: "*Find what you love and let it kill you.*" I think I just did.

"I won't. Don't be with a stupid, shiny guy with boiled balls. You were born for greatness, Princess."

"I won't." I smile.

He lifts my chin with his finger so our eyes lock and says, "Ask me again."

I don't need clarification on this. I know. I know because I feel it, too, and it cracks my resolve. I press my palm against his chest, monitoring his heartbeat.

"Have you ever been in love?" I can't swallow the emotions lodging in my throat.

He grins down at me. "Goodbye, Rory."

My eyes flare, but I grin. "Bastard!"

"What?" He laughs.

I laugh, too. This time it's a real laugh. We both needed this, I realize. An icebreaker.

"Why did you tell me to ask you this if the answer is no?"

"I didn't say the answer is no." He runs his hands along my arms. "But if I admitted it to you, I'd admit it to myself. Then I'd have to look for you, and that'd be a breach of contract. You have to understand, Rory, next time I see you, I'll have you. I won't care if you have a boyfriend, or a husband, or a harem of men vying for your love. If you have children, I'll raise them as mine. So, I guess an apology is in order."

"For what?" I blink.

He turns to leave. I'm not ready to say goodbye, but I know I never will be.

"For no doubt disrupting your life and tearing it apart next time I meet you. All's fair in love and war, yeah?"

But he doesn't wait for me to answer. He gets into his car and drives off, leaving me standing there, with his pulse still beating in my palm.

4

Present

Mal

OUT ON THE BALCONY, AURORA STARES AT ME LIKE I TOOK A shite in her soup.

To be fair, after everything that's gone down in the last eight years, I would have, if the opportunity had presented itself. As it happens, it didn't. So who knows exactly why she's filled with such surprise and terror.

Nevertheless, the years we've spent apart have treated her well, unlike the way they've treated me. She still has funky hair that would look lovely wrapped around my fist, a nose hoop I'm sure she still messes with all the time, legs for miles clad in torn fishnet stockings, and the wardrobe of a fifteen year old crushing hard on Yungblud and 5 Seconds of Summer. She has a Marilyn Monroe-like beauty mark above her upper lip, that prominent, crescent scar I bet she still doesn't know the story of, and lashes so thick, they shadow her cheeks when she looks down.

Positively lovely. The same way many women are.

Many women I haven't thrown my life away for.

The idea that I've been sick with guilt over everything I hadn't told her, everything I couldn't say—*promised* not to tell her—makes me want to laugh now.

Yes, I kept things from Aurora.

But she went the extra mile and *ripped* things from me.

Ask me what drew me to her in the first place that fateful day on Drury Street, and I still won't be able to pinpoint it. She's a fine thing, but too in love with the idea of herself, like all pseudo-artistic pretty girls who can operate a camera and their mouths around a rich guy's cock.

I cut myself some slack. Ages sixteen to twenty-two had been a blur of getting sloshed and treating myself to periodic blackouts. A girl like Aurora had slipped easily into my hopelessly optimistic heart.

Age thirty, however, brings with it a heart that's frosted like a winter garden. Also, I stopped taking destructive lasses into my bed and promising them forever a while ago.

Lesson learned, and Rory was an excellent teacher.

Yeah, Aurora Belle Jenkins hasn't changed.

Me, on the other hand? A completely different fella.

She turns to face me, going for an awkward, hesitant hug. I swivel, also, but with my hands clasped behind my back. When she sees a warm greeting is not in the cards for us, I reach out and use my thumb to lift her jaw, closing her slacked mouth.

"You're here," she murmurs.

"Aurora, always observant and quick-witted." I throw her an impatient smile. My coat is over her shoulders, because I remember she is always cold. What I never got the chance to tell her is that I'm always so unbearably hot.

We really were quite good together. At least for twenty-four hours.

She takes a step back, looking wary, wide-eyed—a frightened

animal who just heard the deadly click of a trigger. She shouldn't be. I would never hurt her. Physically, anyway. Wasn't I the only muppet to give her the time of the day when she was in Ireland? Yes, yes, I was.

There's an elephant in the room, and if she thinks I'll take mercy on her by addressing it, she's about to discover New Mal is nothing like the one she left behind.

"Why...how...what are you doing here?" She blinks.

Seeing her like this, confused and disoriented, is not giving me the instant gratification I'd imagined getting all those years, in case we ever met again. And knowing Aurora, it's not going to last long. She'll find her footing soon.

I had the luxury of spotting her as soon as I walked through the doors this evening. I needn't a single glance to recognize her. She is, after all, tattooed in my mind, permanent and painful.

"Work," I say. "You?"

"Same." She clears her throat, straightening her back, gaining her composure. "You're a singer now? That's great, Mal."

"I write songs," I correct, taking a sip of my whiskey. I can tell she's shocked and hurt by the fact that I'm not hurling myself at her with love declarations. That makes both of us, if you ask twenty-two-year-old Mal.

"You?" I jut my chin in her direction.

"Photographer for Blue Hill Records." She smiles, trying to break the ice. "Gosh, Mal. I never thought I'd see you again. But I see we're still as predictable as the places we come from."

"Speak for yourself." I run my eyes down her body, making a point not to stop anywhere of previous interest. "You might be predictable. I have a few new tricks up my sleeve."

Her smile falls. She opens her mouth to say something. Argue, probably—Aurora's always been feisty, and I doubt that's changed—when the balcony doors open and Jeff Ryner stumbles out.

Jeff Ryner is what happens when every cliché in the fecking book meets a man with zero personality, deep pockets, and an impressive heritage. It's like he was Frankensteined in the basements of some low-budget Hollywood studio. The washed-up, coked-up, slimy, record Suit.

He inherited Blue Hill, a small record label, from his father some years ago and has felt inclined to ruin it. His recent conquests include signing Ashton Richards, a solo artist who is about as talented as a half-empty bottle of lube. Richards looks like an unfortunate cross between a male model, a hobo, and a One Direction dropout. He can carry a note like I can carry a fecking pyramid on my back. Saddled with the vocal range of a battered whale, he relies on auto-tune and his baby blue eyes.

Which brings me to Jeff Ryner's second conquest—yours truly. I'm supposed to write songs for Richards' next album, for the modest sum of one million euros. I say *modest*, because there's no price for my dignity. Yet, here I am, stripping myself of poise for the greater good. Another thing she is responsible for.

Thanks for that, Aurora.

"Jenkins! I see you've met the man of the hour." Ryner slow-claps as he zigzags his way to us, a cigarette dangling from his mouth. He looks like Humpty Dumpty in a Technicolor suit, his sweaty upper lip glistening like garbage juice. "This is Malachy Doherty. Mal, this is Rory, our junior photographer. Mal, Rory shot the cover for Fiona in Wonderland's new album." He waves in her direction.

That cover was brilliant. The pop princess wore a gas mask and a full-blown wedding dress, standing in an open field.

I wonder briefly if it was Aurora's concept before deciding I don't care. So, the traitorous lass turned out to be decent at what she does. Call the fecking press.

"Rory, Mal is one of the biggest poets of our time. He's sold some of the best songs on the billboard, including 'Finding you, Losing Me,' 'On Drury Street,' 'Underneath the Stars,' and 'Princess from New Jersey.'"

If she connects the painfully obvious dots together, she doesn't let it show, and for that, I'm grateful. *Dumb or heartless?* My bet is on the latter, based on what I know about her.

"*Pleasure*," she clips sarcastically, her eyes boring into my skull, trying to make a dent.

She adapts well to the shifting atmosphere. I can tell no part of her is glad to see me again. That's all right. I don't want her to be a willing participant in the game. I just want her to partake in it. It will make everything so much messier, and messy is fun.

"I called you here because I have a good opportunity for you, Rory. Jake, our senior photographer, is with Cold Blaze on their last leg. Once he's done, he's going to stick around in New York for a while—his girlfriend's having a baby. So we need a photographer for this next project."

"I'm your person." Aurora turns to him, nodding.

I pinch my lips, refusing to let my satisfied smirk loose. Ryner saunters over to stand between us, then turns around and leans on the edge of the balcony, looking back and forth at us.

"It's a big one, Jenkins."

She nods, her attention on him now.

She is still deadly beautiful. That's the thing that bothers me most. But it shouldn't. That just means it won't be a terrible inconvenience to shag her, which I fully plan on, before discarding her back to her motherland, this time with no affection and zero promises.

"Deets, Ryner. Give them to me." Aurora starts playing with the hoop in her nose.

You silly, predictable girl.

"Two months in a village just outside Dublin. Tokyo, is it?" He throws me a puzzled look.

"Tolka." I shove my balled fists into my pockets.

"I was close." He laughs.

Sure. You only got the city, country, and continent wrong, arsehole.

"Doherty will be writing the songs, and Richards will be recording them in his home studio—the acoustic version, anyway. Kinda like an artistic workshop, old-school style. Then Richards will come back to New York in March and record it from scratch."

What Ryner means is the singer will come back and have professionals distort his voice to sound like something that doesn't break glass, concrete, and people's spirits. I watch Aurora's face transform from annoyed to terrified in a span of seconds. Her lips are still pursed.

"That means two months in Ireland, Jenkins, all costs taken care of. You're welcome." He winks.

"Wait." Aurora holds up a hand. "Why do I need to stay in Ireland? I can just take pictures for a week or so and then get out of their hair."

Ryner shakes his head. "It's for a documentary of sorts. We need hours of material. Hundreds of pictures. Our marketing campaign is huge. We're bleeding money out of our asses after a butchered colonoscopy exam. We need as much material as possible."

"You can't expect me to live in Ireland for the next couple months," Aurora says through a tight smile.

I know what she did to make me hate her, but I wonder what *I* did to warrant such sour behavior. Other than being a cunt just now.

Come to think of it, that's probably all it took.

Then, of course, there's the matter of the boyfriend.

The rich, shiny boyfriend she said she'd never date, yet I saw her in the ballroom, clinging to his Brioni-clad arm like bad breath on a fecking alcoholic.

What disappointments we are to each other, Princess.

"I can fly in and out of Ireland," she suggests, munching on her lower lip. "It's no trouble, and I bet you'll need me here, too."

Ryner shakes his head, his patience dissipating, just like mine. "Richards' schedule is all over the place now that he's dating that new second-cousin-to-the-royals chick in London. I don't know when he plans to come and go. You need to be there at all times."

"In a hotel?" she asks hopefully.

This time, a smile curls on my face. What can I say? Even I'm not completely unaffected by a good arse-to-mouth situation where Aurora has to taste just how hard I fucked her.

"What would be the point of that? We need you there, with them, under the same roof. Are we having a problem here, Jenkins?" Ryner tapers his eyes at her. "Should I give this assignment to someone else? Someone more experienced, maybe?"

Aurora frowns at him, then shakes her head. Nah, she's not one to back down from a challenge.

"I'll make this assignment my bitch," she breathes.

"I have no doubt, kiddo."

Puke, meet bucket. He didn't ask her to save the world, just take a few pictures of that eejit, Richards, pretending to be hard at work.

Aurora turns her attention to me. I'm ready for her, with the shit-eating grin of someone who not only pissed in her Jacuzzi, but also drowned her boyfriend in it for good measure.

"Mal."

I raise an eyebrow. "Aurora."

"Just so you know, I have a boyfriend," she says matter-of-factly, peeling my pea coat from her shoulders and throwing it my way.

I catch it, and as I do, raise my left hand in the air, palm facing me, so she can see the gold band on my ring finger.

"Good for you, sweetheart," I deadpan, twisting the ring around. "Reached first base yet? Carved your initials on a tree? Maybe you gave each other purity rings," I ponder, then shake my head. "Nah. Too late for that."

I don't think she listened to any of my monologue, though. She is solely focused on the wedding band, following my movements with her eyes. I can see the question behind them, and, of course, charitable bastard that I am, I volunteer the information.

"Kathleen." I shove my hand into my pocket, noticing the way—even though her face pales and her fingers clutch the bannister—she doesn't collapse. "Shortly after you left. Beautiful ceremony, performed by Father Doherty. My sincere apologies for not sending you an invitation."

Aurora's throat works, and it reminds me how delicate it was under my fingers. She elevates her chin, refusing to break.

Night's still young, darlin'.

"Selling songs and marrying Kathleen?" Her face turns to stone, completely void of emotion now. "You're right, Mal. I really don't have the faintest clue who you are anymore."

Ryner looks between us, trying to assess the situation. He knows we know each other, because I told him as much, but I presented us as old friends, not as complete fiends, which is closer to the truth.

"Do you guys need a second?" He sniffs his beaky nose, finishing off his cigarette and putting it out in a plant.

Christ, he's a waste of oxygen. His mother needs to plant a tree for every day he lives.

"*Yes,*" Aurora says.

"*No,*" I snap at the same time.

There's silence for a few seconds before I give Ryner half a shrug and make a show of turning back to the railing, parking my elbows on it, ignoring her.

"All right, then, lovebirds." Ryner rubs his chin.

I can see him in my periphery, moonwalking backward to the doors, like the moron he is.

Aurora drops her voice once we're alone. "In the contract, you said you wouldn't care if we had significant others or spous—"

I cut her off immediately. "You mean eight years ago, when we were both fresh out of diapers? Come on now, Aurora. We were in love with the concept, not each other."

Why is she even bringing this up, after everything she's done and said? It's like being wary of a blood test when both your limbs are cut off and your head is chopped, floating somewhere in the Mediterranean Sea.

Ship's sailed, sweetheart.

I don't bother looking at her. Instead, I stare at the ugly, soulless skyscrapers of Manhattan, reminding myself how much she loves them. And that just like all the ditzy girls I rolled between my sheets before and after her, she's saddled with Instagram-inspired ideas and Photoshopped dreams. She lives a Pinterest-perfect life, and there's no filter to make *my* life suitable enough for her reality.

"Okay…" she drawls, processing. "Just making sure you know I'm not going to honor that contract."

"Excuse me while I go dry my tears with the one million euros I'm here for." I finish my drink in one gulp and place the glass on the wide marble railing. When I turn to her, I have a pleasant, plastic smile on my face. I'd hate for her to think I actually care whether she comes or not.

"Won't Kathleen mind me being there?" She plays with the hoop in her nose. "Considering our history and all."

"Kathleen won't mind."

"Glad to see at least one of you grew up during this decade." She twists the hoop in her nose some more. "And I would ask that Callum could come and go as he pleases while I stay at your house. We'll be good guests and stay out of your way as much as possible, of course."

"That's fine," I snap.

She's staring at me; I'm staring at the view again. I'm not making it any easier for her. Why should I? She's the one who threw everything down the shitter and flushed it a thousand times.

"You still live in your cottage?" she asks.

"Yes."

"Do you have any children?"

"No."

"Is there a—"

"Do I look like a steak?" I cut into her words again.

She shakes her head, looking at me with even more confusion and revulsion than before.

"Then stop grilling me." I twist my head to stare her down.

By the way her face screws in pain, I can tell she got the not-so-subtle reference to the time she asked about her da. I remind myself what I've had to endure in recent years thanks to her and push the guilt aside. To think that every minute spent with her, I was tearing myself apart for not giving her the truth.

About her.

About her father.

Whatever I plan to do to Aurora will only cause short-term damage. She'll land back on her feet. *Eventually.* Me? I'm fucked into the next life, and possibly the one after it, too.

"Look." I sigh. "Ryner is set on sending you to Ireland, and considering the paycheck, and the fact that you mean very little to me, I'm not sure why I should fight him on this. You'll come, you'll do the job, and you'll leave. If you want to bring your shiny boyfriend along, be my guest. We don't have to become *best buds* again." I sign quotation marks with my fingers, sprinkling the insult with a fake, whiny American accent just to walk the extra cunt mile. "No need to get your knickers in a twist."

"Why are you so mad?" she hisses, more shocked than hurt now.

"Mad?" I blink at her like she's crazy. "I'm just not interested in making this more than it is. It's been eight years, and a lot has happened in them."

But not enough for me to spell out the words she wants to hear: *I'm taken. You're taken. It's just a business transaction.*

I won't try to steal you.

I won't try to sabotage your relationship.

I won't try to seek revenge.

Those are all things I don't say. Things I leave out. The things she should be demanding right now.

Luckily, Aurora seems too flustered to read the unwritten fine print of this conversation. She's forever the hotheaded redhead.

"I see." Her jaw squares, and so do her shoulders. "If that's the way you want it to be, then I'll respect that." She nods, taking a step away from me.

I want to throttle her. To tell her it is *not*, in fact, the way I want it to be, but she made it that way. She moved on, and I got stuck. Now I'm angry, and vengeful, and definitely in the mood to inflict some damage myself.

"When do I start?" She parks her hands on her waist.

"Sometime after Christmas, before New Year's. Richards is throwing a party at my house, and Ryner mentioned something about it." I scratch the beginning of my stubble. "Work out the details with him."

"Do you have any plans for Christmas?" She blinks at me.

Poor lass is *still* trying. Is she bipolar? She was quite clear about where I stood with her after we parted ways, so this doesn't make a lot of sense.

"You're doing it again," I point out.

"Doing what?"

"Trying to make pleasant conversation. Being pleasant to you is not on my agenda, Aurora."

She turns around and walks to the door. I decide I'm not done hurting her.

"Kathleen's," I say to her back. "I'm spending Christmas at Kathleen's."

She stops, but she doesn't say anything. I get a good view of her little, round bum.

"And you?" I can't help myself. "Christmas with the future in-laws in England?"

She turns and gives me a serene smile.

"I, too, have no interest in being pleasant with you, Malachy Doherty. The difference between us? Unlike you, I stay true to my word."

I lean back on the bannister and smile, watching her go.

All is fair in love and war, and I'm certainly prepared for battle.

A NOTE FROM JEFF RYNER

History and hysteria have more than a few letters in common.

These two? They definitely share a history, and what I saw on the balcony was nothing short of hysterical.

I've watched it happen time after time in this industry.

Exes working together, thinking they are *mature,* and *moved on,* and *capable of being friends.*

B.U.L.L.S.H.I.T.

I could've told them it would only get uglier from here on out. Warn them not to bother. That the money isn't worth it, and babysitting an asshole like Ashton Richards is only going to put them under more pressure, break more rules, and push them over the edge.

I *could...*

But let's be real. I'm a forty-something cokehead with a sex addiction, and I have absolutely zero doubt that's how they view me and what they think of me. Seeing other people screwing up their lives is not painful at this point. It is even—dare I say it?—therapeutic. Like knitting.

Knitting a disaster.

That's why people gossip, right? To get a kick out of other people's problems. And when other people don't have problems they can see or taste or judge, they create problems for them. Analyze their every move to try to make themselves feel better. Well, this has catastrophe written all over it. How could I prevent it from happening?

Plus, I'm genuinely interested to see how it pans out. Knowing Malachy Doherty's story, I don't know how he can bang up his miserable life more than he already has. Guy is so deep in shit, anything else thrown at him, even a scandal, would frankly be an upgrade.

I pop two pills of whatever my dealer gave me and make my way back to the party, knowing I look like a Eurovision set and not giving a fuck.

Because I don't.

I really don't.

Let people judge. They're not much better. The only difference between us is that I know what Malachy and Rory think about me. They don't know what I think about them.

Rory

"YOU'RE HOME EARLY." SUMMER POKES HER HEAD UP FROM behind the fluffy cushions of the couch before turning back to the TV and shoving another spoonful of Chunky Monkey into her mouth. *Pretty Woman* is playing.

She waggles the spoon at the TV, yelling at the screen, "I freaking loathe rom-coms. Falling in love with a billionaire and ending up marrying him is bullshit with a capital B, especially when you're a working girl. You're more likely to get murdered by him. You know, since working girls are often without relatives. This should have been *Pretty <u>Dead</u> Woman: A Cautionary Tale*."

"Don't wait for a call from Hollywood."

I hang my coat by the door and kick my Toms off as I make a stop at the kitchen counter, which is actually *inside* our tiny living room, pouring both of us large glasses of cheap wine.

Callum wanted me to stay over, but I have an early morning tomorrow, and privately, I can admit that seeing Mal shook me to the core.

"Why the ice cream?" I place the empty wine bottle in the sink, my back to her. I'm trying to act nonchalant, mainly so I can convince myself I'm not having a mental breakdown of epic proportions. Which I'm not. Feeling my pulse pounding against my eyelids is totally normal, I'm sure.

"I was just thinking about the love of my life." Summer lets out an exasperated sigh.

"Shouldn't that be a good thing?" I quirk an eyebrow, turning around and plopping next to her. I hand her a glass of white wine.

"No, considering the fact I haven't met him yet, and it's very likely he's sleeping with someone else *as we speak*, Rory. It's Saturday evening, and the whole world is drunk and stumbling out of office Christmas parties. How could he do this to me?" Summer sniffs. "He's probably screwing another girl right now. The hot girl from HR. Dirty bastard."

I bite down on a smile, working out a way to explain her backward logic in my head. Summer's sunshine blonde hair is tied up in a huge, messy bun, and she's still wearing yesterday's eyeliner. She's clad in gray sweatpants and a black hoodie, a far cry from her usual glamorous, off-Broadway actress persona. Summer is in between projects now, rehearsing for her next show, which is due to start running mid-February. This was supposed to be our time together, but now I have to go to freaking Ireland and work alongside Mal, who had a personality transplant sometime in the last decade and died on the operating table, only to resurrect himself as Satan.

Summer turns the volume down, swiveling on the couch to face me. "What's up, Ror? You look like you sucked off Lucifer and he filled your mouth with ashes and lava."

"No, but close." I put my glass down.

Summer has been my best friend since we were toddlers. We went to grade school and college together. We share an apartment. She knows everything about me.

"I saw Mal at the ball tonight."

She blinks at me. "Mal…?"

"*Irish* Mal."

Her eyes widen, and she slaps the back of her hand over her forehead dramatically. Summer can be scandalized more easily than a seventeenth century duchess in a brothel.

"Say it ain't so."

I nod. "It's so, and it's worse than anything you might imagine."

"I don't know how it possibly could be, unless he's Callum's lover and is after his ass, not yours. You finally have your shit together, Rory. You've been hung up on him for years."

If there's one thing I've learned about this life, it's that you should find friends who love seeing you win and will support you when you lose. Summer is both.

"He's married," I say.

"Ouch."

"To my sister, Kathleen."

"The bastard!" She jumps up on the couch, quilt dropping to the floor, and shakes her fist in the air. "I'm going to kill him."

"The worst part is not even that everything Kathleen said turns out to be true. It's the fact that Mal can't stand the sight of me for some reason. He's mad at me, and he won't tell me why." I grab a throw pillow, hugging it to my chest.

"Who cares why he's an asshole? Just be glad you dodged that bullet. Look how he treated your half-sister. The jerk played her around when you were there. I'm going to go out on a limb and bet their marriage is a clusterfuck of massive proportions."

Summer plops down, grabs my wine glass, and puts it to my lips, urging me to take a sip like it's medicine.

"Besides, you have Callum now, and he is uber hot and doesn't hate money or standing or…you know, life in general."

"Mal doesn't hate life. He loves it."

That's the entire reason he is who he is. Because he loves life so passionately. But I'm thinking about Young Mal. The current version seems about as jolly as a KKK meeting.

Summer huffs. "What was he doing there, anyway?"

"He's working with Jeff Ryner now." I put the pillow behind my head and throw myself over it. "We're about to work together. In Ireland. For two months. I'm going to live with him." I swallow hard. "And his wife."

Summer looks at me like I've just announced my intention to join the circus, where I will be performing a one-hour show doing gymnastics on the back of an elephant in nothing but leopard thongs. Blindfolded.

"What in the fuck went through your head when you said yes?"

"The job opportunity. Plus, the Mal thing happened eight years ago and clearly means nothing."

"Means nothing?" Summer shoots to her feet, pacing back and forth in our tiny living room, arms linked behind her back. "*Means nothing*?! You obsessed over his ass like he was the only male with a functioning dick in the entire universe. It took you years—not weeks, not months, *years!*—to finally move on with Callum. You dreamed about him. You woke me up crying. You thought you saw him on street corners and in festivals and at airports. Remember that time you ran after that poor Asian lady because you thought she was him?"

Do I ever. She hit me with her bag trying to shoo me away.

"She was tall and had the same blue-black hair," I mumble into my drink.

"Point is, he *haunted* you. We had to take turns in college watching you so you didn't break your stupid napkin contract and look for him on the internet. That's not nothing, Rory. That's everything."

I rub my eyes, taking a gulp of air. She's right. Stupid Mal and stupid Kathleen ended up together and somehow reached the convenient (and also stupid) conclusion that I'm the reason for their problems, but I never stopped pining for him.

"You can't go." Summer stops pacing, stomping her foot. "I won't allow it."

"I've made up my mind."

I stare at the TV to avoid her glare. Julia Roberts and Richard Gere are bickering. I think about Callum's reaction when I came back from the balcony and explained everything. He shook Whitney off immediately, then stood up and ushered me to a little bar. There, he told me I should do it. That I daren't pass up a blazing, new opportunity because of an old flame.

He said who knew how long I would keep this job anyway. Once he proposes, he will need me at his disposal, helping with the wedding arrangements, managing our social calendar.

I kind of blocked everything out past the "go for it" part, though. I have no plans of becoming a housewife, but that wasn't the time to broach the subject.

"You're going to screw your brother-in-law." Summer crosses her arms in my periphery. "Let that sink for a second, Lewdy McGrosson. Still wanna go?"

"I'm not going to screw anyone there. Well, maybe Callum." *Definitely* Callum. And unquestionably extra-loud. "Mal's happily married and made that very clear. Here's another thing he made clear: he hates my guts."

"There's a fine line between hate and love, and you two are about to dry-hump on top of it before rolling over to the love side and shitting all over your partners. Mark my words." Summer shakes her finger in my face, collapsing next to me on the couch.

"What does Callum say about all this, anyway?"

Summer was #TeamCallum before I even agreed to go on a date with him—something about him being wholesome, with a well-paying job, and sane. I decide to omit the snow falling on us the minute Mal came out to the balcony. She would laugh at me.

"He's great with it, actually." I perk up.

Well, kind of. His exact words were, "*Look at it as a last hurrah. You'll be needing to make some tough decisions about working at a bar and running around with your camera all day. This could be a great time to clear your head and think about our future together.*"

"Is he?"

I swear, she eyes me like I'm a cat about to hiccup a feather.

"England is a short flight away, and he'll be visiting his family for Christmas and the new year. He's excited. Besides, two months is nothing."

"Two months is one month and twenty-nine days more than you had last time with Mal, and if I recall correctly, you promised to drop your boyfriend, panties, and hypothetical family to be with him at any point."

"If I recall correctly..." I finish my glass of wine and slam it on the coffee table. "I was also eighteen, grieving, and believed in orgasms just a little less than I believed in the Tooth Fairy. I grew up."

Summer throws me a skeptical glance.

"Look, I want the promotion," I say, trying another tactic. "Things are going really well. This project could open so many doors for me. Callum is skeptical about my career, and this could prove to him that I make my own money. I need you to support this."

She takes a deep breath, narrowing her eyes. "Do you really want the promotion, or do you think you *should* want it?"

"What's the difference?"

"Your happiness is the difference."

"I want the promotion," I snap.

"Don't ruin it with Callum, Rory."

"I won't. If anything, I'll probably have Callum over all the time to get rid of the weirdness. I want to see Kathleen again just a little less than I want to have dinner with Hitler, Stalin, and Vlad the Impaler."

"Hey, don't bunch Vlad in with those assholes. He was just misconstrued and loyal to his country." Summer sniffs.

I bump her shoulder with mine. "Point is, I'm dreading every moment of being there. Nothing will happen between *married* Mal and me."

"Call me every day."

"Scout's honor."

"And whenever you want to pork him—remember he also screws your sister, and that's just too Jerry Springer for me to ever be associated with you again."

"I wouldn't risk our friendship like that," I agree.

"Letting him double-dip his wiener into the family sauce again is…gut-wrenching."

"Thanks for the culinary analogy," I mutter. "You really made your point now."

Her eyes on me don't waver. "Promise me, Rory."

"Jeez, Louise. *Promise.*"

She watches me for a long beat, moving her jaw back and forth. On TV, Richard and Julia are wrapping it up. Something about how love conquers all, yada yada. I never much enjoyed *Pretty Woman.*

Then I remember my conversation with Mal all those years ago—about women having to drive men somewhere for it to be a classic romance flick. Julia Roberts did that. I bet Mal likes this movie.

Don't think about Mal. Mal is a bastard.

Summer shoves the spoon into the ice cream and scoops out half the tub, waving it in my face. "Carb up, girl. If that's not a good excuse, I don't know what is."

One week later

Rory

The cab driver deposits Callum and me in front of Mal's cottage and U-turns away, leaving mud splashes in his wake.

It's surreal to see the cottage again after eight years of fixating on what happened between its walls. It looks like the place has been neglected beyond belief. The exterior has turned from charmingly old to decayed ancient. The roof is tattered, falling apart, and the grass is still overgrown, with patches of mud everywhere. I don't know what I was expecting. Maybe a woman's touch from Kathleen, the cardigan-loving, proper-talking demoness? Alas, the place looks like it needs a good scrub, a lawnmower, and a hug. At least from the outside.

"Bloody hell," Callum mutters behind me.

We were supposed to go to England to see his family—the first time I would have met his parents—and instead, he decided to accompany me here for a day to help me settle. He'll have to catch a flight tomorrow morning to England, and I'm already dreading his departure.

"I could get us a room at an inn on the main street," he suggests, his nice way of saying this place is unlivable for anyone who isn't a ghostbuster.

"Ryner said I needed to stay here," I say soothingly, walking up the cobbled path to the chipped, wooden door.

My heart is beating so fast I want to throw up. I'm going to come face to face with Malachy and Kathleen as a couple. They're going to be all loved-up in my face, and I will be working under their roof.

I knock on the door.

"Do they know we're coming?" Callum asks behind me.

"Yeah. Whitney said she sent Mal an email with our flight schedule."

Not that Mal cares, I assume. A knot is forming in my stomach. Is he going to make my life hell here?

"You should text your mum," Callum points out.

I don't turn around to face him. "Uh-huh."

"She's heartbroken over the fact you didn't stop to say goodbye."

"We celebrated Christmas with her," I grumble.

I wasn't in the mood to listen to more of her begging me to cover my birthmark with more makeup, pleading with me not to go to Ireland—her most loathed country in the universe—and generally making me listen to her gossip about people I don't know.

There's no answer, so I knock again, this time harder. It's freezing outside. Callum is shifting from foot to foot next to me. He's wearing a pea coat and a powder blue dress shirt.

He snakes his arm around me, rubbing my shoulder. "Relax, love. It's going to be fine. It's been eight years, he's married, and then there's the matter of you being madly in love."

He says that as a joke, but I can hear the question in his voice. Before I officially signed the contract for this project, I told Callum about what happened with Mal eight years ago, hoping to hell he'd make the decision easy for me and express how uncomfortable he felt about it. I'm not much of a Mary Sue who likes to be told what to do, but it would've been a much-needed nudge in the right direction if Callum wasn't so smugly confident he's the shit.

Okay, so also, maybe I wasn't one-hundred-percent honest.

I left one thing out. A teeny-*tiny* thing. So tiny, in fact, you could fit it in your back pocket. More specifically, the napkin. The contract. But for a good reason: it doesn't matter. Mal clearly hasn't kept it. He's happily married. Plus, it's just flat-out embarrassing.

I knock on the door a few more times, but it's clear no one is home. How fitting of Mal not to be here just to spite me. Of course, Kathleen played along. I decide two (or rather, three) can play this game. I will not be standing outside getting pneumonia just because he has some illogical vendetta against me. The main street is far enough that we'll have to call a cab to take us there if we want to warm up in a pub or an inn, waiting for his highness to arrive, and by the time a taxi gets here, we'll be freezing.

I press my shoulder against the door and take a deep breath.

"Rory?" Callum asks behind me, his voice laced with worry.

"Promise not to judge me, Cal?"

"Promise."

With a shove, I push the door, knowing damn well it isn't locked, because last time—eight years ago—it wasn't, either.

We spill into the house, which also looks a thousand times worse inside than it did before. Callum's lips purse as he walks around, observing the old, ragged furniture and strewn-about newspapers, CDs, and vinyl records. There are poetry books and half-rolled, wrinkly notebooks on the couch and a coffee table and breakfast nook buried under piles upon piles of junk, dust and dirt everywhere.

I look around in shock, trying to spot one inch on the floor that's not suspiciously sticky or covered with something.

I turn around to Cal, and his throat bobs, but he says nothing.

"I'm sorry you have to sleep here tonight." I bite my lower lip.

It *is* a dump. Not because it's small or old, but because it's messy and filthy. It looks like no one has lived here in a while. Cobwebs adorn every corner of the room. Doesn't matter that it's freezing outside, I still find myself cracking a window just to get rid of the stale scent of a thousand takeout boxes left to rot somewhere in this place.

"It's fine." Callum tries to sound calm and collected, even though I know he pays his cleaners extra to come in every day and make sure everything is spotless in his Manhattan penthouse. "Quaint and charming. Besides, a roof is a roof. The people under it are what matters. You're here. That's all I care about."

We spend the next twenty minutes touring the house. We start with the kitchen, where we find the root to the rancid smell: an unattended garbage bag sitting under the sink, a cloud of buzzing flies above it. Even though I don't want to clean these two's pigsty on principle, I also don't want to puke, so I throw it out.

I walk through the narrow hallway afterwards. The master bedroom, which was his mother's before Kathleen moved in, is completely empty, save for the king-sized bed that's unmade. The pillows are a suspicious shade of dirty yellow, and the blanket could use a wash. I move to the bathroom, which has also seen better days, finally stopping at Mal's then-room, and our guest room, I suppose. It has one made-up, *single* bed and a little closet. I turn around to Callum, but he just grins.

"Less room means more spooning. Not a bad Sunday."

I should love this man.

I *should.*

And right now, I'm getting damn close to that elusive feeling.

"No part of this is your fault," he adds. "So don't you dare apologize."

We move to the last room down the hallway, and it is locked—possibly the studio Ryner was talking about. That might explain the deadbolt, padlock, and **STAY OUT** sign on the door.

Callum gets right to business, wheeling my suitcase into our room, while I open the rusty door leading to the backyard to see if the sheep and cows are out and about.

There are no more sheep.

No more cows.

There's no more…anything, really.

I take a step out, and something crunches under my shoe. I look down, frown, and pick up an earring. Just the one. Must be Kathleen's. A drop-shaped pink diamond earring. It looks fake, but then again, so is she. Maybe they're hard up for cash. No other reason for Mal to take this writing gig. I look up, staring at the green hills.

A voice behind me rustles, "Breaking and entering is illegal in Ireland."

I jump, turning around. Mal is leaning a shoulder against the doorframe, his hands shoved in the front pockets of his acid-washed jeans, one Blundstone boot crossed in front of the other. His beauty arrests me for exactly five seconds before I school my face.

"Nice crib."

He pushes off the doorframe, descending the two steps to his backyard and ambling toward me. "Trashed it especially for you."

"And I suppose Kathleen was eager to help. Anything to make me feel unwelcome."

Mal flashes me a breezy smile, tying a red bandana on his forehead like he's getting ready for something. He reminds me of old Mal again—adventurous and boyish, impossible to resist.

"Where is she, anyway?" I look around.

I want to get the initial slap-in-the-face reaction of seeing them together out of the way so I can breathe regularly again.

"Dublin."

"When is she going to grace us with her presence?"

He whistles, then lets out a gruff chuckle. Of course, Kathleen has conveniently removed herself from the situation. I don't know why she's hiding. She's just the type to parade her gorgeous husband like it's a dog show. Obviously, Mal is not going to answer my question.

I gesture toward the nothingness.

"Where's the cattle?"

"Sold it."

"Father Doherty? Is he doing okay?"

He squats down, patting away a patch of mud on the front of his boot. "He's alive."

"How about your mother?"

He stops messing with his boots, looks up, and blinks at me like I stopped speaking English. "I'm not a steak, Aurora," he snarls.

"You need to open the studio. I want to take some photos of it before Richards arrives."

"There's no studio," he says, watching my reaction intently.

Then what the hell is that room? Of course, I don't ask.

"Then how are you going to record the songs?"

"We're not. We're just going to write them."

"Ryner lied," I mumble.

I don't know why I'm surprised. I wouldn't trust that man to give me the time in a room full of clocks.

Mal shrugs.

"You should really clean this place. Richards won't live in this condition in a million years and counting. He's used to pretty, nice things."

"That makes two of you, *Princess*."

I want to ask him what the hell he means by that, but I'm not supposed to care. I haven't done anything wrong. I respected our contract, pined for him for years, and tried to move on. What did he expect? For me to sit around and wait for fate to take control while he wedded my sister?

He shakes his head on a dark chuckle, seeming to take my silence as admittance. He turns around and stalks back inside, leaving me to stand here.

It is crazy how eight years ago, I could feel his pulse against my palm for days and weeks after we parted ways.

Right now, I'd like to rip his heart out of his chest, just to see if it beats anymore.

If it's still there.

And if it's black, like my mother warned me.

Mal

On my way back into the house, Aurora's shiny boyfriend stands up from the sofa and stretches his hand toward me, flashing me his slimy banker smile.

I saunter past him to my room and slam the door. I fling myself onto the dirty bed, staring at the ceiling, ignoring the buzzing of my phone.

Maybe it's one of my regular bells.

Maybe it's my agent.

Maybe it's Richards.

Maybe it's Ryner.

Don't know, don't care.

Aurora. Aurora. Aurora. What am I going to do with you, Aurora?

Not fuck you. Not right now. You're not ready for it yet, and besides, there's the whole boyfriend thing to tackle. He's leaving in a day. I know, because I've read the email Ryner's barely literate assistant sent me, though, of course, I didn't answer it.

Perhaps I should start by educating you as to how badly you've ruined things for me?

No. Too early for that.

Explain how I tried to protect you all those years ago by keeping the truth from you and what you did in return is kill my soul, then feed it to the wolves? Hmm. There's still time for that, too.

The house looks like a kip. It's not always like this, but I wanted her to feel bad. I'm trying to dig into her soul with a spoon and see if she still has a conscience.

I close my eyes, letting another phone call go to voicemail.

"Love?"

I hear the English version of American Psycho calling to Aurora behind the door.

"Mal went to lie down. Would you like me to call a cab so we could go buy some toiletries? I haven't seen any here."

First of all, Mal? I'm not one of his masturbating-in-a-circle Eton mates. Malachy for you, *thankyouverymuch.*

Second, was he expecting The Ritz? I don't owe him anything.

Third…there isn't a third, but I'm positive I'll find something else to get pissy about by the end of his visit.

See, Kiki? You always said I should be more positive.

A few minutes later, I hear a soft knock on the door. I don't want to recognize the sound of her knuckles hitting wood, unless that wood is attached to my crotch. Still, I know it's her.

"Mal?" she asks.

"Leave."

"We're heading out."

I don't say anything, because that's exactly what I said she should do. Go away.

"Can we grab you something? Food? Milk? Bleach? Manners?"

I smirk to the ceiling, my hands tucked behind my head. It's on.

She's here, and she is angry, and she is funny, and she is all mine. Sweet and thoughtful and feisty—the perfect combination. Shiny Boyfriend can do nothing about it but sit back and watch.

"No," I growl.

"When are you planning to start working?"

"When the muse strikes me."

"Can you be more specific? I need to know when to unpack my equipment."

"I need to feel inspired to write," I say in a patronizing tone I just adopted out of nowhere. "Anyone can click a camera. I actually produce, with words and everything. It takes a bit more than having a finger."

Low blow, but that's where she aimed when she made potpourri out of my heart and skipped back to America, throwing it everywhere in her wake. There's a beat of silence on the other side of the door.

"I can email Whitney, Ryner's assistant, to send someone over to clean the house before Richards—"

"Who died and made you Joanna Gaines? Why don't you mind your own business instead of criticizing other people's houses?"

A part of me prays her shiny boyfriend will take offense to the way I speak to his mot, storm in, and punch me. I'm in the mood for a good fight. Alas, Mr. Banker is not planning on ruining his manicure anytime soon, based on the depressing silence coming from outside the door.

"How do you know who Joanna Gaines is?" she asks after a moment of silence, a smile in her voice.

Kathleen's Ma, Elaine, watches her and her husband's show all the time. Sometimes she cries. I'd cry, too, if I had to spend an hour watching people choosing wallpaper for a house that's not even theirs.

"Yeah. Okay. Gotcha." Aurora bangs her palm against the door.

Two minutes later, I hear the front door slam. I close my eyes. My phone starts ringing again. I crack one eyelid open, just to make sure it's not Kathleen's number. When I see it's a US phone number, I turn the phone to silent and take a nap.

By the time I wake up, the crickets are singing. I take my time adjusting to the darkness and stretch—I have nothing waiting for me—then sit up on the edge of my bed, digging the heels of my hands into my eyes.

A sudden thud comes from the living room. Then the front door whines open. I flip my phone over and check the time. Midnight. They weren't solely shopping for tampons and shampoo, that's for sure.

Aurora giggles, her shiny boyfriend grunts, and then they both whisper.

Someone bumps into a piece of furniture. Aurora laughs breathlessly. I hate her laugh. It's throaty and low and *fuck*, which part of me thought this was a good idea, the masochist or the drunk?

Getting revenge by having her come here and spend time with me is like getting laid by wrapping your crotch in sandpaper and joining a monastery.

I hear wet, sloppy kisses. Grunting and chuckling and *oof*-ing. Her muppet boyfriend kisses like a fecking greyhound by the sound of it. So. Much. Tongue. But she likes it. I know, because she whimpers like she did when I did things to her.

He moans.

She sighs.

He groans.

She giggles.

My chewed-up nails are digging into the flesh inside my palms. A nice, sane way to prevent myself from strangling both of them.

"What about our host?" Shiny Boyfriend murmurs.

His host is about to pull a gun from under his wooden floor and blow his fecking head off. The only hole in that plan is that I don't own a gun. And the floor is carpeted. Never mind. This plan clearly cannot work.

"Asleep, probably. His door is closed," she replies.

I listen as they make their way to their room, which I never bothered showing them, bumping into every single object on their way. They sound more sauced than an enchilada. Their door clicks shut, but there's only one, thin wall separating us, and you can hear every-thing through it.

The kissing stops, but something far worse starts. She's moaning now, and I can tell she's not faking it, because I know what she sounds like when she comes.

"Love," Shiny Boyfriend rasps.

I hear a zipper rolling down. I dig my fingers into my skin until I draw blood. It feels like every inch of my body is wrapped in thorns.

"Bite down on your dress. He's going to hear us."

He's already hearing you, you oxygen-wasting pillock.

I jump to my feet like the bed is on fire, throw my door open, and take the two steps to their door. Rather than knock, like a normal hu-man being, I push it open like the manner-less cunt Aurora is starting to become familiar with.

I fold my arms over my chest at the door, watching them la-zily. Aurora is plastered against the wall, and Shiny Boyfriend is on his knees, carpet-munching. She is naked save for a black lace bra, and he is licking the outline of her bare pussy—perfectly, beautifully shaved—when I clear my throat and make myself comfortable against the doorframe. They both crack their eyes open.

Aurora lets out a yelp, but he remains angled right next to her pussy, protecting her modesty.

Don't bother, mate. I've seen it so close I can recognize it in a lineup.

"She likes it when you suck her clit and use your fingers at the same time." I shove my fists into my pockets, yawning the sleep away. "But quite partial to clit-pinching. Go figure."

Rather than appreciating my helpful pointers, Aurora leans down, picks up one of her shoes, and hurls it in my direction with a Celtic roar. I dodge it, yawning again for good measure. I hope she takes photos better than she aims, or Ryner is going to have a problem.

"Had a good night?" I look around.

Really, I should do something with this room. Maybe burn it to the ground so they won't have any privacy.

"Get the hell out!" she screams.

She is so red, her white scar shines bright like the moon. Her spineless boyfriend scurries up, hands her a dress, and rearranges his boner in his trousers.

"I think you should go." The genius advances toward me, but I can tell he's the type to file a lawsuit before he throws a punch.

"Aurora." I ignore him, staring at her with icy boredom.

She puts her black dress on quickly, mumbling something under a breath, doubtful words of praise as to my hospitality thus far.

"I am ready."

"Ready for what? The hard facts of life? Here's one: you're an asshole, Mal. Here's another: there's not one part of you I still even remotely like."

My chest constricts, but it's probably because I haven't had a drink since New York. And before New York, in months. *Years.* I've cut back on the alcohol significantly since The Night That Ruined Everything. I didn't want to become Aurora's father, Glen.

"To work." I pick up her shoe and toss it into her hands. She catches it, her brows diving in confusion.

"Mal, it's midnight."

"She reads the clock; you read social situations." I give Shiny Boyfriend an enthusiastic thumbs-up. "Together, you're a rare force of intelligence and capability."

"I'm serious." She scowls.

"Inspiration hits me at weird hours." I shrug.

"Can it hit you in the face into another fit of sleep? At least until tomorrow morning?" she inquires, her cheeks pink.

She's putting her shoes on, though, like I knew she would. That's the thing about true artists, they cannot deny their art, even—and especially—when they're hurting.

Shiny Boyfriend glances between us, obviously unfamiliar with the full rainbow of human emotions. It looks like this is the first time he's witnessing a fight. He is a bit taller than me and definitely has that Brad Pitt circa 1990, this-is-your-life-and-it's-ending-one-min-ute-at-a-time look down to a T. Unlike Tyler Durden, though, I can search with a magnifying glass and still won't be able to find one alpha bone in his body. There are likely more pheromones in a tutu.

Underwhelmed by my competition, I turn to Aurora and snap my fingers.

"In this lifetime, please. And bring a jacket. I write outside, and you're notoriously more frigid than the iceberg that killed the *Titanic.*"

Aurora stomps toward the door.

"Don't blame the iceberg. Blame the Irish people who built the ship..." she murmurs.

"It was fecking working when it left here for Southampton. We will not be blamed for shoddy workmanship."

I bite down on a smile. Secretly, I can admit to myself that Aurora is not a total bore.

"Besides, what are you, exactly? Last time I checked, your father wasn't a Viking."

She opens her mouth, no doubt getting ready to verbally knee my balls, when the muppet interrupts us.

"Love?" Shiny Boyfriend calls behind her.

I positively loathe that nickname. *Love.* Something about uttering this word so offhandedly makes me want to jam his head into a bucket full of bleach.

Aurora turns around.

He hands her the camera on the nightstand. "Might want to take this with you." He winks.

If possible, her blush darkens even further. Mortified and trembling, she snatches it from his hand.

"Thanks."

"Oh, and you dropped the napkin you were so insistent on taking from the pub." He crouches down, picking up a Boar's Head napkin and holding it out to her.

Look, I have a reaction. Of course, I do—a hot-blooded, red, break-up-with-your-boyfriend-now-because-I'm-bored reaction.

I'm human, after all, even though I haven't been feeling like one lately.

But I keep my face schooled, even as she takes the napkin, balls it in her fist, and throws it into the bin under the nightstand.

"That's an odd thing to take from a pub." I tap my lower lip, oh-so-interested in this unusual turn of events. "Did you catch the flu on the plane? I have tissues and Advil in the bathroom cabinet."

"No, no." Shiny Boyfriend chuckles, obviously delighted with my abrupt shift, playing right into my hands. "Rory is somewhat of a napkin connoisseur. She collects napkins everywhere she goes. It's rather silly, really."

"Rather," I mimic his posh accent.

I still can't believe she fecks this guy, who thinks collecting sentimental stuff is silly. That she hasn't told him about our deal. Actually, that I can believe. She's always been a lying mess.

"Care to elaborate about her fixation with napkins?"

She grabs my wrist, pulling me out the door. "Stop messing around. Let's get it over with."

"Oof, I don't remember her that feisty. What're ya feeding her?" I shake off her touch, smiling at Callum.

He laughs. He thinks we're friends. Jesus Christ, the man doesn't possess one functioning brain cell.

In the corridor, my resolve to be a cunt blunders. I slip and plaster her against the wall. She shoves me back, but her impact is non-existent. Our bodies are pressed together, close, rolling heat and hormones and history Princess Aurora cannot erase, no matter how many frogs she kisses.

I pin my chest to her shoulder and whisper in her ear, *"Busted."*

Outside, I perch on the grass, my notebook open in front of me, pretending to write. The chance of me writing songs tonight is lower than my chance of becoming a blind, Italian nun. But if Rory is going to have sex under this roof, she is going to have it with me. Or not at all.

No gray area, I'm afraid.

"It's dark." She rubs her leather jacket-clad arms, her eyes roaming my backyard.

"You really are on top of your investigative game. Have you considered joining the CIA? A sharp mind like yours shouldn't go to waste." I place the pen behind my ear and frown at the blank page, not looking at her.

Doesn't matter if I draw a dick with a bowtie on the notebook. It's pitch black and neither she nor I will be able to see it.

"Suí síos le do thoil." *Sit down* in Gaelic.

She ignores my party-pooper comment. "Sorry, I don't speak dead languages. Wait here, please."

Aurora dashes into the house and comes back with a plastic bag. She takes out two flashlights, loads of little candles, and a box of matches. I scan her coolly as candles drop from her delicate hands. She is flustered and struggles to keep it all together.

"Are you trying to summon your long-lost, non-existent soul through séance?" I wonder aloud.

She lets out a breathless chuckle. "I just remember how dark the night was in your backyard from when…" She turns the two flashlights on, placing one behind me and one in front of me, then shakes her head.

From when I unknowingly took your virginity because your ex-boyfriend couldn't finish the job and in exchange gave you multiple orgasms. Yeah.

"Anyway, I'm going to drag some of your furniture out here so I'll have somewhere to light these candles. I can't take a decent picture with no light."

"Cheers, Captain Obvious." I watch her face, looking for crumbs of emotion.

Aurora doesn't respond. When she enters the house again, I follow her. No matter how much I'm trying to be a dick—and, in my humble opinion, my efforts don't go unnoticed—I'm slightly above watching her drag heavy furniture outside in the middle of the night by herself.

I carry the coffee table she pointed at and put it outside. She lines it with candles and lights them. I go back to my spot between the flashlights, plucking the pen from behind my ear. I scowl at the notebook again. In my periphery, Aurora is plugging the tube adapter into her camera.

She squats down on one leg and takes a picture of me. I clench my jaw, remembering what she did with the original pictures she took of me. Her cruel confessions. Her pretty, glacier heart.

But then she collects napkins and asks me if I want something from the store and asks about Mam and Father Doherty. Something doesn't add up.

"Napkins." I look up, musing. One word. Five tons of history crammed into it.

"Weren't you the one who enacted the no-mingling rule?" She bats her eyelashes, feigning innocence and taking another picture of me.

She stands up and changes the position of the flashlights, now aiming them at my face. I don't squint. Sitting around in a garden with a notebook is emasculating enough.

"It's a statement, not an olive branch."

"In that case, I choose not to address the statement and tramp all over the un-extended olive branch," she snaps.

I get sick pleasure from knowing I hit a nerve. Hate is the closest thing to love you can squeeze out of the unattainable.

I hurt her back!

I look up, and our eyes meet, just like they did all those years ago on Drury Street. Even then I knew, without a shadow of a doubt, that this girl was put in my life to change it. I didn't know at the time she'd choose to derail it and lead it on a collision course with everyone I cared about.

"Sooner or later, we'll both have to play nice. Shiny Boyfriend is leaving tomorrow," I hiss.

"He has a name." She lowers her camera, her eyes narrowing.

Ken. I bet it's Ken.

"I don't care for it." I press the pen against the page in my notebook until it bleeds, my eyes still trained on her.

"Callum." She lowers her camera. "His name is Callum Brooks."

I hitch one shoulder up. "All I heard is Shiny Boyfriend."

I scribble something in the notebook.

Can you please stop being so beautiful and real and alive all over my house like you own it or something?

Can she?

Can she *kindly* enlighten me as to what went through my mind when I came up with this plan? What I was hoping to achieve, other than dragging her down the miserable road I have walked one too many miles on?

Rory takes a few more pictures. I chew the tip of the pen. I don't know how authors do it, how they bleed words onto the clinical, plastic keyboard. Seems cold and impersonal. I can barely write on a page. I bet Rory could be an author. I bet she could write on a MacBook, the mother of all fancy-schmancy technological diseases. I'm making myself sick just thinking about it.

Also, since when did I stop calling her Aurora in my mind and go back to Rory?

"Do you have a MacBook?" I blurt.

She shakes her head, but doesn't look at me like I'm a weirdo. I've always loved that about her. "Why?"

"Never mind. So, napkins," I repeat the word.

She sighs. "It means nothing."

"Nothing means nothing; otherwise it wouldn't exist."

"Some people collect coasters, postcards, stamps. I collect napkins. It's not a big deal."

Silence.

I look down at the notepad. Back up. "I just find it quite peculiar, since I was under the impression you hated me."

She looks up from the pictures she's scanning in her camera. Her eyebrows pull together. "Why would *I* hate *you*?"

Why indeed.

Why?

I've asked myself the very same question a million times, wondering if I should buy a ticket to America, if I should send her one to Ireland, if I should rip out my heart and dump it at her door.

"I didn't hate you then," she whispers. "But I'm starting to now."

Her eyes are on my face, reminding me why I couldn't let go, even when my entire world crumbled. Some people raise you up, and some people pull you down. And Rory? She pulls me in every possible direction and angle, leaving me tattered.

I remind myself of Kathleen.

Of our families.

Of my top commitment right now, which shouldn't be Rory.

I rip the paper and ball it in my fist.

"Wait, let me take a picture..." She advances toward me, but it's too late. I throw it into my mouth and swallow. She stops, her eyes flaring, the orange glow of the many candles making her look like a medieval witch.

"You're insane," she whispers.

I know.

I write down another sentence.

There's life everywhere you look. Even in objects. But there is death, too.

"Come take a picture of this."

"Your Photoshopped thoughts?" She shakes her head. "No, thank you."

Aurora Belle Jenkins hates me.

But *hate* is a verb.

And I'm about to prove I hate her more.

Present

Rory

THE SUN PAINTS THE SKY LILAC, ITS LIGHT DRIPPING ON MAL, highlighting the perfect arcs and planes of his face.

I take another picture. He hasn't been writing a whole lot, but I'm not here to monitor his progress, or lack thereof.

I don't know how many of them Ryner is going to use for the website, or album cover, or documentary, or whatever he has in mind for this project, but I can't wait to upload these to my laptop and start working on them. I want to study Mal's face alone, without him witnessing what the sight of it does to me.

I stand up and walk around his backyard, looking for my next perfect shot. Mal has been talking about the song "Ironic" by Alanis Morissette for ten minutes now, in a true Old Mal fashion.

"…literally none of her examples were truly ironic. Especially the one with Mr. Play it Safe, who was afraid to fly and ended up dying in a plane crash. It is *not* ironic. It would have been ironic had he died in a car accident. That's the definition of irony. The expression of one's meaning by using language that signifies the opposite. It's like a bunch of people sat and worked on this song, and nobody—not one soul—bothered to tell her nothing about this song was ironic. Other, of course, than the fact that she wrote a song about irony that wasn't ironic. Which is a big irony in itself, I suppose."

I smile to myself, but don't answer him. There's something so deliciously sweet about seeing him in his element. It reminds me that under the bitter jerk he's become is still a boyish, adventurous, wildly creative and witty man.

Who happens to be really good in bed.

"You love what you do," he states, out of nowhere.

We've been talking on and off all night. It's curt—barely civilized—but it's progress. It's still early to be optimistic, and the dynamics might change as soon as Kathleen gets back from Dublin, but I think the realization that I collect napkins defrosted him. I'm not even sure why Mal is trying to be an asshole. He's terrible at it. He is one of the best, most exciting people I know.

"I do. Do you?" I spin the zoom ring, frowning at my camera.

"Do you love him?" He ignores my question.

My breath catches, my thumb halting on the camera ring. I take a deep breath, then walk over to him, ready to take a close-up. We are close enough I can feel his breath on my skin. It's slow. Warm. Wild.

"Do you love her?" I whisper back.

"What I love," he says slowly, "is basking in the knowledge that you will soon be on your knees for me, Aurora Jenkins."

At first, I think he's joking, but then I see the intensity behind his stare and freeze. He means it. He is unhappy with Kathleen. A shiver slithers down my spine.

"You don't love her," I breathe out, closing my eyes.

He is in a loveless marriage.

He opens his mouth to say something when I hear a knock on the doorframe.

My head snaps, and I turn around, finding Callum on the

threshold. He is showered, suited, hair slicked back, and ready to go. A camel-hued, leathered duffel bag is draped over his shoulder. He looks like an Armani ad.

Callum's eyes shift between us with confusion. When I realize my proximity to Mal and withdraw from him like he's fire, my boyfriend's expression softens.

"I'm off." He hooks his finger and motions for me to come to him and say goodbye. I place my camera on the coffee table and move toward him. Something tells me I need to reassure him that whatever he saw meant nothing.

Not that he saw anything. The hand-on-the-shoulder move was a classic are-you-okay? gesture. Nothing about it screamed "I want to rip your clothes off."

I back Cal into the house, knowing damn well Mal is not a fan of our PDA. After his confession, I can understand why. He is unhappy in his marriage, and living under the same roof with a loved-up couple in that state is anyone's idea of a nightmare.

I close the screen door behind me, look over my shoulder to make sure Mal isn't watching, then fling my arms around Callum's neck, covering his face with wet kisses.

"Come to the New Year's party," I say. "Please."

He brushes his nose along mine and frowns. "Have a productive night?" There's an edge to his voice.

I nod. Not a lie. *I* did. Mal, on the other hand...

"Seems like you two patched things up." He rubs his thumb across my cheek.

"Hardly." I kiss his chin. "But we no longer want to kill each other, I think."

"Good. I want you well and alive for the next seven decades," he says.

"Are you still okay with me doing this?" *Am I?*

"'Course. Not only is he married, but he is also an utter weirdo. Why would anyone be attracted to such bizarre behavior?"

He snorts, and I catch myself, biting my lower lip so I don't say anything.

He looks around, shrugging. "Crib could use a bit of a facelift, too. Yeah, you know better than to go with someone like that, love."

Callum tugs me toward the front door, holding my hand. Outside, his cab is already waiting, engine revved up. The driver gets out and flings Callum's bag into his trunk. I rise on my tiptoes to kiss him again. I expect our usual peck goodbye, but to my surprise, Callum grabs the back of my neck, dips his head, and crashes his lips against mine. I open my mouth for his tongue and groan into the kiss, which deepens with each second and feels nothing like our usual kisses.

I don't know how much time passes before his lips desert mine, but the driver is honking his horn and throws an impatient arm out the window.

When Callum finally breaks away, it's not me he's looking at. He's staring behind my shoulder, an easy smile on his chiseled face. I turn, already dreading what I'm about to see.

Mal.

Standing at his front door, like Kathleen did all those years ago when we'd kissed, only he doesn't look shattered beyond repair.

He looks nonchalant and smug and delicious and...*smiling*? Why is he smiling back at Callum?

Like the confession never happened.

Like we didn't share a moment.

Like he knows something I don't.

My stomach clenches and twists. The knots grow like a rubber ball rolled in thorns.

Mal fishes something from his pocket and motions for me to take it.

"Here, wipe your mouth."

I don't move. This could be a trick. He's been hateful before.

"Rory," he coaxes. "Truce?"

Rory.

Are we back on good terms? I'm still not a fan of him bossing me around. I take a few steps toward him and grab whatever it is he holds out for me, my eyes narrowing into slits. His mouth quirks up in one corner, and it reminds me that before he was a jerk, he was the guy who captured an entire street with his guitar and charm.

"Oh, ye of no faith. Is it illegal to be nice where you live?"

"No, but it might as well be. I live in New York."

I take the damn thing, wipe my glistening mouth, and hand it back to him.

He shakes his head. "Keep it. It's yours."

I peer behind my shoulder and realize Callum's cab left. I didn't even get to say goodbye. It makes me want to slap myself across the face, because I know he witnessed at least some of this exchange.

I look down, realizing that what I'm holding *is* mine. Or rather it was, before I threw it into the trash.

I wiped my boyfriend's kiss off with The Boar's Head napkin.

A NOTE FROM CALLUM BROOKS

At this point, you are wondering *why*.

Why did I leave these two alone, considering their history? Ninety-eight percent of logical people in the world wouldn't. This is a made-up statistic, so don't try to look for it on the internet, but still.

Allow me to enlighten you as to why I left.

There's a story my father told me once when the roads to London were blocked due to a snowstorm and I missed a date with the duchess of a-place-I-can't-disclose-in-England. She went on and met someone else while she was waiting for me. They got married. I missed my chance of becoming royalty.

Because of snow.

I thought it was the worst day of my life.

The story goes like this: A boy begs his father to get him a dog.

Not a particular dog, any rat-looking one would do. The boy dreams of owning a dog, breathes the idea, and obsesses over it. Time passes. The father hangs the condition of having a dog over the boy's head. The boy does everything his father tells him to. Makes the best grades, excels at sports, stays out of trouble. He is on the straight and narrow, and does everything he possibly can to get a dog.

One Christmas, his father finally gets him a bloody dog.

The boy is devoted to the dog, aptly named Dog. The dog is his entire life. The boy feeds it the best food, takes it on long walks in green, lush fields. Tends to its fur and takes it to the vet for checkups. One day, during their walk, a storm brews. The boy realizes he and Dog can't get home, so he looks for shelter. He finds a cave in the middle of a forest and slips in. It rains hard. Dog is scared, cold, and shivering. The boy cannot bear the idea of losing his beloved pet, the one he'd done everything in his power to win and keep. He hugs the dog tight the entire time, until the storm passes. When the sun reappears, the boy looks down and realizes to his horror that he suffocated the dog in his quest to save him.

Moral of the story: clutching something desperately doesn't mean you're going to keep it. You might just kill it.

Plus, call me a conceited son of a bitch, but I truly don't see Malachy Doherty as competition. He looks sloppy, his house is an utter mess, and his life is shaping up to look even worse. Those are things women don't find attractive.

And Rory, she is a bit of a wild spirit, this one, but she is not daft. I don't think.

In the cab, I take my phone out of my pocket and wipe away the idea of Rory and Malachy together.

I can keep her.

I have thus far, haven't I?

And let's not pretend she was always into it.

Only a bit more before I seal the deal. Then Weirdo Wackhead can be a distant memory again.

Eight years ago

Mal

WHOEVER INVENTED THE PHRASE "OUT OF SIGHT, OUT OF mind" evidently had the memory of a goldfish. "Out of sight, out of my fecking mind" sounds more fitting.

I miss her.

Oh, how I miss her like a flower misses the sun. Like the Clash missed the mark with "Cut the Crap." I can't stop thinking about her, and that contract is possibly the worst idea I've had since wanking into a Shepherd's pie in tenth grade, straight out of the oven.

My mate, Daniel, claps my back as Sean, his twin, slides a pint of the black stuff across the table of The Boar's Head. They motion for me to drink up with their chins.

"Feck the contract," Daniels spits. "Pick up the phone and call the girl."

I stare at the thick, white foam of my stout. It's not that simple. It's not just the contract part, but whatever comes after it. The making-it-work part.

"What if she's moved on?" I ask my drink.

"In three weeks? Unlikely." Sean lets out a gruff laugh.

Sean and Daniel look alike, as identical twins do. Same blond hair trimmed close to the scalp, green eyes, and I-fucked-your-wife kind of cocky smirks. The only way I can distinguish them is that Daniel makes some sort of sense every now and again when he opens his mouth, and Sean is a complete ape. And I say that with a lot of love. (Not to Sean. To apes. They're lovely, intelligent creatures.)

"I can't do long distance."

I dip a finger into my Guinness and suck the bitter foam. I hear a sigh from the table next to us. Kathleen. She is sitting with her friends, Maeve and Heather. She flicks her straightened hair, smiles at me shyly, and turns back to Maeve.

"Clearly you must, since you can't stop thinking and talking about her. You're a complete puss." Daniel shoves a handful of crisps into his mouth.

"Two people shorten the road." Sean taps his temple. "Think about it."

"Wrong saying, but the sentiment is correct, brother." Daniel laughs. "I know you said you don't want to settle down, but that's exactly what you're doing, and she's not even here. You're settling for misery instead of taking a chance. You haven't shagged a soul since she left. At least give it a shot. You owe it to us, if not yourself. We cannot listen to your whining much longer."

"Mal?" Sean asks.

"Hmm?"

"Is Kathleen…single?"

"As far as I'm aware."

"Do you reckon…"

He completes his question, I'm sure, but my mind is drifting back to Roryland. I pick up my phone and type her name in the search engine. There are only so many Aurora Belle Jenkins in the world, surely. There are a load of pictures of Disney princesses and articles about how to make your own Disney slime before I get to the important stuff.

Outside, thunder cracks, and out of nowhere, it starts to hail.

Random or fate? Sometimes I feel like the world is screwing with me when I think about Rory.

I find her on a New Jersey-based high school website, in an article dated two years ago. She won a photography award of some sort. There's a picture of her holding her cheap statue in the shape of film, staring at the camera, flipping the finger with a mocking pout. Eyeliner, fishnets, and Toms intact. The girl who left me behind.

Why did I have to find out you exist?

"Anyway..." I shake my head. "Even if I wanted to give her a ring, I don't have her number or anything like that."

"Pity," Sean mumbles into his drink, eyeing the girls at the opposite table.

He looks a bit cross. Then I remember he asked me something about Kathleen. Sean and Kathleen are not in the same IQ bracket. A bit of an odd pairing, but stranger things have happened, I suppose.

"Wait, doesn't your granddad know her mam?" Daniel snaps his fingers, his eyes lighting up.

Yes, yes, he does. He would have their home number. Rory is not supposed to know about it—not about him knowing her mother, and not about how I know and kept it from her. There's no chance in hell my granda is going to give me the number, but I could just look at his little phone book. Problem solved.

Of course, there's a chance Rory went back, got to college, and has already met the love of her life. But if she hasn't...

If she hasn't, I'll take long distance.

Or casual dating.

Or anything, really.

I stand up, finishing my pint in one go.

"Keep us posted." Daniel slaps my back.

Sean loosens the collar of his shirt, clearing his throat and sliding into a seat next to the girls.

I get out of the pub, heading toward my grandfather's house on foot. He lives across the village, not terribly far, and I need the fresh air to sort my mind. I hear footfalls behind me, but I don't slow down. Kiki appears by my side. She is wheezing.

"You're actually going through with this?"

"Why not?"

It should bother me that Kath has been eavesdropping on my conversation. She's had her nose stuck in my business as long as I can remember. I chalk it up to Kath being Kath. You take the bad with the good in people.

The good: she's a grand friend, protective, and never steers me wrong.

The bad: she's mad as a box of slimy frogs and likes it when I torture her with mixed signals. If I stop, she crumbles and enters a state of depression.

"It's crazy. You live on different continents. She will never leave America and move here permanently. What kind of future do you have with her?"

"We'll work it out."

I round a corner. She's at my heel.

"That's just something people say when they can't figure out how to make something work."

Kath is practically running to match my stride. We are at my grandfather's door now. I fish the keys out of my pocket—I have a key for granda's lock, because his cat, Saoirse, needs taking care of sometimes when he's on one of his week-long church things.

Kath grabs my arm and yanks me back, jumping in front of the door. "Don't!" She flinches. "Don't call her."

I give her a slow once-over. Christ on a bike, Kath's oddness has an extra shine today.

She pushes my chest away from my grandfather's door, her eyes shimmering. "She is not the girl for you, Mal. I am. I'm the right O'Connell girl." She slaps her hand against her chest, full-blown crying now. "And I don't care that you probably slept with my half-sister. And

I don't care that you have feelings for her. And I don't care that she told me you were nothing but a fling to her. I still want you, and I'm tired of waiting."

I've always known Kathleen had a crush on me. I discouraged it any way I could without rejecting her, by being unavailable and cutting our interaction to the bare, acceptable minimum. But I always thought it was the crush of the same variety I had for Miss Flynn, my middle school teacher, when I first discovered my penis was good for more than pissing—one where you feel attraction toward a person, but also recognize how deeply mental the idea of actually being with them would be.

Kathleen is the most put-together, ambitious, levelheaded, motivated person I know. I'm a busker and a bum and, on weekends, a bloody drunk. We have absolutely nothing in common, other than the fact that we both breathe. Even that is something I'm sure Kathleen is better at.

Wait.

A fling?

"Back up. What did you say she told you?" I hold my palm up.

A part of me acknowledges I'm a heartless SOB for asking about Rory when she just bled her heart out and confessed her undying love, but we'll get to that in a second. Right after we discuss *my* bleeding heart. (*See, Kath? I'm selfish, too. Really, what did you find in me?*)

She stares at her feet, biting on her lip.

"Remember at my house, when you went to the toilet? You got back and saw Rory and me holding hands. That was a minute after she told me she was planning on sleeping with you. I confessed my feelings for you, and she told me she didn't care. She said I got the money and Da and the heritage, and she would get the guy. That she'd ruin you for me. That's why I haven't tried to stay in contact with her, Mal. I was deeply hurt."

I take a step back, digesting.

It sounds nothing like Rory. Not only is she not a cunning cow, but she's also too blasé to voice something like that aloud. It sounds like something out of *Cruel Intentions*, not the mouth of a Disney princess. Then again, Kath is not a liar. At least, I've never caught her in a lie before, and I've known her all my life.

I gather Kathleen in my arms, pulling her to my chest.

"Kath?"

She flinches in my arms. She knows. She can't not-know. I've shagged/snogged/fingered nearly every girl in this village, always careful not to touch her, and not just because her dad warned me off.

"Listen to me. You're beautiful, smart, funny, and make a mean cup of tea. But you also feel a lot like a sister. Too much for me to want to shove my hand into your knickers. And I don't think that'd ever change. I'd rather kick someone's arse for treating you badly than be the wanker to actually mistreat you. You following?"

I feel her body going rigid in my arms. I press a kiss on her shampooed, carefully combed hair, missing Rory's tousled nest of random colors—light roots, dark middle, bleached tips.

"I'm sorry if she said that to you," I add.

"What do you mean *if*? She did." Kath rears her head back, the light in her eyes flickering like a dying flame. "You believe me, right? You know I'm telling the truth." She tugs at my shirt.

"Sean likes you." I change the subject.

"Really?" She sulks like I just suggested she date a bucket of lube. "Well, I don't like him."

"That's fine, but I think it's time to find someone you do."

I'm trying the Band-Aid method. Fast and burning, as opposed to slow and excruciating. If I break her heart once, she'll glue it back together and move on. If I break it one crack at the time, she'll hold on to some silly hope this could happen. It won't. Whether Rory wants me or not, I'll never be with Kath.

I sidestep, push the key into the lock, and close the door behind me, leaving her outside. Then I walk into my granda's darkened living room, take his phone book from the coffee table, sit down on his couch, and dial Debbie Jenkins' number.

"Hello?"

"Ms. Jenkins?"

"Who is it?"

"My name is Mal. Malachy. I'm Father Doherty's grandson."

I expect her to feign recognition. I know she knows my grandfather. But instead of offering some sort of greeting, she says nothing at all. The silence is like a nail dragged over a blackboard. I cram words into it, desperately trying to fill the void.

"I'm calling because…well, I wanted to see how Rory is doing. We got to hang out while she was here, and she was quite emotional, and…"

Put more ands in the sentence, muppet.

I sound like I need to wear a helmet indoors. What the feck is wrong with me? But she is still not saying anything, and now I'm trying to figure out what the feck is wrong with *her*. I tally all stupid things I'm saying and thinking right now, as if this is some sort of a job interview.

"Anyway, is she there?" I clear my throat.

"No," Debbie Jenkins clips.

More silence. Rory Jenkins despises her mother, and I'm starting to see why.

"May I have her number, please?"

"Malachy…" She lets out an exaggerated sigh. "Listen, I know you and my daughter had…a *thing*. We're not as distant as she'd like people to believe. Rory is inexperienced, impressionable, and hopelessly romantic. I'm sure it got blown into this huge something in both your heads, but let's admit it, just between the two of us—it doesn't exactly have a future, does it?"

I'm torn between telling her to feck off and pleading my case. If I thought it didn't have a future, I wouldn't be calling.

She continues, "She moved out. She's in college. She's dating—"

"Dating?" I snap.

"Mmm-hmmm." Debbie lights a fag on the other side of the line.

"A very nice guy, too. In fact, I'm sure she won't mind if I send you the pictures she took of you. They're lying somewhere around her room. She never took them with her. Would you like that? For safekeeping?"

I can feel the napkin with our contract burning a hole in the back of my jeans. I take it everywhere, like I expect to see her, out and about in Tolka or Dublin, and wave it in her face.

See? Remember? We're supposed to be together.

My pride urges me to tell Debbie she can shove the unwanted photos of me where the sun don't shine, but ego is a luxury broken hearts cannot afford.

"Please do," I mutter.

I start to give her my address, but she tells me she'll send them to Father Doherty. I actually prefer it that way, because my house is the farthest from anywhere else in the village, and I'm prone to having my mail lost.

"How is she doing?" I ask again before she hangs up.

I can't help myself, even if I'm starting to believe Kathleen about the whole one-night-stand thing. So what if Rory suggested long distance? She was caught in the moment. The magic wore off quickly for her, that's for sure.

"I told you, Malachy. She's fine."

"Can I call you and make sure she's okay from time to time?"

Hang up the phone, you sorry pile of shite.

"I don't think that's a good idea," Debbie says apologetically. "It'd be for the best if Rory leaves Ireland behind her."

"Okay."

"Bye."

I received the pictures Debbie Jenkins sent me earlier today. I've dropped by my granda's house every single day since our phone call, waiting for them. It took them two months to arrive. Two months of me being a celibate, moody eejit. Two months of me breaking every rule in our stupid contract.

I looked for Rory on social media, but she doesn't have any profiles. Or if she does—they're not under her real name.

I subscribed to her college's newsletter because it sometimes shouts out students, and seeing her name makes me happy. (She's won two photography contests and helped film a short student movie.)

But nothing could prepare me for the moment I flipped the pictures over (fine quality, by the way) and saw the captions she'd put on the back of them.

Picture one, of me singing/busking:

He was a terrible flirt, and he could be soooo cheesy!

Picture two, of me standing on the threshold of The Boar's Head, posing for her like Marilyn Monroe.

He talks too much, and sometimes doesn't make any sense.

Picture three, both of us in bed, *my* bed, after I gave her three hundred orgasms and a part of my heart.

He tries way too hard in bed.

The worst thing is, shortly thereafter at The Boar's Head, I took the napkin out and compared her handwriting on the contract to the words on the back of the pictures. Sean, Daniel, and I all concluded it was the same handwriting. So it's not like her mother could have faked this.

Daniel drums the table. "Well then, I think it's safe to say you can move on with your life now. She sounds like a world-class slag."

"The thing is, she is not," I slur.

I pick up my fifth…sixth pint and chug it down. Kathleen is sitting across from us with her friends again. Sean is staring at her, pining…*again.* She's doing the same—to me. I wish they'd just shag and let me drown in my misery.

"She is not a slag at all."

But the more time passes, the more the crisp memory of her not being a slag dims. The captions on the pictures are now more vivid than her innocent smile in my head.

"I'm going to call her mum," I announce.

"Dumbest idea you've had in a while." Daniel does a thumbs-down, whistling as he crashes his hand against the table. "And you're never short of those."

"Borderline suicidal." Sean bobs his head, dragging his eyes from Kath.

Ever since our conversation by my grandfather's door, she's been dropping by my house quite a lot—always in skimpy dresses that look very odd on her, and always with a fresh platter of something good for me to eat, plus a bottle of wine or a few cans of Guinness in her hands. I invite her in, eat while she tells me stories about whatever is happening in her life, then send her on her way. On the surface, she seems content with being just friends. A dom-girl friend, I suppose, with that kind of attire.

"No, I need to talk to Rory directly." I shake my head and stand. I still keep the napkin, of course, returning it carefully to my pocket, but I've broken every rule under the sun.

Now, here I am, dialing Debbie's number. Again.

She picks up on the third ring. There's a time difference, and I know I'm catching her early in the morning.

"Hello?"

"Debbie?"

Drunk Mal is obviously on a first-name basis with Rory's mother. Sober Mal, however, is worried for Drunk Mal's bullocks.

"Yes?" She already sounds on edge.

"It's Mal, Father Doherty's grandson."

"What do you want?"

Your daughter. Is it not painfully, pathetically clear by now?

"Cheers for the pictures." I hiccup into the phone. "She is very talented, our Rory, isn't she?"

I know I come off as a stalker. The first call was a shot in the dark.

The second one is a shot in my foot. I am unwanted in their lives—that much is obvious—yet I keep coming back.

"What. Do. You. Want?" she asks again.

Tough crowd. All right, straight to the point it is.

"I want to write Rory a letter, but I don't want to send it to you. I want to send it directly to her. I know where she goes to school, so it's not like I won't be able to find out myself. Now it's just a matter of you making it easy or hard for me. I've a feeling she wasn't planning on me ever seeing these captions, and I'm willing to keep this our little secret if you give me her P.O. box."

I'm blackmailing my future mother-in-law. This will make my promise to Rory to invite her for Christmas every year tricky.

Debbie mumbles a few things, but surprisingly, she gives me the address. I write it down on the back of my hand, then on a piece of paper, then as a note on my phone. You know, *just in case.*

"It's not going to do you any good," she murmurs bitterly. "My daughter doesn't want you, Malachy."

"See you next Christmas, Ms. Jenkins."

I'm just acting the maggot, like she's a mate or something, but a part of me wants to believe what I'm saying. Which, of course, speaks volumes about my level of intoxication. See her at Christmas? Ha.

"Cheerio," I sing-song.

She hangs up on me.

Hope Debbie doesn't plan on getting any of Mammy's special mince pies next Christmas.

She doesn't deserve them.

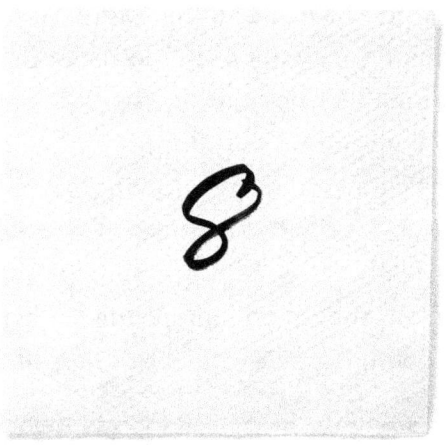

Present

Rory

I DIDN'T LEAVE MY ROOM THE ENTIRE DAY YESTERDAY, DETERMINED to avoid Mal.

Actually, that's not true. I left it one time, when I heard Mal's old car barking exhaust smoke down the road and knew he had gone. Where, I have no idea. I went out then, slipped into my Toms, and marched the entire, rain-soaked way to Main Street, stomping on puddles and flipping the bird to sheep and cows on my way. I stocked up on granola bars and bottled water, then treated myself to a cup of coffee, a chocolate chip cookie the size of my head, and a nice, internal meltdown in a local coffee shop.

By the time I got back to the cottage, Mal's car was parked by the front door. The Lord of the Dumpster was in his room. Hearing whispering behind the closed door, I realized there was someone with him, a woman.

My rubber-ball heart bounced in my chest. *Kathleen.* I tiptoed to the door and pressed my ear to it. I deciphered some of the words and realized it *couldn't* be Kathleen. First of all, she sounded nothing like my half-sister. Second, she had a strong, northern English accent, not Irish, and third, this is what I got from their conversation:

Mal: "It's just for a few months."

Woman: "Then what?"

Mal: "Then I take her and we're leaving. She likes the beach, so maybe we'll go somewhere with a lot of sun. Greece or Spain. South of France, maybe."

Woman: "Isn't she mad at you for having *her* here?"

Didn't take a genius to figure out I was *her*, and I was also about as welcome as gonorrhea.

Mal: "She has no idea about Rory, and I plan on keeping it that way. Makes things simple. I like simple."

Woman: "I could be simple for you, Mal."

Mal: "Certainly you can, and you are."

Whoever she was didn't pick up on the insult. Shame. A punch in the nuts was just what the doctor ordered for Mal.

Then the noises started. The tongues and thrusts and skin slapping skin. My thighs squeezed, and the hollow place between them ached. I thought of interrupting him, too—you know, an eye for an eye and so forth—but didn't want to give him the satisfaction of knowing that I heard.

That I *cared.*

No.

I moved to my room, threw myself onto the bed, flung an arm over my eyes, and shook my head.

Down, girl.

But it was too much, and I was too weak. I shoved my hand into my jeans and played with myself to the sound of Mal having sex with another woman.

It's not cheating, I told myself the entire time. I'm not touching him. I never will. Callum and I just didn't get to finish what we'd started the night before.

I decided not to leave my room unless Mal called me for work. It was stupid to think we could patch things up. He was a different person, and I needed to stop making excuses for him in my mind.

I texted Callum a string of messages telling him I missed him, turned my laptop on, and worked into the night. My mom called a couple times, but I sent her to voicemail. Mal and the woman ended up doing the very same thing Cal and I had been about to do the night before, and extra loudly, no doubt so I could hear.

What kind of merciless, ruthless, immoral monster cheats on his wife and also hides the fact that her half-sister and his once-upon-a-time crush is living with him for two months?

Listening to him drilling into a woman who wasn't his wife put the stamp of disapproval on Mal, and that is very good news.

I am no longer jealous of Kathleen, or interested in being civilized with her husband.

Anyway, that was yesterday, and today I woke up to the faint sound of music and the strong scent of food: bacon, eggs, freshly brewed coffee, and banana bread.

My mouth waters, and I struggle to swallow my saliva. I'd kill for a good cup of coffee. Besides, seeing as I have nothing but negative feelings toward Mal, it shouldn't be too hard to face him.

I crack my door open and step into the living room barefoot, my red plaid pajamas barely covering my legs and messy hair tangled like wild branches around my face. I halt in the cove between the living room and corridor, my heart slowing along with my step.

Ashton Richards (yes, *the* Ashton Richards) is sitting in Mal's living room, smoking a joint and wearing a golden robe with his initials printed on the breast pocket, along with sunglasses indoors. He sips his coffee and reads through something in Mal's notebook, while his staff runs around in the background, cleaning and cooking like magical cartoon animals helping Cinderella get ready for the ball.

I can't help but notice that Richards, despite his many apparent flaws if you believe what the media says, is undeniably gorgeous.

He looks like a really hot version of Jesus—a long-lost Hemsworth brother with long hair.

Mal sits across from him in a recliner, his legs crossed over his coffee table, chewing on an unlit clove cigarette and throwing a rugby ball at the ceiling. "Boys Don't Cry" by The Cure is playing from a portable radio, and I *will* not let the fact that Mal kept his cassettes or his old-school radio endear him to me. He is not a romantic.

There are platters everywhere in the open kitchen, breakfast nook, and on the table. They hold pastries, fruit, a full English breakfast, and coke.

Hold on. *Coke?*

My eyes widen as I zoom in on the silver platter with white lines running across it. Richards lifts his head from the notebook he's reading and waves in my general direction.

"Someone hand the chick an NDA. I'm trying to work here."

A blonde girl who looks eerily similar to Ryner's PA, Whitney, jogs toward me with a thick stack of papers and a pen.

Mal ignores my existence. His cheekbones are ruddy, tinted pink, and I wonder if it's from the cold or from last night's orgasms. He has that lost Peter Pan look—charismatic and unassuming, yet so easily destructive. I can't even hate him all the way, no matter how hard I try.

"Who's the hottie?" Richards nudges Mal's leg with his own, tilting his chin to me.

"My sex slave," Mal deadpans, catching the ball and spinning it on his finger like a pro, his eyes still hard on the ceiling.

Is there anything this man can't do?

Yes, stay faithful.

"For real?" Ashton rips his sunglasses from his face and leans forward, checking me over more closely.

I fold my hands across my chest, aware that my nipples are puckered from the cold.

"Isn't she a little…underdressed?" He raises a thick eyebrow over his crystal blue, Caribbean Sea eye.

I'm going to kill Mal.

Straight-up choke him. Not even in his sleep. I want him to be fully present when it happens.

Mal follows Richards' gaze until his eyes land on mine. I'm still silent because I'm waiting to see how far he's going to take his weird story.

"She has a hobo fetish, so I turn a blind eye to her fashion choices," Mal explains, resuming his ball spinning. "I humor her, but I draw the line at pissing in public and flashing randoms."

I nod, sending a sugary smile to Ashton Richards. The blonde girl hands me a contract and a pen, and I sign it without even looking, my gaze still on her boss.

"Mal is just being humble," I begin. "He's the one with the hobo fantasies. In fact, he *looooooves* trash. Just look at this place." I hand the girl the pen and motion around us. "Sometimes I think he won't rest until this place is a dumpster. I once caught him making love to an empty can of baked beans."

"Tomato soup, actually," Mal amends, straight-faced, but his purple eyes are twinkling with mischief. "And that can has a name. Laura."

Ashton is looking between us now, laughing so hard tears are rolling down his cheeks—a young, hot version of The Big Lebowski.

"Young love. Fucking inspiring. What's your name, honey pie?" He grins at me.

"Rory," I say at the same time Mal volunteers my full name.

"Aurora Belle Jenkins. Her ma's entire cultural education obviously stems from Disney. Personally, I think Cruella de Vil suits her better."

"Personally, I think men who cheat on their wives and keep secrets from them should be stoned to death by a herd of baseball pitchers," I retort, heading toward the kitchen and treating myself to a cup of coffee from the new machine that's been installed since yesterday.

I snag a pastry from a huge platter in the breakfast nook and tear off a piece of it with my teeth.

"You should move to Saudi Arabia," Mal suggests. "Adulterers get the death penalty. Of course, that'd put you at risk, too."

"I've never cheated," I growl.

"*Yet*," he says flatly.

Bastard.

"Why didn't you tell me you guys were working?" I ask with my mouth full, ignoring Mal's third-grade taunting.

Richards is currently trying to count something with his fingers, or perhaps he's *counting* his fingers, and looks completely out of it. It's obvious he and the coke are on intimate terms, and that he's under the influence of multiple other substances.

So help me God, I live in a house where Mal is the responsible adult.

"Because there's enough drugs in here to sedate the entire country of China," Mal clips, looking at me incredulously. "Thought it might be smart not to document it."

"I have a job to do," I say through gritted teeth.

Mal's eyes light up. "Really? You mean a real one, other than walking around with a camera, looking pouty and thoughtful and silly?"

We're locked in a stare down, and I want to snap.

To snap because he screwed someone in the room next door.

Because he is being the meanest version of himself, and then some.

Because he is a cheater and a tool and a liar.

But most of all, to snap because he is ruining this opportunity for me by not letting me do my work.

"We need to talk." I manage not to lurch forward and strangle him. Barely.

"I've tried talking to you plenty of times, and the answer has always been no. Welcome to your own medicine, Rory. Tastes like a year-old used condom, does it not?"

What is he talking about? He tried to talk to me? When? Where? I've been here all along. I'd know if he tried knocking on my door. The guy is unhinged. Maybe he had a few sniffs of the good stuff, too.

"Man, your sex slave has a mouth on her." Richards sprawls on

Mal's couch, snatching a dildo-shaped bong and lighting it up, his eyes crossing as he stares at it. "I hope you're not paying her." He coughs out a cloud of smoke.

"Only in compliments," Mal deadpans.

"Still overpriced for how cheeky she is," Ashton mutters, throwing me a look. "She is dickable, though. Are you sharing?"

Mal shrugs, chewing on the bottom of a lighter. "Certain holes."

"Thanks, I'll make sure to note this on your accolades when I file the sexual harassment suit," I say cheerfully.

That makes Ashton cough and lean forward. He is finally snapping out of it.

"Come on now, Sex Slave. Don't be so uptight." He giggles to himself. "I just said the word *tight*."

I need to get out of here.

I have to. I don't want to spend the rest of my life in jail, and they just might bring me to the point of double murder. There are too many witnesses around. No, thank you.

I storm back to my room, get dressed, grab my backpack and camera, and head out into the bitter cold of late December. They're still where I left them on the couch and recliner when I move out into moss and green hills and naked trees, making my way down the stony path from Mal's cottage to Main Street.

I put my earbuds in and let the words of "Drunken Lullabies" by Flogging Molly seep into me. I kick empty bags of chips and crushed cans of soda along my way down to the village. *I hate this place. I should just buy a ticket and join Cal in England.*

That thought makes the noose around my rubber-ball heart looser. Now *that's* a promising prospect. Staying in Callum's parents' house. They live in Virginia Water, Surrey. I've seen pictures of their estate, and it makes Buckingham Palace look like a studio in Williamsburg. Though being *there* does nothing for my career.

I've spoken to his mother on the phone. To his sister, Lottie, too. They all seem nice and kind and cheerful and *sane*.

Sane. That's what Summer meant when she pushed me into Callum's arms. I make a mental note to talk to her. I promised to call every day, and so far I've only managed to text her a few times. I'm already breaking my promise.

I would give up a lot to have someone to talk to right now, but I don't want to worry Callum over nothing. I need to calm down, chug more coffee, then go back and take pictures of these clowns (Photoshopping out any evidence of Richards' drug use).

My phone vibrates in my pocket, and I take it out, only to see my mother's name flashing. I tuck it back into my jacket with a sigh. Clearly, I'm okay. I sent her two emails reporting as much. Can she really blame me for not wanting to talk to her? All she does is make me feel guilty about coming here.

When I get to the village, I buy a pack of gum from a newsagent. As I reach into my pocket to dispose of the change, I hear chattering behind me—two chicks who sound around my age, maybe slightly older. I don't turn around, even when one of them clearly has a Northern English accent. Liverpool is my guess, though I'm hardly an expert.

"...can't be her."

"Look at her scar, Maeve. It *is* her."

"She's supposed to be American."

"I heard an American accent."

"Stop being ridiculous! Why would she..."

I steal a quick glance—barely noticeable, just to see what they look like.

Maybe they're friends of Kathleen's. Perhaps they know me through Mal, who told people about my birthmark, even though he knows how self-conscious I am about it. Either way, it's in poor taste, and at least one of them—the leggy blonde with the familiar English accent—is in no position to judge me, seeing as she sleeps with a married man.

I grab a napkin from the register, stuff it into my pocket, turn around, and flash them a smile.

"Let me give you a direct answer: yes, I am *her*. What did you hear? That I stole Mal from Kathleen? That my mom is a bitch? That my late dad is a no-show drunk? Been there, heard that, so let me add another rumor into the mix. This one is also true, so listen carefully—I'm living with Malachy for the next two months. Under the same roof. But I won't be screwing around with your friend's husband. I want nothing to do with either of them, so feel free to pass your message to Kathleen."

And by the look of it, anyone else in this village. It's official, I'm the pariah of this godforsaken town, thanks to my lovely host.

Astonishment drips from their faces, their mouths limp, their eyes comically wide. The blonde is wearing tight, white jeans and a huge pink faux-fur coat. Her friend is a petite, curvy brunette, with farmer's boots and a neon green bomber jacket. They're both nursing steaming cups of coffee.

"How dare you talk about Kathleen like that!" The blonde gasps theatrically, snapping out of her shock.

Never mind the fact that she's *sleeping* with Kathleen's husband.

"Let me guess, you're here for your inheritance from your father?"

What? Why would I come here eight years after he died?

"I'm not interested in my late father's money," I clip out.

I wish he'd been broke, so people would stop accusing me of going after his fortune. No wonder Mal hates money so much. It's everything people think about.

"Right," the blonde snorts. The brunette shakes her head, elbowing her friend.

"Stop it, Maeve. I think she really doesn't know. I'm Heather, and this is Maeve."

Reluctantly, I shake both their hands. Maeve still looks upset by my existence, and I'm trying really hard not to out her sordid doings yesterday in front of her friend.

"I'm Rory."

"We know," they say in unison.

"I didn't think she'd be that pretty. Kath said she was just okay," Maeve grumbles, then bites her lip, realizing she said that aloud.

"Do you live around here?" I look between them, trying to break the ice.

Heather nods. "Just down the street. On Christchurch Grove. Ours are the blue and red houses facing each other. We're married to the O'Leary twins, you see. She's married to Sean, and I'm married to Daniel."

This is way more information than I asked for. I smile and step away, toward the street.

"What are you doing living with Mal if you two aren't a thing?" Maeve narrows her eyes at me.

Everything in her face is squeezed in concentration, like her life depends on my next words.

"We work together. I thought he married Kath."

"He did." Heather sighs, as if everyone knows how that turned out.

Well, I don't. I'd kill for an answer. Well, maybe not kill, but seriously injure someone. Preferably Mal himself.

"Did they get a divorce?" I'm starting to think I've gone mad. Either Mal and Kathleen have a super-open relationship or I'm missing something crucial here.

"Mal would never." Maeve's bitter tone does not escape me. "He's loyal to a fault."

Yeah. Loyal. So, so loyal.

"Kath left him, then?"

Their eyes grow so big, I'm afraid they're going to roll out of their sockets. Realizing this is a dead-end conversation, I mutter a goodbye and start backing away, turning around and taking off.

I need to talk to someone, all right. Father Doherty. Yeah, he'll be able to tell me what the hell this entire inheritance obsession is about, and maybe shed light on the Mal-and-Kathleen situation. God knows Mal is not helpful in this regard.

I know Father Doherty lives in this village. It's just a matter of finding him. I'll go door to door if I must.

I tromp my way back toward Mal's cottage and take the long way up, the one between fields of barley and wheat. The air is fresh, and the wheat is brown and beaten by the cold, whooshing back and forth in the wind like silk. By the time I see the cottage, my heart rate is back to normal.

I push the door open and find Mal sitting in the backyard, which has been fully furnished with loungers, a dining table, two fire tables, and a fancy grill. The entire house looks different. Uncluttered, yet full of new, shiny things. I watch Mal sit back at one of the tables outside through the living room window. He's flirting with two American girls from Richards' staff. He is nice, Old Mal again. The one I fell for. I shake my head, roll my eyes, and head to my room, stepping over the threshold.

I blink.

Turn around.

Stalk back to the corridor.

Check it really is my room—it is—then re-enter, looking around.

What. In. The. Name. Of. Jesus. And. His. Holy. Crew?

Someone has removed the bed I've been sleeping on and replaced it with a gigantic, plush, king-sized mattress on an upholstered white bedframe with the initials AR. There are two nightstands, a central sound system, a TV, every game device under the sun, and a clothes rack with robes, fancy coats, and colorful blazers.

I shoot out to the backyard, feeling like my feet are hovering over the floor. I'm not mad. No. I'm *raging*. I can feel my pulse everywhere, including my eyelids and toes. A feral scream lodges in my throat.

I throw the back door open, and it slaps against the wall from impact.

"How dare you?" I fling my arms at Mal. He looks up from something one of the American girls is showing him on her phone—her ass is perched on the edge of the table his feet are on—and all three are staring at me now.

He watches me with quiet amusement. "Care to be more specific? I quit my mind-reading job last week."

The girls snicker, exchanging looks.

"My room! My things! Everything is gone."

I'm finding it hard not to stomp my foot and throw a fit, and Mal knows it, because the more flustered I am, the calmer he looks. He yawns provocatively, leaning back in his chair.

"About that. We had a bit of a space problem with Richards moving in, so I had to put your things in my room. Hey, roomie." He winks, his eyes light and full of mischief.

The girls sigh audibly next to him. I'm about to throw up.

"I'm not rooming with you." I fold my arms over my chest.

"Looks like you are from where I'm sitting. Then again, you're awfully short. Sometimes you don't see the whole picture."

No, he didn't.

"You sit on a throne of delusions if you think I'm sharing a bed with you."

"No one said anything about sharing a bed, silly. I rolled you out a sleeping bag on the floor. Chivalry is not dead, Rory. I'm living proof of that."

"You want me to sleep on the floor?"

He shrugs. "You can stay awake on the floor, if you like. What you do with your spare time—*on the floor*—is not my concern."

More laughter.

He'd better be kidding me.

"Get up," I grit out.

The women exchange bitch-is-crazy looks. They aren't wrong. Not now, anyway.

Mal gives them a meaningful, see-what-I-have-to-deal-with? look. He gets up, swaggering over to me as lazily as he possibly can without standing still. When he's within reach, I grab the collar of his shirt and jerk him indoors. Everyone other than the girls is gone, the house fully prepared for Richards, but I don't take any chances we'll be heard. Richards is probably touring the village, trying out the local beer, butter, and babes. I shove Mal into the bathroom and lock the door. He leans back on the vanity, smirking down at me like I'm adorable.

"Mal," I start, taking a cleansing breath. "We can't sleep in the same room. I have a boyfriend. You have a wife. You care about what she thinks. I know you do."

I don't know if I'm trying to convince him, or myself. "I heard you talking to that English lady yesterday…"

At the mention, Mal's lips curl in satisfaction. Of course, I was meant to hear him nailing Maeve through the mattress, floor, and lower sections of hell, giving her four orgasms and three praises for Jesus, God, Mary, and every saint in the Bible.

"You said you want to take Kath somewhere sunny after this is all over. Maybe you two are going through a hard time—"

"We are," he interjects. "Horrible, really."

I nod, eager to make my point.

"Yes. All couples do. I get it. And maybe you're on a break, and that's why you were with someone else. I'm not judging. But if we share a room, Kathleen will never, *ever* forgive you, and we both know it. And I will never be able to mend my relationship with my sister."

Not that I particularly want that…but still. It would be nice to have the *choice*.

He pokes his lower lip out and tugs at it, his purple eyes raking my face. He is so painfully, unfairly beautiful. I want to lash out at him for abusing the power of his looks by being so impossible. He licks his lips, his eyes dropping to my mouth. I know what he's thinking, and the blood that's buzzing with anger in my veins is now full-blown humming with something that feels deadly close to anticipation. The familiar chill turns hot again, and I know he is my lighter. Ready to set me on fire with a flick of his fingers.

I take a step back, clearing my throat.

"There's also another option," I say.

"You can't go to a hotel. New Year's is around the corner and everything's booked."

"No." I lift my eyes to his. "There's another room at the end of the hall."

I don't mention that I'm dying to know why the room is locked. I simply watch as his expression morphs from easy to very frighteningly dead. His thick eyebrows furrow, his eyes dim, and his jaw squares. I don't need him to open his mouth to know it was a mistake to bring it up, but to leave no doubt, he pushes off the vanity and crowds me, his limbs easy and long and forbidding.

I swallow, but don't cower. I tilt my chin up, not even blinking—not even when he reaches to cup the side of my neck, tilting his head sideways as his gaze scorches a path into my soul and rummages through it like it's a stack of secondhand clothes at a charity shop.

"Let's get one thing straight: you are not to talk about, refer to, or *think* about that room. You are, in fact, the very reason why that room exists. You will sleep in the sleeping bag, or you will not sleep at all. Take the sofa if you're really into pneumonia. There's no central heating, though, and the only heaters working are in mine and Ashton's rooms. After that little stunt in the living room earlier, I doubt he'd let you warm his bed. And just to make things perfectly clear, you're not welcome in mine."

I open my mouth, about to tell him to go screw himself, when there's pounding on the door. I jump in surprise, and he takes a step back, running his hand through his inky hair. I drop my gaze and see that he is hard. Rock hard, fully tented, and turned on. I flush pink, reaching for the door handle, desperate to get out.

Mal puts his hand on mine to stop me. Our eyes lock.

Flick. And just like that, I'm burning.

"Mal! We're off. Make sure to wake Ashton up in about thirty minutes, okay? He has a call with Ryner booked for six pm your time. See you tomorrow. Or earlier, if you want. You have my number." One of the girls giggles. "Ciao, handsome!"

The front door slams. Mal is the first to move. He opens the door, and we both slip out and disappear into different rooms. I go into Mal's room to take my stuff to the living room—lack of heating be damned—and Mal goes into my former room to wake up Ashton.

I'm tucking linens into the sides of the sofa pillow when Mal walks into the front room, his face ashen. I don't ask him what's wrong, because frankly, I don't care anymore.

"Richards is gone," he tells me. "He's not in his room."

Our gazes connect, and we both say in unison, "Fuck."

A NOTE FROM MAEVE

Hullo! It's me, Maeve.

Just one little thing before you go back to your daily schedule.

To be perfectly clear: when Mal called me out of the blue, after years of radio silence, I very much wanted to ignore him. I did. He's been horrible to me the past few years, you see.

Left me heartbroken and shattered when he said goodbye out of nowhere, without giving me a sufficient reason.

Yet I couldn't stay away. A part of me—a small, stupid part of me—thought he might've changed his mind, that perhaps he saw the light and realized I was more than just a shag. That we were soulmates or something.

He proved me wrong as soon as I got to his bedroom. I swear, he was busier making me scream and the bed creak than anything else. It was obviously a revenge shag, and lucky me, I was in the middle of it, while *she* was listening next door.

I know she was, because she was gasping and moaning, too.

Which only made him fuck me with more stamina and speed than ever.

I felt a lot like a condom—like I was the only thing separating them from one another. It wasn't really me he was sleeping with. It was her. And she, she imagined him, too.

Which reminded me why I'd gone and cheated on my husband every single time Mal gave me a ring, even though I'm no silly girl. I knew—*know*—why Mal started sleeping with me: to hurt my husband.

And why he did it last night: to hurt Aurora.

'Tis the truth that sleeping with another man when you have a family of your own is a villainous thing to do. But what about me? What about my feelings? My existence?

Shall I live my entire life washing and cleaning and feeding and cooking?

Loveless and lonely and slaving to kids who don't care and a husband who won't even look at me?

I didn't mean to hurt my family.

To put what I have in jeopardy.

I didn't mean to fall for the unattainable.

To ruin so many things along the way.

Now my Sean knows, but we are not getting a divorce.

No. He is better than that. Better than me. He just told me if I ever see Mal again in private, he would take the kids away.

I know he wants to kill Mal.

I want to kill Mal, too.

But for a different reason. I just saw the girl he fell in love with and realize I don't stand a chance.

There's a reason why fairytales end right after the prince saves the princess. No one likes to see her nursing postpartum depression and a drunken husband, all whilst folding the laundry.

And Mal? He was the prince who blazed by on a horse, heading in a different direction.

Present

Mal

RORY'S SHIVERING.

I told her not to come with. Did she listen? No, she didn't. Does she ever? Also negatory. She just grabbed her camera and flew through the door, taking this as an opportunity to work.

Of course, the fact that I am now the host of a currently AWOL, coked-up rock star whose name is synonymous with recklessness is part of why I'm ready to smash my head against a rock. Ashton Richards is an all-right guy, in the sense that he is unaware of just how irritating he is. He is one of those born-a-cunt people who thinks the world owes them something, and that others should do the job for them. The coke addiction is a byproduct of being an insta-rock star. If Mick Jagger and Steven Tyler had decided to skip on one leg four days a week as some sort of a rebellious statement, he'd have overdeveloped quads and would be late everywhere.

My phone rings a thousand times a minute.

10 Missed Calls From Bigwig Cokehead.

That's the nickname I gave Ryner.

We trudge past the fields by the cottage, and I omit the fact that we are technically trespassing. The fields are no longer mine. I sold every inch of my land except the cottage after The Night That Ruined Everything. I didn't want the responsibility, and I needed the money to buy a new house for Mam, Father Doherty, and Kathleen's mum, Elaine. Then there was that emergency surgery for which we had to fly in doctors from America. That cost me a pretty penny, too.

I stop in front of a shack-like bungalow, the only house remotely close to mine, curl my knuckles, and pound on the door. The place belongs to the Smiths (the family, not the band), and the Smiths know things Rory doesn't, so of course, I'm wary of the exchange.

"Hullo." Brenda, a sixty-something-year-old housewife, opens the door. A warm, yellowish glow and the scent of baked pies spill out from behind her.

She wipes her swollen, veined hands with the hem of the apron wrapped around her big frame. The minute she sees me, her face alters from relaxed to pitying.

"Dear God, Malachy. How have you been? I've been meaning to come check on y—"

"Have you seen a strange-looking man around by any chance?" I cut her off. I did not consider the fact that the entire village treats me like Moses left in the reeds of the Nile River—maybe to survive, probably to die a slow, lonely death.

Surely Rory's going to pick up on my sob story soon, if she hasn't already.

Brenda's brows nosedive. "How do you mean? Dodgy looking? Suspicious?"

"More like crazy looking. Golden robe, long hair. Sort of like a Kardashian version of Jesus Christ."

She *tsks*. "Sorry, dear."

"All right." I turn around. "Cheers."

"Wait! Come in! Have some pie!"

Brenda is calling after me, eager to help the poor, lost boy, but I jerk at Rory's hand before she listens to the questions, and the pleas, and the condolences.

"Must you always act like you've been raised by swamp creatures?" Rory breaks away from my touch, jamming her fists in her pockets.

Her teeth are chattering. The girl is going to die if she tries sleeping in the living room tonight. I don't answer her.

"Ryner is blowing up my phone." She tries changing the subject. "Yours, too?"

"Yeah."

"Should we answer?"

"*We* are not a thing. *I* do whatever I choose to do, and *you* are free to do the same."

Today, when Rory and I had the argument in the bathroom that resulted in all the blood in my body rushing to my cock, I almost told her she could take my bed and I'd take the sleeping bag. Then she had to go and bring up the locked room, and all the dark memories poured in, washing away every good intention I may have had.

"Where could he go? He didn't take the car." She skips to warm up, unfazed by my behavior.

The car is still parked in front of my house. Besides, I highly doubt he can operate a light switch, let alone an actual vehicle. No, Richards must be somewhere nearby. My phone rings again. Ryner. I don't particularly care that we missed the call. I give a shite about this job a little less than I give one about the wellbeing of endangered cockroaches in Madagascar. Richards is the one with the problem.

Rory, too.

"Ryner is pissed." She *ughs*. "This project is going to kill my career."

"We'll find him," I say.

"Yeah." She does weird things in her body, twisting and skipping to keep warm. "Maybe. Other than this house, it's all open fields. I'm surprised you even get mail here."

You'd know.

You sent me one hell of a letter.

We make our way past the Smiths' house and down a valley. It's getting darker, and I know we're going to have a problem if we don't find him in the next half hour. I don't want to call the police and report him missing. It's one thing to lose your wallet, but how does one lose the biggest rock star in the world?

In other news, Rory is on a mission to talk until my ears fall off.

"I think I hear something coming from over there." She points at the sheds out left, a five-minute walk from us. "Let's go check. Anyway, I know how that is. For the first two years in college, the dorms were full, so I got a partly subsidized house off-campus. The place was huge, but it was on this farm that was really far away from civilization. People got their mail maybe once a week. We were constantly late on bill payments. So we ended up having to rent a P.O. box on campus, but those were broken in to all the time because parents were sending their kids money and lots of valuable things. It was a nightmare."

She's babbling. I don't care about her P.O. box.

About her former house.

About dorms and random people's parents, and I definitely couldn't give a toss about what bills she paid eight years ago.

"Finally," she continues, undeterred, "I decided to redirect all my mail to my mom's house. You know how I feel about her, but I just couldn't risk it. I was already drowning in debt. I didn't need unpaid bills with interest on top. Plus, she offered to pay for the entire thing and took care of it herself, so that was a bonus. Here, let's go this way." She stops, pointing behind the barn. "I think that's where I heard the noise coming from."

I follow her, frowning. I believe my views about her verbal diarrhea have changed.

"So you got your mail redirected to New Jersey," I say, controlling the level of interest apparent in my voice.

"Yeah. Living in the middle of nowhere is bad for mail, dude."

"Since when?"

"Like, three months after I moved out? Something like that."

"*Huh.*" I'm keeping it bored, though my mind is screaming *WHAT. THE. FECK.* All in capitals.

Pieces of the puzzle seem to be falling into place, but the overall picture is all wonky and wrong. Different from what I thought. It doesn't paint Rory as the villain and me the hopeless protagonist.

"The house was neat, though. I shared it with eight other girls. One of them was my best friend, Summer. I don't remember if I told you about her. She became an actress in an off-Broadw—"

"That means your mam opened your letters for you," I interrupt, my brain threatening to melt now.

She is still bouncing and shivering. I could put her out of my misery by touching her—getting her hot and bothered has never been an issue—but being rejected by her would crush me.

"Yeah. But I didn't get *letters* letters, you know. Just…bills and stuff. I was starting to build my credit. I couldn't afford late payments." She messes with her camera, which is attached to a strap on her neck.

Through my carefully crafted exterior, it hits me like a ton of bricks.

I've been missing a big part of the truth of it all. The one unspoken. *Her* truth.

I never bothered to ask her version of things—not that I had the chance to. Still. *Still.*

I listened to two sides of the story, but neither of them was hers. Neither of them came from her mouth.

One came from Kathleen.

The other from Debbie, her mother.

And all that time, it seems Rory was oblivious. Her mail was going to New Jersey.

Sure, there are a few loose ends, but with a crushing weight, I know in my gut that everything I've believed all this time was a lie. Everything I believed about her. Rory never set out to destroy me. Rory didn't *know.* Her mother was responsible for this. All of this.

Rory didn't reject me.

She didn't betray me.

She didn't hate me for what happened.

What probably *never* happened at all.

She is still talking, oblivious. Trying to win me over, maybe. She's playing with the hoop in her nose. Nervous.

God, Rory. God.

The earth under my feet is moving. Things inside of me are shifting, too. This changes everything.

Rory is still pure and good and meant to be mine. And I will make her so. Even if I have to fight Callum and her mother, and the entire village.

Which I will.

(I might have to resume my morning push-ups if I plan on starting a full-blown war with the entire universe.)

She's craning her neck now, looking for Ashton, oblivious to the life-changing pep talk I'm giving myself in my head. She has no idea that my whole world has transformed in the last minute.

"...moved to Manhattan, from a five-thousand-square-foot house to a five-hundred-square-foot, one-bedroom apartment. Summer put up a bead curtain to divide our makeshift rooms. But let me tell you, it's awkward when she brings guys back..."

I stop walking.

She stops, too, eventually. It takes her five steps to realize I'm not there with her. She turns around to face me, slanting her head, confused.

All this time.

All this anger.

For *nothing*.

I want to hug her.

I want to fall down on my knees and ask for her forgiveness.

To cry.

To tell her what happened.

To hide it from her, so she won't know how awful it has been.

I want to kiss her. Dip my fingers in her long, currently snow white hair. Press my lips between her eyes and thighs and over her beautiful, flawless heart that always beats faster when it's under my palm. I want to keep her warm. Forever.

"What?" Rory frowns, like a wee child that's been scolded for nothing. "Why are you looking at me like that?"

"Like what?" I smile, happy she can't see the glimmer in my eyes in the darkness.

"Like…I don't know. Like I just saved your life or something. You look upset but happy."

"I am both," I admit. "And you did," I whisper softly, knowing she can't hear.

"Please don't take this the wrong way, Mal, but you're the most confusing, infuriating, hotheaded man I've ever me…"

I'm about to take a step toward her and kiss the living hell out of her—feck Shiny Boyfriend and his shiny family and the shiny engagement ring I found in the nightstand drawer in their room when I went back to retrieve The Boar Head's napkin from the bin (oops).

She'll never know he wanted to propose before I summoned her for work, never know he forgot the engagement ring there, because he has the same amount of brain cells as a Benadryl tube.

Rory is not going anywhere. She's staying with me.

She stops talking, but it's not to welcome my almost-kiss. She lifts her palm and cocks her head, listening. There's a shriek from behind the barn.

"Don't you fucking dare move away. Do you know who I am?"

A cow snorts loudly. Rory and I exchange frowns as we take off toward the back of the barn, the grass muddy and slippery beneath our feet.

We round the big barn and find Ashton Richards, the snog-blocker, looking rather blue and thoroughly crazy, still in his golden robe.

He throws his arms in the air. There's a cow in front of him, but it's backing off, obviously aware of the fact that between them, it is the more intelligent, responsible creature.

Ashton raises one leg in the air while stumbling after the cow, trying to get on top of it. Feck. He is trying to *ride* it.

"Come here. Do you know how many women would give up their families to have me ride them? Do you?" he asks, half-laughing, half-crying.

Actual tears, I notice, which makes the situation considerably more bizarre.

He looks…crushed. Devastated. On the brink of a breakdown.

Rory lifts her camera, adjusts the flash, and takes a string of photos silently. *Badass*, I think. Not just because she's putting her job first, but because of the stoic look on her face. After she's satisfied with what she's captured, she hands me the camera silently and approaches him, yanking at the back of his robe.

"Ashton!"

He spins around and blinks at her, slapping his forehead. "Sex Slave! Damn, girl, your boyfriend has been sulky as fuck since you left. I hope you got it all fixed between you two."

He pats his breast pocket, producing a soft pack of Lucky Strikes. Suddenly, he is smiling again. There's something definitely up with this bloke.

Even though the idiot is not wrong, Rory chooses to ignore the information about me and clamps his back. I don't like seeing her hand on him, but if we don't get him in the house right now, he is going to spend the next week in the hospital, battling a wicked lung infection.

"Can I tell you something?" she asks.

He shrugs into her palm.

"You cannot ride cows, Ash."

"That's not a cow." He points at the cow with his half-lit cigarette, waving it around, like it proves something. "That's a horse, honey pie."

I put my fist to my mouth to cover my smile. Rory nods patiently. She draws circles on his back with her palm, gently persuading him to walk toward me and out of the field.

"What makes you think it's a horse?" she asks conversationally.

"It's completely brown. Cows can only be black or white or both."

"Hmm…" She sounds like she's considering the merits of his argument. "What else?"

"I saw it running from the barn when I walked by. Cows don't run. They're fat and lazy."

That's not true. I've seen cows run plenty. Granted, it's an odd sight, but it is possible. They run heavily, like elderly ladies trying to catch a departing bus.

"What were you doing here in the first place?"

She keeps him talking. They reach the gravel path I'm standing on. We proceed toward the cottage, knowing damn well that Ashton is high enough to make a U-turn at any point and go back to the cow, demanding his ride. We need to keep him engaged until we lock the door with him inside the house.

"I was looking for *you*." He turns toward Rory, poking her arm with his cigarette.

Thankfully, it died because he couldn't light it properly. My jaw twitches, and I slide between them, bracing his back and breaking their contact. It's a relief to be protective of Rory. Trying to hate her was exhausting, and futile.

She had none of my bullshit, for one thing. And for another, I always felt shitty trying to make her sad.

"Why were you looking for me?" Rory blinks, puzzled.

"Because our host here was being a sulky-ass motherfucker. You know, I don't think it's just sex he wants from you, honey pie. The only time I saw him smile was when you were around."

"Our host is married," Rory says, the three of us walking up the road, back to the cottage. "To someone else. There was no need for you to look for me."

"No, he's not." Ashton laughs, wildly and loudly and more annoyingly than legally allowed, I'm sure.

"You also thought a cow was a horse, Richards. Not sure you're in a position to give your opinion about anything, least of all my martial status," I mutter.

I'm not ready for her to find out. Not like this. I want to do this right, so we'll have a chance.

We need to be alone. Somewhere quiet. Somewhere warm. Somewhere I can explain.

"It's not an opinion." He whistles, zigzagging on the road. I tighten my grip around his shoulder. "You ain't married, dude. Ryner told me the story."

How high is this dickhead?

"He has a wedding band," Rory points out.

"That's because he is married," Richards hiccups.

"Richards," I start.

"*Marrieded* is not a word," Rory interjects.

"'Course, it is. It's married. But, like, in past tense."

"Shut up," I hiss, clawing his shoulder in a vise grip, but he is too high to notice.

"Like, divorced?" Rory kicks a stone. She's been kicking it since we were on the gravel path.

"No, like a widower. Like, his wife died and stuff. How do you not know this shit? You're his sex slave. Don't you have small talk after you fuck? While he gets the whip or puts nipple clamps on you?" He tuts, shaking his head. "Kids these days."

Rory freezes, and that means all three of us stop, because we're huddled together, me sandwiched between them. I stare down at my boots.

I can see her shaking her head. Biting her lip hard. I squeeze my eyes shut. *Goddammit, Richards.*

The fecker stumbles out of my grasp and looks between us, trying to light his cigarette again. The cigarette is not even in the same hemisphere as the lighter he's flipping.

"Oh, I see." He places his hands on his knees, laughing hysterically. "I see exactly what's going on."

We're both silent. I want to tell her I didn't lie. I was married to Kathleen. She died, but we were married. And it hurt. All of it.

The marriage part.

The dying part.

The part where Kathleen said I'd kill her one day.

And the fact that I did.

"You guys are not a sex slave and a master at all." He finally gives up, tossing the cigarette aside. "You're like…I don't know. Fucked-up past lovers or something."

More silence.

"You're in love with her." He shoves his finger to my chest. "Dude, you *so* are. And you…" He turns to her. "You're…I'm not sure what you are. Confused as fuck, that's for sure."

"I have a boyfriend," she mumbles, kicking the small stone so hard it flies to the other side of the field.

I can't detect her tone, and it kills me, because *she* kills me. Tonight changed everything for me, but what if it stays exactly the same? What if it's too late?

What if she *will* end up marrying the boil-balled fecker?

"Your boyfriend knows you're looking at another guy like his cum is the nectar of the gods?" Richards asks.

I advance toward him and wrap my fingers around his neck, squeezing.

"Watch your mouth where she is concerned," I warn, "or you will have no teeth to do it again."

I release my bruising grip on his neck. Richards laughs and resumes his walk like I didn't nearly break his bones. Rory and I walk a few steps behind him, at the same pace. He's singing to himself now, oblivious to our existence. I don't know what he's on, but I hope it's laced with cyanide, because every year he gets to live, our generation gets dumber and a (Victoria's Secret) angel loses her wings.

Finally, Rory speaks.

"*Mal.*"

Apologetic. Here we go.

"I'm so sorry for your loss."

At least she's not angry about the lie.

"And I'm also so mad I could kill you right now."

I take that back.

I run a hand through the back of my hair, tugging at it.

"Why didn't you say anything?" she whispers.

Ashton is swinging his arms ahead of us, bellowing a tune. Something about the birds and the bees. I hope he doesn't truly believe in this form of conception, because that means a lot of unmonitored baby Richardses in our planet's future.

"You wouldn't have come if you knew the truth."

"Exactly." She plays with the hoop in her nose.

"Exactly." I lift my gaze to meet her eyes for the first time since she found out. "You deserve this shot. Why throw away an opportunity because of a contract signed on a napkin? Because of an old flame?"

"Because it still burns. Old flames burn you all the same." She looks away.

It starts to rain lightly.

She doesn't ask if I kept the napkin. I'm guessing she thinks I treated it like it was contaminated and got rid of it as soon as I could, considering how I've treated her so far.

"How?" she murmurs instead.

She's talking about Kathleen, but I'm not ready for this conversation. I need four stiff drinks and to have her naked in my bed first. Neither of those things is going to happen tonight.

She gulps. Looks away. I suspect she's taking a moment to deal with the fact that she and her half-sister are never going to make amends again. That this is how it's going to stay. Broken forever.

"When you're ready." She takes my hand in hers and squeezes. "And less of an asshole, of course," she adds, probably not completely joking.

I deserve that.

I know it's friendly. I know it's supposed to be comforting. But I can't help but feel a zing of pleasure and determination course through me.

Ashton Richards is doing cartwheels in the rain, yelling, "We're all going to die one day, and we are so self-observed and obsessed with shit that don't matter."

We don't pay attention to him.

"What are you waiting for, God?" he screams to the sky, opening his arms.

Rory and I exchange looks.

"I'm telling Ryner to throw him into rehab as soon as this is done," she says.

"Good idea."

A NOTE FROM DEAD KATHLEEN

Look, I'm going to admit it right off the bat. I am the villain in this story.

I lied.

I deceived.

I manipulated the situation to my own advantage.

That's what you want to hear, and that's what I'm telling you, but I am *not* one-dimensional, and I'm definitely not as bad as Glen.

I loved Mal from the get-go. I'm talking since age two, not since age fourteen, when all the other girls in Tolka finally noticed that the weird Doherty kid was not so weird anymore, and also happened to be exciting and cool and knew how to ride dirt bikes and pierce his own nose and ears.

I've loved him since he let me play the doctor and dutifully played the patient, asking me humorously to touch him places I had no business even knowing about at that age.

Since he snuck snacks into Sunday Mass because we were perpetually bored and shared them with me.

I loved him when he practiced the guitar and I practiced sewing in my room, and we were both terrible.

I don't regret anything that happened. I did all of it because I thought I could make him happy.

Just remember that as you read on, okay?

Remember that Rory is here for a reason now.

And that before I hate my half-sister, I love my still-on-Earth husband.

So, so much.

In fact, love him to *death*.

A NOTE FROM THE COW

For the record, the farmers who work the shed I live in turn on the soft rock radio station all the time, which is something I am trying really hard not to hold against them. At any rate, that means I'm familiar with Ashton Richards' work, and although I do not consider myself an expert of any sort, I can tell he is no bloody good.

Not good as an artist, not good as a singer, and probably not as a human, judging by the first and last hour we spent together on Earth.

Ashton Richards contributes less than I do to the human effort. At least I produce milk, which gives you calcium, which promotes bone strength. It is depressingly evident that some humans, such as him, clearly decline to use the superior intelligence they were blessed with.

He can walk on two feet. Learn a foreign language. Play Sudoku.

Yet he barely knows his animals.

So, no, I wouldn't let him ride me.

As a horse, a car, a woman, or a spaceship.

Definitely not as a cow.

Just, no.

Present

Mal

Back inside my house, Richards is still higher than the
Empire State Building and seems to be in good spirits. He is in
a touchy mood, though, putting his hands on everything inside
my house. It feels a lot like he's touching me when he touches what's
mine, and I don't particularly like to be touched these days—unless it's
by Rory.

"Mate, stay still, like, won't you?" I sigh.

He turns on the radio and starts dancing in the living room, even
though there's nothing cheerful about George Michael singing that his
heart was broken last Christmas. Why they're playing Christmas songs
after Christmas is a mystery I reckon everyone is too post-holidays
bloated to solve.

Rory is in the bathroom, brushing her teeth and getting ready for bed.

When I look back at Richards, he's fixing himself a martini on the
breakfast nook, improvising with a pickled egg instead of an olive. I'm
about to head into the shower to clean up and go through the script in my

head of what I plan on saying to Rory. I laugh a little to myself, because I brought her here looking for one thing, and now it's like scrambling to welcome a new baby hours before its arrival. Everything is different and exciting and new.

The song ends and another one begins.

"Belle's Belle," written and performed by Glen O'Connell.

No. No. No. She can't hear this.

"Turn it off," I snap, grabbing the rugby ball Richards brought in earlier today ("Dude, this football is hella weird. I had to buy it.") and squeezing it hard to get rid of the tension.

"Why? I love this song! This O'Connell guy was a one-hit wonder, but boy, what a hit." He starts moving to the slow, acoustic tune in a way I think he perceives as seductive. In practice, he looks like a drunk swaying his way back home.

Realizing he is not going to comply, I tuck the ball under my arm and stalk toward the radio on the breakfast nook before Rory comes back from the bathroom.

"I said turn it off." I reach for the radio, but Richards swats my hand away.

"Rain or shine, snow or sun, you will always be the one…"

"No! It's giving me inspiration."

"What inspiration? You don't even write your own songs—probably because you're bloody illiterate."

Truth be told, I'm already furious with him for spilling the beans about Kathleen. And I'm not Instagram. I don't have any filters where people who are not Rory are concerned. If something pops into my head, I say it—the byproduct of having nothing to lose these days.

"Bells are ringing, choirs are singing, it must be Christmas Day…"

"Harsh." Richards pouts. "Take it back, dude."

"Turn it off."

"Nope."

"Lovely as you are, we had to say goodbye, step away from the high, only to hit rock bottom…"

I reach for the radio at the same time he tries to snatch it away. I slam the rugby ball in his face and grab the device. Richards stumbles back, holding his nose, hits the wall, and falls on his ass. I'm fumbling to find the off button, but accidentally turn the volume up. Way up. Now Glen's voice is booming everywhere, soaking the walls.

Feck, feck, feck.

I hear something crash on the floor. When I look up, Rory's standing in front of me, tears in her eyes.

I finally hit the off button, but it's too late. She heard. Obviously. God. That muppet, Richards. He ruined everything.

She runs to the front door, swings it open, and takes off.

I track after her on instinct, not even bothering to lock the door behind me.

Some people are prone to dramatics. Not Rory. I know it has physically rattled her to hear her father's song.

Running after her reminds me of another time—a time I didn't make it.

Not this time. This time, I get the girl.

It's pouring. Rory is wearing her thin PJs, and she's barefoot and surely freezing. I can't stand to think of her uncomfortable in any way.

She is not yours. She's someone else's, I remind myself.

But Shiny Boyfriend is not here. The devil on my shoulder fingers his Salvador Dali moustache.

Besides, making her yours has been the plan all along. My angel smooths his white robe, dangling his leg over my other shoulder.

Wait, isn't my angel supposed to talk me off the destruction-of-her-relationship ledge?

My angel shrugs. *If they marry, he'll move her to a plastic, soulless suburb and cheat on her before she hits forty—with his fresh-out-of-college secretary. I've seen that movie. She's not going to like the ending.*

Fair point. I pick up the pace.

I'm soaking wet, the gravel sinking under my feet with a crunch.

The chase is not only a chase because my legs are moving, but because my mind is racing in one direction.

Mine.

It is primal and carnal and caveman and stupid, but I never fancied myself a particularly bright person.

I knew I was going to destroy her life whether I liked it or not the moment I laid eyes on her again, when she stirred under the chandeliers in that New York ballroom like a mythical fairy.

But being more to her is another matter completely. I didn't think I could. Now I do.

I catch up to Rory and block her way down the path to Main Street. Everything is closed, and miles away, and anyway, running from your problems is a bit like chasing them. They're right there with you, wherever you go, no matter the pace.

"Let me go!" she roars, raindrops dripping from the edge of her nose, her eyelashes, the corners of her pretty, sad mouth. "Please, leave me alone. It hurts. Everything hurts so bad." She breaks down in tears, falling to her knees, her head bowed in defeat.

I put my hand on her head, somehow knowing she needs to be touched. I don't know how. With Rory, I just do.

When I saw her in New York, my first instinct was to put my coat on her, because I knew she was always so cold. I do the same now. I strip out of my waxed hunting jacket and wrap it around her shoulders, pushing her wet hair back because it must be bothering her.

"How did things get so screwed up?" Her voice cracks. "You're a widower. My sister is dead. She hated my guts, and I'll have to live with that for the rest of my life. And I can't even listen to my father's voice without breaking out in hives. There's death everywhere we look. Even the day I met you, I was in a cemetery. It's like we're bound by pain or something. Every minute under your roof rips me to shreds, and I'm tired of feeling tattered."

I lift her up by the arms, even though she resists, sagging back to the ground. The rain keeps pounding our faces. I'm wearing nothing but a V-neck shirt, and I know I'm going to pay for this tomorrow morning, but right now, I don't care.

"Don't say that." I wipe her hot tears with my fingers, like it matters in the rain. But it does. To me, it does.

"Why not?"

Because you're the only thing that makes me feel alive.

"There's death everywhere you look, yes. But there's life, too. You just need to notice it."

"Suddenly you care about that? You told me she was in Dublin," she accuses, trying to pull back.

"She is," I grunt, feeling my ears get hot. "Buried in the same cemetery you just talked about. Right next to your da."

"Mal, Mal, Mal."

She is taking this all in, and it's a lot.

She's drowning in it, and I can't pull her back up. Only time can do that.

"Don't. It's been eight years. Life goes on."

"I need to leave here." She looks around frantically, nibbling on her lip.

I lift her chin up so she looks at me. "You're seeing this through, Princess."

"Now I'm Princess? What is happening here? This is…this is wrong. It's not fair to Callum."

"Giving this up will not be fair to *you*."

"Promise me you'll behave," she says. "Tell me you'll stop being so hateful. But also…" She scrunches her nose. "But also promise you won't be *too* not-hateful, either. Tell me you realize the whole napkin pact was a juvenile mistake, and don't try to pursue me. Callum doesn't deserve this."

I shake my head. "I'm sorry."

I don't add that I can't—or I won't—agree to any of that, or that Callum simply doesn't look like the right guy for her. She's too imperfect for him.

But I'll never say that to her face. And not imperfect in a bad way. He needs a Barbie he can play house with. Rory is too much to handle.

"We need to go back now."

"*Why*?" she shrieks.

"Because we have two more months of babysitting Richards, and falling apart is not an option. Especially if it's because your no-show, mediocrely talented late father popped on the radio for no good reason other than the station couldn't figure out Christmas is over."

She looks up at me now, the entire weight of the world's misery swimming in her green eyes.

"Why am I here?" she asks. Quietly. Darkly. Like a dame.

There's threat laced in her voice, and I want to suck it out of her mouth and scoop up the rest of her venom with my tongue. But kissing her will have to wait. If I do it now, I won't stop, and I have an early morning tomorrow. I made a promise I intend to keep—Rory, Ashton, Ryner, and the rest of the world be damned.

"What kind of question is that?" I run my thumb down her cheek to the corner of her mouth.

She lets me. Though she doesn't realize she lets me.

Goodbye, Shiny Boyfriend.

"I mean, why did you let this happen? Why did you think it was a good idea to work with each other when you spotted me in that ballroom? And why are you so angry at me? What do you want from me, Malachy?" She pounds her fists against my chest, pushing me away and kicking a puddle between us.

It's still pouring, but neither of us cares. She's shuddering again, and this time not from the cold. Her back curves and her mouth slacks and everything about her screams *sex, sex, sex*. I stand there, absorbing her little fists as she launches at me again.

"Surrender," I whisper. "I want us to surrender to this, Rory, like you promised all those years ago." Before life tainted what we had.

"But the contract is gone. It's dead!" she retorts.

"Is that what you need? A piece of paper?" I ask.

"Paper is important. A marriage is a piece of paper."

"Yeah, but people get divorced."

She shakes her head. "The contract is gone."

I pull her up and walk her home wordlessly.

Rory

Sometime in the night, I wake up feeling warm for a change.

I blink my swollen eyes and look around me. Pitch black. The surface beneath me dips, the springs whining. I'm in a bed. Mal's bed.

Whoa.

Panic dries my throat, and suddenly, I'm sweating everywhere. I did *not* sleep with him after breaking down because of my father. No way.

I pat the mattress behind me and find the bed empty. Phew.

Still not convinced, I roll toward the side that's facing the open door, pat for my phone on the nightstand—Mal put it there; I somehow knew he would—and turn on my flashlight, aiming it toward the living room.

It illuminates Mal's silhouette on the couch, his ripped, smooth back facing me, all arches and bows of muscles under the thin fabric of his shirt.

I remember his scent in the rain: male and leather and clove cigarettes and *Mal*.

Then his words come back to haunt me.

He wants us to surrender.

Despite that…I know I should fight this.

I've worked hard to forget about him.

The end game is setting fire to me, like he did all those years ago.

I turn the flashlight off and slide my phone back onto the

nightstand, but there's something on the surface—something soft, yet crisp. I turn the flashlight on again, picking it up.

My heart stops as soon as I see it.

In the unlikely event...

Our contract.

The napkin.

It's here. Intact.

He kept it.

It's on.

A NOTE FROM THE NAPKIN

I know, right?

I didn't think I'd make it this far, either—not to mention get some more airtime. But here we are. And my buddy Mal sure did take care of me. The ketchup stain soaked in deeper and eventually faded, in case you're wondering.

Other than that, I'm feeling pretty rad. Had a bit of a scare there for a moment two years ago when Mal's mother found me and tossed me into the bin (just as I predicted—should've bought a lottery ticket that day). When Mal came back home, he looked for me everywhere. I heard him, frantic, mumbling *no, no, no*. By that time I was at the bottom of the rubbish bag. He flipped it upside down and started sifting through. I couldn't believe my metaphorical eyes. He literally touched trash to retrieve me. And not just any trash: food leftovers and soggy papers and sharp-edged packaging and rubbish juice. He kept mumbling *no, no, no*. I thought he was going to cry.

Full disclosure: I didn't smell too hot before, but since the trash incident, I really do smell like a burning armpit.

Mal doesn't seem to care.

I hope the lad gets her.

I really do.

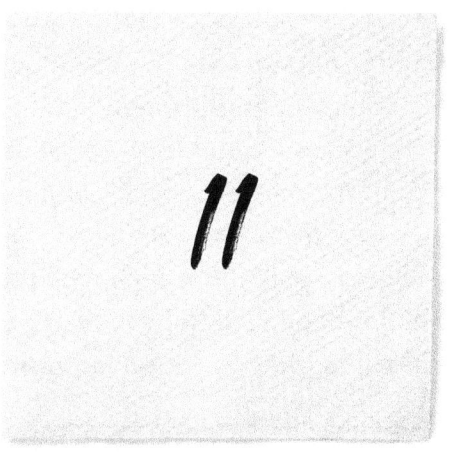

11

Eight years ago

Mal

Dear Princess Aurora of New Jersey,

So. This is awkward.

Mostly because I told you we should leave it to fate, and here I am, writing to you, which is essentially flipping fate the finger while driving slowly by its house after trashing its locker.

I decided I don't want to leave things to fate. Feck fate. I don't know it personally. Why should I trust it?

Anyway, I'm not writing to you about our contract. Forget about it. Well, obviously, don't. I still have it. But I'm trying to give fate a nudge in the right direction.

Thing is, I've been thinking, and perhaps I was a bit rash in my decision not to try this whole long-distance thing. What harm could it do? Let's try.

Also, I would like to point out that I haven't been my flirty self lately. Apropos of absolutely nothing. The edge is gone, I suppose, and anyway, it's never been about the sex, I hope you know. It's more of a validation thing. I suppose you won't relate, because you're brainy and fantastic and go to college and have terrific tits.

Are you still thinking about your father? Stupid question. Of course, you are. I've thought about your da a lot since you left. Not in a weird way or anything. Mam says our loved ones that have passed away are watching us, sitting on fat clouds, which is grossly inaccurate and improbable, as you know, seeing as you've been on a plane and above the clouds. But I'd like to think, especially for you (and a bit for me, because I'm not completely heartless when it comes to my own late da), that they are watching us.

But not all the time, because I do enjoy wanking and taking shits without an audience, and cannot possibly see that changing anytime soon.

Busking is good. Two music producers from the UK tried to buy my songs, but there's just something too bittersweet about being poor and talented and struggling. Once I have the taste of the money, I'll be a goner, and I still want to enjoy what I do.

I don't want to blab, so I'll leave it at that. How have you been? How is college? Do you have any plans for the holidays? Christmas?

Have you ever had a mince pie? (It does not, in fact, have mince in it.)

Attached are some stamps for you to use to send me back a letter. I know the student life can be financially challenging and such.

Love,
Like,
Faithfully,

Mal

Dear Rory,

I realize I might've come on a bit too strong in my previous letter. Perhaps talking about the ghosts of our fathers seeing me wank was not the best way to start up a conversation. I don't know. I'm new to this whole pen-pal thing.

It's just that things have been a bit off since you left. I'm trying to make them better.

My sister, Bridget, had a miscarriage. She was seven months into the pregnancy. We are all quite devastated. Mam went to Dublin for the month to help her out. I'm still busking and looking after the house. I took a side job on the farm so I could help Mam since she stopped working to be with Bridget. They say Bridge is depressed, and they gave her some pills, but I think Mam needs something, too.

Everyone else is fine. Kathleen has started wearing very short skirts and took up cooking. I think my mate Sean has a massive crush on her, so perhaps we'll hear wedding bells soon.

I wrote a few songs I'd love for you to hear, but no worries if you're busy. If you're not, you could always send me your phone number. Also, feel free to answer by email if it's easier (yes, I'm aware I'm breaking more napkin rules):

Malachydoharrr1989@gmail.com

Or you can just snail mail something back. Or just answer through the power of telepathy.

(I'm kidding. Don't do that. It is not a reliable form of communication.)

Enclosed are more stamps, in case you've lost the previous ones.

Snogs and hugs,
Mal

Dear Rory,

Congrats on the photography award. Saw it in your college's newsletter. Very proud.
(And equally pathetic.)

Mal

Dear Rory,

How about just tell me you're still alive and I'll leave you alone?

Cheers,

Mal

Dear Mal,

Good news: I'm alive.
Bad news: Sometimes I wish I wasn't.
I didn't want to write you this letter.
In fact, I never meant to hurt you the way I am about to. Please remember that as you read on.
I need you to stop writing to me. You have no idea how painful it is to see your name. We cannot be together. I've moved on, and I'm trying to rebuild my life.
After I came back from Ireland, I found out I was pregnant. I was

scared, I was alone, and I was at college. I didn't have any means to take care of the baby. I had no one to turn to. Becoming a single mother, alone and financially struggling, sounded like a nightmare I was all too familiar with. Reliving my mother's life was out of the question.

I debated contacting you several times, but what could I say?

You are there, and I am here, and it's not like you could have provided for the baby and me.

I had an abortion. I don't regret it, although a part of me will always mourn the loss of this child. Every year, I will wake up and think what age they'd be right now. What they'd look like. What they'd be up to.

You were a beautiful mistake, but that doesn't mean I don't regret you.

Every time you write to me, it's a reminder of what I shouldn't have done.

Make it stop.

If you care about me at all, you will respect my wishes and leave me alone.

Not yours,
Rory

The letter cuts me open like a sharp blade, guts the parts she left inside me, and dumps them onto the floor. Everything about it makes me want to throw up.

The content.

The confession.

The abortion.

The *mistake.*

The fact that it was printed and not handwritten—I'd handwritten all of my letters to her—the ink smudged enough for me to guess she crammed it into an envelope off the printer in a hurry, not even giving it time to dry. That hurts, too.

She sounds icy and emotionally separated and different—not the girl who asked me about God and ran with me in the rain.

I snap. I finally—*finally*—snap.

Cue a destructive bender.

Mam is away, Bridget is a mess, Rory aborted our child, called me a mistake, and made it clear we are over.

I have nothing to live for, or die for, or look forward to.

I drive down to the village. My plan is to buy whatever alcohol I can afford, which is not much considering Mam hasn't been working and I'm paying all the bills and buying all the food. When I get to the register and slam two bottles of vodka in front of the cashier, I rummage through my pockets to find out they're empty. I had a slow busking day. The weather was a state, and whatever I had, I threw into a homeless guy's mason jar because he looked like he needed it.

My wallet is empty, too. I pretend to look in other pockets, under the scrutiny of the cashier, and I'm contemplating stealing the damn bottles when a delicate hand slips from behind me and hands the lady a debit card.

Kathleen steps forward in one of her teeny-tiny, tight dresses that slashes across her rack, flashing me a seductive smile.

"Mal," she purrs.

She always purrs these days.

I watch her pay for my alcohol and don't attempt to argue, fecking gentleman that I am. She throws a bag of crisps and mint gums into the mix, her smile still something big and dazzling.

"Cheers." I grab the bottles by their necks. I contemplate telling her I owe her, but I don't want to take her drinking. I'd rather stuff the notes into her mailbox.

"Care if I join you? I could use a stiffy."

I bet you could, my mind snarls.

Christ, I don't want to think like an arsehole. It's bad enough to see my mates showing each other naked pictures of their girlfriends. The idea of being someone like that makes my skin crawl.

Kiki plays with a lock of her hair and—shocker—purrs, "Long week. Lots of finals."

"No offense, but I'd rather be alone tonight. Tell you what, I'll give you a bottle and we'll take a rain check. I'll make shite company, anyway."

This may or may not be the understatement of the millennium. I grab one bottle and head straight to my car. I rev up the engine, but it's coughing. That's just grand. A trip to the mechanic is exactly what my overdraft has ordered. I see Kath inching toward my car through the window, waving the second bottle in the air, and I slam my foot against the gas pedal, trying to start the car.

Come on, come on, come on.

Her hand is on the door handle. It's like in a horror film. Will he or won't he? I twist the keys back and forth in the ignition as she opens the door and slips in.

"Me again," she sing-songs, tucking the bottle between her bare legs for balance.

I punch the wheel, staring forward.

"I said I—"

"I don't care," she snaps. "I know you're going to be a miserable sod. I want to be there for you, anyway."

At my house, I open one bottle and we pass it between us at my dining table, filling our tea mugs to the brim. It's pissing outside, and suddenly, I hate Tolka, and Ireland, and myself. No wonder Rory doesn't want anything to do with us. All of us. She's better off not knowing what kind of person her da was. Let's just say there's a reason Kathleen wasn't particularly heartbroken when he died.

Stop making excuses for Rory. She's a world-class cunt who didn't even tell you before aborting your child.

Her body, her choices, I remind myself. A heads-up would've

169

been nice, though. I could've pleaded my case. Weighed our options. Popped the question.

Whoa, time to put the liquor down.

"You look like you need another one. Let me take care of that." Kathleen pats my arm, filling my mug for the third time, the vodka sloshing over.

I notice she doesn't drink hers. Hardly a surprise. Kiki has never been much of a drinker. I stop and wonder why she said she needed a drink in the first place, then decide I'm too busy drowning in self-pity and alcohol to decode her behavior.

"Aren't you going to ask me what happened?" I growl into my already half-empty mug. I polished off my first two servings like they were water.

She sits across from me, shaking her head.

"I think I know what it's about, and it'd only gut me to learn more. I'm exercising self-control."

"Glad one of us can," I mutter, thinking about the stupid letters.

I'll never live them down. Now I truly know I'll never sell a song. The risk of becoming known and having her leak those letters is simply one I cannot take.

"You don't deserve this." Kiki leans forward and rubs my shoulder.

"Trust me, I do." I laugh to the ceiling. "I made a fool of myself. That's on me."

"You could never be a fool, Mal. You're the smartest, most talented man I've ever met."

"You should change your social circle then, milady." I raise the mug in the air, tossing its remaining contents into my mouth in one go.

Everything is spinning—white and slow and sluggish. The air is heavy, stuffy, suffocating. I feel like I'm at the bottom of a murky pool.

At first, I don't notice when Kath slides onto my lap. It's only when her arms circle my neck, heavy as a noose, that I blink and rear my head back, away from her mouth.

"Kiki," I groan. "No."

"Shhh, Mal. Let me take care of you."

She grabs the back of my neck and squeezes my face to her chest, pushing her tits together. It's nice. She has big tits. Bigger than Rory's. They're soft and warm against my nose and mouth. They smell of a flowery perfume and a bit of sweat.

Kath runs her fingers through my hair, kissing the top of my head. My ear. My cheek.

"Your sister. I love her," I grunt into her rack.

Her cleavage is wide open for me. I dip my tongue in the crack between her tits, tasting her salty skin, how wrong it is in my mouth, and it reminds me why I haven't bedded anyone since Rory left.

Kathleen doesn't say a word. She pops one of her tits free of her bra and moves her pebbled nipple across my cheek.

"I don't want to fuck you," I say bluntly, pulling my head back.

It's the truth, but I'm still hard. Because she's here, and she is soft, and she is wanting—something Princess Aurora of New Jersey isn't. Every part of Kathleen is hot, not cold like Rory is, but it's easy to ignore that when you're bollocksed. Especially as there's a part of Kathleen that's Rory, too—a chunk of DNA and genes that Rory could never take away from this village. From me. Kiki is right here, in Tolka, ready for me to screw her to death. And I'm hard, so fecking hard I'm straining against my Dickie's.

Oh, how I wish I were more like Daniel or Sean or Jake or any of my mates who could just sleep with Kiki because she is here.

"Get off," I huff, shaking my head. "Please, darlin'. You're better than what you're doing right now."

But Kathleen's hands are everywhere. They're on my chest and shoulders and back and face. They cup my jaw, and she dips down and kisses me, deep and punishing and cruel. With tongue and hatred and frustration. She kisses me like I did something horrible to her, and now I need to pay.

My head spins like a broken roundabout. I mumble, "*Stop. Stop. Stop.*"

She presses her palm against my hard-on and squeezes. "If you didn't want it, you wouldn't be hard."

"Younedda stop," I slur.

She unbuckles my belt, ignoring my command. My mind is a gray fog of floating thoughts, but I still manage to put things together. Her new fondness for short skirts and dresses makes for easy access. She planned this all along. And she always brings something to eat and alcohol when she is over. Coincidence? I think not.

I feel her warm, wet cunt descending over my throbbing cock.

"Kathleen, I don't want to fuck you," I repeat, as coherently as I possibly can.

The thought of this happening makes me sick. Because I know Rory would never take me if she knew I slept with her sister. Selfishly, that is the first reason, with the second being I don't want to hurt or delude Kiki.

"You *are* fucking me," she hisses, licking the length of my neck. "And you're going to continue until you come."

She slides up, then down, building friction, and my balls tighten.

"No."

"*Yes*. Mal, I'm so wet for you," she says.

And it is true. She is the wettest I've ever had, I think.

Fuck Rory.

Fuck Rory who fucked me over, thinking we were only just a fuck.

I'm shagging her sister now, and they say revenge tastes sweet, but the bitterness that explodes on my tongue is so tangible, I want to puke.

Kathleen's cunt, however, is not at all bitter. She is straddling me fully now, moving slowly and deliciously up and down my shaft. I hear the slap of our thighs together. Feel the slick of her wetness, her juices dampening my pubic hair. She moans into my mouth, her lips sweet and sharp. She bites my lip and makes me bleed as she clenches around me.

I close my eyes and throw my head back to an angle where she can't put her lips on mine. The kissing part is not my favorite. The fucking part, on the other hand...

"Go faster, Rory."

If Kathleen notices my slip of the tongue, she lets it slide. She moves faster, my balls tighten, and I know I'm close.

I've always tried to be a good lover. To go down on the girl, to hit deep, to feel what she likes and doesn't like. But right now, all I want is the personal gratification of being inside Rory's sister, spiting her somehow, without her knowledge.

Still, I squeeze my eyes shut and imagine it's her I'm fucking.

"Rory, Rory, Rory," I chant shamelessly, too out of it to be good, to be fair, to be present. "I'm coming."

"Come," Kathleen drones.

And in that moment, I swear her voice is throaty and low, just like Rory's. I shoot my load inside her, growling in frustration and pleasure.

I can feel the spurts of cum shooting straight into her, and that's when I realize I didn't wear a condom.

And *that's* when I realize I don't particularly care.

I've only ever gone bareback with Rory, only once, and it didn't end well.

But Kath, Kath is nothing like Rory.

She is dedicated to me. She's not the hunter, but a willing prey.

"I don't mind, you know," she tells me quietly. "If you call her name. I really don't. It's kind of kinky, I think. I like it."

I clutch her waist in one hand, her jaw in the other, and kiss her mouth hard, ignoring the blood between us, filling my lap.

What it means.

What she just did to me.

What I just unwillingly took.

And the calamity that's waiting for us around the corner.

Present

Rory

Rory: Are you sitting down?

Summer: Bitch, what kind of question is that? Who's standing up for no reason? This is the 21ˢᵗ century. We sit down unless we're in the gym or in line for Jamba Juice.

Rory: Mal is a widower.

Summer: ???

Rory: What part didn't you understand?

Summer: The one where you're being short and snappy with me for no apparent reason, in fact.

Rory: Sorry. Sorry. I'm just shocked. Kathleen died some time ago. He wouldn't give me the details. I'm shattered, Summer. She was my sister.

Summer: Half-sister. And as you should be. But don't forget she wasn't a saint to you.

Rory: Still. What do I do?

Summer: You pack a bag and say goodbye to Cillian Murphy Junior. This has trouble written all over it. He is officially available and after your ass.

Rory: A. We're working together, and B. He looks NOTHING like Cillian Murphy.

Summer: A. I don't care, and B. Shame, huh?

Rory: Seriously, what do I do?

Summer: Mal. You are about to do Mal.

Rory: How could you be so callous about her death?

Summer: After the things she told you before you left, how could you NOT?

Rory: I need to tell you something else.

Summer: I knew it would get worse. I knew it. Tell me.

Rory: He kept the napkin.

Summer: How do you know?!?!

Rory: He left it on my nightstand last night.

Summer: $#%$%&^^*#%#!!%%^&^%&%^

Rory: After he told me he wanted us to surrender to our promises to each other.

Summer: <GIF of J. Alexander, America's Next Top Model judge, looking scandalized>

Rory: I can't believe you're making fun of the situation. This is serious.

Summer: It's serious that he is a widower. It's serious that I told you this wasn't a good idea. It is NOT serious that you're about to live on a cloud of orgasms for the next few weeks, which will cost you your perfect boyfriend.

Rory: I'm not going to cheat on Callum.

Summer: Mark my words. By the end of today, you are naked in his bed.

A NOTE FROM SUMMER

I have a confession to make, but guys, it's going to be an awful one.

It's not that I'm an awful person. It's that I'm real. I wish I could be less real. I wish I could be a bubbly TV or book character who is always helpful and nice and loyal. But I'm not.

We all have baggage, and mine landed me in hot water a few months ago.

All I want you to know at this point is that I love my best friend very, very much and always will.

But love comes in different sizes and shapes, and it's not always the full range of positive feelings you imagine when you think about it.

I love Rory, but sometimes I want her to snap out of it.

She is so naïve, so self-centered, so clueless.

Who goes to Ireland to work with the love of her life for two months, leaving a boyfriend she clearly doesn't love behind?

She does.

This is going to end in tears.

I just hope I'll be there to wipe them.

Oh, and as for the confession? You'll see.

Present

Rory

I wake the next morning when the scent of freshly baked cake wafts into my nose, and I follow it like a cartoon character, practically floating to the living room. Cocoa and sugar and warm, crisp goodness. I find Mal in the kitchen with his back to me. His damp, ruffled hair suggests he is freshly showered, and a dark gray sweater clings to his lithe body and dark jeans. He moves around in his dirty Blundstones, the cake cooling on the counter beside him. The minute our eyes meet, my smile drops.

He looks like shit.

His bronze skin is pale, his eyes droopy and watery, his nose red, and he looks flat-out drained. There's a mist of cold sweat coating his face and neck. He places the cake in the breakfast nook to cool, then produces a small gift bag from behind the nook, putting it on the counter.

"I'm off," he says flatly.

His gruff voice is extra gravelly, extra throaty, extra *different*. Something happened between last night and now, and I'm hunting through my brain to try to figure out what it was.

"You're sick." I ignore the birthday stuff. I don't care who's celebrating, getting out of the house in his state is a bad idea. "Stay."

He shakes his head. "It's important."

"Whose birthday?" I ask.

"Please don't ask." He touches his eyebrow, looking down.

An odd response, but then again, Mal is an odd person. Then I remember my presence here is largely unwelcome, and maybe he's going to celebrate someone's birthday and doesn't want to invite me. The thought pierces my heart with shame and pain, but I let it go.

"Where is Ashton?" I ask, mainly to drown my grumbling stomach with my voice.

"Eh." He flashes me a tired smile, traces of Fun Mal appearing in his crinkled, smiling eyes. "Our fine lad took off in the middle of the night, while we were sleeping. TMC reported he got on his private jet at Dublin Airport and took off to Thailand to ride elephants."

"You're kidding me." I can practically feel my eyes bulging out of their sockets.

Mal shakes his head, then coughs. It's dry and loud and almost makes him pop a shoulder. "Ryner just called to give me the gist of it."

"He must be freaking out."

Mal shrugs. "That's what you get for signing a forty-million-dollar contract with a heroin-shooting, coke-snorting, LSD-enthusiast rock star and expecting him to be holed up in Ireland for two months. Here. Look at this."

He turns his open laptop to me and hits a TMC link. Ashton is sitting on an elephant, swinging his arms back and forth, sandwiched between a guide and a gorgeous woman who can't be much older than eighteen.

"Elephants, motherfuckers! The biggest force of nature since dinosaurs! Woo-hoo!" he bellows.

I cover my mouth, struggling not to smile.

"Actually, you're thinking of blue whales. They're the biggest animals on Earth," his assistant, the chick who gave Mal her number, mutters from beside the elephant as she walks with the rest of Ashton's entourage.

"Yeah, but I mean, like, mammals," Ashton huffs.

"Whales are mammals."

Ashton lets out a piercing scream. "Well, that's just fucking great. Get me down from this stinking asshole right now. They all look like wrinkly, purple balls, anyway."

I click the X icon to close the video, trying not to let the two million views and counting on the sidebar freak me out.

I turn to Mal. "You look like death."

I decide to cut him some slack about the napkin and bring it up later. He doesn't seem eager to discuss it at the moment. My first priority is to make sure he doesn't walk out this door anytime soon. Lightning booms outside, the rain beating down hard on the roof. The light flickers off for a second.

Again with this supernatural nonsense.

"Cheers." He lifts his tea mug in the air, taking a sip.

I round the breakfast nook and press my palm against his forehead. He is burning.

"You're not leaving," I whisper.

"I'm afraid I'm not asking for permission, Rory."

"You're not," I insist, wiping the sweat off his forehead. "You'll die out there. And then I'll be all alone here, which would suck."

I meant it as a joke, but I forgot about Kath. It's a foot-in-mouth moment. *How did she die? Was she sick? Did you take care of her?* Until I find out, I should be more careful with my words.

"You're not alone." He gives me a friendly peck on the forehead. "There are mice in the attic."

"Mal," I warn, following his gaze and looking at the car keys between us. I shake my head. "Promise me you won't leave."

"What did I say about promises, Rory? I only make them if I intend to keep them. What about you?" More coughs.

There is only one place he needs to be right now. In bed.

Mal was right. The living room is not a place to sleep, and it's my fault he's in this condition. I should've given in to the sleeping bag in his heated room. Yet, I insisted we not share space. Now he's sick as a dog because he tried to please me.

I scoop up his keys, turn around, and run to Ashton's room, locking myself inside. Mal is at my heel, and after I slam the door, he slaps his palm over it with a growl.

"Rory!"

"Get into bed!" I yell back.

"I need to go."

"Not in this state. I don't care who it is, Mal. You're not going. If you want, I can call and make an excuse for you."

I hear his forehead sliding along the wooden door as he squats down, probably too exhausted to stand. He chuckles bitterly. "I very much doubt they'd like to hear from you."

Ouch. And there's the jerk again.

"Who is it?" I ask, trying to sound unaffected. My voice is frayed around the edges, though, cracking mid-sentence.

"Rory, darlin', this is not a joke."

"You can't leave the house, Mal, unless you're going to urgent care—in which case I'm driving."

There's silence from the other end. The first minute, I'm guessing he's contemplating my offer. The second minute, I suspect he might've fainted. I open the door timidly, looking left and right, but he isn't there.

I step outside, frowning.

"Mal?"

I stride into the living room. The front door is slightly ajar. Surely, he didn't…

The keys are in my hand, and it's raining hail, so there's no chance he just left. My eyes dart to the breakfast nook. The cake is gone. The little gift bag, too.

Jesus.

I jump into the car, still in my pajamas, and drive down the road. I catch him walking on the shoulder, cake wrapped in a plastic bag in his hands. He is soaking wet. I slow and roll down the window.

"Mal!" I yell.

His hair drips water into his face. His eyebrows are crinkled in determination. He is also a very unnatural shade of blue. "Get in! I'll take you wherever you want to go."

"No, thank you."

"Mal!"

"Go back home, Rory."

"Please. I didn't know…"

"Home." He stops, turns around, and stares me down.

The finality of the word strikes me somewhere deep. Wherever he is going, I really am not welcome there.

"You can't come with me, and I'm going no matter the cost. So your best option is to wait for me at home, really. You're just wasting my time, and every minute I'm out in the pouring rain trying to convince you to *stop* following me is a minute I am still, in fact, standing in the rain, my condition worsening. Follow my logic here?"

Why is he so harsh? So broken? So...*mad*? He was completely different yesterday, and I refuse to believe this is all due to the fact he woke up with the flu.

But I'm confused, and furious, and a little forlorn over the way things have progressed this morning, so I throw an accusing finger his way.

"Keep walking, but I'm ordering you a cab, and you better be home by one o'clock or I swear to God I'll find your mom and grandfather's numbers and call them."

I smash the gas pedal with my foot, leaving him there, with a soggy cake, a gift bag, and that invisible cord between us he seems to tug whenever I wander too far away for his liking.

I'd let him have the car, but he is in no condition to drive, and I'm scared he'll black out on the steering wheel.

At the next stop sign, I call a taxi company on the outskirts of Tolka and urge them to pick up Mal where I left him. I tell them I'll Venmo them a hundred euros if it happens within the next five minutes. Then I continue my journey to Main Street and park in front of the newsagents, shaking with a humiliation I cannot fully explain.

Truly, I have no idea what I'm doing. I just know I have at least a few hours to burn before Mal comes back from his mysterious birthday bash. I open the glove compartment and find fifty euros. Considering I just spent more than that hauling Mal's ass to his date, I think I'm okay to borrow it. I slip out of the car and get into the store, grabbing a small basket and throwing in flu medicine, herbal tea, a fancy Cadbury chocolate bar, chips, and a triangle-shaped sandwich to calm my grumbling stomach. When I hand the beautiful, dark cashier the note, she flips it and shakes her head, handing it back to me with an apologetic smile.

"I can't accept it. The money is ruined."

"Ruined how?" I blink, confused. I'm starting to think everyone just flat-out hates me in this town. They won't even take my money now?

"Someone wrote all over it."

I take the note and flip it. Sure enough, I see my name on it, and a date.

The date I threw it into Mal's guitar case.

He kept it. For good luck. For fate. For whatever reason, he kept it *and* the napkin, and what does that even mean?

Heart pounding like a restless, caged animal, I tuck the note back into my pajama pocket.

Did you feel the same way I did, Mal? Did you walk around with a hole in your chest?

But if he had, he wouldn't have married Kathleen. I'm reading into things. Not the first time I've done that. Besides, Callum. I love like Callum.

Callum, Callum, Callum.

"Look, it's the only money I have. I stay right up Main Street, in the Doherty cottage. Is it okay if I come back in a few hours with the money? I'm starving. Also, my host is sick, and I—"

"I know who you are." The woman lowers her voice, her eyes softening. She has this weird mix of Irish and Indian accents, sweet and round and warm, like spices and honey.

"You do?" I let out an audible sigh.

News sure travels fast in small villages. I wonder if that's why people feel so strongly about country life. Because it defines you so profoundly, it's a part of your identity. Then again, I *did* have a show-off with Maeve and Heather here not even forty-eight hours ago.

She starts shoving my things into a stripy, nylon white and blue bag. "I arrived in Tolka three years after your mother left. They told me how you got the scar. I'm so sorry, Aurora."

"Huh?" I look up at her, no longer smiling.

My mom wasn't here to begin with—she said she never set foot in Ireland—so how could she possibly leave? And I was born with this birthmark. That's what she said. This is not some Harry Potter scenario where the scar has deeper meaning. It is what it is: a birthmark. Knowing me, I probably punched myself in her uterus by accident.

The cashier hands me my bag.

"On the house. I'm just glad you survived." She shakes her head a little, her long side braid moving back and forth.

"Survived *what*?" I'm trying not to lose patience. "What did you hear about me? About my mom?"

The bell above the door chimes, and someone walks into the shop. The light flickers, just for a second. *On. Off.* The universe is trying to tell me something. The universe can also go screw itself. It hasn't helped at all so far. It just messes with me.

As soon as the woman sees who it is, her eyes widen and her mouth clamps shut. I turn around. It's Father Doherty, and he's already holding a bottle of wine, obviously in a hurry to pay and leave.

Fancy everyone having a party and not inviting the Wicked Witch of the West.

I wish I could say I am happy to see him, but more than anything, it's panic that washes over me. I'm panicked about Mal being sick and walking around in the rain, panicked I'm losing grip on what I have with Callum, but most of all, I'm terrified that there's some big secret about me I'm not privy to.

And all the answers are around me, in a demonic circle, dancing ritually and laughing. Only they're invisible, and I can't see them.

"Rory," Father Doherty gasps, stumbling backwards. His back hits the magazine shelf.

I raise an eyebrow. There's no way his grandson didn't tell him I was here.

"I've been meaning to come up and say hello." He clears his throat, mustering an embarrassed smile.

He looks even more ancient than he did eight years ago. Weaker, too. Tragedy has a way of painting your face in a different shade. You can always spot people who are grieving before they open their mouths.

"I'm sure you have." I smile patiently, knowing there's no point in confronting him.

"I wanted to give you time to settle. How have you been?"

"Oh, you know." I wrap the bag handle around my fist. "This nice lady over here was in the middle of telling me a story, weren't you, Ms..."

I turn around and watch her watch him with pure terror in her eyes.

What the hell is going on?

"Patel," she says. "Divya Patel. Actually, I...I..." She looks at me, smiling apologetically. "I don't know what I was thinking. I mixed you up with someone else. It's all a bit of a blur. A lot happened when I first came to Tolka."

I look between them. Unbelievable. He just silenced her without more than a look.

Father Doherty knows something I don't. Divya, too.

"Please." I drop the polite charade, turning back to her. "I deserve to know how I got my scar."

She looks between me and Father Doherty. There's a scream lodged in my throat. She's asking him for permission. He has no right. She shakes her head and grabs the bottle of wine he's handing her.

"I'm sorry." Her voice is quiet.

I storm out of the store, ignoring the sting in my eyes. I drive around for a while, trying to piece together everything, see if Mom ever mentioned anything about being in Tolka. But if she had, I would certainly remember. She never talked about Tolka. When it's late lunchtime, I finally decide to come back to the cottage. But instead of eating, I dump the bag with the food onto the counter and call her.

"Rory!" She picks up on the first ring. "Gosh, I knew you'd call at four in the morning. I've been trying to reach you for *days*. Text messages don't cut it, young lady. What about your mom? You knew I had those injections two days ago."

"It's Botox, not bone marrow. This, too, shall pass," I bite flatly. *After six months or so, depending on where you got it.*

"You're too sarcastic for your own good, Daughter."

"No such thing, Mother."

"How's Ireland? How's your wretched half-sister?"

Dead, I want to scream. I'm in the Twilight Zone, and I'm not talking glittery vampires. Since breaking the news about Kathleen would only make her ask a trillion more questions I'm not prepared to answer, I keep this piece of information to myself.

Instead, I say, "Have you ever been to Tolka, Mom?"

"Hmm, what?"

"You heard me."

"Where is this coming from?"

"It's a simple question. Its origin is of no importance. Have you or have you not visited Tolka?"

"Your father used to live there for a hot minute, you know." I hear her flicking the lighter and inhaling the first drag of a cigarette. "When your half-sister was younger."

Of course. Of course, she would never call Kathleen by her name. Of course, she's hostile toward Dad, even when he moved closer to his kid and tried to be a decent father.

"You're not answering my question."

I want to punch a wall. I think I just might. But I'm afraid a trip to the hospital will result in more revelations. Maybe they'll run some tests and find out I'm half-leprechaun. Who knows?

"No," she says finally. "No, I haven't. Are you sleeping with that infuriating Irishman yet? You've always had a weakness for the ones who are irreparable."

"He doesn't need repairing."

"He *is* broken."

"Everyone is broken. Some show it more than others."

I made the mistake of telling Mom how I felt about Mal when I came back from Ireland—the first and last time I opened up to her about a boy. She threw a fit, especially after she found the rolled-up sanitary pads in my bathroom trashcan and asked how come my period was so early. Then I had to tell her about the morning-after pill I took, and she flipped and dragged me by the arm to get tested for STDs.

I've never felt more like an idiotic child than I did then, and I haven't shared much with her about anything since.

"I have a boyfriend, so, obviously, no. I haven't slept with him, nor am I planning on it."

"You never know. You and I, we're made of the same self-destructive material. When I met Glen, I had a boyfriend, too."

"You did?" I ask mildly.

I don't really care. I'm not her.

It doesn't even matter if Callum and I break up down the road. I still won't do this to him, for the simple reason that I won't do it to *me*. I'm not a cheater.

"Yup." She pops the P, taking another drag. "Good Italian boy. Went to the police academy. Could've had a good life, Aurora. Instead, here I am, cutting coupons for soap and working double shifts at Hussey's Pizza. Pretty darn sure the Lord chose it as my workplace to remind me what I did to Tony."

I'm about to ask her about my scar when I hear a loud thud coming from behind the front door.

Hoof.

"Talk later, Mom."

"Wait! I need to talk to you about—"

I kill the conversation and boomerang the phone across the breakfast nook. Padding toward the door, I wonder what inspired me to put the phone down when I heard a strange, foreign, scary sound from behind the door of this deserted cottage. If photography doesn't pan out, I sure could be an extra in the first five minutes of a B-grade scary movie. Then again, staying on the phone wouldn't have helped.

I wouldn't trust my mom with my wallet, let alone my life.

Please be Callum, surprising me to whisk me off to England, and not an axe murderer.

I fling the door open, only to find the usual fields, gray sky, and endless rain. I look left, then right, and still—nothing. I'm about to close the door when I hear a low, gritty groan at my feet. My eyes slide down. Mal is lying on the ground, soaked to the bone, looking positively green.

I gasp, clutching the collar of his jacket and dragging him inside. He is heavy as hell and ice cold to the touch. I can only get him to the middle of the living room before I start taking off his drenched clothes. He's limp, and mostly unconscious under my hands. I don't ask him why he decided to walk instead of calling a cab or—God forbid—me. I don't ask where he's been. My main concern is keeping him alive right now.

After I manage to strip him down to his briefs, I throw his heavy arm over my shoulder and pull him up, using all the strength I possess. My quads burn under his weight as I lead him to his bedroom. We bump into things on the way, but I don't think he is conscious enough to notice. He is freezing, and he is always so hot. It terrifies me.

Once he's in bed, I turn the radiator on and jog to the bathroom, coming back with a towel. I start to pat him dry everywhere, then tuck him under the duvet like a burrito, wrapping him like a mummy.

"Tea and flu medicine are on their way. Don't go anywhere," I joke—because he's unconscious and can't hear a thing—running off to the kitchen like a headless chicken.

I flick the kettle on, unscrew the bottles, then turn the kettle on. (Again? Again!) I head back to the bedroom with a glass of water, waiting for the water in the kitchen to boil.

"Heat up, heat up, heat up," I chant to myself as I run my palm close to the radiator to check for warmth. Nothing.

"Electricity is down in the entire village." Mal coughs, rolling in bed. His voice is so weak I can barely hear him. "Don't bother."

This is why the kettle didn't work. I shove the pills and water in his face, trying not to appear as frazzled as I feel.

"Drink."

He perches himself against the headboard and dutifully swallows the pills, not bothering with the water. Did I mention he is green? Yes. Because he is. He is shaking, too. And I, the girl who is always cold, am responsible for making him an icicle. He gave me his jacket in the pouring rain when I felt like running away spontaneously—barefoot and underdressed in the middle of the night. He slept in the living room for me, with nothing to shield him from the cold.

"We need to get you to the hospital."

"In this storm? Fat chance, Rory. It's probably overcrowded, anyway. Christmas fecks all the drunks up, and winter does the rest."

"Why did you have to leave?" I seethe, trying to gain control of my temper. "What kind of stupid asshole wakes up in the morning sick as a dog and decides to take a long-ass stroll in the rain?"

My New Jersey-based bad cop is slipping into my speech, and I bare my teeth at him. I tuck the edges of his blanket under the mattress, again caging him to the bed.

He doesn't answer, just presses his eyes shut. His chest is barely moving. I stand up and go to Richards' bedroom to grab another quilt for him.

When I come back, he looks:

1. Ashen
2. Dead

I run a finger under his nostrils. He is still breathing, but barely. Cold mist covers his skin. My entire body turns rigid.

Be okay. I can't lose you, too.

"Fuck you." I feel the tears prickling my eyes as I begin to undress.

He needs body heat. He needs body heat, and for the first time in a long time, I am actually not cold. My blood is boiling with fury at what he did to himself. At what I did to him. I dump my clothes by his bed, leaving on only my white cotton panties—I never bothered to wear a bra or brush my teeth, things were too hectic today—and slide in next to him.

I think he is out of it enough that he doesn't even realize when I roll him to his side and clasp my arm and leg over him. His heart beats against mine, dull and weak, struggling to keep up with the rest of his body. Hot tears run down my cheeks.

Everything is falling apart. Summer was right. I am naked in bed with him—only not for the reason she thinks. I can't let him die in the name of loyalty to Callum. Richards is a runaway, my boyfriend is in another country, Mal is a widower (and possibly bipolar?)—plus, surprise! He kept the napkin—and there's this huge secret hovering over my head, but I can't seem to untangle it from the cloud of lies and deceit that follows my every step in Ireland.

I rub the length of his bulging arms, up and down, up and down. I press my forehead to his lips to check his breath and temperature. His pulse is slow, his breathing labored. I wonder if I should take his phone and call someone.

I sing him a lullaby my mother sang to me when I was a kid to help me fall asleep. Honestly. It was the only beautiful thing she ever did for me. It always soothed me and calmed me down.

"*Oh blow the winds o'er the ocean/ and the trees, and the seas/ and the little pigeon, that never sleeps.*"

Mal groans, his eyes still closed. A sign of life.

"Rory."

"Yes?" I ask hopefully.

"You're terrible, darlin'. Please stop."

Then he is completely out of it, leaving me to shake with laughter next to him, so entwined I can feel him everywhere on my body.

"You're a total pain in the ass, Doherty," I mumble into his chest.

Goosebumps rise along his smooth, bronze flesh, and I smile. I doubt he can hear me, but I know the gooseflesh is him responding to what I'm saying.

"You make everything so hard." I sigh, and as I say it, I realize he *is* hard.

One of my legs is thrown over his, and his penis is pressed against my groin. It's hot and velvety and swollen, even behind his briefs. I shudder, closing my eyes, feeling the delicious clench inside of me. I open my eyes again to glance at him. But he's not pretending. He really is dead to the world.

And he is getting warmer. Because of me. The ice queen.

"Of course, you would be hard when I say that. You always had the sense of humor of a cabbage," I add as an afterthought.

He lets out a soft snore, his body tilting away from me, heavy with sleep, but I'm not ready to let go. I press my thigh harder against him, tightening my grip.

"Please get better, Mal. Please, please, so I can sing you lullabies you hate and read your songs and give you shit about the napkin and ask you a million questions."

I don't know why I'm talking. It's obvious Mal is not going to answer. Somehow, I manage to doze off in his arms, too tired now to eat the food I left on the counter.

I wake up a couple hours later. The winter blankets the sky, dim and black, but it's still not nighttime. I glance at Mal's face. He seems to be sleeping peacefully, and some of the color has returned to his face. One good thing is that he is very, very hot and sweaty against me. He is fighting the fever off, his hair sticking to his forehead and the nape of his neck.

His dick is still wonderfully erect. Okay, time to untangle, call Callum, and tell him I'm coming to England. No way I'm staying here when Ashton is a continent away and Mal is hard and beautiful and available and kept the napkin. Mom might be a handful, but that doesn't mean she's not right. Mal is trouble, and I'm not a huge fan of trouble anymore.

I try to withdraw from his body, only to find he's now the one with his arm clasped over me, and not vice versa. I slide to the edge of the bed, but Mal clasps my arm. I gasp and turn to look at him.

He smirks, his eyes still closed.

Bastard.

"Going somewhere fancy?" he inquires, his voice deep and rich and gravelly.

Pouty, broken-boy charm has always been my kryptonite, and when he is Imperfect Mal, the urge to love him overwhelms me.

Food for thought, though: Kryptonite also has the power to completely destroy Superman.

"Yeah," I say. "England. To meet my boyfriend's parents."

These plans have been brewing in my head for a while, but I've yet to do anything about them. Now something tells me it's time I should. *Must*, if I want to save my relationship.

His eyes are still closed, his smile widening.

Did he listen to what I just said? Maybe he woke up with brain damage. Poor soul. But I'm sure there are women lining up to take care of his screwed-up self. There are two types of women—the ones who want to save, and the ones who want to be saved. The entire population of the former would take Mal and his goodie bag of issues happily.

"Stop smiling." I groan.

"Why? Life is beautiful."

"Is that so?" I quirk an eyebrow. I think—I *think*—he just rolled his hips against my groin, essentially pushing his dick between my legs, but I can't tell for sure, because the movement is very gentle. What I *am* sure of is the fact that I'm drenched to the bone and currently clenching my womb, wishing his throbbing member was in my tunnel. And yes, I just said *throbbing member* in my head, because admitting the obvious—I am insanely, deliriously in lust with him—is hard to swallow.

There's heat swirling in my lower belly, and if I don't escape this bed right now, I will do something I won't be able to forgive myself for.

His eyes pop open, purple and bright and full of mischief. It's like he woke up a new, healthy man. The tables have turned again, and now I'm the one at his mercy.

"Are we still doing this I-have-a-boyfriend routine? Because Shiny Boyfriend lost the girl the minute you found the napkin."

I get out of bed and walk out of his room, flipping him the finger without turning around. Screw him and screw Tolka. Screw his goddamn grandfather (sorry, God) and the unpredictable Ashton Richards and Jeff Ryner himself.

I head to the living room, unzipping my suitcase and rummaging through my stuff for an appropriate flight outfit.

After a moment I see Mal sauntering into the living room, lazy and confident and *OH MY GOD, WHY CAN'T YOU BE UGLY?*

"You might want to reconsider that." He picks up his cigarette-holed Joy Division white tee from the floor, but doesn't put it on.

"Oh, yeah?" I park a fist on my waist. "Why?"

"Because you're naked, and although I'd personally pay good money to keep you in that state, there are rules to abide by in this wonderful country."

I look down at my naked body, then up at him, frowning. I pick up the first thing in my vicinity—the triangle sandwich I never ate—and throw it at him. He catches it in one hand, cracks it open, and takes a bite. *Dammit.*

"You kept the napkin and you didn't tell me!" I ignore my stomach, which at this stage is glued to my inner organs, screaming for food. Guess that's what happens when you're too busy having three internal meltdowns and an anxiety attack due to emotional overflow. You forget to eat.

Mal shrugs, putting his shirt on and taking another bite, talking with his mouth full. "You wouldn't have come here if I had."

"Because I wanted out of our contract!" I yell, throwing my chocolate bar at him.

I should really stop doing that. I really *am* hungry, and the electricity is still down, and I don't trust any of the glitzy, organic, gluten-free, sugar-free, taste-free stuff Richards' people crammed the fridge with anyway.

Mal catches the chocolate bar in his spare hand, tearing the wrapper with his straight, white teeth and biting off a chunk.

"That's not how contracts work, darlin'," he notes, chewing vigorously.

"Where have you been?" I ask again. "Whose birthday did you go to?"

He tilts his chin down and stares at me seriously. "You'll find out when you're ready."

"Fine. Next question. Why are you screwing Maeve? She's a married woman."

"Same answer. There's a reason, but I need to ease you back into my life. A lot has changed, and I don't want to overwhelm you."

"I don't want to be in your life!" Only I do, and I hate the discourse between my heart and my brain. "And even if I did, you screwing Maeve didn't earn you any brownie points."

"Well…" He pushes off the wall and stalks toward me, disposing of the sandwich on the coffee table without breaking his stride. "Shagging her still, while we're together, has never been the plan. Honestly, she was a bit of a one-off. I hadn't…" He pauses, poking his lower lip out, trying to figure out how to say it. "I hadn't been with anyone in quite some time. And even if I was that sort of person, I'm not a cheater."

I shake my head. "Me neither, and I sure as hell don't plan on starting now."

"Oh…" His smile drops. "But darlin', you already have."

I blink at him like he's crazy. Because he is. Completely *mental*, as they say in this neck of the woods.

"What the hell are you talking about?" I unzip my suitcase frantically, fishing for some clothes. I can feel my hands shaking, and I don't know how to stop them.

He places his foot on the suitcase above me, slamming it shut with a thud and preventing me from getting dressed, and that's when I realize he is still without pants. Just his shirt and briefs, and the mammoth erection pressing against them, pointing at me.

"You've already been in bed with me. Mostly naked. You've already had your wet-as-feck panties pressed against my cock—and yes, I noticed, thank you very much. You've already masturbated to the sound of me plunging into Maeve—imagining it was you, by the way, forever the romantic. Face it, Rory. Emotionally, you didn't only cheat on Shiny Boyfriend, you basically fucked his entire immediate family, pet parrot, and rude neighbors."

I rise to my feet, and angry blood whooshes between my ears. I'm no longer chilly. My cheeks are aflame with shame and mortification. He heard me coming from the next room. Of course, he did. The only reason he interrupted Callum and me in the first place was because his walls are paper-thin.

"Mal…" I take a step back, raising a finger in warning. "I don't want you."

"You don't want me?" He takes a step forward, crowding me toward the kitchen. "Or you don't *want* to want me? There's a difference."

"How is it different?" I play into his game, mainly so he'll talk and not do something else to me I won't be able to stop.

"Well, if you simply don't want me, I have no choice but to respect that."

He closes the distance between us, and my back bumps against the cold fridge. His bare body is flush against mine, and my heart is pounding so fast and hard, I think it's about to leap out of my mouth, like a fish, if I open it to tell him not to touch me.

But Mal doesn't touch me.

He *almost* touches me, knowing it frustrates me even more.

He gets in my face, smirking. "But if you don't *want* to want me, then I'm sorry, but I'm not going to let you screw up both our lives because you feel committed to a guy you aren't sure about to prove a point nobody cares about."

"I got in bed with you because you were freezing. I haven't cheated on Callum." I shake my head, reminding him. Reminding myself.

My eyes drop to his lips, and there's a fireball growing in my lower stomach, a sensation akin to nothing I've ever experienced.

You will never forgive yourself.

He leans forward, regarding me with thinly veiled amusement. I feel his hot breath on my face when he speaks. "You just did the right thing by me, right?"

"Right." I nod with gusto. "*Exactly.*"

"Do you know this rumor?" He frowns thoughtfully, his hand snaking into my panties in one smooth motion.

I gasp, reaching for his arm, but he grabs my wrist and pins it to the wall with one hand, his expression unchanged by my resistance.

"About Mick Jagger and Marianne Faithfull in 1967? When they were allegedly caught in Keith Richards' estate during a drug raid, while he ate a Mars bar out of her cunt?"

I feel something shoved into me and think, *oh, God. Oh, Jesus.* The chocolate bar is *inside* me. It's so filthy and crass, I want to spit in his face, but I can't help but shiver with pleasure, clenching around the thing.

"Do you think there's truth to that rumor?" Mal's lips are practically moving on mine now.

I can feel my puckered nipples rubbing against his body. My breathing is so labored, I am practically heaving. It feels like I'm tipping over an edge of something huge, like I am never going to be the same again.

"I think—" I start.

He pushes the chocolate bar in and out, in and out, thrusting it inside me deeper and faster, and I squeeze my eyes shut and hate myself, because I'm about to come.

You're cheating on your boyfriend, I scream inwardly. *He is making a point, and you are falling for it. Tell him to stop.*

"Answer?" Mal asks indifferently, his lips still ghosting mine. "Yes? No? Maybe? Unsure?"

"St…st…sto…"

"Say it," he urges, his lips crushing mine, but not kissing them—punishing, more like. "Tell me to stop, and I will."

I can't do it.

I can't do it, and I break down in tears as wave after wave of pleasure begins to crash over me, head to toe, and I'm coming hard against the chocolate bar. It's the ultimate sensation of pleasure and pain, but the guilt thrown into this makes it somehow, shamefully, even more erotic.

My knees buckle, but Mal keeps me on my feet, his hand clasping the back of my neck as he withdraws what's left of the chocolate bar slowly. I can feel my sticky thighs gluing together, the gooey, melted milk chocolate dense over my flesh.

Mal lifts the bar between us, and it's ruined, molten, the white waffle sticking out.

"Hungry?" he asks coolly.

I shake my head, feeling my tears fly everywhere.

I cheated on Callum, just like my mom cheated on the guy she left behind for Glen. I'm no better than her.

Mal takes a bite of the chocolate, shrugging, and suddenly, my mouth waters. I am so, so hungry. Without asking me again, he angles the bar toward my mouth.

"Tastes like you." He licks his lips.

I take a tentative bite, then another one. I finish off the bar. I barely have time to swallow before his lips crash down on mine, and I moan into his mouth, helpless.

I wish I could rewire my thoughts back to my boyfriend. Or that Callum was an abusive, awful man who had it coming. But this is not the case.

But the truth is, I can't.

The truth is, I don't think I ever could, even before I met Mal in

New York again. The cracks were always there, weeds slipping through them, even when Callum and I were a normal couple facing normal issues. I always compared him to Mal. I longed to feel Mal's lips on mine, his heady scent wrapped around me like a collar, owning me without even trying. The difference was, I didn't feel guilty, because the possibility of that ever happening seemed unlikely.

In the unlikely event.

I whimper as Mal takes my face in both his hands and deepens the kiss, growling like a beast. His tongue meets mine halfway, and my eyelids drop shut.

My phone pings, and I rip my mouth from his, snapping out of the moment. I'm cupping my face as I scurry to the breakfast nook. I flip it over to see the number on the screen.

Callum.

It's like he has a sixth sense. How did he know?

"Hey, love," he says, sounding cheerful when I answer. "Summer called me. She told me about Richards running off. What a wanker. She suggested I hop on a plane to keep you company. What do you reckon? Still want me to come for New Year's?"

I look up and see Mal with his elbow propped on the side of the fridge, raising his eyebrows in a *really?* look. I shake my head. My thighs are cemented together with dried chocolate. *What have I done?*

I look away from Mal, clearing my throat.

"Yes!" I say, trying to match his jovial tone. "Please come over. I would love to have you here."

When I end the call, I press my forehead against the breakfast nook and close my eyes. Do I get a special award for being so stupid? A discount at my local library? Anything? Seems a bit surreal I'd be left to my own devices after pulling something like this.

I need to tell him. I need to tell Callum.

"I just want you to know," I say shakily, my lips moving on the surface of the counter, "that this meant absolutely *nothing*."

"Say that to your puckered nipples and wet cunt, darlin'." Mal breezes into his bedroom on a whistle, picking up the half-eaten triangle sandwich on his way.

All the lights in the house turn on at the same time. The microwave *dings*. The television turns on, and two guys in suits talk heatedly about football.

The electricity is back. Mal lets out a sigh of contempt.

"Real funny, Kiki. I'm trying here, too, but you see that she's stubborn."

I whip my head toward him and scowl. "You think your dead wife wants you to hook up with me?"

"I know she does," he says, matching my thunderous look.

"How so?"

"She loves me, and I love…" he trails off, slanting his head sideways. "I love chocolate bars. Love is like that, don't you feel? Deadly, kind of. The more you prolong and stretch it like a leather leash, the more painful when it finally snaps and hits you. When you're ready for answers, let me know."

A NOTE FROM THE CHOCOLATE BAR

Best. Day. Ever.

Present

Mal

I T'S NOT THAT I DIDN'T ANTICIPATE HER REACTION.

But it still shocks me, because while Rory is swimming (or drowning, I don't know) in the eternal question of whether she can respect and forgive herself at some point for what she's done to Shiny Boyfriend, I mourn the fact that she hasn't yet broken up with him.

I'm locked outside my room now, Rory inside and refusing to speak to me. I can still taste her sweet, earthy pussy on my tongue, along with the chocolate.

This situation is ridiculous, which, of course, I don't point out.

I make it a game. I put trays of food at her door, like she's a prisoner. I knock every now and again and ask her if she needs anything.

Alas, Rory is a tough prisoner.

At bedtime, I get a call from Ryner telling me Rory and I need to pack our suitcases and head to Greece. Why? Let me tell you why. Because Richards is on his way from Thailand to Spinalonga Island.

"Spinalonga?" I hold the phone between my shoulder and ear, right in the middle of dying lollipop sticks pink above the sink. The artificial color drips everywhere, including on my clothes, but I still dip the sticks in paint meticulously, because those sticks need to be bright pink, glittery, and ready for usage.

As for me? I'm living the rock-n'-roll life, clearly, thankyouverymuch.

"The leper colony. He read a book about it." Ryner *tsks* on the other line.

"You mean he watched a video," I deadpan.

Ryner laughs humorlessly. "Probably, man. Probably."

"Did you tell him there aren't any lepers there *now*?" I ask.

Something is obviously going on with Ashton Richards, and no one is saying anything, because everyone has a horse in the race to produce his new album.

"He's not listening. He's gotta check into rehab."

"No shit."

But I don't further promote the idea of Richards checking in, because that'd kill the entire Rory Project. I'd have to finish the songs and hand them to Jeff. Which means Rory would run back to America before we sort our situation. That's simply not a possibility I am willing to entertain.

"I still think we can chain him to my sofa and make it work," I say.

"Yeah? Go pick him up, then. I'll throw you a nice bonus when this is all over."

"Ryner." I squeeze my fingertips into my eyelids, smearing pink dye all over my face. "I can't leave Tolka. It's in our contract. You know exactly why."

We go back and forth a few more minutes before Ryner asks me how Callum is doing in that smug way that implies I have a lot to lose if I say no. I ask him who the feck Callum is, and he tells me he's Rory's boyfriend.

I know that, but I like to pretend he means so little to me, his name hasn't registered. I know what Ryner is doing here. He's reminding me that Greece is a great opportunity to whisk Rory away from Callum, who is planning to come here tomorrow, on New Year's Eve, and save their relationshit.

I mean, *ship*. Relationship. Not like I shat all over it or anything.

Look, I want to be better than knowingly sabotaging their relationship.

Actually…no. That's not true. It *sounds* like something honorable to say, but the truth is, I don't want to be honorable about this duel. I would kick and bite and break every man-rule to have Rory. Throw sand in his eyes. Anything to win.

'Tis the truth, and the worst part is, I still sleep at night like a baby. (Though I don't know why they say that. Babies are horrible sleepers. Sleeping like a knocked-out drunken sod sounds more accurate.)

Once Ryner and I come to agreement, I slide Rory a napkin with the news under my bedroom door and slip out of the house to say my goodbyes before I leave Tolka, even if it's just for twenty-four hours.

When I'm back, Rory is all packed, sullen and ready to go. It looks like she's been crying the entire time since I fucked her with a candy bar.

I feel awful, but I'll feel worse if she ends up with Prince Preppy Pants. He will bore her to death, and I don't want her death on my conscience.

I drive us to the airport in complete silence. It's only when we get comfortable in our first-class seats on the plane that Rory opens her mouth again. I think she is about to tell me I'm a cunt, but she surprises me.

"How did I get my scar?"

I spit my soda all over my lap. A sincere *burn in hell* would have been nicer than this loaded question. I frown to buy time, but my heart rate accelerates.

"You're asking me?"

She nods, staring me down.

"Didn't you say you were born with it?" In my head, I envision myself running with a cart through aisles in the supermarket, desperately shopping for more time.

"That's my mother's version, and I'm starting to doubt it. Ms. Patel from the newsagents told me there's a horrible story behind my scar. Your grandfather walked in before she had a chance to tell me."

"Ms. Patel also believes in ghosts and that people with blue eyes see everything in a blue hue."

That's a flat-out lie, actually, but I'd rather jump off this plane using Rory's knickers as a parachute than hurt her the way the truth would.

It is not that I don't want to tell her the truth, but when so much of it is about to be unveiled, it is best to wait, to ease her into a situation, then sit her down properly.

"I still want to know what the rumor is," she insists.

"Yes, of course, I suppose. Thing is, I'm not exactly attuned to small-town gossip."

I don't add that most of the gossip in Tolka relates to me.

"But your grandfather knows," she persists. "Why would he keep that from me?"

"To protect you?" I pick up a travel magazine and pretend to flip through it.

In my head, there are red sirens blaring everywhere. *FUCK, FUCK, FUCK.* Mini Mals are running around, yanking their hair out.

She's onto us! Somebody do something!

"I'm going to ask him." She taps her knee with her fingers, munching on her lip.

"You do that."

She stares at me skeptically. I think she knows I know, and it's killing me not to be completely honest with her. I wish I could telepathize to her that I will explain, soon. That there are stages. That she doesn't know everything about me yet, and before she makes up her mind, she needs to really understand.

We all pitied the American girl with the backpack and the camera and the broken dream.

I screwed her and kissed her and promised her marriage and took all her secrets, while not giving her the only truth she ever cared about and came all the way to Ireland for.

Rory clamps her mouth shut, then opens it again.

"You won't tell me whose birthday it was, and you refuse to tell me about the rumors surrounding me. You won't talk about Kath's death. Can you at least show me a song so I can take a picture of it for my project? It's coming together well, by the way. Thanks for asking."

I know it must be a nightmare for her to live in Tolka.

People either hate her for being the girl Kathleen was forsaken for or pity her for being the girl who made that thing with Glen happen. Between me being a massive, purple dick and Richards being Richards, Rory—the only person who takes this project seriously—is helpless.

I lift my arse from the seat and take my notebook out of my back pocket, handing it to her. She opens it to a random page, her green eyes gliding over the text, line by line, as she moves her lips in the shape of the words.

He calls you love.
I call you darlin'.
You say you're happy.
I think you're drowning.
We promised each other so many things.
Now I don't even think you know what they mean.

Call the press.
You're a mess.
You make me so fucking depressed.
Trying to make everything right, shiny, pretty, and tight.
So tired of waiting for you to see the light.

He calls you love.
I call you darlin'.
You say you're safe.
I think you're spiraling.
If you want the truth, kiss me hard.
Or at the very least, lower your guard.

She gives it back to me and looks away to the window. The sky is wooly and gray.

"I'll find my truth, Mal. I will." She ignores the words she just read.

My chest tightens. I seriously underestimated Shiny Boyfriend's grip on her. Or maybe it's not him. Maybe it's the idea of him. The idea of me. Maybe dating an idiot who spent the last decade making a living writing hate songs about her doesn't sound too hot.

We look in opposite directions.

"My truth shouldn't be conditional," she whispers.

I take a deep breath. "Neither should your promise."

By the time we land in Crete, Richards is back from Spinalonga and throwing a party in his presidential suite. Earlier, he tweeted that he was in town, and a bunch of starfuckers brought down the hotel's glass doors, leaving them shattered on the lobby floor. Then Richards sent some of his staff out to pick up the hottest groupies and invite them up to his suite, making them dispose of their phones at the entrance.

Rory and I walk in on him getting a blow job from a lass while fingering her friend's arse. Which, naturally, makes Rory roll her eyes and squeeze hand sanitizer into her palm, passing it over to me. I shake my head.

"Not gonna wash my hands until the next time they're on you."

"You mean, never?" she asks dryly.

I give her a little smile. Sometimes we say things because they sound right. That's what she's doing right now. I think we both know there will be a second time, and soon.

She shivers, and not from the cold, because she hasn't been particularly cold since she came to Ireland—something I hope she notices. Knowing full well that Richards' cooperation is what my entire Rory Project depends on, I saunter in, grip the jerk's shoulder, and yank him from his blow job. The girl is still bobbing her head with an O-shaped mouth when I shove Richards onto the plush leather sofa by the wall, crowding him with my arms crossed over my chest.

"Party's over. We're getting back to work." I kick the sole of his sliders.

He mimics my movements, knotting his arms together, pouting. "Ever been to Thailand, Mal?"

"Can't say I have."

"Well, I just came back, and let me tell you, it's a magical place. I had a lot of time to think about shit."

He was in Thailand exactly twenty minutes, during which he rode an elephant, made an embarrassing video, and decided to visit Greece on a whim.

"I broke up with my girlfriend—who is a duchess, by the way—and now I'm all about finding the one."

"Do you think you're going to find her in a stranger's asshole?" I ask evenly.

Rory nearly coughs out a lung behind me, a combination of laughter and horror.

"Look," Richards rolls his pretty-boy, bluest-blue eyes, "you got this writing-songs part under control. You told me yourself that the songs are all done and read—"

This time I cut him off by kicking him in the shin before he's able to do some serious damage. He shuts up.

"Your boss paid you extra to do this documentary project," I remind him. "He paid me. He paid Rory. You're screwing up her work, too. You can burn through money and blow and women all you want after we're done with this. You have all the time in the world."

He laughs bitterly. "No one has all the time in the world."

I don't want to start explaining figures of speech to him. He is not my spawn. So I just look at him, waiting.

"Anyway, Ireland depresses me," he whines, throwing an arm over his face like a teenage girl who just found out her crush likes the cock, too. "You live in the middle of fucking nowhere, dude. No offense, but you actually do. It's, like, scientific."

"Do you know what the word *science* means?" I ask, just as Rory slides into the conversation diplomatically.

"If we put a good dent in the project, we can all go somewhere else for a while." She claps her hands together and appears by my side. "A vacation."

"Really?" Richards drops his arm, his eyes lighting up.

This feels a lot like we're his parents, promising him a trip to Disneyland if he makes good grades. Only there's no way we could conceive someone like him, because I've met goats more sophisticated than this man.

I hitch one shoulder up, not correcting Rory's soon-to-be-broken promise.

Richards frowns. "Sex Slave chick needs to give it to me in writing. I don't want her to run off with her boyfriend and fuck it up for us."

I turn around to Rory, but she is no longer standing next to me. I think she got a phone call. Probably her boyfriend whining because he can't see her after all.

When I turn back to Richards, he's jumping to his feet, buttoning his jeans, and tucking a joint into the corner of his mouth. He slaps my back.

"Thanks, man. I appreciate you coming to get me. I was getting this weird vibe, you know? Like you didn't like me very much. Like we didn't *gel*."

He says the word *gel* like I say the word *cunt*.

I remove his hand from me. "Couldn't be farther from the truth."

Rory

Double shit with a side of crap.

Callum is here. In this building. Checking into a room with the receptionist.

Summer's work, I'm sure.

After Mal slipped me the napkin with the new developments and our sudden Greek trip, I beckoned Summer for an emergency freak-out. I told her about the chocolate bar incident, which prompted her to slap Mal with the pet name Mal-Teaser. I also heard her plugging her vibrator into the charger and am pretty sure she was swiping left and right on Tinder, trying to find a playmate for the night.

"Please don't do something stupid." I closed my eyes and threw my head skyward, praying silently.

"Oh, honey, that's rich," she said, "considering you just out-stu-pided an avocado after less than a week in Ireland. I'm trying to make things better for you. Trust me, okay?"

I didn't know if I should. I still don't.

I love Summer, but she has very precise, very definite ideas for my life, and I don't necessarily agree with them all.

She must've told Callum where I was, redirecting him from his pending trip to Ireland to Greece. And he, the charming boyfriend that he is, decided to surprise me. When I got a text from him, I couldn't stay in the room watching the face-off between Mal and Ashton. I ran down to the lobby, threw my arms over Callum's neck, and pretended to be elated to see him.

As I should be.

"Missed you, love. Have you lost a little weight?" He frowns, chuckling. "Looks good on you,"

He leans down and gives me his customary peck on the mouth. The kiss seals my guilt on my lips, like a closed envelope.

Mal kissed those lips yesterday afternoon.

Right after shoving a chocolate bar into them that had been shoved between my *other* pair of lips.

"Let's get you settled!" I grab his hand.

I already know I'm going to tell Callum what happened. And I already know he is probably—rightfully—going to break up with me. What I have yet to find out is whether it's possible to live with myself after doing what I did to Callum.

I tug him toward the elevators, frazzled, and punch the button five hundred times, turning back to him with a giant, fake, plastic smile.

"Yay!" I wave my fist around. "Reunited. Again. Awesome."

Just shut up, you idiot. You're making it worse.

"Rory." Callum's voice is laced with worry, his eyebrows pulled together. "Are you drunk? You know I don't take well to public lewdness."

"Totally sober." I let out a nervous laugh.

The elevator doors slide open, and, of course, Mal is standing on the other side, looking devilishly gorgeous—for a homewrecker, that is.

"I was looking for you." His expression softens until he notices Callum behind me.

His whole face changes again. It's painful to watch. He looks… disappointed. Not that he has any right to be.

"Malachy," Callum greets him from behind me, stepping into the elevator. I step in as well, swiping the electronic card over the screen and pushing the button for Callum's floor.

"Shiny Boyfriend," Mal answers, his voice dripping ice.

"How's the writing going?" Callum asks.

I jump into the conversation before Mal gets the chance to offend Callum.

"Well, Richards is flying back to Ireland, so Mal can see to his arrival. You and I can stay here."

I just want to save face. Truth is, in approximately ten minutes, I am going to deliver some harsh truths to Callum, after which neither of us will have the ability to stomach my existence.

Tonight is New Year's Eve, and the party Ashton was planning with Mal back in Ireland has been canceled. It would have been a great opportunity to take pictures, but clearing the air with Cal is of higher importance.

"That's a wonderful idea." Callum smiles down at me, and my heart breaks into a trillion pieces.

You did this. You basked in Mal's warmth, not even realizing he was burning everything around you.

"It really is," Mal agrees, shifting toward me. "There's only one, tiny obstacle standing in the way."

"Which is?" I narrow my eyes.

"Reality," he deadpans. "Richards and I have decided to stay here until Monday, too. You know, change of scenery and all. Great way to get the creative juices flowing." Mal grins down at me wolfishly.

Must.

Not.

Kill.

The.

Gorgeous.

Poet.

My jaw locks so hard it's about to snap, and it occurs to me that Mal is just crazy enough to tell Callum what happened before I get the chance to. Mal is probably reading my mind, because the way he looks at me says *trouble.*

"Well, we'll get out of your way, Malachy. Rory and I certainly have a lot of catching up to do."

Callum turns to me and drops a kiss on my head, no doubt thinly veiling his sexual intentions.

"No truer statement has been spoken in this elevator." Mal smirks, looking skyward, shaking his head.

Bastard. Why can't I like the sane one? Why?

I turn my head to flash Mal a warning look, but he refuses eye contact with me, staring straight ahead.

The elevator dings, and Mal gets out, walking right behind us, even taking Callum's suitcase and rolling it along the corridor. "Before I forget, there's been a change of plans," he says. "Richards is throwing a party tonight in his penthouse after all. Stars are coming from all over Europe. I think Alex Winslow is cutting short his vacation with his wife and kids in the south of France just to say hi. It's going to be wild, and therefore not a place for a *sweet* lady like our Rory."

He knows there's no chance in hell I'm going to leave the hotel now. This is the stuff Ryner dreams about. The kind of crazy, old-school, rock-star party full of familiar faces, where people swing from chandeliers and write songs in the corner of the room and create plaster molds of penises and drive Rolls Royces into swimming pools.

We stop at Callum's door. I look up at him and play with my nose hoop. He shakes his head with a smile.

"Let's stay and go to the party. Who cares where we are, as long as I'm inside you?"

Mal is standing in front of us, watching the entire exchange. I want to throw up. I don't know why Callum said what he just did, but that makes me feel even worse than I did a second ago.

I rise on my tiptoes, giving Callum a chaste peck on the cheek.

"Let's get inside," I whisper brokenly.

I slam the door in Mal's face, leaving him out. Physically. Figuratively.

Leaving him with the lies.

With the secrets.

With the weight of his affair with married Maeve.

And the guilt of keeping Kath's death from me.

With our sins.

When I turn from the door to face Callum, I drop the charade.

"We need to talk."

Present

Rory

I NEVER GET TO TELL CALLUM ABOUT WHAT HAPPENED WITH Mal. As soon as we shut the door behind us, he gets a call he has to take and locks himself outside on the balcony. He uses his hushed, I'll-make-meatballs-out-of-you, hedge-fund-analyst tone that makes my skin crawl.

The phone call lasts nearly two hours and reaches octaves better suited for the jungle. I feel sorry for him that he has to work on New Year's Eve. But by the time he's done, I'm getting ready to hop into the shower before the party.

When he walks back in, his face flushed and pouty, he glances at my half-naked figure and perks up, plastering a lazy smile where a scowl rested seconds ago.

"Me. You. Shower. Sex. Let's go."

"We need to talk."

"I don't reckon anything is more important than a quick shag, especially with your hipbones poking out Bella Hadid-style. Despair suits you." He runs his tongue over his upper teeth. "Go on. You can't tell me you haven't been longing for my cock all this time."

I sit on the edge of the bed, hunched and defeated, racking my brain for how to deliver the news—how to rip us open like a mummified body and dump all the internal organs.

I hate that Summer was right in her prediction.

The napkin didn't mean nothing.

It meant *everything.*

Mal warned me years ago that he was going to break whatever I had going with someone else if we met again.

And he kept good on his promise.

Callum tugs at my sleeve, and there's something in his expression that makes my heart rattle my ribs like they're metal bars.

I burst out in tears, covering my face, feeling ashamed not only for what I did to him, to *me,* but also for being such a coward. For not coming clean like a grown-up. He stands there, the summer blush vanishing from his face, watching me.

"All right then, no shagging. I didn't think the idea would upset you quite so much…" He scratches his head, trying to make light of things. "I *did* give my willy curls a good trim, if that's the reason you're distraught."

I try to laugh to make him feel better, but the truth is, we don't have time right now to have the conversation we obviously need to have. I slip into the shower and turn the water to sizzling hot, staring ahead at the powder blue tiles with their tiny cracks of old age, wondering when it all went so wrong.

I know exactly when. The minute I took this job.

Because being around Mal and not wanting him is impossible.

I can deny myself of a lot of things, but he's never been one of them.

Mal makes me burn. Crackle. Melt. My love for him is thick and sturdy. Metallic and alive. A beating organ, co-existing with my heart.

I get out of the shower and face Callum, who is choosing cufflinks from a little velvet box he takes with him everywhere.

"When we get back, we really need to talk," I mutter.

He answers without turning to look at me, his voice surprisingly dead.

"You're the boss."

Spin the bottle.

We are playing spin the bottle.

This party is a total shitshow.

And Alex Winslow never showed up.

"Winslow?" Richards puffed on a suspicious-looking cigarette and laughed when I asked him about it. "His idea of partying is curry night in front of the telly with the wifey. A total straightedge, that fucker," he said with the worst impression of a cockney accent to ever be recorded on planet Earth.

Instead, the music is crappy (mostly Ashton's stuff), the place is ninety-nine-percent semi-naked women in togas, and there's a self-proclaimed tattoo artist taking spontaneous customers on Richards' rotating bed while it's rotating, which anyone with three brain cells can see is not the best idea of the century.

There are servants walking around the suite offering platters of grapes, cheese, crackers, champagne, and schnapps. New Year's Eve balloons adorn the room in gold, silver, and black.

And as I mentioned, we are sitting in a circle, playing spin the bottle like the big, screwed-up, dysfunctional pile of random people we are.

"Rules." An English chick with fake boobs and highlighted hair twirls like a fairy around the room, batting her eyelashes in every direction. "Since we have a proper couple here, we need to make sure they're both all right with seeing other people snogging their significant other."

She directs her big, hazel eyes at me and raises a daring eyebrow. I glance at Callum, fully expecting him to shut it down. That was one of the points I always brought up to Summer when I wanted to break up with him after we started seeing each other—his conservative, traditional streak that drives me nuts.

"I'm always up for a bit of fun." He smiles, much to my amazement.

He slices his gaze toward me, narrow-eyed, like this is some kind of test.

I glance at Mal across from me, briefly, so as not to raise any suspicion. His face is stoic, his eyes zeroed in on the empty champagne bottle between us. Maybe he's finally getting it. That it's not only because of Callum that I refuse to entertain the idea of us.

It's because he *is* Glen.

I'm starting to see that my father wasn't the lovable, village-drunk martyr I'd imagined him to be. The secrets and lies swarming around Tolka have a root, and that root might be his grave.

Everyone is staring at me now, assessing my reaction. This could go south fast, and I'm too old to cave to peer pressure. On the other hand, I can't pretend to be a prude. Not when Cal is game.

"Go on. You're the one who always tells me to lighten up." Callum elbows me with a chuckle.

There's a threat laced in his voice for the first time since I've known him, and I don't have time or the ability to crack it open and study its inside right now when I'm already tipsy.

I shrug in acceptance, and all the girls in the circle *woo-hoo* and *meow* like cats in heat. Callum is prime meat in this testosterone-deprived environment. Plus, Ashton looks too tanked and Mal too unattainable to promise any type of real action. The English chick goes as far as shimmying her boobs in Callum's direction and winking. Very understated.

"Are you good with seeing Rory snog other lads?" she taunts.

"No one can kiss her the way I do, love." He flashes her a predatory smirk.

Love. He calls everyone love. Mal is right. It's not romantic. It's kind of annoying.

"And what about other birds?" she pokes.

I choke on the beer I'm nursing, but say nothing,

"*Especially* birds." Callum laughs.

"And what about you? Are you open to kissing a bloke?" She continues grilling Callum.

She is flirting up a storm with my boyfriend. It occurs to me that I should be mad, but all I can muster is irritated apathy, like when you see someone being a bigot online, but all you can manage is *Liking* the comment that argues with them, not actually entering the exchange.

Callum clears his throat. "Let's keep it straight, yeah?"

Of course. Me kissing girls is great, but him kissing guys is out of the question.

"What about you?" British Bombshell turns to Ashton, who's sitting next to Mal. "Are you okay with snogging a bloke?"

Ashton gives a brief, nonchalant nod, sliding his gaze to Mal. Mal looks between British Bombshell and Ashton, his face blank. I realize I am holding my breath, waiting for his answer, when he opens his mouth.

"I don't discriminate when it comes to hating and fucking."

"Hallelujah!" Bombshell giggles.

I cross my jeans-clad legs, feeling my panties lined with wetness. I don't know why the idea of him kissing Ashton is so erotically pleasing to me. Maybe because they're both so aesthetically beautiful. Maybe because I know Mal hates Ashton, and that Mal is the kind of guy who can hate-fuck anyone into a coma, despite his eccentric, contradictory nature. And suddenly, I'm imagining Mal dicking Ashton from behind, and the air gets hot and heavy and incredibly thick in my lungs.

"Rory?" Callum turns to me.

"Hmm?"

"You're fanning yourself. Is there an issue with the air conditioning?"

Shit. I drop my hand and steal a glance at Mal again. His purple eyes shine as they laser their way into my pupils. *Busted.*

Ashton is the first to spin the bottle. It lands on a Greek brunette. They both crawl on all fours, meeting halfway in the middle of the twelve-person circle. Knowing they're about to set the bar for the rest of us, they grin at each other conspiratorially and plunge in with force.

Callum and I exchange looks when we realize it's much more than just kissing. Richards' hand slides into her shirt, and she cups his erection through his jeans as they kiss deeply. She lifts one of her legs and straddles him in the middle of the circle.

"All right," Callum says in his cheerful tone. "Let's break it off before someone gets pregnant."

Everyone laughs nervously, and the flushed brunette scurries back to her spot. British Bombshell spins the bottle, eyeing Callum like he's pizza to someone in ketosis, and sure enough, karma decides to spit in my face, and the bottle lands on him.

Maybe it's because I don't have the right to be angry, but I'm oddly okay with this outcome. It doesn't even surprise me much. Mal says Kathleen has been messing with his life in a roundabout way since she died, and maybe he's right. So many coincidences happen when we're together. It's like we're sewn into one piece, entwined in the same pattern, on the same path, and every time someone else tries to get close to us, life rips it to shreds.

Callum searches my face—for approval or jealousy, I have no clue. My pulse escalates. There's a ball of guilt the size of my fist lodged in my throat.

I give him a small nod. "Make the most of it, stud."

They both shoot to their feet and meet outside the circle, by the bed. He cups her cheek like he does to me when he wants sex. It is technical, familiar.

"Hi." He smiles down at her.

"Hi," she breathes.

I realize I'm smiling, too, because they're cute together. But

I shouldn't think that way. When his lips meet hers, half the girls in the circle turn their heads to watch me. I force myself to stare at Callum and the girl, willing myself to feel something—*anything*— but it's pointless. It's like watching a TV show, a half-engaging one at that. After ten seconds of a slow, sensual, French kiss with tongue and awkwardness and a healthy dose of anxiety, they break away, and something in the air crackles with tension. She's still clinging to his body as he takes a step back, shaking his head like he can't believe he did that.

He glances at me. My heart breaks, but for all the wrong reasons.

She can make him happy, and I'm standing in her way.

Not for long, I tell myself. Callum deserves more, and it's time he gets it.

"Okay, thank you for the PG-13 exhibit of sloppy first base." Ashton yawns. "I'll make sure to recommend your asses next time Ed Sheeran needs to write a church-friendly song. Brandy, your turn."

Brandy is his assistant, I discover. The one who gave Mal her number back in Tolka. Yup, same one with the long, tan legs and flaming red hair that looks like fine cherry wine. She leans forward, her cleavage more generous than Oprah Winfrey's charity work, and spins the bottle. I already know where it's going to land. My heart feels like an iron fist trying to break the bony wall of my ribcage.

Thud, thud, thud.

And then…*it happens.*

The bottle lands on Mal, and Brandy's smile is so wide, I can comfortably fit a baseball bat into it. Horizontally. *Not* that I'm thinking about doing that.

Maybe just a little.

She crawls to the center of the circle, probably wanting a rehash of the way Ashton manhandled the Greek goddess, but Mal stands up, walks toward her, and yanks her up. *By her ponytail.* He does it so casually, so effortlessly, I hear a collective sigh from all the women in the room and realize I contributed to it with my own little moan.

Mal looks down at her. She tilts her head, a seductive smile stamped on her lips.

"What are the odd—" She can't even pronounce the S before his lips smash into her mouth, and they kiss so deeply, so brutally, so cruelly, I want to cry. It feels like a tiger slashing my chest with its pointy claws, ribbons of blood spurting from my heart.

I'm not okay.

Actually, I feel like I can't breathe.

When his tongue slides past her lips and conquers her mouth, I inhale sharply and force myself not to squeeze my eyes shut. Her moans and groans of pleasure seep into me like poison.

When they're finally done sucking each other's faces, Callum clears his throat. I turn and realize he's been looking at me the entire time.

"Enjoy the show?" His lips twitch in annoyance.

"More than the company," I mutter.

I'm so fed up with his passive-aggressive BS. But I also acknowledge it is my fault for not spitting out what happened between Mal and me in Ireland. Though it wasn't my fault he had to be holed up with a business call. I tried. I couldn't do it twenty minutes before we left for the party.

Mal and Brandy go back to their places, and I can feel my face heating up, like I did something wrong.

"Rory, your turn," Callum clips.

I try to ignore his tone as I grab the bottle, look up at the ceiling, and say a silent prayer.

Please don't let it be Mal.

I'm fine with anyone else. Preferably a girl. Even kissing Ashton would be okay. He is cute, a rock star, and not conscious enough to even remember this tomorrow.

My fingers clench the bottle.

"Are you planning on spinning it, honey pie, or just staring at it, hoping it'll turn through the power of telepathy?" Ashton inquires, snickering.

I close my eyes and inwardly scold my no-show dad for the very first time since I was born.

Hey. So…we don't really know each other, but if you're up there, spare me the awkwardness. It's the least you can do.

I spin the bottle, suck in a deep breath, and watch. It turns and swirls one, two, three, four times before it lands on…

"Mal," Callum states with conviction.

"Ashton," Brandy says at the same time.

Of course, she wouldn't want me to kiss her crush.

Oh, and by the way, *Thanks, Glen.*

"I think it landed on Ashton," I contribute.

Though I have to say, on the off-chance Glen is up there, trying to make amends by pointing the bottle toward Ashton, he is not keeping sober in heaven, because it does seem like the bottle is pointing smack between Ashton and Mal.

"It's definitely pointing at Mal," Callum disagrees, tapping his smooth chin.

What the hell is he doing? I'm not stupid enough to actually ask this when we're with company.

"Guess it can only mean one thing." British Bombshell cackles like a hyena, staring at Callum with a look pregnant with lust.

Everyone here has a dog in this fight, and hers seems to be the hungriest, most vicious one.

"And what would that be?" Callum turns to her without patience.

"A three-way kiss," she purrs, twirling a lock of her hair over her finger.

"Yes!" Ashton pumps his fist in the air. "Fuck yes. Sex Slave and Pouty Poet in the same pot. Sign me up."

"Sex Slave?!" Callum loses his cool.

"Chillax, it's a pet name." Ashton laughs out a curling ribbon of smoke.

I swear I will get stoned just from kissing him.

"Works for me," Malachy says tonelessly.

I feel Callum giving me a shove toward the center of the circle.

"Go on, then," he says.

"Wait, I don't know about this," I mumble.

"We had this conversation!" the British girl cries. "Don't pussy out on us."

"Yeah, don't be a party pooper, Rory," Callum presses.

I turn toward him, scowling.

He shrugs, a private, secretive smirk on his lips. "You're not the only one who's good at sharing. That's good news, right?"

I walk toward Mal and Ashton, feeling my palms getting clammy.

"How are we going to do this?" I put my hands on my waist. "Do we want to start kissing just two people, and the third one will join in, or is it going to be…"

Without further ado, Ashton grabs the back of my head, pulls me in, and kisses me silly. He shoves his hot, alcohol-soaked tongue into my mouth, and that's when I realize we're all kind of drunk—Callum included for once.

Shitty music aside, Ashton Richards can kiss. I'm starting to enjoy it when I feel a second tongue wrestling its way into the mix, and now I have *two* tongues in my mouth. One of them is Malachy's, and I know exactly which one's which.

I can feel my clit swelling, my lower belly tingling in anticipation as we kiss slowly and passionately, Ashton nibbling at the corner of my mouth and Mal Frenching me to oblivion and back. It becomes clear that this is not a three-way kiss as much as it is two guys kissing one girl. They have minimal contact with each other, and they are here to serve me.

Just when I begin to wonder if I'm the only one getting carried away in the situation, Ashton puts a hand on my waist and plasters me to his body. I feel his thick, throbbing erection against my thigh and let out a groan. Mal is having none of it and pulls at my other side, tugging me close. I'm nestled between them, feeling hot, liquid lust slithering down to my panties.

I should feel ashamed, or self-conscious, or embarrassed, and I do—I feel all three, I swear. But I mostly feel like taking my clothes off and kissing every inch of their bodies until they screw me from both sides. My mouth is full, and my nipples are erect and painfully sensitive.

It occurs to me that this is the shot of a lifetime—the one Ryner wants to see on the cover of *Rolling Stone*—of his rock star, his song-writer, and his photographer making out fervently. But he can't have this shot, because all three of his artists have gone rogue, and there's no one to take the picture.

We kiss for long minutes before I feel someone tugging me back by my shirt. I snap my eyes open and find out it is Ashton. I also realize he's a step away from us. He's not a part of the kiss anymore. He hasn't been a part of the kiss for a while, I notice when my mind adjusts to the fact that there was only one tongue in my mouth for a few good seconds, if not minutes. My legs are clasped around Mal's thigh. I've been riding it. *Jesus.*

"C'mon," he whispers to both of us through a mostly closed mouth. "You've been soloing for a full minute now. People are starting to rub their genitals on the floor to get off."

My eyes flare, and I look over at Callum, who stands up from the circle, turning toward the door. He grabs my camera before dashing out, and the thick, red cloud of lust I'm engulfed in evaporates. In a knee-jerk reaction, I launch myself after him, chasing him down the corridor.

"Callum, wait!"

He thunders toward the elevators, swinging the camera here and there. By the time I catch him punching the elevator button, I'm out of breath. I put a hand on his shoulder, but he turns around, swatting it.

"Don't touch me."

"Please," I beg.

I don't even know what I'm begging for. It's pretty obvious what happened there got out of hand, that Mal and I shared more than a kiss. There were feelings there, too.

"Please, what? Please, let me make a fool out of you, Callum? Please, let me go suck someone else's cock? Please, leave me alone so I can pick up where I left off with a man who so very willingly let me go?"

He screams in my face, and he is red and angry and no longer the Callum I know and feel comfortable and safe with. The elevator dings, and he walks in. I follow him.

"*I* wasn't going to let you go, Rory. I was supposed to be the last man standing. I put up with your bullshit attire and stupid quirky dreams and boring colleagues."

He stares at the corridor, the elevator doors still open. I don't know what to tell him. I don't even know if it's worth coming clean about what happened, because this is a breakup, and even though I did something vile, he is being no less despicable.

That night on the balcony, at that Christmas party, I took one look at Mal and knew with certainty what he'd said was true.

Loving someone is willingly accepting that they can destroy you.

Mal ruined me.

I wrecked Callum.

I think you were put on this Earth to destroy me, Callum said all those months ago.

Was that the truth, or did Callum simply want to be destroyed?

"I wanted to play the stupid game so I could see how you'd react. You didn't care when I snogged that cow over there." He points sideways to where we were, in the presidential suite.

I flinch at his offhanded insult. The doors slide shut, and we begin to ride down to his room.

"But when Mal kissed that bird, you almost exploded. Then you went and continued kissing him long after Richards withdrew."

"I'm sorry," I mumble, cursing Summer inwardly for creating all this mess, even though I know I'm more responsible for it than anyone else. "God, Callum, I never meant to hurt you."

Even *I* know how lame I sound. I wish I could turn back time.

I'd change one thing and one thing only—I wouldn't have touched Mal before I broke up with Cal.

The elevator dings, and Callum steps outside and turns to face me.

"By the way, if you'd waited just a little longer, you could have broken my heart *and* my bank account, walking away with half my shit." He shoves his hand into his front pocket, produces a small, velvety black box, and throws it at me. I catch it, but don't open it, already aware of what must be sitting there.

God, Callum.

"I bought another one in London, because the first one was left in that godforsaken dumpster in Ireland, and I wanted to propose as soon as possible." He stops, looks down. "But not soon enough, apparently."

My eyes are full of tears. My head hurts. I'm losing it. I'm breaking apart, and suddenly, all I want to do is make him feel better, no matter the cost. I take a step toward him, but he shakes his head. He punches the button to call the elevator when the doors begin to close, not quite done hurting me.

"This is the line." He juts his chin to the threshold between the elevator and the corridor. "You don't get to pass it anymore. We're done here, Rory. We've been done from the beginning. I was always temporary, a starter to pass the time until the entrée arrived."

I fall to my knees, letting out a sob.

He slings the camera into the elevator, and it lands next to me.

"You're always so obsessed with taking the perfect picture. Well, I took photos of your little threesome. That'll keep your slimy boss happy. You're welcome."

I look up, my eyes blazing with shame and anger.

He is going far.

Too far.

Twisting the knife in my chest, watching me bleed.

Yet I'm full to the brim with guilt.

"I know we should break up. I know. But if it's the right thing to do, why does it hurt so bad?" I ask, feeling snot running down to my mouth.

Nothing about this situation is pretty, me included.

"Holding on to something that never existed is far more painful," he spits. "Trust me, Rory, I've tried."

A NOTE FROM SUMMER

Time to air the dirty laundry, and boy, there's a suspicious-looking stain the size of Alabama on my conscience.

Okay—insert deep, cleansing breath—here goes.

A month after Rory and Callum started dating, he dropped in unannounced while she was at work. It was supposed to be a surprise. He brought flowers and champagne and sashimi from her favorite sushi place and wore a bowtie—and not even in a hipster, looks-good-with-skinny-jeans kind of way. Rory was supposed to be home, but Ryner had called her in—some emergency about a pop star who lost a bunch of weight and decided she wanted a reshoot of her album cover.

Rory never turns down work. I think she'll die clutching her camera to her heart.

Anyway, so Callum knocked on the door with all this stuff, and I happened to answer it. I'd just broken up with the guy I'd been dating for three years who had cheated on me *that day*. Suffice it to say, I was not in a good headspace.

Callum stuttered, apologized, and said he'd drop in at her work. I laughed, knowing she'd probably take the opportunity to dump him if he did that.

We ended up sharing the bottle of champagne Callum brought. He wasn't much of a drinker. That's what he told me, anyway, but he said he was feeling really on edge. He said he knew Rory was going to break up with him. He thought she found him boring and too straightedge and overtly proper.

He thought correctly.

Rory *did* find him boring. And she always compared him to Mal. Which grated on my nerves, because yes, Mal was awesome, gorgeous, and great in the sack, but that was over, and it was time to move on.

When she came back from Ireland all those years ago, she showed me the pictures she took of him. I had a brilliant idea of how to help her get over him. I told her to come up with negative things about Mal and write them on the back of the pictures, so every time she thought about hopping on a plane and begging him to be with her (which happened more often than logically acceptable), she'd remember.

But all we could come up with was that he was a flirt and tried (and succeeded) to be really good in bed. It was useless. He was perfect. Other than, of course, the fact that he'd let her go.

Anyway, back to Callum and me. That night, one bottle of champagne led to two others.

"I don't get it. I have demons, too, you know?" he said. "I'm not the squeaky-clean bastard she thinks I am. I can be a horrible person, Summer."

"I don't believe that," I said.

"I'm selfish," he replied.

"We all are."

"Me more than most."

That was the last thing he told me before his mouth descended on mine.

We slept together.

He cheated on her.

I cheated on her.

It was brief, quick, four-minutes-and-he-came sex. So anti-climactic in every sense of the word. I still consider it the worst thing

I've ever done. And I wasn't even close to climaxing. I didn't enjoy it, but Callum had always been the fantasy—well-bred, well-endowed, and well-hung. Not to mention, the guy in a suit was the eighth wonder of the world, I'm pretty sure. It was a moment of weakness.

"See?" he said as he put his shoes on in a hurry. "I told you. Selfish."

I said nothing to that.

"But I thought she'd be different, you know? I thought she'd get me out of that behavioral pattern. I don't know. Maybe I have a sex addiction."

I stopped answering him because I didn't pity him. I had my own problems, my own issues with life.

The thing is, I didn't know she would come back home, plop down next to me on the couch, notice the roses and sashimi on the counter, the traces of the masculine cologne he'd left behind, and say: "You're right. I'm so stupid. I should just get over Mal and give this thing with Callum my best shot."

That's what she said when I could still smell the rubber of her boyfriend's condom wafting from my pajamas, even after I took a shower. And Callum wasn't doing much better guilt-wise. I'd watched from the window half an hour earlier as he shoved himself into the back of an Uber, on the verge of sobbing.

"I think you should," I told Rory, thinking, *but please don't.*

So now you see why I'm carrying five tons of guilt on my shoulders.

I never thought it would pan out this way. And even though I want to throw up every time the three of us are together in the same room (which doesn't happen often), I just can't be the one to let her break up with Callum.

My conscience can't handle the failure of their relationship, no matter the reason. But secretly? If you asked me in a closed room—padded and soundproof—what I thought, I'd tell you my best friend, whom I love to death, is a brat.

She should just choose a guy and put everyone out of their misery.

I wish I had a pouty napkin boy who would rip the world apart to be with me.

I wish I had a rich, selfish-but-irresistible boy who would do anything he could to make sure Napkin Boy couldn't.

Present

Mal

I T IS WORTH MENTIONING HOW I ENDED UP WRITING SONGS FOR A living, when initially, I made having people beg to buy my songs somewhat of a competitive sport.

The answer—as it is to many questions—is Rory.

After she left, I worked through the pain. I wrote songs about love, and about hate, and about indifference. About loneliness and alcohol and the dark corners of my soul that frequently sent a hostile breeze through the rest of my body.

Hundreds of songs became thousands of songs, and thousands of songs became something bigger than me. Like a monster in my closet, lurking every night. Every song became a demon, and each demon was out for my blood.

I bled onto the pages until there were no more words to be written. Still, I wouldn't sell them. I couldn't sell them because I didn't want to change my circumstances. I didn't want to become big and famous and rich (not that I thought I would, but one can't take any chances). I didn't want to brush shoulders with Ashton Richards and his likes. I wanted to busk till I died, and come back home to my small cottage, and live a life where I didn't chase inspiration—it chased me. Where my art didn't stem from the need to have a bigger house or a fancier car or more money in the bank. I did it because I wanted to, a luxury not many paid artists have. It helped that I'd never been a particularly materialistic person.

But then the accident happened.

Katherine died. But before she did, there were a series of surgeries that required specialists to fly out from Switzerland and America and whatnot. The medical bills began to pile up. Mam and Elaine, Kathleen's mother, needed a place to live. There was shite to buy and people to pay, and I felt the world cornering me into a place I couldn't get out of.

So I sold out.

I unchained my demons and sold them to others as pets. These people put leashes on those demons, slapped them with a cheery tune, and sold them to the masses as Billboard hits.

I sold out, hoping Rory would hear, listen, make the connection, and hopefully find me.

It was the kind of stupid, boyish hope I'd admire in a fictional, hopeless character, but hate in myself. Then again, what were the odds of her not deciphering the unmistakable words?

"...summer rain on Drury Street. Stupid me, I thought you were mine to keep."

"...underneath the stars, you ask, do you believe in God? Sometimes I do, sometimes I don't, but after we're through, I think I won't."

"Across the ocean, there's a girl, made out of marshmallow and cyanide and shiny dew."

Then I thought, I don't know, maybe she simply hadn't had the chance to listen to some of the BIGGEST FUCKING BILLBOARD HITS IN THIS DECADE because she had something against the radio and YouTube and TV and Western culture.

But I promised myself not to be bitter—especially after finding out Rory hadn't, in fact, sent me the pictures and letter. She might've written those nasty-ass things on the backs of the photos—okay, fine, it was her handwriting, she did—but she didn't intend for me to see them. To *read* them.

As for the abortion—that's still a mystery. I want to ask her about it—if it's even true—but that means dragging her into World War III with her mother. As much as I think Debbie Jenkins is a cunt—and trust me, no part of me *doesn't* think that—I don't want Rory to hate her mam more than she already does.

I hear a knock on my door and ignore it, still staring at the ceiling. If it's Richards coming to get fucked, he's in for a disappointment. I may have pretended to be more into snogging a man than I actually am. Not that there's anything wrong with kissing men, but it doesn't get my dick hard.

I just knew Rory would get a kick out of it, and I wanted to feck her mind before I bedded the rest of her.

Speaking of the F-word, she's probably giving Shiny Boyfriend backdoor access right about now to make up for letting me own her mouth for long minutes. I wouldn't be surprised if I got her pregnant (possibly again) from kissing alone.

Bang, bang, bang. It's progressed from knocking.

I groan, unplastering myself from the mattress and making my way to the door. Why are there no peepholes in these hotel doors? What kind of feckery is that? I swing it open with a frown.

Rory is standing on my threshold, eyes swollen, nose red. She's been crying, and I'd pull her into my arms and hold her tight, but I need to know why she's here, what we even are anymore. She lets me shove a chocolate bar into her pussy one day, but is (rightfully) mad at me the other. Getting my hopes high is a sure recipe for a heartbreak. And I'm not talking three-to-four-pieces break. My heart would completely shatter if Rory decides to ditch both Callum and me.

It's like men are from Mars, women are from Venus, and Rory is from Pluto—faraway, mysterious, and nowhere near the rest of us.

I wait for her to say something. Preferably that Shiny Boyfriend finally got the hint, packed his Prada bags, and ran home to find himself a Botox-ridden lady friend who shares the same values. All three of them.

By the way, of all the shitty things I've done to get her—and the list is quite impressive for someone who doesn't fancy himself a psychopath—kissing her today the way I did in front of him was not one of them.

We were both lost in that kiss. *Found* in it, too.

She is standing outside.

I'm standing inside.

And between us is a small, significant distance I really need her to be brave enough to cross.

"Where is the napkin right now?" She sniffles, shifting between her feet.

I fish for it in my back pocket—I still take it everywhere I go—and hold it up. I've imagined this moment so many times. The feelings of triumph and certainty coursing through me. But now, in reality, I feel…morbidly pathetic.

That I still have it. Always. With me. *On* me.

She storms in, slamming the door behind her with a kick. I expect it to be like in the movies: she finds out—a little later than I'd have liked her to—that I'm the one, and now it's going to be fifty shades of every position in the *Kama Sutra*.

But this is not what happens.

What happens is she launches herself at me, throws her arms over my shoulders, and starts sobbing. Rory is not the sobbing type, so I wrap my arms around her and kiss her forehead, sheltering her from the rest of the world. If Arsehole Boyfriend wants her back, he is welcome to try to pry her out of my grasp.

"It's over," she breathes into my shoulder.

My heart is a mess of massive proportions. It hurts for her, but it's thrilled for me, too. I can feel my shirt getting wet from her tears and snot. Her entire body is quivering with wave after wave of misery, and my initial sense of triumph is replaced with dread.

"Darlin', it wasn't meant to be." I run my fingers through her hair. "He didn't stand a chance. It was always us."

She shakes her head into my shoulder, bawling even harder. "It's not just that. I mean, I'm horrified by what I've done to Callum, and I'm ashamed of what we did…" *Hiccup.* "I've tried to fight what we have for so long, Mal. I no longer remember what it feels like to let go and allow you to pull me down the rabbit hole."

I take her face in my hands, move her away so she can look me in the eye. "Newsflash, Rory: you're already there. There wasn't one moment in time, from the second we met, that you weren't mine. Just like I've always been yours."

She stares at me with emotions floating in and out of her pupils, like passengers on a train. I can see all of them.

Shame. Anger. Fear. Elation. Excitement.

"I kept the napkin, didn't I?" I twist a lock of her hair between my fingertips.

Marry me, Rory.

Then she does something so unexpected, I nearly swallow my tongue.

She drops to her knees and unbuckles my belt with frantic movements. I say nothing, because I'm not above getting an emotional blow job, and because a weird, fucked-up, highly convenient part of me thinks she needs to suck my dick to prove something to herself.

When she pulls my briefs down, I'm hard as a baseball bat. My cock pops out with comic enthusiasm. She fists it and groans, closing her eyes and shoving it into her mouth. My eyes roll back in their sockets, and I thrust a hand into her hair, tugging for moral support. I feel her tongue swirling against my tip and forget what planet I'm on.

"Aurora Belle Jenkins," I growl, "one day, you'll be the death of me. But what a fecking way to go."

Twenty minutes later (okay, six), I come hard inside her mouth—after asking for permission—and yank her up by her hair. I know that's what she wanted all along when she gives me that glossed-over, may-I-be-fucked-now? look—to be manhandled like that Richards' assistant lass.

Sometimes the dissonance between the way I act to win her over and my real self makes me wonder if I'm a sociopath.

"This was the part where we were supposed to make sweet love." She laughs, her lips red and swollen.

She dives into my bed. I'm still standing, propping a shoulder against the wall and watching her.

"You were the one who got on your knees, Princess."

"I missed it, and I'm single now." She shrugs, tying her arms over her chest like a rebellious teenager.

"No, you're not."

She blushes. "Did you enjoy kissing Brandy?"

"Yes," I answer her honestly.

Her gaze shoots to me, thunderstorms brewing.

I laugh. "I enjoyed feeling your eyes burning holes in her skull. Meant I was still in the race."

"You won the race."

"There shouldn't have been a competition."

She stares at me with heavy eyelids, begging to be fecked. I deny her. This is the only leverage I have.

She has my heart. I have my dick.

I turn around, grab her purse from the nightstand, and leave. I come back ten minutes later with her suitcase, which I retrieved from Callum's room using the card she had, and start unloading it.

She asks me questions, but I'm too deep in my head to answer.

When I'm done, I go into the bathroom, splash my face with water, and stare at my reflection in the mirror.

I point at myself, narrowing my eyes. "You're going to go out there and feck the shit out of her. So hard she won't remember what day it is. What year it is. What Shiny ex-Boyfriend's name is. But this time, you're going to be cool about it. You need to screw her like you don't *want* to screw her. You're going to—"

"Mal?" she calls out from outside.

I stop dead, my eyes widening.

"The walls are kind of thin, and anyway, I've slept with you before. I know you can deliver the goods."

A rush of laughter courses through my throat as I throw the door open. She stands on the other side with her arms open.

She jumps at me, and her legs wrap around my waist, my hands firm on her arse, and we kiss so long and intense, I'm certain our oxygen supply runs short. I move up the length of the bed with her in my arms—before remembering I want to make it epic, yet casual, and look-I'm-not-trying-too-hard-at-all—and shove her front against the full-length window. We're on the fifteenth floor or so, and there's another room, in another hotel, facing ours.

I jerk her jeans down so fast the sound of ripping fills the air, and I tug her panties to the side.

"Mal," she moans.

"Shut up," I growl, remembering the writing on the photo.

Tries too hard.

Talks too much.

I sheath my cock with a condom, spitting the wrap into her hair and plunging in.

"Ahhh," she hisses, holding on to the windowsill. But I just stay there, cock inside of her, not moving.

"Mal?" she asks, still facing the Mediterranean view and the opposite hotel room.

The balcony's sliding doors are wide open. There are shadows of people moving around inside the room. They could watch the entire thing if they just bothered looking, and it gives me a possessive thrill.

"Yes?" I ask conversationally.

"Are you having a case of stage fright?" she asks, her tone matching mine.

I bite my lip to stop myself from laughing. Feck, I missed her sweetness and sass. "Nah. Just enjoying the view."

"Can you enjoy it while thrusting into me?"

"Pass. You wanna get fecked? You do all the work. Go on, then. Feck *me*. Whenever you're ready." I give her arse a little slap. "Just move back and forth. Not exactly astrophysics."

"Are you for real?" She cranes her head around to stare at me. I'm still hard, and still inside her, and dead serious. She said I was a terrible flirt and tried too hard in bed. Well, here I am, completely unattainable—if you don't count Rory herself—and the laziest lay on Earth.

I run the tips of my fingers over her back, making her shiver all over.

"The friction is not going to create itself, darlin'."

She turns around and starts thrusting, back and forth, her arse cheeks jiggling deliciously as she does all the work. I look down, enjoying the porn-worthy vision. She picks up the pace, and I feel my balls tightening.

I groan. *Not good.* I mean, *very good.* Too good. I can't come after five minutes, though. Especially after she listened to my bathroom pep talk.

I pull out of her without warning to stop myself from coming, and she turns around, scrunching her nose.

"Mal!" she cries.

"Bullocks." I tap her arse with my cock. "Guess you try too *hard*."

Before she has the chance to get offended, I throw her onto the bed, headfirst, and scoot on my knees toward her. I pick her up by her stomach, so she's on all fours, and plunge in again without warning.

"Jesus." She sighs. "You're lucky you're good at that."

Well, I *try*.

I feck her good, fast and deep, playing with her clit, and when I feel her thighs shaking and her breath hitching, I stop again, turning her around on her back.

She growls, "What the hell is wrong with you? Let me come!"

I'm trying here. But I'm about to blow my load before you do.

"Coming is so overrated, darlin'. Making love is about *giving*." I fist my cock and tease her cunt in slow circles, not plunging in.

"In that case, *give* me an orgasm before I pack my suitcase and head upstairs to Ashton's room. I'm sure he's more generous in that department."

I can't help it. I start laughing. I know I'm killing the mood, but hell, it *is* funny. I throw her leg over my shoulder and start pumping into her again, swirling my thumb over her clit as I do. She closes her eyes—ignoring the man my cock and fingers are attached to—and whimpers softly, her tits jiggling to the rhythm of my thrusts. I love seeing her like this. At my mercy.

"Faster." She bites on her lip.

"Too lazy." I keep my pace, thrusting deeper and deeper, not quite satisfied unless I feel like I'm tearing her apart.

"*Mal*," she begs, although she is being fucked really hard and not very pleasantly. "Just a bit more."

I deliberately slow down, putting her through delicious torture. I can feel her legs shaking again, and know she will enjoy her climax so much more if it comes gradually. I move in and out of her, watching as her skin blossoms in goosebumps as I give her what must be the best orgasm of her life by the look of her O-shaped mouth.

Once I'm done delivering the goods, I finally let go, pump into her a few more times, and find my own release.

I collapse beside her, staring at the ceiling, enjoying the dead hum of the air conditioning and our in-sync breaths.

"Let's stay here for the entire week." Rory is grinning at the ceiling, her eyes glossed over.

I roll over and throw an arm over her midriff, kissing her temple.

"Can't."

"Why?"

"Because my pumpkin carriage turns into dust come midnight."

"I'll let you bum a ride in my Honda, in that case." She laughs.

"Because I've got shite to take care of back in Tolka," I amend, grinning.

"Define 'shite,'" she presses.

I make a sizzling, steak-on-a-frying-pan sound, trying to keep it light, but I still avoid answering.

She has the right to know. I can't deny that anymore.

"No, you're keeping me in the dark. *Again*." She removes my arm from her body ever so promptly. "What's in Tolka, Mal? Why do you need to go back? Where do you go when you randomly disappear?"

If I thought she could handle the truth, I might consider telling her. But I know, with a clarity that makes me want to heave and throw up, that she would turn around and walk away if she found out. And I'm not ready for her to go. Not yet.

Maybe she'll eventually leave me.

It's an option I'm not eager to entertain, though I force myself to try to come to terms with it.

But even so, I still have a few good weeks in me—a few weeks of screwing her, picking her quirky, somewhat twisted brain, and enjoying whatever she has to give. A few weeks of remembering what it means to be alive. A hit of my favorite drug after years of being sober. Never mind what going cold turkey again might do to me.

"Answer me, Mal."

I stand up and walk toward the bathroom, stark naked.

"You're a dick," she huffs from the bed.

"Evidently," I deadpan, slamming the door behind me.

"You can't keep things from me forever," she calls. "The truth always catches up with you."

I smile at the bathroom mirror, a sad smile that knows she's right, but also so very wrong. Because she's still in the dark about some things.

"Pack your bags, Princess. We're going home."

Present

Rory

L IKE A MOTH TO A FLAME, A JUNKIE TO HIS FAVORITE DRUG, A girl with daddy issues to a destructive bad boy, I'm hooked again. Five rounds between the sheets with Mal and three apology emails to Callum later—which remain unanswered, much to no one's surprise—Mal is fast asleep next to me. I'm still guilt-ridden and feeling low about Callum, yet somehow high about being here with Mal. It's an emotional overdose that makes me feel scattered. Bittersweet remorse dipped in ecstasy.

I send Summer a quick text informing her of the latest development in my love life and ask her to leave her judgment at the door. When she starts blowing up my phone with text messages and calls, I flip it over and slip out of bed. I take the elevator up to Ashton's room.

I know I'm bypassing Mal's direct request, but I've come up with a plan. He's so secretive about whatever's going on in Tolka—like Father Doherty, Ms. Patel, and Maeve and Heather—I decide to beat him at his own game.

I knock on Ashton's door, and he opens up a minute later, his golden robe wide open and revealing his loose anaconda, which flips from side to side like a wiggly tail. I blink, focusing really hard on his face and trying not to blush.

"Do you have a minute?" I ask.

He nods, sparing me the sex-slave jokes—even though, for the first time since we've met, I do look thoroughly screwed—and steps aside to let me in.

As I suspect, there are two girls in his bed, sleeping soundly. One of them is Brandy, and it feels like some sort of validation of an unkind thought to find her there. He leads me to a separate room—a living room of sorts—and we sit across from each other. I pitch him my idea—stay in Greece, soak up the sun and some culture, *and* write the album. I bring out the big guns and my selling points: this place is so much warmer, and close to big cities, and the sea. It is full of tan, gorgeous tourists he can sample. Besides, it's only for a week out of the entire project. We'll be back in Tolka in no time. What's the rush?

Ashton nods vehemently, though he seems kind of distracted, a faraway look stamped on his face. "Yeah. Great idea. Yeah."

I realize it's the first time I've caught him semi-sober.

"Are you okay?" I scratch at my eyebrow.

He laughs, reaching for a bottle of whiskey. "Why wouldn't I be, honey pie?"

I shake my head. *Not your business, Rory.* But isn't that what people say when they turn a blind eye to truly devastating things that happen in the world? I make a mental note to bring Ashton's drug problem to Ryner's attention next time I email him, which should be tomorrow.

When I get back to the room and tuck myself under the blankets next to Mal, I think about how I'm putting him in a position he doesn't want to be in. If whatever's waiting for him in Tolka is that important, he will have to spit it out in order for us to up and leave. If it turns out to be nothing—well, I earned a week in the sun.

I close my eyes, trying to fall asleep, but all I can see in my dreams is my mother, running down Tolka's Main Street, crying hysterically with me in her arms. In my dreams, I'm tiny. Still a baby. And I'm bleeding all over. We leave a trail of blood as the entire village follows us, running.

They are *chasing* us.

And we are running away.

I wake up in a cold sweat and feel the familiar chill wrapping itself around me. I'm shaking so hard my teeth are chattering.

I maneuver myself between Mal's arms and borrow his heat, but sleep doesn't revisit me.

A NOTE FROM ASHTON RICHARDS

Despite what y'all think, I'm not a world-class idiot.

I can tell she broke up with Hugh Cunt or whatever that suited, English dude's name is. I mean, when she and Pissy Poet are in the same room, you can cut the sexual tension with a butter knife. Also, I'm privy to the fact that Pissy Poet and Sex Slave want to spend the next few days going at it like the world's about to end.

I'm a pretty decent human, believe it or not, despite how the media portrays me. I mean, sure, I love my drugs. MDMA keeps me happy and bursting with colors and inspiration, and that's the type of shit I'm known for. I'm the smiley, carefree guy.

Weed is a necessity at this point—who doesn't smoke it these days? And my doctor prescribes the painkillers, so it's not like I played God and decided I needed to cram them into my body on my own accord.

Also, I'm not going to defend my cocaine usage. But you try to live in the public eye since age seventeen and see what it does to your self-esteem. Every single mistake you've ever made is recorded, documented, aired on TMC, and stored—ready to be thrown in your face at any given moment.

And don't get me started on dick pics and public breakups and Taylor Swift-like starlets who write songs about how bad in bed I am.

(Let the record show that I didn't even try with that particular chick. Eat shit, Jordan Jackson. Come to think of it, you're probably into that BS. You were always too kinky for my taste.)

But I digress.

So, yeah, I mean, okay. I may have had my own motivation for this whole staying-in-Greece plot that doesn't have anything to do with Sex Slave and Pissy Poet's sexcapade.

It simply made perfect sense for my master plan.

Them keeping each other occupied = less people on my case.

Less people on my case = more time to do drugs and get drunk.

More drug and alcohol time = less time to think about how this album is never going to materialize, because I'm never going to record it, because I won't be alive by March.

Because I have terminal cancer, you see. Stage fucking billion cancer, which has spread to every single part of my body. And here I thought I was just permanently hungover, never expecting to find out that while I was partying, my body was eating itself to death.

It is all fun and games until the fat lady—in this case my doctor—sings the sad news to me, and I choose to go out with a bang, not like a faded version of my old self—a sad, bony, shadow of myself, lying in a hospice bed staring at a pleasant, generic picture on a wall.

Yeah, that's the money shot I won't allow TMC to ever have: me dying in a hospital gown, looking like a corpse.

Wanna hear the best part? With the amount of drugs I'm using, people are never going to suspect I'm anything other than a twenty-seven-year-old rock star who died from an overdose. A good ol' tragic legend who worked hard and partied even harder. I'll slip into the Amy Winehouse and Brian Jones club with a fake ID, so to speak.

If any of the goddamn idiots surrounding me just looked closely—not even too close, just enough to smell my sick-person's breath and see all the rotting behind my eyes—they'd have realized nothing I've done makes sense.

Riding cows? Traveling to Thailand? All the other *Jackass* shit?

I'm seizing the day, one second at a time, because I'm not counting years, or months, or days. I'm counting seconds.

Yo, Hendrix, Morrison, Cobain—I'm coming for you. Make room on the couch and put a good record on.

Over and fucking out.

Rory

I wake up trembling from the cold and immediately know Mal is not in bed. I can hear him in the corridor outside our room, talking on the phone. His hushed voice skates over my flesh even though he's nowhere near me, causing my nipples to pucker. I jump out of bed and plaster my ear to the door, every bone in me aching for answers.

It's not that I don't respect Mal's privacy; it's that he knows everything about my life, and I know nothing about his. There's a big gap between us, and I'd just like to build a bridge over it, bring us both into the light.

I strain my ears, but hear nothing.

The door flings open suddenly, and I get hit in the face, stumbling down on my butt. I rub my ass cheek, feeling my ears turning red.

"Oh, shit. Sorry." Mal rushes around the door and pulls me up, frowning. "Were you eavesdropping?"

Hmm?

"No," I groan, wiping the hair out of my face. "I was about to open the door to look for you. Why, were you talking to your secret lover?" I joke lamely.

"No, but close. Ryner," he clips.

"Didn't think he was your style."

I try to lighten the mood. Anything to make him forget I *did* try to eavesdrop on him.

"Did you know Richards wants us to stay here for the remainder of New Year's week? The nerve on this wanker."

"Oh, yeah?"

Another lie in our deceit bucket, which is piling up quite nicely. I don't even feel so bad this time, since Mal is lying through his teeth every day we spend together.

"That a problem?" I cock an eyebrow, daring him to open up.

"You know it is," he retorts, storming into the room and shoving clothes into his open suitcase. "I agreed to two nights in Greece. Just the two. Even that was a stretch, and against my contract with Ryner. I'm done here."

I'd ask him again why, but I know better than to think he'd answer.

"Pack up your stuff, Princess. We're leaving, with or without the project."

"How do you mean?"

He turns toward me, scowling. "I mean, I don't give a damn about this album, and neither should you. Let's go back."

He can't stay.

But *I* certainly can. And should. This is my job. In a moment of pure, sharp clarity, I realize that nothing's changed. Mal still wants me to make gigantic sacrifices in the name of our unstable relationship. And I still humor him because…why? His pretty purple eyes? His bulging biceps? His panty-melting songs?

Move to Ireland at eighteen.

Give up on college.

Leave my job.

It's a good thing he still hasn't asked me to lick his shoes clean.

I pick up my purse, throw the strap over my shoulder, and advance to the door.

"Where are you going?" He grabs my wrist.

I shake him off, laughing bitterly. "Not sure, but wherever it is, you won't be there, acting like a jerk who thinks I owe the world to him. I broke up with my boyfriend because of you. You pursued me relentlessly, and for what? To act like I need to up and leave my work just because you said so?"

Mal's face twists in agony. He understands how badly he is screwing up. He shakes his head, sighs, and drops to his knees, pressing his forehead to my stomach. It is not an act of begging or kneeling, but a simple, sweet gesture.

"I'm sorry. I am being an arsehole, but I don't mean to. And trust me when I say the last thing I do is take you for granted. Let's do something fun today. I'll make some calls and see what I can do about postponing going back to Ireland. What do you want to do?"

You, I think with exasperation. *That's what got me into this pickle in the first place.*

He reads my face and starts laughing, rubbing his cheek.

He's blushing. I am melting despite my best efforts. This is how it's always going to be.

"Other than the obvious, mutual answer." He presses his hot lips to my midriff through my pajamas.

"Surprise me," I whisper.

"Surprise you?"

He grins, the same grin the wolf flashes before he opens his mouth and swallows Little Red Riding Hood whole.

"Your wish is my command, Princess."

I wore a yellow summer dress and a slightly unhinged smile on my wedding day. The groom wore a red bandana on his forehead, Blundstone boots, cargo shorts, and a black V-neck tee that smelled of warm beer.

We looked too young and too drunk and too careless, but we both somehow knew it wasn't a mistake.

We just needed liquid courage to be able to do this despite the secrets.

Mal and I got married in Cyprus eight hours later in honor of our napkin contract.

We took a ferry first thing in the morning, right after our mini-argument, and spent our time on it eating clams and drinking white wine. By the time we got to Cyprus, Mal's nose was sunburned, and I was tipsy and giddy—but not enough to think this was a good idea just because the alcohol in my bloodstream told me so.

The truth is, I wanted to marry Mal.

I've always wanted to marry him, from the first time I met him. What seemed impossibly juvenile and destined for failure at age eighteen, seemed…well, just as unlikely right now, at nearly twenty-seven, but the contract was a great excuse, and a big chunk of me just wanted to promise him forever and take it one day at a time.

After the mayor of Larnaka performed the ceremony (no kidding), during which we were surrounded by three other couples who'd come to get married, Mal bought me a drink at a nearby English pub.

Now we are sitting here, basking in the surreal, and it feels a little like a parallel universe I never want to step out of—one without Mom or Ryner or Callum.

I'm telling myself this could work. That it *will* work.

So what if we live an ocean apart? I can visit him for long periods of time. He can do the same. He works from home, for crying out loud. I might make him fall in love with New York and move in with me.

How hard is it to fall in love with New York? All the best artists did.

"Don't you think it's weird how we just ran into each other at Ryner's event a few weeks ago, and now we're married? I never actually thought I'd see you again."

I pop my martini's olive into my mouth. I'm sun-kissed, have a good buzz going, and I'm sexually satisfied.

"Positively mental," he agrees, kissing my nose.

His entire face is hot and smells of sea breeze, sand, and ice-cold beer.

"It's like fate intervened."

Summer is going to kill me when she finds out I tied the knot with my Irish fling from a decade ago, my mom will finally have that heart attack she's been threatening me with, and Callum…I don't want to think about his reaction. I'm hoping he'll never find out. It's not like there's anything tying us together. We hang out in different social circles and work in different jobs. He hasn't left anything at my apartment. He's always been weird about coming over. Come to think of it, I'm not sure he liked Summer very much.

"We haven't discussed where we want to live. I didn't even sign a pre-nup," I point out.

The way Mal lives, he doesn't really give the impression of swimming in money—which I don't care about—but everything about his track record of selling hundreds of songs—songs I listened to over the years and thought sounded familiar, but I couldn't put my finger on why until I came face to face with him again—tells me money shouldn't be a worry for him.

Mal shrugs. "Why would you?"

"I'm officially entitled to half of what's yours," I joke.

I'd never touch a dime he's earned, and he knows it. The money from Glen remains untouched in my mother's bank account to this day.

"You can take my money. I never much cared for it." He dips his head, kissing the side of my neck.

"What do you care about, then, Malachy Doherty?"

He smiles, takes my hands in his, and kisses my knuckles, his purple, magnificent eyes still trained on mine. "*You.*"

We stumble back into our room at three in the morning, not expecting any company. I head toward the little bar by our window to fix myself a gin and tonic. Mal is bending down next to me to grab a bottle of water from the mini-fridge when the door to our suite flings open.

"Mal? Are you there?" calls a soft voice.

Brandy. My blood immediately boils to an unhealthy temperature, because:

A. What the hell is she doing in this room, and how did she get the digital key?

B. She just slept with someone else—her boss!—not even twenty-four hours ago, for crying out loud.

Whatever. I don't need a reason to be mad at her. She is after my husband. My *husband.* I want to wave the ring he purchased for me earlier today at a local jewelry store—with a heartfelt promise to get me something bigger and fancier soon.

Like I'd ever care about the size of my ring.

I look down at Mal, who is holding the bottle of water at my feet. He unscrews the cap, takes a big gulp, and presses his index to his lips, smirking, so childlike in his mischievousness.

I get to break the news to her uninterrupted. Sweet.

"Over here," I sing from behind the bar. She can't see Mal from his position.

Brandy strolls in, looking like a high-class street worker: red mini dress and blow-dried hair intact, all wrapped in perfect makeup and crimson-red lips.

"Oh, I wasn't expecting to see you here." Her smile falls.

She stops a few feet from the bar. I take a sip of my gin and tonic.

"Can I get you anything?" I bat my eyelashes.

"Is Mal on his way? Is he in the shower?" She looks around.

"He's around."

As soon as I say that, I feel Mal's fingers wrapping my bare thigh. He levels his head in front of my groin and hooks his thumbs into my underwear, pulling them down slowly.

What is he doing? We have company.

"What are you doing here at three in the morning?" I ask, trying to keep it as casual as possible when I feel his hot breath against my exposed self, now free of panties. My pulse quickens, and I feel the familiar pool of want coating my insides.

"I just thought...I mean..." She looks around again, like Mal is going to materialize through the turned-off TV at any moment. "Ashton said he works into the night, so I thought maybe he needed something."

Like a dirty one-night stand?

"It's okay. We work closely. I help him wherever I can."

I trace the rim of my gin and tonic glass. I still haven't gotten used to the weight of the ring on my finger, but it makes me feel empowered. Like I can conquer the world. It's what Mal's love does to me. Even though he hasn't spoken the words aloud, I can feel them soaking into my skin when he looks at me.

"Have you ever been in love?" I should ask him that again, and soon.

Mal swipes his tongue—still cold from the water—along my slit, and I shudder violently with uncontrolled desire. Brandy takes a step toward me and parks her elbows on the edge of the bar.

"No offense, but I don't think you're helping him in the way he wants me to help him."

"None taken," I manage to say on a suffocated moan, just as his tongue digs deep between my walls.

I can feel how wet I am on his tongue, and I can also feel his smile, the rumbly, dark chuckle he emits in response to her last, stupid comment. He is eating me raw while she's telling me it's her he wants to bed.

Now *that's* ironic. Although I doubt Alanis Morissette would've wanted to use it for her song.

"Anything I can pass on to him? Doesn't seem like our guy is coming anytime soo—" I try to control my breathing as Mal thrusts his tongue in and out of me, swirling it around my clit every now and again to remind me what's to come (me).

"Well, I…"

"Ohhh, God," I wail, holding on to the edges of the bar, white-knuckled, and throwing my head back shamelessly.

He uses his nose to massage my sensitive nub and digs his tongue so deep into me, I see stars. I lose my ability to keep my eyes open somewhere along the way.

"Is everything okay?"

I can practically hear her frown.

"You look like you're getting sick or something."

Mal can't help it. He full-blown laughs into my pussy as he eats me, nibbling on my lips, sucking, tonguing me ruthlessly. He wants me to come on his face and in *her* face. And I do. I climax hard, spreading my legs apart while my dress is mostly hoisted up and biting my lower lip as I splay my fingers on the bar, my gin and tonic knocked to the floor.

After a few seconds, I open my eyes and bat my eyelashes at Brandy.

"Yeah, I'm good. I had a bit of a…" I clear my throat. "Pulled a muscle or something."

Brandy takes a final step toward me and peers down, her eyebrows still drawn together in annoyance.

"Mal!" she gasps, clutching her invisible pearls while wearing a dress as short as a napkin.

I tumble away from my husband, watching as he flashes her a completely charming, casual smile and stands up. He is sporting a huge erection through his cargo pants, his lips are swollen and look as if he just ate a glazed doughnut, and his hair is messy and delicious and silky as flower petals.

Right now, he looks so delightful, I know there's absolutely no way on Earth I will ever give him up.

"Hey, Britney."

"Brandy." She exposes her teeth, her cheeks red with fury.

"Right." He puts his hands on his hips. "How can I help you?"

"Is this a fling or...?" She points her finger between us, narrowing her eyes at Mal.

He exhales sharply, blowing away a lock of his shiny, overgrown hair that has fallen across his bandana, and pretends to think about it.

"Well, I asked her to marry me this morning. Actually, that's not entirely accurate. I asked her eight years ago, but she said no. This time she said yes. And so, for the past few hours we've been legally married, which makes me lean toward serious. What say you, Mrs. Doherty?" He turns to look at me, stroking his chin. "It's not friendship bracelets, but it's a step in the right direction, no?"

I offer him a noncommittal shrug. "Looks like I'm going to keep you for now. *No offense*, Brandy," I mimic her condescending tone.

I've never seen anyone rush out of a room so fast. She looks horrified. I'm half-sad for her. But I'm completely happy for myself, because when Mal scoops me in his arms and lifts me in the air, and we're both defying gravity and logic and the worlds we've built for the past decade.

I swear I don't even notice when he puts me back down.

I'm floating on a thick, heavenly cloud.

But because I'm still in the dark, bathing in the unknown, a minute from forcing the truth out of him, I know the bubble is going to burst.

A NOTE FROM BRANDY

Taps mic

Is this thing on?

Oh. Hi. Brandy here. I guess I should explain myself.

Let me start by saying, the token trashy girl never *knows* she plays that role, you know?

No one would ever audition for the part, let alone willingly play along.

If you ask me, I had every right to go after the tortured poet. Every time I saw him with the weird silver-haired girl, they either looked like they were about to kill each other, or they actively *tried* to sabotage each other's lives in one way or another. How was I to know there was more to them than just two professionals who weren't getting along?

Oh, and don't even try me with the whole sleeping-with-my-boss incident.

Yeah, yeah, I sleep with my single, available, generous, rock-star boss. The one with the huge dick and thirty-two million followers on Instagram. Who wouldn't? He is effing Ashton Richards!

Besides, since when is it wrong to go after a single, hot man? And when the guy looks like Malachy Doherty, it is legit my *duty* to try to seduce him.

Also, let the record show that I'm not the worst, most dreadful person in the world.

Just ask my sister, Whitney, who works for Ryner.

She hooked me up with this job, and she knows better than to warn me off my gorgeous employer.

Because I might be sleeping with my boss (technically, I don't, because I was hired by his manager), but she's the one having a baby with an English banker who apparently has a girlfriend.

A fancy, hot, photographer girlfriend who has no freaking clue he's been messing around for months behind her back.

The banker doesn't even *like* Whit, but does she care? No. Because he's going to pay her way through the next nineteen years.

Now that I think about it, Callum Brooks totally fits the bill.

I need to make a mental note to ask Whitney about this. Maybe when she isn't so emotional and complaining about her sore breasts.

Oh, well. Back to the perfect-husband drawing board I go.

Present

Rory

MAL CONCEDED TO TWO MORE DAYS IN GREECE, BUT HELL IF
he wasn't Bitter Betty about it. We're making the best of it
by staying in bed all day, catching up on more sex, more
seafood, and more of the sun on our balcony.

We talk about the songs he wrote about me ("How could you not
know?" "How was I *supposed* to? You told me you were never going to
sell them. Besides, listening to a hit song and assuming it's about me?
How bigheaded do you think I am?" "Well, your head is a little dispro-
portionally large, but I've heard all movie stars are like that, so I suppose you're in good company."), listen to music, and use every napkin
we get with the room service to sign more contracts between us.

*In the unlikely event that we have a fight...we promise not to walk
out on each other.*

*In the unlikely event that we have three boys and no girls...we
promise not to have everything in the house blue and watch footie all
weekend.*

In the unlikely event Mal moves to New York...I promise not to allow him to wear tweed jackets and become the cliché tortured artist.

All those things seem important, but they're still hanging in the air like stars, unreachable and far away. We don't talk about what counts. About his secrets. About the mysterious calls he takes every few hours in the hallway.

We don't talk about the fact that I don't want to move to Ireland, because my life is in America, and he doesn't want to move to America, because his heart is in Tolka.

We don't talk about Kathleen.

Or Father Doherty.

We don't talk about my nightmare.

At some point, Mal slips to the hallway to take another phone call, and I pick up my phone to text Callum and ask him how he is.

After I'm done with the message, I slide into my unopened text messages to face the Summer music. It's more like a scream, if I get the vibe right, and what I see makes me want to throw up.

Summer: Please answer.

Summer: I guess he told you.

Summer: I NEVER meant to sleep with him, Rory. You have to believe me.

Summer: And I knew he loved you so much. Please, please forgive me.

Summer: Omg, stop! You were going to break up with him, anyway. You told me so a million times. In my mind, you weren't even, like, fully together. It was always Mal you wanted. Pick up.

My mouth is slack when Mal returns to the room, looking around.

"Shall we pack up?" he asks with his fists balled at his waist. I force myself to look up and ignore the way my heart shatters like windows.

Boom, boom, boom.

"Three more days." I muster a weak smile, playing dumb again.

That's what Ashton said. Three more days. And he actually sent for Mal to come work with him today for an hour, to justify our stay here. I joined Mal to take pictures, and we broke the news about our wedding to Ashton, who was elated. But then again, he was also very, very high. I've a suspicion he would have been just as excited if I told him I'd bought a new keychain of the Temple of Hephaestus at the local market.

Yup. Ashton looked higher than an airplane. I remind myself yet again to tell Ryner he needs to send Ashton to rehab after this project is over. It's obvious things have gotten way out of control.

"I need to go back," Mal repeats his usual mantra.

"You do? Awesome. I'll meet you there in three days."

I read Summer's last messages again and again and again. I'm tired of being kept in the dark. Mal stares at me with wild, white anger that I haven't seen on him before. Heat rolls off of his body in waves that crash at my feet.

"Fine," he spits.

"Fine."

He grabs his suitcase, which is already packed and zipped, and blazes to the door. I'm still in bed when he stops, sighs, and comes back, looking wasted and empty. It's like those ten steps away from me drained him completely.

"Please," he says quietly.

I know what he is asking.

He is asking me not to make it any harder for him. To come without question.

I think about Callum sleeping with Summer.

About letting Mal do unholy things to me while I was still with Cal.

About cheating and being cheated on. I never thought either of those things would happen to me.

But I also know they happened for a reason.

They say once a cheater, always a cheater.

But I think sometimes things do not appear broken, but they are, and through the crack, bad things slip in.

I'm screwing up my something whole because Mal is in a desperate situation. I'm starting to see I'm not being fair to him.

"Mal," I breathe.

He slowly looks up. I see bad things have already slipped into his broken interior.

"Have you ever been in love?" I ask.

A huge smile breaks on his face. It is true and big and real, and it can keep me burning forever. I know as long as I see this smile every day, I will never be cold.

"Funny you should ask. Yes, yes, I have been. I still am. It started eight years ago, in the most unlikely event, and it has no expiration date."

I stand and walk over to him. I cup his stubbled cheek.

He shakes his head. "Just trust me, Rory, when I say we need to go—not because I think you should give up on something for me, not because I'm only half-alive when I'm not in Tolka, and you deserve the full experience, not just part of me."

His mouth meets mine, but he is not kissing me. Just tracing his lips along mine as he speaks to me.

"I love you, Princess Aurora Belle Jenkins Doherty of New Jersey, you little heart slayer."

"I love you, King Malachy Doherty of Tolka, my bigger-than-average-but-not-uncomfortably-so soul crusher. Now, let's go say goodbye to Ashton before we leave."

The first thing to tip me off that something's wrong is the smell. It smells like urine and rotten meat. I push the door open while Mal loiters at the door, texting.

Brandy and the rest of Ashton's crew are nowhere in sight,

probably downstairs drinking at the bar, and I tiptoe my way toward the master bedroom, where he probably is.

Bingo.

I find Ashton asleep, with the robe open—fully naked, of course—taking a nap with a pool of piss all around him. I swear to God, I'm going to blow up this entire project and have him thrown into rehab right here and right now, no matter how much money Ryner is going to lose. I walk over and shake his shoulder gently.

"Wake up. You need to get into the shower right now and pull yourself together."

I look around and find traces of crushed pills and cocaine on his nightstand. Mumbling "screw it," I gather all of them and walk over to the bathroom to flush them down the toilet.

I come back into the room and do the unthinkable. I grab Ashton's cellphone from his nightstand, place it on the floor, and smash it with my foot. That way, he won't be able to score anything in the near future.

Not that he'll get the chance. This is rock bottom, as far as I'm concerned. He is coming back to Ireland with us, and I'm locking him inside Mal's house until this thing is finished. He is going to record this album sober and experiencing withdrawals.

"Ashton!" I shake his shoulder more aggressively now. "Wake up."

Nothing.

Mal comes into the bedroom, tucking his phone into his back pocket.

"Why does it smell like the wanker pissed all over the room, including the ceiling and neighboring countries?"

"Because he did." I turn to him, rolling my eyes. "He won't wake up. Can you get me a bottle of cold water from the mini bar, so I can pour it on his face?"

Mal frowns and approaches the bed. He ignores Ashton's nakedness, and runs his hand under Ashton's nose. His face turns ashen.

"Darlin', do me a favor and wait outside, okay?"

"What? Why?"

"Because." My husband turns to me, his purple eyes full of misery. "He's dead."

The ambulance is here within two minutes. The police arrive shortly after. I don't know how they find out, but all the major gossip websites send local journalists to cover the story, and Ryner, who is going through a mental breakdown with a side-dish of a heart attack an ocean away and lands himself in the hospital, commands us to go back to Tolka, not talk to anyone, and stay there until further notice.

After a brief interview with the police, we are released and driven back to the hotel. We pack our things, still in shock, and leave Brandy and the rest of the staff in tears behind us. There is nothing I want to do more than stay and console people and figure out what happened, but I know how badly Mal wants to go back home, and now is not the time to defy Ryner.

On the plane, we stare at nothing and stay quiet.

Mal is the first one to break the silence.

"I feel like shite for treating him the way I did, you know."

"He really liked you." I swallow.

I kissed the guy this week. His mouth was hot and alive, his heart beating against mine. Hell, I talked to him just a few hours ago, and he was funny and sweet and easygoing—not a care in his madman's world. I don't know why I'm so deeply devastated by the loss of his life, but I just want to crawl into myself and cry.

"I hate that we could have prevented it," I mumble.

"We couldn't."

"He was high all the time. We let it happen."

"You obviously haven't met an addict before. There was nothing you or I could have done to prevent him from using. This is not on you, Rory." He kisses my shoulder.

I feel my eyes coating with tears again. "Then why am I so sad?"

"Because you're a good human. Because essentially, *he* was one, too."

We don't talk about the project, about the album, about the absurdity of us reuniting to work on something that will never materialize. Now that the project is officially dead—along with its star—something fundamental has snapped and shifted in the world we created together. We no longer have ground on which to operate. I don't have a deadline in Ireland.

I tap my phone where it rests on my knee, pushing away Summer's nonstop unanswered calls and Mom's book-long messages begging me to come back home before something terrible happens.

"You're crying." Mal squeezes my shoulder.

I realize I am.

I shake my head. "I'm sorry. I've just never dealt with death up close before. My grandparents were dead before I hit three, and even though Glen died when I was a teenager, I didn't know him and never witnessed it. It sounds ridiculous. I'm almost twenty-seven, yet up until now, death seemed like this vague, abstract idea. It was there, but not really. Now I feel it everywhere."

Mal takes my hand in his and kisses it.

"It is," he agrees.

"You probably miss Kathleen all the time," I say.

"I do," he admits, pausing to think about it. "But then I also think, when you lose someone when they're young and in their prime, it reminds you how fragile life truly is. It reminds you that you were not put on this Earth to work. You weren't put on this Earth to do the dishes or pay your taxes on time or, I don't know, count your weekly alcohol units or goddamn calories. We're not here to win awards or make money. What flashes through your mind in that fraction of a moment, when you realize this is it for you, that you're about to die, is the kiss you stole from your first crush under the old oak tree. The cartwheels on the beach on a perfectly sunny day with your brothers. The first time your niece said your name, and you knew you were a goner—you were going to give her every single thing she asked for, including but not limited to your limbs. Losing someone when they're young is like surviving a fatal disease. Life gifts you a second chance of not fecking it up. It can either dim you or make you shine brighter. It's a great reminder that what we have is rare and fleeting and not to be carelessly wasted. You want to honor Richards' legacy? *Live*."

"That's why you didn't want to make it big." I sniff. "You always wanted the family life. Your little corner in the world."

And he almost got it, too, with Kath. But then she died. A part of me wants to go back to Ireland and start making babies with Mal right away. I've never admitted to anyone what crossed my mind when I got back home from Ireland after my first trip there.

How a part of me—and not a small one—was regretful that I took that morning-after pill. Because that would have been a great excuse to drop everything and go be with him. I'd have done what my mother hadn't. I'd have tried to make it work.

Mal rubs his thumb across my cheek, frowning.

"Now you get it, Princess."

The next couple days are a blur.

Mal and I have long, emotional, grueling sex. We talk for hours, wrapped around each other. I cry a lot, and he listens—a lot. Mal makes elaborate plans to tell his family about our marriage, and I do the same with my mother.

In reality, however, I don't pick up the phone, and he doesn't arrange any conversations with his family. He visits them every day, but never allows them to pop into the cabin. I'd say he avoids having them meet me like the plague, but even the plague gets the royal treatment compared to the way he handles his family when I'm around.

One morning, I hear whispers rising from the front door while I'm still in bed.

It's Mal—clipped, asshole, this-is-not-the-man-I-married Mal.

"…poor timing. I'll ring you in a bit."

"When exactly is a bit?" asks an old woman's voice, brittle and wary.

"Eternity and beyond, Mother."

"That's what it feels like, since *she* came along."

A hushed, heated reply comes from the other side of the door. They're fighting.

"No. Absolutely not," Mal rumbles. "I've got this under control. Just go."

Sometimes Mal disappears. When he does, I spend my time arguing with Ryner on the phone instead of facing the Summer and Mom music.

"Just send me the goddamn material. I'm throwing a special tribute for him, okay? Oh, and in case it escaped you, you *work* for me!" he screamed at me one day shortly after he was discharged from the hospital.

"He hasn't even been put to rest," I noted. "Which begs the question—is it a tribute to the late Ashton Richards you're working on, or a tribute to your pocket and record label? Seems to me, you're milking the best out of this horrific situation."

"I just had a heart attack." He sulked. As if this, in itself, was a reason to grant all his wishes.

"True, and I don't want you to have a second one, which is why I'm asking you to let it go. Don't pay me for the project. Let Ashton rest in peace."

I'm not going to let Ryner capitalize on his death. All he cares about is selling a few posters and releasing half-finished songs to earn a few bucks.

"Welcome to unemployment, sweetheart. You've really done it this time," Ryner then shouted into my ear.

"Thanks for the warm greeting. I'll be sure to make the most of it." I hung up.

I caught Ashton Richards in private moments, while he was suffering from a horrific addiction that led to his death. I don't see why anyone should witness it. He was obviously desperately chasing happiness, but never quite reaching it.

Mal doesn't say Ashton's death wrecked him, but then he doesn't talk about it much—just listens to me when I do—and he is adamant about not going to the funeral in the States.

Though that could also be because he has a secret lover/family/life here that he keeps disappearing off to. I say this completely lightheartedly, but of course, there's a void in my stomach that opens an inch every time I wake up and his side of the bed is cold.

Every day I think to myself, *This will be the day he opens up to me about the situation.*

Every day I am wrong.

Then, a week after we're back in Ireland, Mal announces he's ready to go busking again. He needs to unclutter his mind, he says.

"You can tag along. Take pictures of Dublin."

"I think I'm good." I give him the thumbs-up.

I finally have a plan. I managed to track down Father Doherty's new address in an old-school phone book—the kind of fat, yellow thing grandparents usually use to stop doors or as a makeshift coaster. Father Doherty lives bang in the middle of the village, and it's time to pay him a visit, have him shed some light on my situation.

Mal, of course, can see through me. We haven't spent an entire month together the whole time we've known each other, yet he can somehow read me better than anyone else.

"You sure?" He furrows his brows.

I nod. "Positive."

"Hmm."

"What?"

"Nothing has been positive about you these last days, so I find your choice of words somewhat alarming."

"It's been a rough week." I saunter over to him, linking my arms around his shoulders. "One wedding and an upcoming funeral. I just want some me-time. Maybe I'll finally call my mother back and catch up with her."

Mal's face twists at the mention of my mother, but he nods and kisses my forehead. I don't know why *he* acts like he has an open beef with Debbie Jenkins, but if he's flinching every time I mention her out of solidarity, he's doing a fine job being empathetic.

"Want to talk tonight?" He skims his lips along my temple.

"About what?" My heart speeds up with hope.

"About everything."

"Will you finally tell me what's going on?"

He bends his head down, closing his eyes. "Yes," he croaks. "God, I don't want to, but yes."

I walk Mal to the door, kiss him goodbye again, and wave him off, the Stepford wife that I am not. As soon as I see his car racing down the graveled path, I slip into my Toms, grab my army jacket, and run down to the village on foot.

The weather is crisp and chilly, but no longer freezing, and I'm high on adrenaline from knowing how close I am to the truth. I can feel it at my fingertips, tingling, waiting for me to grab it.

This time, I'm going to corner Father Doherty until he relents. He must. A man who serves God for a living can't lie, can he?

Besides, I have the perfect thing to lure him into telling me the truth.

It's simple, really.

My mother is holding out on me.

Father Doherty is holding out on me.

They're keeping the same secret, obviously.

If Doherty *thinks* I already know something I don't, he'll open up.

My calves burn, and my breath rattles somewhere between my chest and throat. I am running out of oxygen, but I'm not slowing down. This is what I've been waiting for. Not just Mal, but also the truth.

The truth about Callum.

The truth about my father.

About my mother.

The story of *me*.

I slice through the streets of Tolka, passing the newsagents, the pubs, the quaint inns, the spilled flowerpots, and Gaelic-graffitied brick walls of the alleyways—the beautiful, pastoral lie covering the rotten secrets I am about to unveil. And I don't stop until I'm at the door of the address I found.

I clutch the little note to my chest, the paper so thin and inky my jacket and fingers are stained, and manage a few knocks on the door before my legs give in and I collapse on the stoop.

The door swings open, and I straighten up, clearing my throat.

"Hi, is Father D…"

I stop dead when I see the person in front of me. Because that person? It's not the old man with the bushy eyebrows.

It's the person Mal never told me about.

Purple eyes like Mal's.

And features so eerily identical to mine.

Kathleen's features.

Seven years ago

Mal

KATH IS PREGNANT.

I don't even pretend to be surprised when she shows up at my door, sans the skimpy clothes, clad in her usual sensible cardigan and thick leggings and carefully combed hair, and rubs her flat stomach tellingly.

"May I come in?" She clears her throat.

She knows as well as I do that we fucked up royally that night. It's not about the fact that I didn't use a condom, or that I was completely ossified when it happened, or that she was a virgin (who'd always proclaimed, as long as I can remember, that she wanted to wait till marriage). And I don't even want to touch the dubious-consent subject. But the worst of it is the fact that I had to tell Sean what happened—he was one of my closest mates, after all—and Sean and Daniel cut Kiki and me off from their lives completely.

Apparently, Sean had confessed his love to Kath one night. I was aware of his feelings, too. Bit of a shit thing to do, I admit.

Well, maybe a lot.

Kath and I deserve it—every nasty eye roll from the O'Leary twins and shake of the head from Maeve and Heather.

I could tell Sean I wasn't fully there, that I didn't know what I was doing, and it'd be the truth. My memory of that night is vague at best. But I don't want to throw Kath under the bus, even if she ran me over with that particular decision.

Mam and Bridget went to visit Dez in Kilkenny for the month to clear their heads, and so I'm still tremendously alone. I write songs, sing them on street corners, get offers, and turn them down. Then I go home, and since my mates won't talk to me, and since I stopped sending letters to Rory, as per her request, I no longer reject Kathleen's attempts to spend time with me. I can't afford to avoid her.

Sometimes she studies while I write.

Sometimes we feck with the lights off, always with a condom, and she lets me chant, "Rory, Rory, Rory."

Most times, though, we share dinner and watch whatever is on the telly and I drive her back home before it gets too dark.

Today Kiki shoulders past me, into my living room, seeming to feel right at home. Unlike me, the living room is in a good condition. The rest of the house is pretty tidy, too.

She sits at the table, and I follow her with two glasses of water. I have no particular reaction to the news she delivers. I'm not happy, nor am I sad. I had a feeling it was going to happen. I've used condoms every other time we had sex—despite her protests—but apparently, I have super sperm, at least where the O'Connell girls are concerned.

Now, I'm just waiting to hear from Kath if she's going to keep it or not. My chest feels tight, but I don't want to assume.

"How are you feeling?" I ask, sliding the glass her way.

She takes a small sip, her eyes clinging to my face, trying to read me.

Why can't I love her? Why can't I love the girl who'd never leave me? The girl who'd die for me?

"Good. A bit nauseous, but good. Thanks for asking."

"When'd you find out?"

"This afternoon. I went in to buy the test after school. Called Heather and Maeve to come with. You know Maeve is dating Sean now? I think they make a cute couple. Heather is fit."

"So they know about the pregnancy," I say, keeping my temper in check. And here I was under the impression that baby daddies are the first to learn of the news.

"Yeah. Hope it's okay. I didn't want to take the test alone, and I knew you were busking and didn't want to bother you or freak you out for no reason. It could have been negative."

"Are you going to keep it?" I ask, flat out.

Her face morphs from happy to shocked, her eyebrows dropping.

"What kind of question is that? Of course, I'm going to keep it. I'm bloody Catholic, Mal."

I nod.

"I think it's more a question of what are *you* going to do." She sits back, folding her arms over her chest.

"I'm going to take care of it, of course," I say, feeling my eyebrows jumping up in surprise. Was there even a question?

Kathleen huffs. Wrong answer, I guess. I try again.

"Both of you. I'm going to take care of both of you—financially and otherwise. It's not going to be just you. I'll find a real job. And I'll have it half the time if you let me."

"It's not *it*."

"Of course, it's not." I blink. *Jesus. What more does she want?*

"It's a boy," she says smugly, grinning now. "A little fella, Mal. I can practically feel it. Women know those things."

I try to smile, but it feels weird on my face. Right. A boy. I reach across the table and take her hand in mine, stroking her inner wrist with my thumb.

"I mean it. You're not alone. You won't have to drop out of uni or anything. I'll take care of him all the time, give him everything I have."

She looks away. Sniffs.

"What?" I press.

She needs more, but I can't figure out what *more* consists of. Suddenly, I want to give her whatever it is that she wants. Even if it kills me. Maybe I could start by not mumbling her sister's name when I feck her from behind.

Probably, arsehole. Probably.

"I called your ma," she says softly.

She's not crying, though, which makes me wonder if it's an act. I let go of her hand and sit back.

"You did?"

"I told her. I had to. I had to get her blessing, Mal. Plus, she's been so down since what happened with Bridget." Kath looks up and smiles, tears in her eyes.

Perhaps it's not an act after all. Maybe Rory turned me into a jaded bastard.

"She is so happy to get a grandson, Mal. So is Bridget. Perhaps Dad is up there making things right for us. It's like kismet. Like it was meant to be."

Kismet.

I told Rory we should leave it to fate, and guess what? Fate flipped us the bird, turned Rory against me, and made sure I impregnated Kath. If fate exists, it is working extra hard to make sure Rory and I are never going to be together. Kath is still talking in the background. I'm catching up on her speech.

"…told her I completely understand. Your mam is very adamant we should get married, especially considering how religious I am, but I told her we could wait. I respect your wishes and know that making your mam and girlfriend happy is not a good enough reason to propose."

Girlfriend?

It feels bizarre to argue the point that Kath and I are not a couple, especially considering she's carrying my child. But marriage?

Really? It's not that I don't like Kath; it's that I like her for all the wrong reasons.

Because she is here and available and familiar and open-legged and reminds me of her half-sister. Those are quite horrible reasons to be with someone, let alone marry her. But now that we carelessly threw a kid into the mix, I know Kathleen is right. My family—Mam, brothers, sister—absolutely expect me to do the right thing by her. Even if I feel horribly tricked and cornered. Even if I can barely remember that night.

But you can certainly remember all the other times you fecked her with a condom, and sober.

"Say something," Kathleen whispers, gawking at me.

"I…" *Don't want to marry you.* "I need to think about it."

"Okay."

"But regardless, I will be there for you. For both of you. Always," I add fiercely.

Of course, I don't know what I'm saying.

I don't know where life is going to take me.

And I definitely have no fecking clue how badly I am going to break that promise.

I marry Kathleen eight months into her pregnancy, her round belly looking like the gleaming moon in the shapeless, white dress.

It's a small, quiet ceremony at Father Doherty's church—late December, on the heels of Christmas. Kiki radiates happiness and triumph, Mam and Elaine are fawning over her, all my brothers and sister are weeping with pride and joy, and Sean and Daniel are here with Maeve and Heather—reluctant, but present.

During my stag party, which Daniel threw, he laughed and said Mam and Kiki finally wore me down and made me propose. I sipped my drink, smiled, and told him to feck off. But he wasn't wrong, and that bothered me.

I promise Kathleen forever, she does the same, and we exchange rings. These past few months have been intense. Kathleen didn't want to know the gender of the baby, but spoke only of that. She moved in with me as soon as Mam came back from Kilkenny with Bridget. I was there when the peanut kicked for the first time, I was there when it started moving in her belly—especially at night, and I was there when we could see the imprint of one of its limbs stretching her stomach.

Kathleen and I turned from sometimes-shagging to always shagging soon after we found out she was pregnant. I stopped calling her Rory, but still couldn't face her when we were doing it. Thankfully, there were enough positions from which all I could see was her naked back.

After the ceremony, we go back to our house. Kath can't drink, and I've been cutting back on alcohol, too. Mam and Elaine decided to move in together, since they're friends and since Kathleen and I apparently need our privacy, especially since we're about to welcome little Glen into the world.

About that name.

Aside from me being surprised and confused by the choice, Glen is a terrible name for anyone under sixty-five years old, and our Glen is expected to hit that mark sixty-six years from now.

We burst into the cottage, and Kath is taking off her big, white dress, groaning as she does. She looks like a cloud in that white thing, but I know better than to say that to her.

"Have you given any more thought to selling your songs?" she asks, removing the bobby pins from her hair one by one and clutching them between her teeth as she speaks.

I shake my head and fall to the sofa with a sigh.

"Mal," she pleads.

I turn on the telly, crossing my legs. *Cash in the Attic.*

Bloody hell, Glen. You're laying it thick, now, aren't you?

"I don't understand you at all." Kiki sulks, removing her brace-lets and jewelry with sharp, frustrated movements. "You're a brilliant writer. We could get good money for them instead of relying on my da's inheritance, which is already dwindling. We could actually buy real, expensive furniture for Glen's room, as opposed to the second-hand crap we have now. I just cannot for the life of me fathom why."

"Because my songs are *mine*."

And Rory's. She inspired them. No part of me wants to show the world what went through my head that day I spent with her, the day she left, and everything after. All the other songs I wrote and got offers for before her are no longer relevant. Rory changed me.

Kath doesn't know any of this—not the story behind the songs, and not that being asked about them constantly feels a lot like being stabbed in the chest.

"You're being so unreasonable." She gales into the bedroom.

It used to be Mam's bedroom. Now it's ours. We moved all our furniture in yesterday. Well, I did. Our nightstands, bed, and Kath's huge mirror that's tilted so she looks skinnier. ("Don't judge, okay? Ha-ha.")

I've just closed my eyes to take a few moments to breathe when I hear a shriek from the bedroom. I jump to my feet immediately. My first thought is—*the baby.*

"What's going on? Is the baby okay?"

"What in the ever-loving *fuck* is this?"

I'm temporarily taken aback by the fact that Kathleen has said the word *fuck.* I wasn't even sure she was aware of its existence, let alone able to produce it from her good, Catholic lips. Of course, we've done the deed countless times, and in less than Christian positions, but...

Wait, what the feck *is* this?

A napkin. She is holding a napkin. *The* napkin.

The contract.

I snatch it from her hand and mentally kick my own arse for not putting it elsewhere when I arranged our nightstands by the bed. She must've gotten them mixed up and opened it to take out one of her gazillion hand creams, finding this instead.

"It's nothing." I shove the thing into the back pocket of my suit pants. Kathleen's eyes are two big planets, pregnant with misery. She slaps my chest, then covers her mouth, her face twisting in anguish behind her hands.

"You two had a deal?"

"She doesn't want me," I say—a spur-of-the-moment reaction and definitely up there among the dumbest things to say to your newly wedded wife, who by the way, is also heavily pregnant.

But in my mind, I know this is the most efficient way to assure her the napkin means nothing.

Which, clearly, is also a massive problem.

The napkin shouldn't mean anything, but not because Rory buggered off to another continent to shag other people and take pictures of them and write on the back of those pictures how much they suck in bed and in life and in small talk. (I'm paraphrasing here, of course.)

The napkin shouldn't mean anything because I'm about to have a baby with my childhood friend, turned lover, turned wife.

Yes, arsehole. Wife.

I advance toward my wife. My patient, saint-like partner who groaned and took it when I called her something else again and again and again for months.

"We both moved on. And *we* are married, in case you failed to notice."

I clasp her arms, draw her close.

She pushes me away. "Get rid of it," she barks.

I let out a dark chuckle. "What?"

"You're not deaf, Mal. Get rid of the bloody thing. It shouldn't be in the house in the first place. I cannot believe you."

She cannot believe me?

Can *I* believe *her*? After she fecked me when I was half-dead and a quarter functioning? Making me take her virginity, and coming back to ride my cock, always begging me not to wear a condom?

Calling Mam, manipulating her and Bridget to pressure me into this marriage, convincing Mam and Elaine to move in together?

But I'm not dumb enough to start a massive fight on our wedding day.

I smile instead. "It's just a silly memory. I'll tuck it in a photo album. You'll never see it again, and we can move on with our lives."

"Are you fucking kidding me?"

Again with this word.

"Kiki…"

"*Mal*," she mimics my voice. "I'm so sick and tired of people giving you slack because of some bloody, magical hold you have on them. You're stalling."

"I'm not stalling. I'm simply rejecting your request."

"You're a cunt, is what you are."

"All right, then," I say.

Can't really dispute that. I certainly feel like one right now. But she is not the little saint she makes herself out to be, either.

She advances toward me and slaps my face.

I can feel my skin burning, my cheekbone aching. I clench my jaw. Something tells me I'm being a stubborn son of a bitch, that I should just get rid of the fecking thing. The napkin means nothing. It meant nothing from the moment Rory said goodbye. And even if it didn't, her letter didn't leave room for doubt.

Now, let's play devil's advocate and say there *is* doubt, that it's not over on her end.

Let's say we meet again, four years from now, because fate has a twisted, sick sense of humor.

Let's say Rory is no longer a bitch from hell and decides to honor the contract.

Then what? I leave little Glen and Kathleen and my entire family—who will disown me for taking off with the Yank, no doubt—and go live happily ever after with the same girl who aborted my child without consulting me about it?

I stalk toward the kitchen, hearing Kathleen's bare feet padding behind me. I stop by the bin, take the napkin out of my pocket, and crumple it in my fist, ready to throw it out, along with Rory's stupid memory.

I clutch it above the open jaw of the bin, squeezing hard, my fist shaking.

Do it already. What is the matter with you?

"Do it!" Kiki yells.

I stare at my fist, the trashcan, the fist again, then lift my eyes to the ceiling, letting out a ragged sigh.

Feck you, Rory.

I withdraw my arm, yanking at my hair with the other one. I can't do it.

I don't notice when Kath jams her feet into her shoes, but I snap to attention when the door slams behind her. I take off after her immediately. It's late, cold, and dark.

Kath slides into my car, revs it up, reverses, and then gallops down the path to Main Street. I chase her by foot, yelling at her to slow down. That only causes her to slam her foot against the gas pedal to get away from me faster.

As I run after my own car, my own wife, my own future, I contemplate stopping. I can see through the rearview mirror she's in quite a state. She's shaking and crying so badly, I'd be surprised if she sees anything. Maybe if I leave her alone, she will slow down.

Maybe if you leave her alone, she will finally find proof of what you haven't said in so many words thus far: that her sister will always be the love of your life, and she's the consolation prize.

Bile rises in my throat as I speed up. I try calling her, fumbling with my cell as I chase her, but she doesn't pick up.

Pick up, pick up, pick up.

She's heading straight to a busy, two-way intersection, and she's not slowing down. I don't know if she realizes what she's doing. She is losing control over the vehicle. My eyes sting, my heart thrashes against my ribcage, and I'm a stupid bastard who is about to pay for his silly fantasy.

Everything happens in slow motion.

Kathleen ignoring the stop sign at the end of the road.

A lorry with a frozen meat slogan blazing straight into her path from her left.

Metal hitting metal.

Big bang.

Silence.

Silence.

So much silence.

The scent wafting in the air makes me choke on my breath. Metallic blood and burned flesh and the end of my life.

I round my smashed car and try to open the driver's door, but the metal is too hot to touch, and there's thick smoke everywhere. The lorry driver stumbles out, holding his right leg.

It's Sean.

God, it's Sean.

He looks sober—of course, he is, he didn't drink a drop during the wedding because he had a shift tonight—and in hysterics, running his palm through his buzzed hair, his teeth chattering.

"Oh, Lord." He runs toward me. "I didn't see her. She came out of nowhere."

He's right. It wasn't his fault. She did come out of nowhere. But why Sean? Why him? And why am I so irrationally angry right now?

"Is she okay?" he asks dumbly.

"The baby," I gasp, wrapping my hand in my dress shirt and jerking the door open. The sting of heat scorches my skin through the fabric. "Call an ambulance."

"She looks dead," Sean blurts, obviously in shock. "I can't go to jail. I don't want to go to jail. Jesus."

That's what he is thinking about right now? Going to jail? Kathleen's life is over. Mine, too. And the baby's. Please, please don't let it be the baby.

I have so much to say.

I say nothing.

Sean turns around, looking at me. He is pale as a ghost. "This wouldn't have happened if she'd dated me. You hurt her, Mal. You did this. It's all your fault."

Kathleen is dead.

But the baby is not.

"It was a close call, Mr. Doherty. You are blessed," the doctors say.

Yeah, I snort. *I fecking feel blessed.*

I look down at the small, purple thing. Only reason I don't cry is because someone needs to look in charge.

I'm sorry, little one. So terribly much.

Kathleen was wrong all along.

It isn't a boy.

It's a girl, and she looks just like both of us.

All I can think when I look at her is not all the things I gained, or all the things I lost in the past year.

But how all of them are connected to Rory.

How she ruined everything.

And how badly I want to ruin *her.*

Present

Rory

"MAY I HELP YOU?" THE LITTLE GIRL ASKS FROM THE doorway, her voice honey sweet and soft. She has the most glorious hair. Deep brown, but not quite as dark as her father's.

Her. Father's.

See also: My husband.

See *also*: The man who hid the truth about his daughter from me.

That was one of the first things I asked him when we met in New York again, when he threw his marriage to Kathleen in my face.

"Children?"

"No."

He didn't even hesitate. The answer was flat, like the void behind his pretty eyes. But there's no way this kid is anyone else's. She is a perfect blend of Kathleen and Mal. Suddenly, I'm hit with the awful, complicated truth. He kept this secret from me, even *after* he married me. His true family was something he never planned to share.

He didn't trust me enough to tell me he was a father. He thought I'd leave him if I found out, if he ever did care enough about us to want me to stay.

I wouldn't leave a single father. But I sure as hell would dump a compulsive, dirty liar.

All the times he disappeared. The birthday party. The glitter. The tiny, fake diamond earring tucked between grass blades in the backyard. The rush to head back to Tolka when we were in Greece. All because of his baby girl.

A mixture of anger, frustration, and overwhelming protectiveness toward this kid, who never knew her mother, swirls in my stomach. And guilt. So much guilt, for a reason I cannot pinpoint right now.

I offer her a little wave.

Say something. Anything. You are probably freaking her out.

"Um, hi?"

Not that, you idiot.

"You look like a princess." She giggles, covering her little mouth.

How old is she? I'm guessing seven at most. Maybe six. Jesus, this cuts it close to the entire napkin ordeal. Is it possible she was conceived that soon after I left?

"That's because I am." I plant my fists on my waist.

"You are?" Her eyes nearly bulge out of their sockets.

"Well, kind of. My name is Aurora Belle. I came here because I heard there's another princess living in this village—a prettier one I must meet. Guess I found her." A lopsided grin appears on my face.

She chuckles with delight, cupping one of her cheeks to hide her blush. My heart squeezes in my chest. Her smile is dimpled. Neither Mal nor Kathleen had dimples. They were probably given to her by the almighty, to remind her she should smile despite her circumstances.

"You came to the wrong address. I'm no princess; I'm just Tamsin."

Tamsin.

"Tamsin! Yes! That's the girl I was looking for." I produce my planner from my backpack, opening to a random page and nodding vehemently. "Yup. There you are. Princess Tamsin of Tolka. Everybody is talking about you back in our kingdom. They say you are the sweetest, kindest princess in all of Ireland."

If she could burst glitter right now, she would. She jumps up and down, clapping her hands, and that's when I realize what she is wearing: cowboy boots, a little leather jacket like her daddy's, and a pink dress. Her sense of style is all over the place. I like that so much about her. And I hate her dad so much right now for not giving me enough credit to know I could easily love her.

"Would you like to come in?" she asks, taking a step aside.

"Why don't you call your grandfather and ask him if I can?" I smile nervously, tucking the planner back into my backpack.

"Grandpa-great is not here yet. He comes shortly before teatime, which means in just a bit. Grandma's here. Would you like me to call her?"

"Oh, that's not necessary. I'll come ba…"

"Nana!" Tamsin's mouth opens to the shape of an egg, producing a shriek that could cause the earth to move. "Na-naaaaa!"

Before I find a good hole in the ground to swallow me into the next dimension, a woman appears at the door. She looks nothing like Mal—not even a little—which makes me suspect the worst. My suspicions turn out to be correct when she opens her mouth.

"Aurora, you said?" She wipes her hands on a paper towel, as if sullied by my presence.

She looks old enough to be my mother—not quite Father Doherty's age. Ireland is not exactly full of priests who live in sin with women who look like they want to burn me alive, so I'm guessing this is Kathleen's mother, who lives with Father Doherty and Mal's mother.

"Yes, ma'am. I'm here to see Father Doherty."

"Tamsin." She pats the little girl's chubby cheek with one hand, her eyes still zeroing in on me. "Go get your room tidy before supper."

"But I want to stay with Princess Au…"

"Off you go," she quips, and Tamsin scurries away into a house that looks newly refurbished, extremely spacious, and plush. Nothing like Mal's modest crib.

The woman throws a warning finger in my face. "I knew you would eventually come back. We don't have your money. Everything you see here Malachy paid for. Your drunken sod of a father wasn't half as rich as he made his harem of flings believe."

Whoa. I can see where Kathleen got her cut-a-bitch streak. Kathleen's mother could teach mobsters a thing or two about tough talk.

"I'm not here because of Glen. I'm here on a work assignment. You don't have to believe me, but it's the truth. And while I'm here, I'd appreciate exchanging a few words with Father Doherty."

I leave my marriage to Mal out because I still feel like an outsider, a pariah, an interloper in this village. And also because she lost her daughter. Grief is a fiend. It takes over swiftly, then makes you do and say things your normal self would not even think about.

"Whatever the reason you're here, I'm telling you to leave. My granddaughter was never supposed to meet you. That was the deal we had with Mal. He promised us. It's bad enough you're probably warming his bed—"

"Well, I'm not looking for Mal. I'm looking for Father Doherty. Please tell him to meet me at The Boar's Head in two hours. If you do, I promise I will never bother you and your granddaughter ever again."

Knowing that the message will be passed, that Kathleen's mother would never give up a chance to see me gone, I turn on my heel and leave.

Mal

There's no good way to offhandedly mention to your wife that, by the way, you have a seven-year-old daughter, and oops, her mother was her dead half-sister who absolutely loathed her. Oh, and just for the record, you are ninety-nine percent sure Tamsin (the daughter—see? already getting ahead of myself) was conceived when you were drunk off your arse and raped.

Yet Mam's surprise visit, paired with the fact that Rory is understandably starting to lose patience with me, plus that little, nagging thing called my conscience, means I'm going to tell her tonight.

I play the inevitable conversation in my head as I park my coughing, five-hundred-year-old car in front of the cottage. The fact that Rory married me and not Shiny Boyfriend without knowing I make seven figures annually only multiplied my love for her to dangerous quantities I'm not sure my heart can contain.

"Hey, darlin', what do you fancy eating tonight? I'm thinking risotto, wine, and you. Oh, by the way, I have a kid."

Though, maybe it's best to warm her up with some good news.

"Hello, Princess. Did you know I'm busking as a hobby and am actually a reluctant millionaire? I have a lot of fun facts in store for you. Here's another one—I'm a father."

I push the door open, my hands full of presents for Rory and Tamsin. I got Rory chocolate and vintage CDs of the Irish music she likes, and Tamsin a princess dress and...*what the feck?*

Rory's in the living room, stuffing her belongings into her handbag. Her suitcase appears to already be fully packed and standing at the door like an impatient mother, waiting. She has her phone pinned between her shoulder and ear as she struggles to fit her scarf into her purse—she's always cold when she's away from me; why can't she understand that?—and she is growling into the phone.

"I don't care what vehicle. You can send a freaking donkey, and I'll ride it out of here." Pause. "Yes, sir, I know that's not the business you're in. My point is, I just need to get the hell away from this place as soon as possible. Please. Honk when you arrive."

She lets the phone drop to her hand and kills the call. She mumbles something incoherent about calling her mother and punches the screen when I clear my throat.

"Are we going on a honeymoon?" I ask, unloading my hands on the breakfast nook in front of her.

Stay cool. There might be a logical reason for her packing.

She looks up and scowls, like she wasn't expecting me. Then she takes a step back, as if I'm going to strike her.

"You scared me." She tugs the scarf out of her purse and throws it over her shoulders, getting ready to leave.

"Right now, I could say the same about you," I hiss through gritted teeth, doing everything in my power not to launch at her.

I'm not stupid. I knew from the get-go this had a very low percent chance of ever working out.

Still.

Still.

You fall in love with a girl named after two Disney princesses, and you believe in the unbelievable, because…well, Disney and shit.

She folds her arms over her chest.

Uh-huh. This can only mean pissed-off Rory, and that can only mean *run for shelter.*

"What's going on?" I round the nook toward her, but she raises one hand to stop me.

"I ran across someone interesting today."

"You did?" I play along.

She nods.

I say nothing, because I have a bad feeling, and there's something clogging my throat, probably the amount of confessions I should have spat out to her a long time ago.

She takes a step toward me. "Someone you know very well. A little girl called Tamsin. Ring a bell?"

My mouth goes dry. What can I say to this? That I refused to talk to her about Tamsin because I didn't think I'd fall in love with her again? That I hadn't realized I never fell *out* of love with her in the first place?

That at first, I was simply protecting my daughter from her and Richards and their urban, heathen lifestyle by sending her off to live with her grandparents while I worked on this project—oh, and also on ruining her life?

That the secret, locked room actually belongs to Tam, and it's beautiful, and so is she, and the house is normally on point, because I raise her alone, just the two of us? That I was mad that she got near it because I was so protective of Tam, even when she wasn't physically *in* the room? That I messed up the house in advance to make her experience crappy, leaving Tamsin's pristine room untouched.

That by the time I realized she could be mine, it was too late? The lie had grown too big, too threatening, and I was running like a headless chicken between my lover and my daughter?

Does she even want to listen?

"Cute kid, by the way." Rory shrugs, making a show of looking like she doesn't care. "Then I was informed by your mother-in-law that I am a monster."

She is a hurricane, and I'm pushing against the storm when I stride toward her, wanting to explain myself, but she shoves me away and stalks toward the door. I jump in front of her and block her way, plastering my back to the closed door.

"Let me explain."

She throws her head back and laughs, not an ounce of humor in her voice. "What's to explain? That you're a liar? That you're a fraud? That you're a shitty dad for sending your daughter to live with relatives while you screw your new wife, living the perfect double life?"

When she puts it like that, it does seem impossible to find justification for the clusterfuck I've created with my own hands (and cock). But it's not that simple. I know this well, because I walked into this thing demanding revenge, but I never planned to take it this far.

Honestly, I thought Rory would be long gone. I expected her to quit.

"Rory…"

A car honks outside our door. Rory throws up her arms with faux delight.

"That's my carriage, as you like to charmingly put it. I'll see that our equally enchanting divorce papers hit your mail in a timely manner. Hey, Mal, remember our conversation about epic romance movies?"

I glower.

She is making fun of the breakdown of our marriage. No matter the fact that I was stupid enough to cause it, and she is clearly pissed off, I'm still finding it difficult to watch her shitting all over what we have.

Rory doesn't wait for me to answer, making a show of bypassing me and throwing the door open. She stands on the threshold as she delivers her last line.

"You said all great romance movies have a scene where the woman drives the man. Here's an unscripted twist: our romantic, amazing, sweet, *perfect* movie was a parody. Bravo." She claps, taking a little bow. "You won the Razzie for this one, Mal. It really was *that* bad."

Then she takes out the napkin—*our* napkin with the contract—from her bag and rips it to shreds in front of me, throwing the pieces in the air and watching them float down like confetti.

"The contract was dumb. So were we. Maybe it's my fault. Maybe it's in my DNA to attract lying asshats. But if I have to thank you for one thing, Malachy Doherty, it's for opening my eyes to the fact that Callum was just as big a douchebag as you are. Congratulations. You're just as bad as—what did you call him? Shiny Boyfriend? Make sure you give him a call and invite him next time you're on the prowl."

With that, she slams the door in my face and leaves.

Rory

Still reeling from finding out my husband has a secret daughter, and that he promised his family he'd keep me away, I show up just in time for my emergency meeting with Father Doherty at The Boar's Head.

He is already there when I arrive, twiddling his thumbs and glancing left and right, like he's committing some sort of crime. When I slide into the booth, he stands up and stares at the table, hard.

"On one hand, it is highly frowned upon for me to socialize with women of your age, publicly or otherwise. Especially at a pub. On the other, I am deeply worried for your wellbeing in Mal's house when both Elaine and Lara are in Tolka."

"Which one is which?" I plop down on the wooden seat opposite to him, cradling my tall glass of water. I don't mention that I will no longer be staying at Mal's house.

"Elaine is Kathleen's mam; Lara is Mal's."

I didn't even know my mother-in-law's name, and just found out she'd likely to stab me in the eye before shaking my hand. What a wonderful start to obviously long-term marital bliss.

I rub a drop of water on the table, back and forth, wondering how this day could possibly get any worse. Of course, I believe it can. Today hasn't met a negative challenge it couldn't conquer. I wouldn't be surprised if a UFO kidnapped me on my way to the airport to perform a full rectal examination on me, sending me back to Earth with nothing but lubricated ass cheeks, anal scars, and a T-shirt that says "My Wife Went to Kepler-22b and All I Got Was This Lousy T-Shirt."

"I'm guessing they both hate me." I frown at my drink, because examining Father Doherty's face is too painful.

He says nothing to that.

I should really get what I'm here for and move along. There's a flight to New York in four hours, and I don't want to miss it or I'll have to stay another day.

Mal hasn't kept something small from me. He kept an entire child, with personality and freckles and purple eyes and hobbies. And she's my niece. My half-sister's child. Why do people insist on hiding things from me?

Mom.

Father Doherty.

Mal.

Summer and Callum.

"Father?" I slant my head. "Is there anything more unholy than preventing justice? The truth is all around me. If I don't get your version of things, I'll get Ms. Patel's. Or Maeve and Heather's. Or Mal's, eventually. We both know I'll get a far worse version from any of them, or at the very least, not as accurate as yours."

"I promised your—"

"Mother?" I arch an eyebrow, mustering the courage to lie to a priest. If I burst into flames right on the spot, I will only have myself to blame. "She told me her side of the story."

"She did?" His eyes flare.

Bingo. They are in this together. I decide to run with the only thing I have. It's a shot in the dark, but on the off-chance it's a memory and not just a dream, I fire it out.

"Yeah. How she was here. How she ran with me."

My heart is beating so hard and loud in my chest, I'm surprised he doesn't hear it. Maybe he does, and he wants to spare me the embarrassment. It was just a dream. A nightmare of sorts. But it seemed so real.

To my surprise, Father Doherty plants his head inside his palms and bursts into tears—the gut-tearing sound of a mewling animal being ripped to shreds by a pack of coyotes.

"Please forgive us. All of us."

"Tell me." I lean down, careful not to touch him as I beg for more of his words. "Everything. Please. Don't I deserve to know? There's a chunk in my life—the first chunk, the most important chunk—that's missing, and nobody here is telling me anything."

My voice sounds so urgent, so crisp, so wild, I scare even myself. I sound unhinged.

He looks up and exhales sharply. "I don't know how much your mother has told you."

"Then tell me everything. From the beginning."

"When you weren't even a year old, she decided to take a leap and give in to your father's pleas to come to Ireland and try to work things out. She was lonely here. An outcast. She came to church often. Less to confess, more to…vent, I suppose. She told me—outside of the confession booth, of course—that two things brought her here. She wanted to try to help Glen get sober, but even more important, she didn't want it on her conscience to have you live without a father knowing she didn't even try. She moved in with him and they became—how do you call it?—an instant family, making Kathleen and her mother take the backseat in Glen's life."

Molten ache seeps under my skin. I had no idea Mom came here. I had no idea she ever set foot in Ireland. Why wouldn't she tell me? Seems like the kind of thing she would gloat about. "*Look. I tried.*" Yet, she never mentioned it, even though she knew it would put her in a positive light.

"Continue."

"Things weren't easy for the couple. Glen struggled to stay sober for more than a few hours. Your mother felt lonely and isolated. She tried to befriend some of the village women, but naturally, they felt loyal to Elaine, who was absolutely devastated. Elaine—Kathleen's mam—had held on to the hope she'd reunite with Glen for years after Kathleen was conceived. Debbie took this hope from her. Or so she felt."

I realize he is saying this about a woman with whom he lives and is probably fond of. I refrain from letting a string of profanities exit my mouth.

"Okay," I say, my heart pounding fast. "Then what happened?"

Father Doherty stares down at his hands on the table, like they've committed some sort of horrible crime.

"Your mother came to me one day and told me she would like to leave and take you back to America, that things had not worked out so well between her and Glen. That was no secret. She said he'd been verbally abusive and prevented her from going out with you three separate times, accusing her of flirting with the villagers. We had a lengthy discussion, during which I gave her my opinion on the matter. Principally, that families should remain together and that she should consider encouraging Glen to try harder, perhaps by agreeing to his marriage proposal."

I bite my lower lip. My mother was in an abusive relationship with my father, here in Ireland. And I gave her hell for putting a buffer between him and me.

"Then the weight of my words crashed down on me." Father Doherty's lower lip trembles, and he chokes on a sob that never quite makes it out of his throat. "She went back to Glen that day and told him she was willing to marry him if he went to rehab. He said she'd been nagging him for months and that he liked the drink better than he liked her. He sent her on her way. Debbie was relieved to leave. She tried to take you, but he wouldn't let her—said you were going to stay with him because you didn't need a pesky mother like her.

"They almost tore your limbs fighting over you, snatching you from each other. You were only a year old at the time, still so fragile. Finally, your mother took you. She gathered your passports and her bag and flew out the door. Glen grabbed a bottle of whiskey and threw it at her. Luckily, he missed. But the glass shattered against the wall and part of it…part of it…"

He swallows, his eyes shifting to the scar on my temple.

The one my mother told me I was born with.

Everything inside me shatters. Glen did this to me. He gave me this scar. Father Doherty squeezes his eyes shut, and when he opens them again, a zing of determination flashes through them.

"It cut you open. You were bleeding badly, and it was close to your eye. The blood came gushing out. I remember getting to their house shortly after the incident and throwing up from all the blood, which I knew belonged to an innocent baby. But Glen wasn't shocked by what he'd done. He was too far gone, too drunk to realize his actions. He started chasing after your mother, who took off with you in her arms. She ran up the road on Main Street, toward the entrance of the town, to try to catch a cab to the hospital. He raced after her. People on the street noticed. They thought your mother was running away with you. She didn't have the best reputation in Tolka. She was seen as the woman who came for the man Elaine had pined for all those years. Some of them ran after him and her, to see what went on."

"The gray squirrel," I say quietly.

He nods, his eyes telling me I've gotten exactly what he meant all those years ago.

A flashback of my dream shoots like an arrow through my head.

The mob.

Chasing after my mother.

With me, bleeding in her arms.

Father Doherty drops his head to his hands again. "I was looking for your mother at the exact same time she was running from him. First, I made a stop at Glen's. When I saw the blood, I ran out and drove around the village, and when I found you, I immediately stopped my car and let your mother in. We drove to the hospital. The entire journey, I apologized for giving her the wrong advice instead of shelter."

I rub my eyes, trying to keep myself together. It's difficult, especially when I want to cry for my mom as much as for myself.

"It doesn't make any sense." I shake my head. "She always told me she's never been to Ireland."

"She wanted to protect you from the truth, to keep your scars minimal—on the surface—and make sure they only marred your skin, not your heart. She didn't want you to know who your father really was that day. And after the incident, when you were discharged and Debbie went back to New Jersey, Glen was prosecuted and jailed for a couple years. He got sober in prison, but it didn't last quite as long as we'd hoped. The time inside changed him, though. He no longer wanted anything to do with—"

"My mother and me?" I finish for him.

I have so much hatred for Glen right now, I'm afraid I'm capable of digging up his grave just so I can kill him all over again. My poor mom. She dealt with everything all by herself.

And let me think she was the coldhearted one between them.

"Well, yes." Father Doherty rubs his cheek, embarrassed on Glen's behalf.

"I don't understand any of this. Then why did my mother show me letters and gifts from him every birthday and Christmas? He always gave me the thoughtful presents. The ones that meant something."

"It was important to your mother to make you believe you meant something to him. She took the role of the martyr, even though it killed her. She took the blame for the fact that you and your father weren't in contact, not wanting you to feel rejected by Glen. She gathered the letters you sent him, read them, and made sure you thought he bought you all the things you wanted. But *she* was the one doing all the buying. And when you asked something that was specific to Ireland—a chocolate bar or Irish music—I'd buy it for you, and your mother would pay me back, despite my refusal to accept her money."

"She wrote the letters on his behalf?" My eyes flare.

He nods solemnly.

"And the child support?"

Father Doherty shakes his head.

Jesus. Glen didn't pay. It was just Mom and me.

He sighs. "She only wanted the best for you. She would send me your gifts, spending hundreds of dollars a year, so I could send them back to you and have it appear completely authentic."

I remember the Irish stamps, the wrinkly boxes that put butterflies in my stomach. I've never wanted to hug my mother tighter. A rush of sympathy for her courses through me. She's been through so much, and I've been a brat to her. The entire time, I thought she was jealous of the relationship I wanted to have with Glen.

"Is that why Kathleen hated me so much? Because I took her father, monopolized his time, then sent him to jail for a while?"

He sighs again, evidently feeling the strain of having to admit just how awful the man who left me his DNA and a mountain of daddy issues was.

"Kathleen was desperate for love. Always had been. Feeling loved was a need for her akin to breathing. Glen limited their communication to Sunday visits, and even then, he took more interest in Mal and his music than in her. But Kathleen wasn't jealous of Mal. She'd always loved that boy, since they were wee babies. In her head, I suppose, it was the easiest to blame you. Then, when you visited here after he died, she was worried you showed up solely for the inheritance. Your mother sent me a letter informing me of your arrival, so I waited for you. When we met, I wanted to keep you as far away from Kathleen as I could. I sent you to Mal, after warning him never to tell you the truth about Glen and your scar. But then you both went to Kathleen, and she realized not only did you take her father, you were also about to take the lad she'd been in love with since birth."

"Hold on." I lift a hand. "Mal was aware of all of this? He knew this when I came here at eighteen?"

But, of course, he knew. If Maeve and Heather knew my story—and they didn't even have the slightest business knowing me—how could Mal not?

By the pained look on Father Doherty's face, I realize he did not think this implication through.

"He didn't mean..."

"I have to go." I dart up, my throat itching with the ball of tears lodged inside it. No truer words have ever been spoken by me. I *have* to leave. Not just The Boar's Head, but Tolka, too. I have to leave Ireland behind. Every green, rolling hill, charming, cobblestoned pathway, and red door is haunting me.

I have to listen to my mother, who's been telling me, begging me, warning me about this place. Telling me to run away and never look back. Maybe I can get the marriage with Mal annulled. It hasn't even been a week.

Mal. Mal, Mal, Mal.

A secret daughter.

The truth about my father.

The lying, deceiving, manipulative piece of—

"Wait!" Father Doherty rises to his feet, staggering forward, holding on to the edges of the table. He's so frail that he groans involuntarily as he does. He puts his hand on his lower back, wheezing.

I stop, my shoulders sagging. "Do you need me to call you a cab?" I ask, my voice softening.

He shakes his head. "Please don't be mad at him. He just did as he was told. He, like your mother, like myself, didn't want the truth to consume you, to have your past dictate your future."

With all due respect, Father Doherty sounds like a fortune cookie. I'm not going to accept this excuse.

"It's not for *him* to decide what I should or shouldn't know. Or for you. Or for her. For anyone." I let out a feral yelp, throwing my hands in the air.

All heads in the pub snap toward me, and I turn my volume down a notch, leaning forward and whispering hotly, "No one ever appointed Mal to be my Prince Charming, and if he were such thing to me, he'd be doing a crappy job. I deserved to know. I came to him begging for answers. He lured me into his net and made me think it was of my own free will. I never would have…"

Slept with him had I been up to speed on what my father had done.

Let him hold me all night.

Fallen in love with him.

My relationship with Mal would have been completely different, had he told me the truth when I met him the first time.

Then something else occurs to me.

"Tell me, Father, did Tamsin celebrate her birthday recently?"

The glitter.

The cake Mal baked.

The present.

Father Doherty showing up at Ms. Patel's newsagents unexpectedly, buying booze.

Of course, that's another event I was shunned from because I'm the daughter of the devil—the devil whose only crime was trying to save me from my father.

"Yes." He tucks his chin, staring at his shoes. "Her seventh."

"I see."

For the first time in my life, I can say this with certainty. I *do* see. And as precious as Tamsin is, I cannot afford to stick around and watch her grow.

"Are you going to need that cab?"

Even I flinch at the callousness of my voice. This man is pushing eighty-five. I have no business talking to him like this. He coils his fingers over the table, still unable to lift his gaze and meet mine.

"Oh, Rory. My dear Rory. Your mother didn't tell you anything, did she? She never would."

I purse my lips, staring down at my Toms, like a punished kid.

Please don't light me on fire, God.

Father Doherty eyes my suitcase by the table, finds the courage to look at me, and speaks.

"Don't go. Don't leave for America. If you go, you will only lash out at Debbie, and she doesn't deserve it. She loves you so much, Aurora. She always tried to protect you from everything surrounding Glen. I remember when she named you, she sent me a letter, explaining why she chose those names for you. Because she wanted you to have the fairytale, something perfect and uncomplicated. She never wanted all this mess to touch you."

"Yet it did," I seethe, feeling my teeth grind against one another.

He wipes his tears with the base of his thumb, sniffing.

"It most certainly caught up with me, and blew up in my face."

* * *

Mal

The best (and perhaps only good) part of being from a small town is that people look out for you. Fifteen minutes after Rory stormed out, while I paced a hole in the floor trying to figure out my next move, I got a ring from my barman Dermot at The Boar's Head, letting me know my grandfather was having a lively conversation with a young woman.

My woman.

I run to my car and drive like a rabid dog after snapping back to reality. I throw it in park without turning off the engine and look up to see her getting into a cab. The vehicle is an ugly, seventies Renault that coughs its way down the road. Rory is in such a rush to leave, she didn't want to wait for a decent ride.

This is how much she hates you.

I run, motioning to my wife to lower her window, and guard, and *feck—will she just listen?*

Rory pretends I don't exist, staring straight ahead at the back of the driver's seat, her sunglasses perched on the tip of her button nose. I rap on the window with my fist, coughing out fifteen years' worth of sex as my sole physical activity.

"*Slow. Down.*"

My request falls on deaf ears.

"The hell with you, woman." I slap the roof of the car, and the driver speeds up in response, so I run even faster. (Who in their right mind does this for fun?)

I can't let her go. Well, I guess technically I can. Perhaps I even *should*, but I won't. Not without a fight. And she needs to learn the entire truth, even if it rips us both to shreds.

"I didn't tell you about Glen because I was sworn to secrecy. Because look at you—you're devastated. Because I knew, selfishly, that if you found out about Glen, you wouldn't have room in your heart to fall in love with me eight years ago. Which you did, Rory. We fell in love in less than twenty-four hours. And it took us less than a week, almost a decade later..."

I slap my hands on my knees and pant, sucking in as much oxygen as I can, before resuming my chase. She is still staring at the back of the driver's seat as if it's the most mesmerizing thing since fiberglass manufacturing. (No, seriously. Look it up on Google. It's fantastic.)

"...to remember how we can't live apart. Not really. Exist, maybe, but not *live*. And it's not like I completely shielded you from the truth. Trust me, I battled this shite internally. I did. That's why I took you to Kathleen. It was my coin-flipping moment. I told myself if you really were meant to know, she'd tell you the truth. She didn't, Rory."

She still gives me nothing.

"Yes, I fecked up. Yes, I kept the truth from you. About you. About me. But none of it was because I wanted to hurt you. I wanted to protect you. To shield you from the past. It's called past because it passed! We have a present, Rory. A future."

Her nose twitches in annoyance. It's the slightest movement, but it gives me hope—not that she will forgive me, but that she might be pissed enough to stop the cab, get out, and smack me in the head.

"Fine. A part of it wasn't entirely altruistic. Of course, I wanted to feck you again when I saw you. Who wouldn't? Look at you."

Her nose tics under her sunglasses again, her lips folding under her teeth.

She is angry.

I'm about to make her angrier.

"Want to know if you love someone? Watch them suffer and see how much it tears *you* apart. Because when you were down, when you hurt, Rory, every fiber of me burned right along with you. You leaving without listening to what I have to say simply solidifies my suspicion all along: Your skin is not the only thing cold about you. Your heart is frozen, too. I loved you from the start. You, however, were always more interested in my dick and my Irishness. You really took daddy issues to a whole new level, darlin'."

I can see her hand gripping the door handle. She barks something to the driver, and the car slows down gradually, not yet coming to a full stop. I know I'm close, so I put the final nail into the coffin. The one I was waiting to share with her on another, happier occasion.

"Oh, and another thing: That napkin you just tore apart didn't mean jack-shit. You said you didn't believe in kismet when we first met. I forgot to mention—neither do I. I sought you out eight years ago, after you left. I sent you letters and gifts and tried to track you down. I called your house and your mother and your dorm, trying to get to your cell number. Want to know something else? I hunted you down last year, too—saw your name on the back of a Blue Hill Records cover and put two and two together. I knew you were working for that wanker, Ryner. So I accepted his offer to write Richards an album, because I wanted you near me. It was never fate. It was never luck. I *demanded* to have you at my disposal, Aurora Belle Jenkins. You were a part of a package deal. It's not fate; it's us. From start to finish. Twisted, screwed, obsessed, destructive, wonderful us."

The car comes to a stop, the driver punching the steering wheel with frustration. I watch as Rory bursts out the back door like fireworks, shaking her fist in my face.

"How dare you! We said no seeking each other out. You used that napkin to make me marry you! You lied!" She pushes my chest.

She is completely red, her hair a mess.

"Bullshit!" I laugh in her face, shoving her away, no longer able to tolerate anything less than the truth. "You married me not because of that stupid napkin, but because you let me shove my fingers, and a chocolate bar, and my tongue into every hole of yours I had interest in invading while you still had a boyfriend. Because that's what we do. We run people over to get to each other. We destroy everything in our way, other than ourselves."

The cab driver gives me a look of interest, listening with his tongue out, practically panting. Probably should've kept the chocolate bar bit to myself.

"You're lying. You've never sought me out." She points at me, manic.

I laugh harder. I can't help it, because now that the truth is coming out—why not let it *all* out? She deserves to know what her mother did, even if it makes both her parents intolerable arseholes.

I turn around and stomp back toward my cottage (feck the car), and she follows me, because I hold the one thing she wants—the truth.

"Try again, Rory. Why do you think I hated you so much? Why do you think I married Kiki? Why do you think all the bad shit happened? I chased you around, and your mother told me you wanted nothing to do with me. She said I should move on. That you'd found another lad to keep you warm at night. She sent me the pictures you took of me, with the god-awful things you wrote about me on the back of them."

I turn around to see her face morphing from angry to horrified.

Her features twist in pain. "Oh, God."

"Yeah, that's what you said when I screwed you six ways from Sunday and gave you enough orgasms for a decade of PornHub material. Yet apparently, I tried too hard. And you know what? I did. I did try far too hard, because I wanted no one else to compare."

"No one did compare!" she screams in my face. "Happy? No one compared, which is why I didn't date until Callum came along. There was no other guy. I wrote those things on the back of your pictures because I couldn't stop thinking about you, and Summer gave me an exercise in trying to find the bad things in you, and those were the only things I could come up with. You were damn near perfect. When I came back from college, I turned my room upside down so many times, desperate to find your photos, because they were the only thing I had left of you. And I didn't want to look you up on social media, because I still honored the stupid contract. I cried days and nights about those pictures, Mal."

I pinch the bridge of my nose, taking a deep, cleansing breath. "I sent you dozens of letters. They were redirected to your New Jersey address, and you never saw them."

"Jesus."

"The cherry on the shit cake? Your mother told me I got you pregnant and you had an abortion."

There's radio silence from her side of the bare shoulder of the road, so I open my eyes to look at her. She is staring back at me, stunned.

"Is it true?" I ask quietly.

She shakes her head slowly.

Thank God.

"I'm speechless right now," she admits.

"I'm sorry," I say. "But also, sort of relieved, because now you're angry at someone else."

"Is that why you and Kathleen got married? Had a child?"

"Yes. I mean, no…I don't know." I shake my head, pacing back and forth.

The cabbie dumps her suitcase and backpack onto the side of the road and drives away, leaving us in this field, and it's getting dark, and cold, but neither of us seems to care.

"This is how it happened: I got so furious with you, I pulled a Glen and went to get myself two bottles of something terribly strong to knock myself unconscious. Kathleen was there, at the newsagents, and she sort of jumped into my car without my consent, but I was so lethargic, I didn't even have the strength to kick her out. We got piss-drunk. Well, I did, anyway, and that's how it happened."

There are tears clinging to Rory's lower lashes, and I wish I could kiss them away, but I don't think we're there yet. I don't know if we ever will be. I try to ignore the possibility of never kissing my wife again.

"You slept with my sister, Mal."

"She…"

I know this will be the first and last time I say this. Not just because Kathleen is dead and I honor her memory, but mainly because I never, ever want Tasmin to know how she was conceived. She doesn't deserve this horror of a story. I refuse to saddle her with a truth that has nothing to do with her.

"I wasn't conscious, Rory. I mean, well, not fully. I said no. Several times, I think. But I wasn't completely there when Tamsin was conceived. This marriage I dangled in your face…it was a sham. A lie. Kiki knew it, too."

The tears fall from Rory's cheeks to her feet, and she is quivering like a leaf dancing on the ground in fall.

I continue, undeterred, "I'm not going to lie, though. Kathleen reminded me of you, and at that time, I was under the impression *you* were something I would never be able to have. So I settled for the closest thing. *Her.* I'm not proud of what I did or how I did it."

"*Rory, Rory, Rory,*" I remember chanting every time I was inside Kiki. Like an unanswered prayer. A requiem for a broken heart.

"When we found out she was pregnant, I was pressured by every-one we knew to tie the knot. She'd been a virgin before, and our fam-ilies would have killed us. And, frankly, I stopped trying. I thought maybe becoming a father would distract me from you."

"Did it?" She's sobbing openly now.

I want to wrap my arms around her and tell her to let it all out. Yet, I'm rooted to the road's shoulder, waiting for her to come to me just once in this lifetime.

I'm tired of doing the chasing. I'm tired of losing just so she can win. I'm exhausted from plotting how to court her, how to have her, how to ruin her, how to keep her, while she keeps fighting it.

Sure, initially, I didn't tell her about Tamsin because I thought she wasn't going to stick around long enough to need to know, and I wanted to protect my daughter. But the minute Rory said "I do," things became real.

And that was the moment I shoved my reality under the carpet for a woman.

I hid my daughter for a lover.

Never again.

"Nothing made me forget you. The night Tamsin was born was also the night Kiki died. Consequently, it was also our wedding day." I let all the events sink in. "I know I was more than a bit short with you the day Tam celebrated her birthday. Actually, I was a full-blown arsehole. But I was hurting, the pain coming from so many directions. I didn't want to be touched, not to mention prodded."

Her eyes meet mine with understanding.

"After the wedding, we came back home, and Kiki found the napkin. Our contract. She told me to throw it away." I wait a beat, watching her face.

She stops breathing altogether and waits for me to continue.

"I couldn't do it."

She lets out a ragged breath and starts crying harder.

"She ran. And I chased her, like I chased you just now. But with you…"

I suck in a breath. The truth hurts. It cuts you open. That's why we hide it from the ones we love. From the people whose opinion we care about.

"With you, I chased harder."

Rory

She died because of us.

She didn't stop at a stop sign, because the only thing she cared about was running away. After the accident, Kathleen had been rushed to the hospital. Tamsin's heartbeat was faint, but the doctors were also concerned for the life of her mother. The baby wasn't getting enough oxygen and was in distress.

My sister's last words were, "Save him. I know I can't make it. He can."

She thought Tamsin was a boy, and that he would live.

She got one thing right. The important part.

Kathleen was pronounced dead shortly after Tamsin was delivered—close enough that she didn't get the chance to hold her daughter in her arms. Because of the impact caused by the collision with the truck, Tamsin was born with spinal damage and had to undergo a complicated operation when she was barely old enough to see shapes. Mal shelled out some serious cash to make sure his daughter was given the best medical treatment. Experts were flown from all over the world. He's been writing and selling songs ever since, never looking back or stopping to consider what he wanted for himself.

The first songs he sold were about me.

He was furious with me. He blamed me for the argument leading to Kathleen's death. He became a single father before he'd even turned twenty-four. And for what? A girl who'd allegedly had an abortion with his baby and told him to stop writing to her after he confessed his family was falling apart.

On our way back to the cottage, while we are both in too much shock to touch the Kathleen subject, Mal opens up about Maeve.

"Her husband, Sean, was the lorry driver who collided with Kathleen. We were friends, before..." He looks up and shakes his head. "We were mates once. But when the accident happened, when he was bursting with adrenaline, his truth came out. He told me I never deserved my wife. That I never truly loved her. He screamed that she died because of me."

I wince. The truth has a way to hit you harder than any lie. It's what you need to face when you look in the mirror every day.

Sean had reminded him he was unworthy of his wife.

So Mal reminded Sean he wasn't worthy of *his* either.

"I took Maeve as a lover to prove she didn't love him, just like I didn't love Kiki. I paraded her around Tolka as retaliation, making a point of doing it openly. I kissed her in public places, pinched her arse in the queue when we were at the bank. In short, I was a cunt. I hurt so much, I wanted to hurt others. I'm just grateful you weren't around when I was at my worst."

"Then you took other women to bed, too? Why?" I ask, my voice barely audible.

"Being with Maeve gave my loneliness a kind of…I don't know, a stubborn quality. She was in it because she thought we had a future and she wanted her hands on whatever money she thought I had, but I was in it for revenge. What finally made me stop was hearing her kids were being bullied at school because everyone knew their mam was sleeping with a man who wasn't their dad. I couldn't stomach it. I broke it off and wrote Maeve a check to send them to a school where no one knew them and they could start fresh. Then I tried to erase the aftertaste of Maeve with an ever-growing line of women who knocked on my door. But the longer the line became, the shorter my attention span grew. In the last few years, I've been solely focused on Tamsin. She's the only thing that's kept me sane, the only person who's mattered. Until you."

I say nothing to this, because even though I'm flattered, I can't help but also feel angry.

"When I saw your name on the back of that cover, I had a Pavlovian response," he continues. "I picked up the phone and accepted the job Ryner had offered me months before. I laid down my ultimatums, and one of them was doing things my way—demanding *you* as the photographer. Ryner desperately needed a hitmaker for Richards. He agreed to all of my requests, including this crazy one to transport you here. It's amazing what you can get away with in the name of the creative process. I could've told him I needed the entire Victoria's Secret cast and ten kilograms of cocaine to write this album and been the happiest pig alive."

I swat him when he says that, and can't help but laugh because he *could* have said it, and still, it's me he asked for.

"So, I moved Tamsin to her grandparents' house for a couple months and planned on making your life miserable and sabotaging your career. I know, extremely toddler-like of me. Trust me, it didn't sound as outrageously stupid when I thought about it without saying it out loud. I wanted to make your boyfriend break up with you, to shove your face in the reality I've lived. But very early on, I learned two things that stood in the way of my Marvel-villain-like master plan."

Mal rubs his cheek. His hair is a tousled perfection, his eyebrows furrowed, and the curves of his cheeks are so angular and prominent, I can't believe he is truly flesh and blood.

"One, I discovered you didn't really do all the horrible things I thought you'd done to me. That definitely put a damper on my Rory-is-Satan quest. And two, even if you had, even if all of it were true, I found I still couldn't knowingly and maliciously hurt you. I didn't *want* to hurt you. I still loved you too much, regardless of how you felt about me. I loved you when you hated me, I loved you when I thought you were indifferent to me, and I loved you when you were on the fence about me. But when I realized you loved me back? All bets were off. The world kept spinning. Days went by. Things changed—other than one thing, my love for you."

When we reach the door, I look down at my feet. Shame consumes me. Shame for all the times I wasn't here for Mal when he needed me most. Shame that I became a person he thought wouldn't love Tamsin wholeheartedly and unconditionally.

Not only does she belong to the man I love, but she also belonged to my half-sister, and no matter how I felt about her, she will always be a part of me.

I swallow. "I want to meet Tamsin. Properly, I mean."

I look up, and there is so much relief and love in his eyes, I'm surprised my heart doesn't pop like a piñata—all colorful ribbons and candy and joy—through my chest.

It's hard to stay mad at Mal for keeping Tamsin a secret, knowing he had every reason to believe I was a monster. I even find it hard to stay mad at Glen for nearly killing me when I was a baby. After all, those events led me here, after all these years. I'm not upset with Mal anymore for keeping what he knew about my father a secret when I came here the first time around—not because he was right to keep the information from me, but because I found out something important about Mal today. He puts his loved ones first. And sometimes he does twisted things to keep us safe and sheltered, just like Mom.

Love makes you do twisted things.

I'm not justifying it—hell, I'd like to maim Mal every single day for how he handled everything with Sean and Maeve—but I'd be hypocritical not to see where their actions came from. I cheated on Callum, too.

"You can't play God anymore." I point at Mal's face.

He nods. "Who says I *play* Him?" He rubs the back of his neck, grinning.

I swat his chest. "You can't keep any secrets from me. I mean it."

"I won't," he promises.

"What do I do about Debbie?" I play with my nose hoop as Mal pushes open the door.

He shoves my suitcase into the cottage and steps in after me.

"On one hand, I'm overwhelmed with gratitude for what she's done, sheltering me from the truth in a way that would make me feel loved and appreciated by a father. I know she did that to protect me— portrayed herself in a bad light to make sure I thought highly of him, even though she had a wonky way of going about it, and even though we had such a weird relationship throughout my teenage years. When I left the bar earlier, I was ready to go back home and patch things up with her. Then you told me all the lies about the abortion and her sending you letters and the pictures I took of you, not to mention hiding your letters from me. How do I forgive that? She almost took my happiness from me. Almost."

How do I forgive my mother for wanting to keep me away from the love of my life?

Mal cups my cheeks, smiling down at me. I never considered just how perfect we fit. He is tall enough to tuck my head under his chin. Just enough wider than me to cover me completely, but not comically so. Everything about us is in sync. It's like we were made for each other, two pieces of an elaborate puzzle that can only go together.

"You talk to her. You hear her out. You give her shite, then you move on and let it go, focusing on your happiness. Because, Rory?"

I blink up at him.

"Blood is thicker than water, and it's only when you're about to lose someone in your family that you realize just how much you truly love them."

A NOTE FROM DEBBIE (RORY'S MOM)

Before you judge me, consider this: I did everything I could, and I worked with what I had.

Can we please just keep in mind that I had Rory when I was eight-goddamn-teen? I was supposed to go to college, for Christ's sake. To have a life, a future, a steady boyfriend. The wedding of my dreams, a big Italian family with a good boy from the right side of the tracks. All of that—*poof!*—gone. And for what? One mistake? Everyone makes mistakes. Some just have more weight than others.

Mine happened to crush my entire life.

Of course, I love my daughter. But that's why I did what I had to do.

It seemed a little unfair that I was put in this situation. Single mother, struggling to put dinner on the table, forever late with paying the bills. I dwelled on the unfairness of it all for years, when I clocked in and out of a drugstore I hated, working double shifts and leaving Rory with a sixteen-year-old babysitter who occasionally forgot to feed her. Unfortunately, she was the only sitter I could afford, so I had to shove some food into Rory right before I left for my shift.

I've done some things I'm not proud of to make sure we had a roof over our heads. My folks weren't mighty thrilled to find out I got knocked up overseas, and they definitely didn't offer to help me, let alone house me. In fact, their exact words were, "You're done here, young lady. Pack a bag and leave, or we'll do it for you."

They died months apart when Rory was three, so they didn't even get to see how great she turned out. How well we both did. How we made it.

The day they told me I was no longer welcome in their house, I vowed to make sure she'd have everything I didn't.

What did I do to support us? Well, what *didn't* I do?

I worked double shifts, scrubbed diner kitchen floors on weekends with Rory in her little sling carrier attached to me, taking cat naps and staring at me periodically with her kind, intelligent silence. I started doing women's hair in my apartment whenever I didn't have a shift or a cleaning gig. The rules were they needed to bring the hair dye along with them, so I wasn't responsible for the shade, and a tip was mandatory, because the blow dryer blew my electricity bill through the roof.

I went on dates with men I didn't like and got paid by the hour. I took advantage of my killer legs. I didn't do anything but cling on their arms, but I still threw up every time I came back home and watched my daughter sleeping soundly next to my bed. I didn't know what I would do if she ever did that to support her kid, to make sure they had formula, clothes, and medical insurance in place.

I remember the day I started smoking. I'd put Rory to sleep—she was two years old then, exactly one year after I ran away from Glen—and slipped into my tiny, dated bathroom. I looked in the mirror, adorned with puke-green seventies tiling, and couldn't believe the dark shade under my eyes.

I wanted to cry.

I wasn't beautiful anymore, even though my entire life was still ahead of me. I was a few months shy of twenty-one, for crying out loud. All my friends were dating, studying, going out, or focusing on their exciting, new careers, and I was either working or begging Rory to stop crying.

I wanted to do something for myself—something destructive but indulgent. Alcohol was out of the question. I'd seen what it did to Glen. So I checked on Rory again—still asleep—and slipped out to the local mart down the block. I bought myself a pack of something fancy-looking and a Zippo and came back home. Made myself a cup of coffee, cracked a window, and lit up.

The first cigarette made me nauseous.

The second calmed me down.

I've never bothered to kick the habit. It's my small way of telling the universe to fuck off.

As for the letter I sent Malachy…*look.*

At this point I was acutely aware of the fact that Ireland was not for the Jenkins girls. I ran away from it, leaving the father of my child arrested and eventually thrown in jail. Everyone in Tolka hated me, and Rory by proxy. Malachy reminded me of Glen every single time my daughter spoke about him.

The music, the guitar, the songwriting, the charm, the alcohol, the hysterical impatience, the whirlwind romance, and the ability to drive women to madness. I was terrified, and sure, he was just a phase—the first real, exciting guy she'd ever met.

I only half-lied in that letter. I told him the truth about the thought process of being pregnant at eighteen. I just lied about my identity.

It wasn't Rory who wrote to him; it was me.

And I didn't abort the baby; I kept her.

Not that I didn't think about having an abortion at the time. I went as far as booking an appointment at the clinic. But when I arrived and flipped through the leaflets, the clock moving at a snail's pace, each *tick-tock* sound flicking my skin like a welt, I realized I couldn't do it.

Not to her. Not to me. We were in this together.

Then there was her scar.

Of course, I wanted her to hide or remove it. But I couldn't afford the plastic surgery. I hate it, okay? That's the truth. It's a constant reminder of how I failed my daughter. I couldn't keep her safe from her own father, even when the writing was on the wall, smeared in a drunk's man vomit.

There are the good souls asking me why I didn't tell Rory the entire story. Well, what kind of good would it have done her? It was easier to keep her innocence intact, to send Father Doherty gifts, which he sent back to her, and pretend her father was functioning and loving and present. Should I really have told her we sent him to jail? Should I have scarred her again before she even knew how to spell her own name?

I let her think what she wanted to think.

That he was some kind of a hero, that she was deeply loved.

She already thought I was lame. So I scored a few more lameness points. Big deal.

All I ever wanted was to protect my daughter.

By hiding the letters.

By telling Malachy to back off.

Sure, the way I did it may offend some people. I definitely took it too far. Most parents in my position, I believe, would have ignored Mal's letters. Or simply not opened them in the first place. But I thought I was saving her.

And I'll do anything in my power to help her.

Even if it kills me.

Even if it villainizes me.

That's what they don't tell you in the movies. Bad guys have hearts, too.

Present

Mal

INDING DEBBIE JENKINS AT MY DOORSTEP WAS AKIN TO finding dog shit on my porch, lit on fire, attached to a ticking time bomb, which had been secured to a school bus full of kids.

This woman has messed with my life more than anyone else I know, and still, I called her here, knowing that Rory needs her. I put her on a plane—first class, in case you were wondering, a luxury I'd never indulge in myself—so she could salvage her relationship with her daughter.

When I open the door, she's staring at her pointy, glittery cowgirl boots with a frown, drawing a circle with the tip of the right one. Rory wasn't exaggerating about the hairspray, highlights, and *Coyote Ugly* outfit. Her mother looks like a Vegas showgirl who fell asleep under the blazing sun and woke up twenty years later.

Rory is in the bedroom, dead to the world after a turbulent few days, and I want to make this as painless as possible for my wife.

"Debbie." I open the door, stepping aside. "Do you need help with your suitcase?"

"I didn't bring one. I wasn't expecting her to—"

"Forgive you? I wouldn't, either. But Rory's better than that." Than *us.*

She still refuses to look at me. If nothing else, her shame is evidence that she has a soul. That's good. Souls are rolling, organic, never-dying things. Bodies are born and die and decay in between.

Debbie steps in gingerly. I make her a cup of tea without asking if she needs it, while she perches her arse on a stool by the breakfast nook.

I slide the cup toward her and stand at the other end, waiting. Her chin is still tucked into her neck, and she's doing everything she can to avoid eye contact.

"I didn't…" she starts, then clamps her mouth shut. She opens her mouth again. "I mean, my daughter has always been my number-one priority. She still is. You should know that."

"Funny thing is, she was my priority, too," I answer evenly.

"You can't blame me for not wanting her to repeat my mistakes," she says to her thighs. "You know what went down when I was here. The entire village does."

"No, but I can blame you for naturally assuming I'm as bad as Glen."

She finally looks up at me, her eyes big and green, like Rory's. Unlike Rory's, they're also sad and crinkly and bloodshot. They've seen things they never wanted to witness. We have that in common.

"You were a young boy, a drunk, a busker, a shameless flirt." She shakes her head. "Look, I'm not here to fight. Thanks for the ticket, but I'm here to see my daughter and go. And I'll be taking her with me."

"Fat chance." I yawn, cupping my mouth and revealing my wedding band.

Just to be clear, it is not the same wedding band I wore when I

311

married Kath. I couldn't chance jinxing my marriage to Rory with a band that was a constant reminder of the biggest tragedy in my life.

Debbie's eyes widen, and she opens her mouth, about to say something, just as we hear a groggy voice from the corridor.

"Mom? What are you doing here?"

Rory is rubbing the sleep out of her eyes, and whaddaya know? Her ring twinkles as she does. Debbie looks between us, her mouth slacking in shock. Guess I should've given her a heads-up before I got her on that plane. *Oops.*

I stand up and rap the counter.

"I believe you have some things to discuss. Have fun, ladies."

"Mal! What the heck?" Rory grabs my wrist as I make my way to the door.

I need to visit Tamsin and explain to her with my usual delicacy (of a tank) that there's someone new in our lives. Someone I love dearly.

I kiss the side of my wife's neck. "Tamsin only has two grandmas. Don't you reckon she deserves three?"

That's all I need to say to make her melt and smile at me cunningly.

"You're a pig," she whispers.

I steal another kiss, laughing as I march to the door. "Then you're my shit."

Rory

"Explain yourself," I tell her.

I flick the kettle on and try to calm my heartbeat. Talking to my mother right now is the last thing I want, but it needs to happen. On one hand, I'm grateful and surprised she's put on a show for my entire existence, feeding me sweet lies to protect me. It's kind of endearing, in a screwed-up, totally dysfunctional way. On the other, she tore Mal and me apart for years. Everything would have looked so different had she just given me his letters.

But then again, Tamsin wouldn't have been born.

Mal wouldn't have her.

I would never know that Summer is a backstabbing friend who slept with my boyfriend.

And I never would have landed the job with Ryner that taught me who I am as an artist.

"No, *you* explain yourself to me, Rory. What is this marriage nonsense? You hardly know the guy! Plus, you have a boyfriend." Mom shoots on her feet, waving her hand in the air, her bangles clashing, creating a wind-chimes kind of sound.

It transports me back to adolescence, and I find myself touching the hoop in my nose, gritting my teeth.

"Callum and I broke up."

"What? Why?"

"Because I cheated on him. And before you say anything—please remember you cheated on your boyfriend with Glen, too."

Mom's face falls. She raises a finger, about to defend herself, but I interject.

"Besides, I found out afterwards that he cheated on me first—with Summer, of all people. Although, to be honest, looking back, I've always had my suspicions. He always tried to change me, to clip my wings in small, roundabout ways. And anyway, Mal and I are married, and after the bullshit Ryner pulled when Ashton Richards died, I'm not in a hurry to get back into the glitz and glamor of this industry."

I didn't know this to be true until the words escape my mouth. But as soon as they do, it becomes crystal clear to me.

I should be doing something different.

People like Ryner don't inspire me. I'm a photographer. I take photos. It brings me, and others, joy. I could be a photographer anywhere. I could take pictures of things that are far more interesting than pampered, delusional, plastic pop princesses and self-entitled rock stars who think the sun shines from their buttholes.

Mal sold his soul to the devil and started selling his songs because he had to.

I don't *have* to.

I don't need any special medical treatment. I am perfectly content making pennies.

"Rory! Oh my goodness. How am I supposed to react to this? You didn't even invite me to your wedding!" Mom slaps the back of her hand to her forehead.

"Mom, we married in private. Just the two of us and witnesses."

"Like, in Vegas?"

"Like, in Cyprus."

Her eyes are wide and frighteningly, radioactively green. "But Rory, what if he isn't the one?"

"He is." I take both her hands, ushering her to the backyard. I want her to see where we fell in love. On that piece of green grass, under the sky that was lit with a thousand stars.

"Look here." I point at the backyard. "Eight years ago, almost nine, I sat here with Mal and knew that no other boy would ever make my heart beat as fast and hard. And you know what? No one ever did. I know you are wary. I know Ireland brings many harsh memories to the surface. Father Doherty told me all about them. I'm sorry, Mom, but I knew you never would, and I needed to learn the truth."

She blinks at me, clearly willing her tears away, and I wrap my arms around her, speaking into her hair.

"But I don't have a baby to take care of, and I'm not doing this out of fear or desperation or because my conscience won't allow me not to try. I'm doing this of my own free will. Because he makes my reality better than my dreams. Because I am so painfully aware that we will all end up like Glen and Kathleen one day. We come from dust and return to dust. But while I'm here, on this planet, breathing, *living,* I want to do this alongside the person who makes me laugh. Who loves me unconditionally. Who kept a tattered, stained napkin that was a complete lie for nearly a decade, on the off-chance we'd meet again."

"Kathleen…" Mom shakes her head.

I realize no one has explicitly said that to her, that Kathleen is dead. She would have been just a little older than me, were she still alive.

I nod solemnly. "Car accident."

"Oh God."

Mom breaks off the hug and sniffles, grabbing my cheeks in her oily, wrinkly, mom-hands. She examines my face with the precision of a hawk to see if there's a crack in my mask, if I'm telling the whole truth.

"It's real, isn't it? This thing with Mal," she asks brokenly.

"The realest." I laugh, happy tears sliding down my cheeks.

"And you know all about what happened with Glen?" She looks at me from under her fake eyelashes, blinking slowly.

I nod. "About the scar, too. I'm not mad, Mom. I just wish you'd told me. I could've handled it. You didn't have to go through all this effort."

"Oh, but I did." She rushes into my words, sliding her hands from my cheeks to my arms, squeezing. "I wanted you to know you deserved to be loved. You are the most precious thing in my world, Aurora, even if you don't always feel that way. I wanted you to think he adored you, but I had to keep you far enough away from him so you'd never know the truth."

"Is that why you didn't want me to come to Ireland?"

She sighs. "That, and we seem to have it hard for Irish men. I didn't want you to move across the ocean and leave me in America. It was selfish, but you're my only family." Pause. "I mean, you and the cigarettes and the hairspray."

We both laugh, until I remember I have something I still need to clear up with her.

"The pictures. You sent Mal the pictures with the mean things I wrote about him. You sent him a letter saying I aborted his baby. It started a chain reaction that caused everything to fall apart over here. You have no idea."

I'm not going to pin Kathleen's death on Mom, obviously. But she did manipulate the hell out of our lives.

She sniffs, wiping her nose with the sleeve of her glittery denim jacket, which has pink patches and a sequin collar. That's a sight I didn't think I'd live to see. Usually my mother will grab anything within reach, including the Bible or a kid in a bubble, and use them to wipe off her snot before tarnishing her precious clothes.

"I know. There's no better way to describe it than I was being manic. I didn't trust Mal, and I didn't want you to end up in a bad situation like me. When I sent him the pictures, I thought that'd be it. I should've known your love was stronger than that. When he kept sending letters, I lost it. I knew he'd get to you soon enough. So when I sat down to write him my own letter, I described everything I'd gone through when I found out I was pregnant with you—with one little alteration. I wrote it as if *you* had an abortion. I couldn't stomach it. It took me three days to write the letter, and I went back and forth. I threw up every hour. But it just cemented the fact in my head that you shouldn't be put in this position. Only now I can see what kind of damage it must have caused the three of you. Please know, I thought it was a fling. Puppy love. Something you'd grow out of in no time. At no point did I think you wouldn't find a better man for yourself in America."

The sad part is, I believe her.

I know she did horrible things, and still, I cannot help but feel compassion for her. I saw how hard her life was. We lived under the same roof. She always provided for me. She always did her best.

I wrap my arms around her again, and we sob into each other's shoulders. It's the toughest—and by far best—conversation I've had with my mother. And it hurts like a bitch.

"I love you, Mom. But if you do something like this again, I swear, I'm going to go apeshit on your ass."

She laughs, grateful for the fact I lightened up the mood.

"Oh, trust me. I know better than to mess with kismet, fate, and their peers. So what are you going to do about Summer?"

She pulls away, running a loving hand along my arm. It's the first time she's ever done that, and I feel a rush of excitement, like we're morphing into something different. More real. "You know, in the spirit of forgiveness and moving on and all the mumbo-jumbo you millennials are into?"

"Oh, you know… I think I'm going to let karma beat her down for a little while."

A NOTE FROM GLEN (RORY'S DEAD FATHER)

I cocked up.

That is a blanket statement, of course, because that happened quite a lot, literally and figuratively. I can't pinpoint the exact moment I threw everything in the shitter. Maybe when I had my first drop of alcohol, when I was eleven. Uncle Paddy left the bottle on our kitchen counter, and my parents, who'd fought all night, slept in. It made sense to try whatever it was that made grown-ups in my family able to tolerate each other and put a smile on their faces.

I was hooked after that.

Or maybe it was when I knocked up Elaine, Kathleen's mother. It was all fun and games until I had someone else to take care of, and I didn't know how, because my own parents had expected us to raise ourselves. I had a few more brothers—six or seven, I don't remember—but I was the youngest. My parents were in their forties when I was born, and they never showed the slightest interest in me.

Maybe it was when I ran away from Elaine and Kathleen and locked myself in my parents' old house and wrote "Belle's Bells." Not a day passed when I wasn't asked about that song—on the street, in a letter, a fan email, or by a prodding radio host who remembered I was still alive and called me for a brief interview, usually around November.

I wish I could tell you it was about Elaine.

Or the girl before her.

Or the girl before *her*.

I wish I could tell you it was about Kathleen.

But the truth is, this wonderful song about love and heartbreak and addiction and angst and all the things that make people's hearts move is about…alcohol.

A stiff drink to take it all away.

Which is why, till the day I died, people speculated as to what it was about.

Now, Rory and Debbie were a different story altogether. I think I actually fell in love with Debbie in Paris. When she told me she was pregnant, my gut reaction was to tell her to move to Ireland with me. So I did.

She tried to make it on her own in America, but when she realized it was harder than she'd thought, she finally accepted my offer. By which time, I was a deadbeat drunk, not an artist drunk. Quite a difference.

I could tell you I didn't move to America because I had a daughter I couldn't leave, and later a son, too. But I wasn't that great a da. I was torn and messed up, but had only myself to blame.

The day I hurt Rory was the day I lost hope. It is hard to rationalize and make excuses for a no-show father, but it is impossible to justify one who hurt his own baby.

I came out of jail worse than I went in, with one big difference—I stopped trying to reach out to Debbie and see Rory, and I started putting an effort into what I had.

Kathleen knew I was a terrible, abusive drunk, but I did my best with her.

With Mal, too. It broke my heart to see my daughter pining for a boy who was waiting for the big bang. She was just a floating star in his universe. I knew those things couldn't be changed.

I knew because her mother wasn't it, either. Debbie was.

But being dead is actually centuries better than being a guilt-ridden drunken fool. If you're wondering what it's like on the other side, let me tell you, it's not that bad. Weather's nice all year round, though you can't really feel it. I don't have a body, so that's a bit of a downer. No one does. I'm not above the clouds, nor am I under the ground. There's no heaven, nor hell. I'm in everything, though. In the air and in the trees. On butterfly wings and in the cow shit and between the cracks on the floor. I'm on top of skyscrapers in Beijing and on a dandelion in a small town in Nebraska.

Being dead, you don't always feel the spirit of other people who are dead, unless you know them really well and they're beside you.

Right now, I can feel Kathleen. She's standing right next to me, asking if we should go for it. Not with words. It's unspoken, like the meaning behind really good song lyrics.

We do things we shouldn't do all the time, Kath and I. There's no protocol against it, and if there is, they didn't hand it to us when we switched over to the other side.

I've turned off lights in a pub when Mal and Rory needed to get the point.

Made it snow.

Shut down electricity.

I did everything I could to signal to Rory that Mal is the one, that he is not like me.

That he will not let her down—he will love her forever.

But I've never made an entire street light up before, especially a street as crowded as Drury.

"Think we can do it?" I ask Kathleen voicelessly.

I'm tucked between the bricks of a red Drury Street building, and she's on top of a bus stop. I can feel her nod.

"Let's give them something to freak out about."

(ANOTHER) NOTE FROM KATHLEEN

I told you I'm not the villain.

P.S. She better be good to my kid.

P.P.S. Yes, of course, I regret telling Aurora Rory I would never take care of her child. A bit late to change it now, though.

P.P.P.S. Fine. They do look cute together. Happy?

(ANOTHER) NOTE FROM SUMMER

Me again.

I mean, like, duh. I needed closure with my best friend—didn't I?

Even when it became painfully clear that Rory wasn't going to come back to our apartment in New York. Not that I didn't understand. She was now with the love of her life, living the charmed little existence she'd always dreamed of.

Plus, I screwed up. I know I did. It doesn't matter that she wanted to break up with Callum, that she never felt for him an ounce of what she feels toward Mal, that I was pretty sure their relationship wouldn't last another day, or that we were both very drunk.

I made one mistake. I wouldn't allow any more of them to stack up. I needed her forgiveness to move on.

I flew out to Ireland. Extreme, huh? I think so, too, considering the amount of rehearsal I bailed on just to be able to patch things up with my BFF (best fucking friend). I took a cab to Tolka straight from the airport three months after she found out about Callum and me. Three months after she started ghosting me.

I found her in a compromising position on the grass in her backyard, being nailed by her new husband. I swear he was planting her like a flower. I interrupted them mid-fuck, but only by accident. The door was unlocked—I remembered Rory used to complain that Mal always kept it unlocked—and I waltzed in. When I realized what was happening before my eyes, I started backing up, but my butt hit the breakfast nook and knocked a Guinness bottle to the floor, and they both turned around to see where the noise came from.

The first thing Rory did was throw her dress at me, then she proceeded to bolt up on her feet and chase me naked around the cottage, yelling, "You screwed my boyfriend" really loudly.

Mal leaned against a wall, arms crossed, a smirk on his face, watching the entire thing half-naked and fully hard. He was gorgeous. I finally realized why she couldn't shake him all those years. Not only did he look a thousand times better in person, but he also has this cocky, sweet, you'll-never-tame-me expression that just speaks to the inner fixer-upper women have.

Mal then made us all coffee and tea before he announced that he was going to pick his daughter up from school.

On the couch, Rory grabbed my hand and told me, "You know what the worst part is? I wasn't even mad at you for sleeping with him. You're right. I did tell you I was going to break up with him a gazillion times, though it was still a mistake. I was mad because you didn't tell me. And because you kept pushing me into his arms for your own, selfish reasons, despite my doubts. The lie is bigger than the sin."

"I know." I broke down in tears.

I was tired from the flight and from being eaten alive by my own guilt (AKA not the way one likes to be eaten). I just couldn't take it anymore.

"I know all those things. I just thought I could sweep it under the carpet and pretend like it never happened. I wanted it to work out between you guys—right up to the point you were in Greece, actually." I gnawed at my lower lip.

"Why? What happened?" Rory asked, taking a sip of her tea.

She was normally a coffee drinker. Another thing that changed after she moved to Ireland.

"I ran into Whitney, Ryner's assistant, at Saks. Before you growl at me, I was just looking around, not working on inflating my overdraft situation." I cleared my throat. "Anyway, I could swear she was sporting a baby bump. It was so easy to figure out with her malnourished self. Of course, I had no intention of saying hi to her, so I did what every character in a B-grade romantic comedy does and hid behind the mannequins. Whit was walking around with someone who looked like she could be her mother, rubbing her swollen belly. The woman asked her, 'Do you really think he's going to leave his girlfriend for you?' And Whitney replied, 'I don't know, and I don't care. He got me an apartment next to his so he can be close to the baby. If Callum wants to marry Little Miss Awkward, I'm not going to ruin his plans as long as he keeps the cash flow coming. Which he will.'"

Rory's eyes flared, and she sucked in a breath, straightening her back. More than anything, she looked casually outraged. Like, when you tell your friend about something insane that happened to one of your colleagues at work. She seemed completely emotionally detached from the story, which made it easier to tell her.

"What happened then?" she asked.

"Well, at first I thought, *What are the chances?* But then, I remembered you always told me Whitney was extra touchy with Callum and totally had the hots for him. Pieces started falling together. He'd cheated on you before, why wouldn't he do it again? I tried to call when you were in Greece, but you didn't pick up. Then what happened between us came out, and it was too late. I swear not telling you was the worst thing I've ever done, Rory. I swear. There's never any way a boy could come between us."

Rory put her hand on mine and smiled. "I know."

"You do?" I felt my entire face twisting in pain.

She nodded. "I've known it for a long time—that I was going to forgive you, that is. I figured we should have this conversation face to face, so I was going to do it when I came to visit Mom in a few weeks. But you beat me to it. Look, I know how crappy it feels to cheat on someone. I agonized over what I did to Callum. Still do. Because it doesn't matter that he cheated—I'm better than that. Or I should have been. I don't regret being with Mal, but I regret that it happened before I broke up with Callum. That's for me to live with, a permanent stain on my conscience, and yet here I am—living. So I'm asking you to do the same. Live with your mistake, Cinder-freaking-rella. Learn from it, and go find your Richard Gere."

We stared at each other for a while, smiling quietly. It felt like a promising hello, but somehow also a bittersweet goodbye. Nothing would be the same, I knew, with or without Rory's forgiveness. She was not coming back—not to live in New York, anyway, and yet she chose to give me the beautiful gift of forgiveness.

"For the record, I hate your new husband for taking you away from me." I sniffed, crossing my arms and looking the other way to further prove my point.

"For the record, he resents you, too, for what we did to his pictures," she snorted.

"You told him!" I grabbed a throw pillow and threw it in her face.

She caught it in the air and tossed it back at me, laughing.

It hit my face and fell in my lap.

"Bitch," I shrieked.

"Traitor." She waggled her eyebrows.

We both collapsed to the floor, holding our bellies, giggling, and I knew that with or without her, I'd eventually be all right.

Now I'm at the Dublin Airport, waiting for my flight back to New York.

There's a tall, dark, handsome-type guy sitting across from me, waiting for the same flight and reading a paperback of *The Historian* by Elizabeth Kostova. By the pace at which he flips the pages—barely every minute or so—I know he's focused on me from the corner of his eye.

I slip one foot out of my pump and wiggle my hot pink toenails, popping the mint gum between my lips and eyeing him brazenly.

He looks up, a polite smile on his face. "May I help you?" he asks.

"No, but I can help you." I flash him a grin.

His brow rises. "You can? Please enlighten me as to how."

"I can move somewhere else, so you won't be distracted and can finish your book. It's a wonderful novel, you know? Vlad the Impaler was the real MVP."

God bless my weird obsession with Eastern European folklore.

Tall, Dark, and Handsome closes the book and rests it on his crossed legs, sitting back and giving me his full attention.

"Do you have a name?"

"What am I, Arya Stark? Of course, I have a name."

He bursts out in laughter, which instantly makes me smile. My heart is pounding all over my chest. I steal a glance at his left hand. No ring. But that doesn't mean he isn't involved.

I will never repeat my Callum mistake.

It appears TDAH is also a mind reader.

"Single, in case you're wondering. Which, let's admit it, you are."

"And Irish," I point out after hearing the accent.

I don't want this to be a fling. I don't *want* a fling. I want a *Pretty Woman* moment (sans the part where I sell my body, obviously). I want my Richard Gere. I want to know if Tall, Dark, Handsome, and Irish slept with someone else the night of Rory's Christmas party. If he is the one. If I should be irrationally furious at him about bedding that ho on Christmas. Somehow, I can't bring myself to be mad at him, though. Because he's so here now, so alive in front of me, and it feels like the entire world—the sky, the earth, everything between—is ours to explore if we wish to.

"And Irish." He nods. "But I live in New York."

"You do?"

He nods again.

"What do you do?" *That's my quota of dos for the rest of the week.*

"I own a shop."

"What kind of shop?"

"One that sells sex toys and other high-end toys of the variety you won't be buying your godchildren," he says flatly.

I stare at him, unblinking, waiting for him to tell me he's joking. When I realize he isn't, I smile. "Just my type."

He grins. He has a glorious grin, not to be confused with a smile. No, his looks are cunning and mischievous and drugging.

"I'm Kirby."

"Summer."

We both lean forward at the same time, still in our seats, to shake each other's hands. When we sit back, we both cross our legs. He picks up his book; I pick up my phone. We go back to whatever was keeping us occupied, but we're both smiling.

"Are you a member of the Mile-High Club, Summer?" he asks, flipping a page casually.

I post a story on Instagram with a picture of his feet, captioned: "Look at these feet! Just imagine the rest of him? #WinkWink!"

"Well, no, but as Groucho Marx once said, 'I don't want to belong to any club that will accept me as a member.'"

Please be my Richard Gere.

Please be my Richard Gere.

Please be my Richard Gere.

He smiles.

"Then how about dinner? Fully clothed."

"Partial clothing is fine, too, you know."

"Sounds like a plan."

Epilogue

One year later

Rory

A LITTLE HAND GRABS MINE, PULLING ME TOWARD THE THRONG, her tiny feet secured in shiny, red Dorothy-style shoes.

"Pu-leeeeeease. You said five minutes. Surely at least a thousand have passed!"

"It's been barely two." I laugh, lowering my camera.

I give the subject of my photo shoot, an engaged couple, a helpless shrug. They don't seem mad. Maybe because they haven't paid me.

When I officially resigned from Blue Hill, I promised myself no matter what I do, I will always leave room to have one photo shoot a month that's completely pro bono. Chicken soup for my inspiration, if you will. Last month it was the 100th birthday party of a woman named Joselyn O'Leary in North Dublin. I came to her retirement home and took pictures of her dancing with her new beau, Finn, who at the tender age of eighty-five, is fifteen years her junior.

Today, it's a couple of teenagers—nineteen, I believe—who fell pregnant and decided to make it official. They don't have a budget to speak of for their wedding. They're going to use the bride's mother's living room for the party next month, and the dress and ring were bought at a secondhand store. They wrote me a touching letter asking if I'd be willing to take a few pictures of them, so here I am.

Their wedding will be held at a local council flat, and not only have I been invited, but I promised to come, too.

"Two or a thousand, it is time to go." Tamsin pouts adorably, the way she does when she's trying to get me to give her chocolate.

The couple laugh and shake their heads.

"Your daughter is just precious," the girl tells me, adjusting the polka-dot dress that's a little too tight on her swollen midriff.

I don't tell her Tamsin is not my daughter, because frankly, it feels like she is. I move my hand along Tamsin's ponytail, brushing flyaways behind her ear and smile down at her. I've found bringing her when I take pictures brings brighter smiles to everyone's faces, and my photos have never been better.

"We'll see you at the wedding, then? Next month?"

"You bet!" the soon-to-be-husband says. "Hopefully she'll like us more when there are snacks and drinks around, aye?"

Tamsin and I walk hand in hand down Drury Street and toward the growing crowd in front of Mal.

It doesn't matter that Mal is a millionaire. He will always busk, and I will always love him for that just a little more than I did the day before, because his passion and integrity for his art inspire me.

It also doesn't matter that we are in the midst of refurbishing the cottage completely, gutting it from within, and are currently staying with Elaine, Lara, and Father Doherty while we're waiting for our home to be ready.

It took a while, but Elaine and Lara warmed up to me. Father Doherty did his best to bridge the gap, but I think what did it was my relationship with Tam. They could hate me all they wanted, but the truth of the matter was—*is*—I am the one who fixes her hair every morning, does 2,000-piece puzzles with her, helps her with her homework, and binge-watch vintage *Sabrina the Teenage Witch*. It was also helpful that I turned out to be just as frugal and unaffected by money as Mal is, so they can *see* I'm not here for an inheritance or some other sort of free ride.

"May I have chocolate milk? And apple candy? And this dress? And these boots? Rory, can I? Oh, and can you do my hair tomorrow for school? Brantley McCay likes me. Mia thinks so, anyway." Tamsin stops by a little boutique shop for kids, pointing at a mannequin of a girl her age.

"Tomorrow is Sunday." Laughter rolls out of my mouth, bouncing on the ground ahead of us. "But yes, I'll French braid your hair on Monday. And you can have one thing out of the three, preferably the boots, because they are super cute, and also because your grandmothers will maim me if I feed you junk before dinner." I answer all of her questions at once, and we make a stop at the little store and get her glittery, leopard boots I'm sure she will flaunt for my mother during their next weekly Skype session.

When we get to the crowd, I work my way past onlookers to the only available spot from which I can see Mal and place Tamsin before me, putting my hands on her shoulders. She bobs her head and smiles, and it's only when I know she is secure and not going to be pushed around by the dozens of people standing around Mal that I allow myself to drown in his voice, his music, his words.

They said that love was beautiful,
I asked them if they were high,
Because when you barged into my life, you made me taste the sky,
But then you left me here, and the ashes on my tongue turned blue,
Darlin', what more can I say? It ain't easy loving you.
I know we said forever, a promise born a lie,
Though I really want to do it the right way before I die.
Marry me right, and true, and in all the colors you injected into my life.
My Disney princess, my shiny savior, my sharp, bleeding knife.

Mesmerized by his lyrics, it takes me a moment to realize he's put down his guitar and is now approaching me with his unnerving swagger and foolhardy smirk that burns panties in its wake, leaving a trail of tattered hopes and dreams of something more.

I cover my mouth with both hands, not knowing what to make of it.

We *are* married. In the last year, we've acted it more than most married couples I know. And yet, here he is…

On one knee.

Squinting up at me like I'm the sun, Tamsin between us as I hug his daughter from behind.

"I got you something a little more impressive than the ring from Larnaca this time, Princess Aurora of New Jersey."

He fishes in his back pocket for a black, velvety box and pops it open in front of me. I feel Tamsin squealing and giggling under my palms, her shoulders shaking in delight.

Everyone around us sucks in a breath as I stare back at a huge diamond sparkling in front of me in different shades of pale gold. I've never seen anything like it.

"Yes." I choke on my own laughter.

Mal's face changes from delighted to confused as he grabs my left hand from Tamsin's shoulder—kissing his daughter's cheek first—and slides the ring onto my finger, securing my original wedding band.

"Oh, darlin', that wasn't a question."

Everyone around us laughs, Tamsin included.

"Then why are you on your knees?" I wipe tears of joy from the corners of my eyes.

"Great angle to check out your t-i-t-s," he retorts.

"Daddy!" Tamsin hoots, holding her little belly. "I know how to spell! I got second place in the spelling bee at school, remember?"

"Why, how could I forget, little TimTam? It was a test, and you passed with flying colors."

He pulls her into a hug, and she drowns between his muscular arms, a ball of giggly happiness.

This past year, I've had the pleasure of watching Mal be a father to Tamsin. It was enough to confirm I want to have approximately five hundred babies with him. And an indefinite number of pets. We started out with two dogs named Jim and Morrison. Both rescued. It wasn't even a discussion. We knew where we'd get them: the shelter.

Mal and I came a long way with the people we hurt and who've hurt us. Mom and I are working things out. She comes over every Christmas. I send her elaborate gifts from Sephora on Thanksgiving. And yes, that includes hairspray.

Mal apologized to Sean and Maeve. He actually went as far as helping them open their new business—The Tolka Inn. No matter how much they despised him, in time, and with a lot of groveling, they've tentatively allowed him back into their lives.

As for Tamsin? She has been the missing link I didn't know I needed in my life. The reason why my snow globe was beautiful from the inside, tranquil, but also so incredibly still and boring. She shook it up and makes it snow like every day is Christmas.

Mal gets up, grabs me by my waist, and pulls me close, Tamsin slipping to the side coolly. She's made it an art to escape our make-out sessions by now.

"Hello, stranger." He grins at me.

"King Malachy of Tolka," I answer, producing the fifty-euro note Father Doherty gave me almost a decade ago and sliding it to his waist-band, as if he's a stripper.

"You're the four seasons, Rory. And I promise to be your shelter in the winter. To bask in you in the summer. To crash into love with you in spring like it's the first time we've met. And when you fall? I promise to always pick you up."

Everyone erupts in claps and whistles, and goosebumps dance all over my skin. I feel loved. Cherished. Invincible.

"Play me a song?" I ask.

"What would you like to hear, Ms. Rothschild?"

"Surprise me." I bite down on my lip, not surprised in the least that he remembers our entire conversation from when we were practically kids.

He jogs back to his place, just like he did almost a decade ago.

Lowers his head and gives me a sideways I'm-going-to-fuck-you-tonight smile, which I believe now, exactly as I did nine years ago.

He opens his mouth and starts singing my father's song, "Belle's Bells."

And for the first time since I heard it and knew Glen wrote it, I feel nothing but contentment and peace.

No pain. No shame. No need for closure.

Because no matter who Glen O'Connell was, he led me to the love of my life. To my new home. To the place where I matter. Where I take pictures of babies for a living and don't chase coked-up, glitzy starlets and dodgy, sexually harassing bosses. Where I go up to Northern Ireland from time to time to hang out with my half-brother, Taron, putting fresh flowers on his grave and telling him all the stories I couldn't have when I still lived in the US.

I visit Kath, too.

I even visit Dad—and yes, it helps that they were buried in the same graveyard.

Kathleen might've said she'd never accept a child of mine back when Mal slipped into the bathroom, but I am lucky enough to raise a child of hers, and that's all that matters.

And when Mal's eyes meet mine, and people shout and whistle and laugh, because it is so stupidly clear what he's thinking about while he's singing this completely innocent Christmas song, Tamsin cringes and waves the bag with her brand new boots in the air. She says the words I never thought I'd hear her say.

"Ma, Da, get a room!"

In this moment, I'm not burning.

Not ice cold.

Just…perfectly *warm*.

Fifteen years later

Mal

I will not strangle my child today.
  I will not strangle my child today.
  I will not…
  "Da! Kiki said I'm not tall enough to be a basketball player." Grayson elbows his sister, Kathleen, in the backseat. I loosen my bow-tie (bowtie!) as I maneuver my Volvo SUV from our plush cottage (yup, you heard that right, too) toward Dublin, where I am going to watch my daughter, Tamsin, get married.
  "Well, your sister is right," Rory interjects, kneading my thigh to calm me down.
  Look, I like the lad Tamsin is marrying fine. He doesn't appear to be a serial killer/wife beater/Manchester City supporter. I'm just uncomfortable with handing my baby over to someone else.
  And I don't mean that in the literal way, of course. Tamsin can take care of me better than I do her. But there's something so final about letting go, about not being the main man in your daughter's life anymore.
  "That is slanger!" Grayson throws his hands in the air.
  "It's *slander*, you eejit, and it's not," Kiki huffs.
  Grayson's name is close enough to Glen, but also far enough that we all feel comfortable about it. Kathleen, however, was named after my first wife and Rory's sister to honor her legacy. They're the most infuriating twelve year olds in the universe. Not even my brothers, sister, and mother can handle their lip. After Rory and I said I do (again), we decided to try for a sibling for Tamsin. Good thing we already knew life was not a smooth ride. After two years of trying unsuccessfully, we turned to IVF. And surprise, surprise, now Tamsin has two siblings, and they're both hellraisers.
  "You let her get away with everything. It's so unfair."

"Your face is unfair," Kiki retorts.

"At least it's not ugly," Grayson deadpans.

"But it's very unwitty." Kiki crosses her arms over her chest, flashing a taunting smile.

"She wins." I shrug, tapping the wheel and feeling my beautiful wife squeeze my thigh harder in warning. "What? She had the better comeback. I do appreciate a good taunt."

When we arrive, I allow the valet to park our vehicle, and Rory rushes into the hotel where Tamsin is getting ready for the ceremony. I'm at her heels, and the twins are somewhere behind, probably arguing about what shade of yellow the sun is and who'll walk through the door first.

My phone is buzzing in my pocket, and I stop and motion for the twins to join their mother down the hall, to help their sister get ready. I plug one finger into my free ear.

"Yeah?"

"Mr. Doherty?"

"Depends who's asking."

"Michael Corr. Real estate agent. We spoke on the phone a week ago. You put a bid on the Tolka house on Henrietta Street."

The house closest to our cottage. The Smiths own it. Well, their children, now that Mrs. Smith is baking cakes in heaven.

"That's right."

"Just wanted to congratulate you. They accepted the offer and are happy to go through with the sale."

I let out a sigh of relief. The past few years, Rory's mother hasn't been doing so grand. Thing is, Debbie found a boyfriend six years ago, and she is bloody gaga for him. There's no chance in hell she'd agree to move in with us, even though we have plenty of space. So I purchased her a house close to ours, so Rory can keep an eye on her. And as for her old-new boyfriend, Antonio Romano? I'm sure he'll appreciate the proximity to Italy.

Another plus: they'll be living right across from Tamsin and her husband, James. Which means another set of eyes on my baby. (Yes, this will never get old.)

"Thank you," I drawl. "You just made a fantastic day even better."

I kill the call and advance toward the slightly open door of my daughter's hotel room. I peek inside, letting my heart fill with warm, unfiltered joy.

Grayson and Kiki are on the couch. She is trying to tame his impossible hair, which he got from me, and for once in their lives, they aren't fighting.

My older daughter is sitting in front of a vanity, a makeup artist and hair stylist fussing around her, holding my wife's hand.

My beautiful, gorgeous wife's hand.

"Just remember, you'll always be my little girl, even when you're eighty," Rory says.

Tamsin looks up and smiles at her. "Thank you," she whispers.

"What for?" Rory smiles.

"Making a family out of Dad and me. Giving me the only thing I truly wanted. Filling a void that couldn't possibly be filled by anyone but you."

It's crazy, but I feel the exact same way about Rory.

I've never told my wife what her father said to me when I was a wee lad. I didn't want to blend her tarnished memory of him with something so pure as our love. But one day, when he was teaching me how to play guitar, he turned around and said, "You know something, Mally-boy? I think one day you'll be my son-in-law."

"I'm not going to marry Kiki." I scrunched my nose.

I didn't like her that way—that much I knew, even when I was about ten.

"No, not Kathleen. I'm talking about Aurora."

"I don't even know her."

"Not yet."

"She lives in America."

"Love is bigger than this planet, son. Much, much bigger."

We were destined, Rory and I.

I knew that with each flickering light when we were together that first time she came to Ireland.

Each slammed door.

The spontaneous drizzle.

Unexpected snowflakes.

For years, I knew Glen was up there, eventually with Kiki by his side, playing matchmaker.

I look up toward the ceiling and smile at the old bastard. He couldn't take care of his child while he was living, so he atoned for it after he died.

"Thank you."

Acknowledgements

This year, I decided to grant myself the indulgence of writing one, completely crazy, utterly out-of-character book for me. And boy, did I show all my crazy. I wrote the points of view of a cow, a napkin, and a chocolate bar.

#NoRegrets.

This book was supposed to be a rom-com treat for Christmas, but somehow ended up as something else completely. Still, I embraced it, and so did the wonderful people who helped me through this process.

I would like to thank my editors, Angela Marshall Smith, Paige Maroney Smith, and Jessica Royer Ocken for being so unbelievably amazing, talented, and meticulous with each of my manuscripts.

I'd like to also give a huge shout-out to Hang Le for the beautiful, unique cover. It is absolutely gorgeous in every way. And to Stacey Blake of Champagne Formatting for making the interior so, so pretty.

Big thanks to the girls at Social Butterfly PR (Jenn, Brooke, and Sarah, namely), who put up with me, and to my wonderful agent, Kimberly Brower at Brower Literary, who helped make the audiobook for *In the Unlikely Event* exactly what I wanted and envisioned it to be when I decided to write so many points of view.

A huge shout-out to my wonderful street team, my momager Tijuana Turner, who has read this book approximately one thousand times, and my beta readers, Amy Halter, Lana Kart, Sarah Grim Sentz, and Josephine McDonnell (thanks for upping Mal's Irishness!).

Special thanks to the people who put up with me on a regular basis, Charleigh Rose, Helena Hunting, and Ava Harrison.

Also, to the Sassy Sparrows, my reading group, and to my readers, who make me strive to become a better, more daring writer and artist. Thank you for pushing me in the right direction. Always.

On a personal note, I would be so grateful if you could leave a brief, honest review for the book when you are done reading.

All my love,
L.J. Shen

Standalones:

Tyed

Sparrow

Blood to Dust

Midnight Blue

Dirty Headlines

The Kiss Thief

Sinners of Saints (all interconnected standalones):

Defy

Vicious

Ruckus

Scandalous

Bane

All Saints High:

Pretty Reckless

Broken Knight

Enjoyed *In the Unlikely Event*? Make sure you stay in the loop!

Join my reading group. (https://goo.gl/eqDz46)

Sign up to my newsletter. (http://eepurl.com/dgo6x5)

Follow me on Instagram—@authorljshen

Like my author page. (www.facebook.com/authorljshen)

Preview of

DIRTY
HEADLINES

Prologue

Jude

ON HER DEATHBED, MY MOTHER SAID THE HEART IS A LONELY hunter.

"Organs, Jude, are like people. They need company, a backup to rely on. That's why we have lungs, tonsils, hands, legs, fingers, toes, eyes, nostrils, teeth, and lips. Only the heart works alone. Like Atlas, it carries the weight of our existence on its shoulders quietly, only rebelling when disturbed by love."

She said a lonely heart—such as *my* lonely heart—would never fall in love, and so far, she wasn't wrong.

Maybe that's why tonight happened.

Maybe that's why I'd stopped trying.

Creamy sheets tangled around my legs like roots as I slipped out of the king-sized bed in the swanky hotel room I'd been occupying for the last several hours. I rose from the plush mattress, my back to the stranger I'd met this afternoon.

If I stole a glance at him, my conscience would kick in and I'd never go through with it.

I was choosing his cash over my integrity.

Cash I very much needed.

Cash that was going to pay my electricity bill and fill prescriptions for Dad this month.

I tiptoed across the room to his dress pants on the floor, feeling hollow in all the places he'd filled in the previous hours. This was the first time I'd stolen anything, and the finality of the situation made me want to throw up. I wasn't a thief. Yet I was about to wrong this perfect stranger. And I wasn't even going to touch the one-night-stand issue for fear my head would explode all over the lush carpet. I didn't normally do one-night stands.

But I wasn't myself tonight.

I'd woken this morning to the sound of my mailbox collapsing from the weight of the letters and bills crammed into it. Then I'd failed a job interview so miserably, they'd cut the meeting short to watch a Yankees game. (When I'd pointed out there was no game—because, yes, I was *that* desperate—they'd explained it was a rerun.)

Defeated, I'd stumbled my way through the cruel streets of Manhattan, the early-spring rain loud and punishing. I'd figured the best course of action would be to slip into my boyfriend Milton's condo to dry off. I had the key, and he was probably at work, polishing his piece about immigration healthcare. He worked for *The Thinking Man*, one of the most prestigious magazines in New York. To say I was proud would be the understatement of the century.

The rest of the afternoon played out like a bad movie piled with clichés and reeking of bad luck. I'd pushed Milton's door open, shaking the raindrops from my jacket and hair. First, low, guttural moans seeped into my ears. The unmistakable visual followed immediately after:

Milton's editor, Elise, whom I'd met once before for drinks, bent over one side of the couch we'd picked out together at my favorite flea market, as he relentlessly pounded into her.

Thrust.

Thrust.

Thrust.

Thrust!

"The heart is a lonely, cruel hunter."

I'd felt mine shooting an arrow of poison straight to Milton's glistening chest, then heard it crack, threatening to split in two.

We'd been together for five years. Met at Columbia University. He was the son of a retired NBC anchor. I was on full scholarship. The only reason we hadn't lived together was because Dad was sick and I didn't want to leave his side. But that didn't stop Milton and me from crocheting our plans into the same colors and patterns, entwining our lives one dream at a time.

Visit Africa.

Get assigned to the Middle East.

Watch the sunset in Key West.

Eat one perfect macaron in Paris.

Our bucket list was etched in a notebook I'd keenly named Kipling, and it was burning a hole through my bag right now.

I hadn't meant to throw up on Milton's doorstep, but it was not a big surprise, considering what I'd just walked into. The bastard had skidded on my breakfast as he chased me down the hall, but I'd pushed the emergency stairway door open and taken the stairs two at a time. Milton had been very much naked, with a condom still dangling from his half-mast dick, and at some point he'd decided bursting into the street in his birthday suit was not a good plan.

I'd run until my lungs burned and my Chucks were wet and muddy.

Bumping into shoulders, and umbrellas, and street vendors in the pounding rain.

I was angry, desperate and shocked—but I wasn't devastated. My heart was cracked, but not broken.

"The heart is a lonely hunter, Jude."

I'd needed to forget—forget about Milton, the stacks of bills, and my unfortunate lack of employment the past few months. I'd needed to drown in alcohol and hot skin.

The stranger in the suite had given me exactly that, and now he was about to give me something we had never agreed on.

Judging by this place, though, he won't have trouble paying for the cab to the airport.

A curved, wrought-iron staircase that cost more than my entire apartment stared back at me, leading to a Jacuzzi the size of my room. Plush, red-tufted velvet couches taunted me. Floor-to-ceiling windows dared me to drink in the view of well-heeled Manhattan with my poor eyes. And the teardrop chandelier looked eerily similar to little sperm.

And to make it through next week, Judith Penelope Humphry, you will stop thinking about jizz and move on with your plan.

I reached for the back pocket of his Tom Ford dress pants, where he'd tucked his wallet shortly after sliding out a chain of condoms, and examined it in my shaking hands. A Bottega Veneta leather creation, black and unwrinkled. My throat bobbed, but I still couldn't swallow my nerves.

I flipped the wallet open and slipped out the stack of cash. Turned out Stranger Junior wasn't the only thing thick about this one. I counted hurriedly, my eyes flaring as they took in all the cash.

Hundred…two…three…six…eight…Fifteen hundred. *Thank you, Jesus.*

I could practically hear Jesus scolding me. *"Don't thank me. Pretty sure* thou shalt not steal *was way up there on my not-to-do list."*

Yanking my phone out of my shoulder bag, I searched the brand of the wallet in my hand. Turns out it cost a little less than seven hundred bucks. My dysfunctional, albeit heavy heart pounded as I began to toss out plastic cards without giving them a second glance. The wallet was sellable, and as it turned out, so were my morals.

My gut knotted in shame, and I felt my face growing hot. He was going to wake up and hate me, regret the minute he'd approached me at the bar. I wasn't supposed to care. He was going to leave New York come morning, and I would never see him again.

Once his wallet was empty, and all his cards and IDs neatly arranged on his nightstand, I slipped back into my dress and electric pink—although crusted in mud—Chucks and chanced one last look at him.

He was completely naked, his groin haphazardly covered by the sheet. With every breath he took, his six pack tightened. Even in sleep, he didn't look vulnerable. Like a Greek god, he rose above susceptibility. Men like him were too conceited to be played. I was glad there was going to be an ocean between us soon.

I opened the door and hugged its frame.

"I'm so sorry," I whispered, kissing the tips of my fingers and brushing them over the air between us.

I waited until I was out of the hotel before I let the first tear fall.

Five hours earlier.

I stumbled into a bar, hiccupping a whiskey order to the bartender between sniffs and shaking the rain out of my long, dirty-blond hair.

I tugged at the collar of my black dress and groaned into the drink he slid across the bar for me. My Chucks—I'd opted for low-top pinks this morning as I'd still been foolishly optimistic when I left the house—dangled in the air while my 5-foot-2 frame sat on the stool. My earbuds were firmly tucked into my ears, but I didn't want to taint my playlist of perfect songs with today's shitty mood. If I listened to a song I liked now, I'd forever associate it with the day I found out Milton liked it doggy-style after all, just not with me.

I tried to give myself an internal pep talk as I gulped whiskey I couldn't afford like it was water.

My job interview had gone horrifically bad, but my heart had never been set on working for a Christian gluten-free-diet magazine anyway.

Milton had cheated on me. But I'd always had my doubts about him. His smile always dropped too soon after we'd hung out with my dad or met someone on the street. His right eyebrow always arched when someone wasn't in agreement with him.

As for the growing medical bills—I would find a way to tackle them. Dad and I owned our apartment in Brooklyn. Worse came to worst, we'd sell and rent. Besides, I didn't need both my kidneys.

I was sniveling into my drink when the scent of cedarwood, sage, and an impending sin skulked into my nostrils. I didn't bother to raise my head, even when he said, "Semi-drunk and conventionally beautiful: a predator's wet dream."

He had a strong French accent. Smooth and raspy. But my eyes were locked on the amber fluid swirling in my glass. I wasn't in the mood for small talk. Usually I was the person who could make friends with a brick. But right now, I could stab anyone with balls simply for breathing in my direction. Or any other direction, really.

"Or a horny man's worst nightmare," I responded. "Consequently, I'm not interested."

"That's a lie, and I don't do liars." He rolled a cocktail stirrer between his teeth in my periphery, shooting me a wolfish smirk. "But for you, I'll make an exception."

"Cocky *and* full of yourself?" I inwardly slapped myself across the face for even answering him. I had my earbuds in. Why had he talked to me in the first place? That was the international signal for leave-me-the-heck-alone. Never mind the fact that I wasn't actually listening to anything, just wanted to push away potential conversationalists. "Good thing you didn't say you put the STD in *stud* and now all you need is U."

"I take it you've been hit on by extremely unsophisticated men. How rough was this day of yours, exactly?" He erased the rest of the distance between us, and I could now feel the heat of his body radiating from beneath his tailored suit.

I had a feeling if I turned around and looked at him—really looked at him—he would steal the breath from my lungs. My heart, angry and wounded from earlier today, thudded dully in my chest. *We don't want any intruders, Jude.*

Tall, French, and Handsome slipped a one-hundred dollar bill to the bartender in front of me. His eyes caressed the side of my face as he asked him, "How many drinks did she have?"

"This is her second one, sir." The bartender offered a curt nod, wiping the wooden surface in front of him with a damp cloth.

"Get her a sandwich."

"I don't want a sandwich." I yanked my earbuds out of my ears and slammed them on the bar, finally looking up and spinning on my barstool to stare back at him.

A colossal mistake if I'd ever made one. For the first few seconds, I couldn't even decipher what I was seeing. He was a level of gorgeous most people were not programmed to process. I'm talking Chris Pine perfect, Chris Hemsworth mammoth, and Chris Pratt charming. He was a triple-C threat, and I was S.C.R.E.W.E.D.

"You'll have to eat one." He didn't bother sparing me a look, tossing his phone on the bar. It was lighting up like crazy, with dozens of emails pouring in every minute.

"Why?"

"Because I'm above fucking a drunk girl, and I would very much like to fuck you tonight," he said calmly, peppering his casual statement with a dimpled, bewitching smile that turned my guts into warm goo.

I tried to blink away my shock, still staring, cataloging his face. Deep blue eyes—tiger-slanted and dark, dark, dark like the bottom of the ocean; mud-brown hair tousled to a fault; a jawline that could give you a papercut if you touched it; and lips made for saying filthy things in a sexy language. He was a specimen I had yet to encounter. I'd lived in New York my entire life. Foreign men were *not* a foreign concept to me. Yet he looked like an improbable cross between a male model and a CEO.

His navy suit made him look severe. The curves and edges of his face were ruthless. Filling in between those cutthroat cheekbones and square chin were a pouty mouth and straight nose.

I averted my gaze to his fingers to check for a wedding band. The coast looked clear.

"Excuse me?" I straightened my spine. Just because he looked like a god didn't mean he had the right to act like one. The bartender slid a hot plate with a roast beef, mayo, tomato, and cheddar cheese sandwich on a brioche bun in front of me. I wanted so badly to remain defiant and tough, but unfortunately, I also wanted to not puke up pure whiskey in about an hour.

Hot Stranger Guy leaned against the bar, still standing—*six one? six two?*—and cocked his head to the side. "Eat."

"It's a free country," I quipped.

"Yet you seem chained to the idea that fucking a stranger is somehow wrong."

"I'm sorry, I didn't catch your name, Mr. Not Getting The Hint." I yawned.

"Will Power. Nice to meet you. Look, you're obviously having a bad day. I have a night to burn. I'm flying back home tomorrow morning, but until then…" He jerked his arm, allowing the sleeve of his blazer slide up as he glanced at his vintage Rolex. "I'm going to make sure whatever's on your mind is forgotten for the night. Miss…?"

Screw it. And him. He was the kind of hot I very much doubted I'd even get to *meet* again in my lifetime.

I could put the blame on Milton.

And the medical bills.

And the whiskey.

Hell, I could blame the entire state of New York after the day I'd had.

"Spears." I narrowed my eyes and took a bite of the sandwich. *Darn.* I flipped the napkin that came with the sandwich to check the name of the bar. *Le Coq Tail.* I made a mental note to return in about twenty years, after I'd finally paid my dad's medical bills and stopped living off ramen noodles.

"Like Britney Spears?" He arched an incredulous eyebrow.

"Correct. And you are?"

"Mr. Timberlake."

I took another bite of the sandwich, nearly moaning. When was the last time I'd eaten? Probably this morning, before I left the house for my job interview.

"You're getting on my nerves, Mr. Timberlake. And I thought it was 'Will Power'?"

"Cry me a river, baby. I'm Célian." He offered me his hand.

His poise unnerved and fascinated me at the same time. He was carved like a god but looked vital and warm to the touch like a mortal. It clouded my judgment, messed with my senses, and made my stomach feel like hot tongues of lust licked it from within.

"Judith, but everyone calls me Jude."

"I take it you're a Beatles fan."

"Presumptuous. Your list of negative traits is never-ending."

"Not the only long thing about me. Eat, *Judith.*"

"Jude."

"I'm not everyone." He threw an impatient smile my way, looking like he was over our conversation.

Bossy bastard. I took another bite. "This doesn't mean anything."

I was pretty sure I was lying, but I was too emotionally exhausted to deny myself things tonight.

He leaned toward me, entering my personal space the way Napoleon blazed into Moscow, with the pride and discretion of a pagan warrior. He brushed his thumb along the column of my throat. A simple touch, and my entire body broke out in violent goosebumps. It was the combination of his feral, male ruggedness, his accent, and his sharp everything else—suit, scent, and features.

I was helpless.

I wanted to be helpless.

"The heart is a lonely hunter." But my body needed company tonight.

He leaned forward, his lips close to my ear, and whispered, "Oh, but *this* does."

"You're not my type." I grinned into the rest of the whiskey I downed.

"I'm everyone's type," he said matter-of-factly. "And I'll make it good for you."

"You don't know what I like," I shot back. Ping-ponging with him was fun. He was curt, sharp, and unaffected, but oddly, I didn't find him rude.

"Bet you all the cash I have on me that I do."

This is interesting.

"What if I fake it every time I have an orgasm and act like I don't?" I tucked my iPod and earbuds into my bag. This conversation couldn't possibly be weirder. He smiled a smile I'd never seen on a human face before—so predatory my insides clenched on nothing, my panties dampening between my thighs.

"Clearly you've never had a real orgasm. When I make you come, you'll be lucky to keep your fucking kneecaps from snapping."

"Self-endorsem—"

"Save me the sass, Spears."

Ten minutes later, we were crossing the street on the way to his hotel. I tried hard not to lose my cool when we entered the glitzy lobby. The Laurent Towers Hotel stood across from the LBC skyscraper, home to one of the largest news channels in the world. The place was buzzing with people, but we were the only ones waiting for the elevator. We both stared at it silently while my heart screamed, nearly bursting from my chest. My knees shook under my cheap black dress. I was doing this. I was really having a one-night stand. Granted, I was twenty-three, newly single, and freshly vindictive. I knew there was nothing immoral about sleeping with him. But I also knew this was a one-off I would likely laugh about years from now.

"I don't normally do this," I said when the doors to the elevator slid open and we stepped inside.

Célian didn't answer. When the doors glided shut, he stalked toward me, his eyes cool and detached, his mouth pursed. He cornered me against the wall, every step more voracious than the last. My pulse wrestled inside my throat. He considered me with those cocksure eyes, and I lifted my chin, feeling my nostrils flaring.

Célian cupped me through my skirt, and I whimpered, my body arching against the wall behind me. His thumb found my clit and dug its way through the fabric, pressing hard and massaging it in lazy circles.

"Don't try to convince me you're a good girl," he hissed, his breath—mint and fresh coffee beans—skating along my throat. "I don't give a fuck."

"Your English is very good for a tourist," I noted. His accent was thick, but he used words like a weapon. Strategic, sparse. Each syllable a vicious strike.

He took a step back, watching me through a curtain of indifference. "I'm quite good at a lot of things, as you're about to find out."

The elevator dinged, and he disconnected from me.

The doors opened and an elderly couple smiled at us, waiting for us to leave the elevator. Célian looped his arm in mine like we were a couple, and dropped it casually the minute they were out of sight.

The walk to his suite was silent, but I nearly drowned from the noise inside my head. I convinced myself this was the right thing. A no-strings-attached night of pleasure with an inhumanly beautiful tourist would take the pain away. I trailed behind him, watching his broad back and lean figure. He looked like he worked out for a living, but dressed like he had no time to hit the gym. His profession, however, would remain an unsolved mystery. He was flying back to France tomorrow, and whether he was a hot-shot lawyer or an assassin made no difference to me.

Once we were in his suite, he handed me a bottle of water.

"Drink."

"Stop ordering me around."

"Then stop staring at me, doe-eyed, waiting for instructions."

He removed his blazer and kicked off his shoes. The suite was plush and tidy—too much so for an occupied room. It was huge, but I couldn't detect any suitcases, phone chargers, a desolate shirt lying on the ground, or any other telltale objects.

On one hand, it looked suspicious. On the other, he looked exactly like the kind of psycho to not leave a trace behind. And I was in his room. Fantastic.

Note to self: After your actions today, try to base all your future decisions on fortune cookie advice. You'll do better.

I drank the water he'd handed me without realizing I did so, then dropped the bottle in the trash like it was on fire, my rebellious soul dying a little.

It's not too late to bail. Tell him you're not feeling well and leave.

"I think I should—" I started, but I never got to complete the sentence.

He slammed me against the wall, his lips fusing to mine, shutting me up. My eyes rolled from the sudden pleasure and stars exploded behind my eyelids. I clutched the collar of his shirt as he hoisted me up in his arms and dug his fingers into my butt. My legs wrapped around his waist in no time. He gyrated against me, igniting lust in my lower belly, and when I moaned, he pinched the side of my thigh so hard I tried to fight him off, only to find sinking my claws into his skin felt a lot like drowning in an eternal kiss. His lips were crushed, hot velvet. His body stony marble, and hard everywhere.

Célian slid his tongue into my mouth, and I let him.

He rolled his hips, his hard—*very* hard—cock pressing against my slit, and again, I let him.

He bit my lower lip harder and growled, then sucked the pain away. I cried for more.

He slipped his hand between us, nudged my panties aside, and dipped two fingers into me.

I was embarrassingly soaked.

The sexy stranger tore his mouth from mine, staring me down. "Time to finish your sentence, Miss Spears."

"I… I…" I blinked, flustered.

He began to thrust his fingers in and out of me—slow, so tauntingly slow—his face still dead serious.

Who was this guy? He looked so unaffected, even when an involuntary groan escaped my lips every time he dug deeper and deeper into me, his fingers curling and hitting my G-spot. His other hand traveled up to my breasts, twisting one nipple roughly.

"You said you should do something." His hand left my sex momentarily to paint my lips with my desire for him, before returning to its new favorite place between my legs. He tasted me on my lips. "What was it, Judith?"

Judith. The way he rolled the J between his teeth made me want to die in his arms. His hot tongue was on my neck, chin, lips, and then between them again. We were tangled together like we needed each other to survive. I knew it was just one night, but it felt like so much more.

"I…eh…nothing," I said, fumbling for his zipper between us. He pressed one of his hands over mine, pushing my palm against his huge hard-on. Now I had a whole different reason for panic. That thing could maybe fit in my gym bag. Not my vagina.

"I set the pace," he said.

I shook my head. He wasn't the boss of me. He slipped two more fingers into me—most of his hand—and I was so full I thought I was going to smolder. A growl escaped my mouth. He swallowed it into our filthy kiss, and I came on his fingers in an instant.

The pleasure was so intense I turned to mush against the wall, sliding along it like spaghetti. Célian elevated me back up, digging his fingers into my cheeks, holding my jaw in place and tapering his eyes at me. "You better taste as good as you look."

He slid to his knees in one swift movement, flipped my dress up and threw one of my legs over his shoulder. His tongue drove into me with my panties still nudged to the side, and rather than licking and sucking, he started fucking me with his tongue. I threaded my fingers through his hair, noting that it was softer than mine, and rolled my head against the wall as he awarded me with the kind of oral sex I'd never thought was possible.

Milton was a generous, albeit robotic lover. This man was a walking, talking orgasm. I was pretty sure I would come if he sneezed in my direction. An intense desire to clamp my thighs around his face and keep him there forever slammed into me. My second climax soared from my toes to my head like an electric shock, sending me to heaven, and when he closed his lips over my swollen clit and sucked it with force, I was pretty sure every angel in my vicinity got their wings. By the time he stood up, rid himself of his dress pants and shirt, and ripped a condom wrapper with his teeth, I knew that whether I could accommodate him or not, I was willing to end up in the ER trying.

Célian drove into me all at once, crashing me against the closet behind us, lacing our fingers together and essentially handcuffing me to the surface. The pleasure was so penetrating I writhed between his arms, fighting his hands so I could claw and touch and rip to match him, thrust for thrust.

"Fuck," he hissed. "Judith."

"Célian." It was the last thing I said to him for a while, before we both drowned in hot sex.

On the floor, like two savages.

Doggy-style on the bed while he was facing the TV—watching CNN.

Then when I told him he was about as gentlemanly as a sack of rocks (he let out a soft curse when Anderson Cooper presented an exclusive item about voter fraud that even I was half-tempted to listen to), we got into the shower and he ate me out again, this time paying extra attention to my clit.

Then we went at it again against the sink.

Finally, when I collapsed into the bed, he handed me another bottle of water and said, "I'm leaving at six. Checkout is at ten, and they don't appreciate tardiness at the Laurent Towers."

I wanted to tell him to: A, take a hike, and B, that it was a brilliantly bad idea for me to stay the night. But I wasn't entirely sure I could face my ill dad after all the sex I'd been having, and *not* with my newly ex-boyfriend. I didn't have to stare at the mirror to know I looked thoroughly screwed, with cracked, engorged lips, stubble marks covering every inch of my red skin, and three bite marks on my neck—not to mention my eyes were deliriously drunk, and not from the whiskey I'd consumed hours ago.

Reluctantly, I texted Dad that I was crashing at Milton's and scooted up Célian's bed, closing my eyes. I felt orphaned in the world. No one knew where I was, and the only person who cared—Dad—couldn't particularly help me, as he barely left the house anymore.

That's when I decided I wasn't even going to tell Robert Humphry about my breakup with Milton Hayes. Dad had put all his Hope chips on my boyfriend, counting on him to take care of me once he was gone. Everybody needed someone, and other than Dad, I had no one.

Célian slid into bed behind me, his swelling cock pressing between the backs of my thighs.

He traced a rough-padded finger over the side of my ribcage, along the tattoo I'd gotten the day I turned eighteen.

If I seem a little strange, that's because I am.

"So you don't like The Beatles, but you do like The Smiths." His breath caressed my shoulder blade.

I grew up with a single dad who was a construction worker in New York. Money was tight, and sitting on the floor listening to his vinyl records had been our favorite pastime. We read books about Johnny Rotten and invented deliberately misleading music trivia games to pass the time.

"Careful, you might get attached if you get to know me," I said quietly, staring out the floor-to-ceiling window overlooking New York.

He began to drive into me from behind, silent. "I'll take my fucking chances."

The position reminded me of the front-row seat I'd had for Milton and Elise's adulterous performance. My feelings tangled and knotted. My body was elated, but tears gathered in the corner of my eyes. I was glad my one-night stand couldn't see them, though they were definitely a mixture of happy from all the orgasms and sad at the prospect of going back home tomorrow morning to face reality.

No boyfriend.

No job.

A dying father and a pile of bills I didn't know how to pay.

After we both finished, he kissed the back of my neck, turned over, and went to sleep. And me? I had a direct view to his dress pants and the outline of his fat wallet, which seemed to glare back at me.

My heart was a lonely hunter.

Tonight, I'd let it feast.

Dirty Headlines is available now!